THE STARS SHINE DOWN

Books by Sidney Sheldon

THE STARS SHINE DOWN
THE DOOMSDAY CONSPIRACY
MEMORIES OF MIDNIGHT
THE SANDS OF TIME
WINDMILLS OF THE GODS
IF TOMORROW COMES
MASTER OF THE GAME
RAGE OF ANGELS
BLOODLINE
A STRANGER IN THE MIRROR
THE OTHER SIDE OF MIDNIGHT
THE NAKED FACE

THE STARS SHINE DOWN

SIDNEY SHELDON

William Morrow and Company, Inc.
New York

Copyright © 1992 by Sheldon Literary Trust

All rights reserved. No part of this book may be reproduced or utilized in any form or by any means, electronic or mechanical, including photocopying, recording, or by any information storage or retrieval system, without permission in writing from the Publisher. Inquiries should be addressed to Permissions Department, William Morrow and Company, Inc., 1350 Avenue of the Americas, New York, N.Y. 10019.

ISBN 0-688-08490-7

Printed in the United States of America

This One Is for Morton Janklow,
a Man for All Seasons

Acknowledgment

I owe a debt of gratitude to those who were so generous with their time and expertise:

Larry Russo, who led me through the arcane maze of the biggest gamblers of all—the real estate developers.

The musical mavens who invited me inside their private world—Mona Gollabeck, John Lill, Zubin Mehta, Dudley Moore, André Previn, and the Trustees of the Leonard Bernstein Estate.

I wish also to express my appreciation to the citizens of Glace Bay for their warm hospitality. I hope they will forgive me for the few dramatic licenses I felt it necessary to take.

The expertise in the book belongs to those listed above. Any errors are mine.

The stars shine down
And watch us live
Our little lives
And weep for us.
 —M<small>ONET</small> N<small>ODLEHS</small>

THE STARS SHINE DOWN

BOOK ONE

Chapter One

Thursday, September 10, 1992
8:00 P.M.

The 727 was lost in a sea of cumulus clouds that tossed the plane around like a giant silver feather. The pilot's worried voice came over the speaker.

"Is your seat belt fastened, Miss Cameron?"

There was no response.

"Miss Cameron . . . Miss Cameron . . ."

She was shaken out of a deep reverie. "Yes." Her thoughts had been drifting to happier times, happier places.

"Are you all right? We should be out of this storm soon."

"I'm fine, Roger."

Maybe we'll get lucky and crash, Lara Cameron thought. It would be a fitting end. Somewhere, somehow, it had all gone wrong. *It's the Fates,* Lara thought. *You can't fight the Fates.* In the past year her life had spun wildly out of control. She was in danger of losing everything. *At least nothing else can go wrong,* she thought wryly. *There is nothing else.*

The door of the cockpit opened, and the pilot came into the cabin. He paused for a moment to admire his passenger. The woman was beautiful, with shiny black hair swept up in a crown, a flawless complexion, intelligent eyes, cat-gray. She had changed clothes after they had taken off from Reno, and she was wearing a white, off-the-shoulder Scasai evening gown that accented a slender, seductive figure. Around her throat was a diamond and ruby necklace. *How can she look so damn calm with her world collapsing around her?* he wondered. The newspapers had been mercilessly attacking her for the past month.

"Is the phone working yet, Roger?"

"I'm afraid not, Miss Cameron. There's a lot of interference because of the storm. We're going to be about an hour late getting into La Guardia. I'm sorry."

I'm going to be late for my birthday party, Lara thought. *Everyone is going to be there.* Two hundred guests, including the Vice President of the United States, the governor of New York, the mayor, Hollywood celebrities, famous athletes, and financiers from half a dozen countries. She had approved the guest list herself.

She could visualize the Grand Ballroom of the Cameron Plaza, where the party was being held. Baccarat crystal chandeliers would hang from the ceiling, prisms of light reflecting a dazzling diamondlike brilliance. There would be place settings for two hundred guests, at twenty tables. The finest linens, china, silver, and stemware would adorn each place setting, and in the center of each table would be a floral display of white orchids mixed with white freesias.

Bar service would have been set up at both ends of the large reception hall outside. In the middle of the hall would be a long buffet with an ice carving of a swan, and surrounding it, Beluga caviar, gravlax, shrimp, lobster, and crab, while buckets of champagne were being iced. A ten-tier birthday cake would be in the kitchen waiting. Waiters, captains, and security guards would all be in position by now.

In the ballroom a society orchestra would be on the bandstand, ready to tempt the guests to dance the night away in celebration of her fortieth birthday. Everything would be in readiness.

The dinner was going to be delicious. She had chosen the menu herself. Foie gras to begin with, followed by a cream of mushroom soup under a delicate crust, fillets of John Dory, and then the main course: lamb with rosemary and pommes soufflés with French beans and a mesclun salad with hazelnut oil. Cheese and grapes would be next, followed by the birthday cake and coffee.

It was going to be a spectacular party. She would hold her head high and face her guests as though nothing were wrong. She was Lara Cameron.

When the private jet finally landed at La Guardia, it was an hour and a half late.

Lara turned to the pilot. "We'll be flying back to Reno later tonight, Roger."

"I'll be here, Miss Cameron."

Her limousine and driver were waiting for her at the ramp.

"I was getting worried about you, Miss Cameron."

"We ran into some weather, Max. Let's get to the Plaza as fast as possible."

"Yes, ma'am."

Lara reached for the car phone and dialed Jerry Townsend's number. He had made all the arrangements for the party. Lara wanted to make sure that her guests were being looked after. There was no answer. *He's probably in the ballroom,* Lara thought.

"Hurry, Max."

"Yes, Miss Cameron."

The sight of the huge Cameron Plaza Hotel never failed to give Lara a glow of satisfaction at what she had created, but on this evening she was in too much of a hurry to think about it. Everyone would be waiting for her in the Grand Ballroom.

She pushed through the revolving door and hurried across the large spectacular lobby. Carlos, the assistant manager, saw her and came running to her side.

"Miss Cameron . . ."

"Later," Lara said. She kept walking. She reached the closed door of the Grand Ballroom and stopped to take a deep breath. *I'm ready to face them,* Lara thought. She flung open the door, a smile on her face, and stopped in shock. The room was in total darkness. Were they planning some kind of surprise? She reached for the switch behind the door and flicked it up. The huge room was flooded with incandescent light. There was no one there. Not one single person. Lara stood there, stunned.

What in the world could have happened to two hundred guests? The invitations had read eight o'clock. It was now almost ten o'clock. How could that many people disappear into thin air? It was eerie. She looked around the enormous empty ballroom and shivered. Last year, at her birthday party, this same room had been filled with her friends, filled with music and laughter. She remembered that day so well. . . .

Chapter Two

One year earlier Lara Cameron's appointment schedule for the day had been routine.

September 10, 1991

5:00 A.M.	Workout with trainer
7:00 A.M.	Appearance on *Good Morning America*
7:45 A.M.	Meeting with Japanese bankers
9:30 A.M.	Jerry Townsend
10:30 A.M.	Executive Planning Committee
11:00 A.M.	Faxes, overseas calls, mail
11:30 A.M.	Construction meeting
12:30 P.M.	S&L meeting
1:00 P.M.	Lunch—*Fortune* magazine interview—Hugh Thompson
2:30 P.M.	Metropolitan Union bankers
4:00 P.M.	City Planning Commission
5:00 P.M.	Meeting with mayor—Gracie Mansion
6:15 P.M.	Architects meeting
6:30 P.M.	Housing Department
7:30 P.M.	Cocktails with Dallas investment group
8:00 P.M.	Birthday party at Grand Ballroom—Cameron Plaza

She had been in her workout clothes impatiently waiting when Ken, her trainer, arrived.

"You're late."

"Sorry, Miss Cameron. My alarm didn't go off and . . ."

"I have a busy day. Let's get started."

"Right."

They did stretches for half an hour and then switched to energetic aerobics.

She's got the body of a twenty-one-year-old, Ken thought. *I'd sure love to get that into my bed.* He enjoyed coming here every morning just to look at her, to be near her. People constantly asked him what Lara Cameron was like. He would answer, "The lady's a ten."

Lara went through the strenuous routine easily, but her mind was not on it this morning.

When the session was finally over, Ken said, "I'm going to watch you on *Good Morning America.*"

"What?" For a moment Lara had forgotten about it. She had been thinking about the meeting with the Japanese bankers.

"See you tomorrow, Miss Cameron."

"Don't be late again, Ken."

Lara showered and changed and had breakfast alone on the terrace of the penthouse, a breakfast of grapefruit, cereal, and green tea. When she had finished, she went into her study.

Lara buzzed her secretary. "I'll do the overseas calls from the office," Lara said. "I have to be at ABC at seven. Have Max bring the car around."

The segment on *Good Morning America* went well. Joan Lunden did the interview and was gracious, as always.

"The last time you were on this program," Joan Lunden said, "you had just broken ground for the tallest skyscraper in the world. That was almost four years ago."

Lara nodded. "That's right. Cameron Towers will be finished next year."

"How does it feel to be in your position—to have accomplished all the incredible things you've done and to still be so young and beautiful? You're a role model for so many women."

"You're very flattering," Lara laughed. "I don't have time to think about myself as a role model. I'm much too busy."

"You're one of the most successful real estate developers in a business that's usually considered a man's domain. How do you operate? How do you decide, for instance, where to put up a building?"

"I don't choose the site," Lara said. "The site chooses me. I'll be driving along and I'll pass a vacant field—but that's not what I see. I see a beautiful office building or a lovely apartment building filled with people living comfortably in a nice atmosphere. I dream."

"And you make those dreams come true. We'll be right back after this commercial."

The Japanese bankers were due at seven forty-five. They had arrived from Tokyo the evening before, and Lara had arranged the meeting at that early-morning hour so they would still be jet-lagged after their twelve-hour and ten-minute flight. When they had protested, Lara had said, "I'm so sorry, gentlemen, but I'm afraid it's the only time I have. I'm leaving for South America immediately after our meeting."

And they had reluctantly agreed. There were four of them, diminutive and polite, with minds as sharp as the edges of samurai swords. In an earlier decade the financial community had wildly underestimated the Japanese. It no longer made that mistake.

The meeting was held at Cameron Center on Avenue of the Americas. The men were there to invest a hundred million dollars in a new hotel complex Lara was developing. They were ushered into the large conference room. Each of the men carried a gift. Lara thanked them and in turn gave each of them a gift. She had instructed her secretary to make certain the presents were wrapped in plain brown or gray paper. White, to the Japanese, represented death, and gaudy wrapping paper was unacceptable.

Lara's assistant, Tricia, brought in tea for the Japanese and coffee for Lara. The Japanese would have preferred coffee, but they were too polite to say so. When they had finished their tea, Lara made sure their cups were replenished.

Howard Keller, Lara's associate, came into the room. He was in his fifties, pale and thin, with sandy hair, wearing a rumpled suit and managing to look as though he had just gotten out of bed. Lara made the introductions. Keller passed around copies of the investment proposal.

"As you can see, gentlemen," Lara said, "we already have a first mortgage commitment. The complex will contain seven hundred and twenty guest units, approximately thirty thousand square feet of meeting space, and a one-thousand-car parking garage. . . ."

Lara's voice was charged with energy. The Japanese bankers were studying the investment proposal, fighting to stay awake.

The meeting was over in less than two hours, and it was a complete success. Lara had learned long ago that it was easier to make a hundred-million-dollar deal than it was to try to borrow fifty thousand dollars.

As soon as the Japanese delegation left, Lara had her meeting with Jerry Townsend. The tall, hyper ex-Hollywood publicity man was in charge of public relations for Cameron Enterprises.

"That was a great interview on *Good Morning America* this morning. I've been getting a lot of calls."

"What about *Forbes*?"

"All set. *People* has you on the cover next week. Did you see *The New Yorker* article on you? Wasn't it great?"

Lara walked over to her desk. "Not bad."

"The *Fortune* interview is set for this afternoon."

"I changed it."

He looked surprised. "Why?"

"I'm having their reporter here for lunch."

"Soften him up a little?"

Lara pressed down the intercom button. "Come in, Kathy."

A disembodied voice said, "Yes, Miss Cameron."

Lara Cameron looked up. "That's all, Jerry. I want you and your staff to concentrate on Cameron Towers."

"We're already doing . . ."

"Let's do more. I want it written about in every newspaper and magazine there is. For God's sake, it's going to be the tallest building in the world. *In the world!* I want people talking about it. By the time we open, I want people to be *begging* to get into those apartments and shops."

Jerry Townsend got to his feet. "Right."

Kathy, Lara's executive assistant, came into the office. She was an attractive, neatly dressed black woman in her early thirties.

"Did you find out what he likes to eat?"

"The man's a gourmet. He likes French food. I called Le Cirque and asked Sirio to cater a lunch here for two."

"Good. We'll eat in my private dining room."

"Do you know how long the interview will take? You have a two-thirty with the Metropolitan bankers downtown."

"Push it to three o'clock, and have them come here."

Kathy made a note. "Do you want me to read you your messages?"

"Go ahead."

"The Children's Foundation wants you to be their guest of honor on the twenty-eighth."

"No. Tell them I'm flattered. Send them a check."

"Your meeting has been arranged in Tulsa for Tuesday at . . ."

"Cancel it."

"You're invited to a luncheon next Friday for a Manhattan Women's Group."

"No. If they're asking for money, send them a check."

"The Coalition for Literacy would like you to speak at a luncheon on the fourth."

"See if we can work it out."

"There's an invitation to be guest of honor at a fund raiser for muscular dystrophy, but there's a conflict in dates. You'll be in San Francisco."

"Send them a check."

"The Srbs are giving a dinner party next Saturday."

"I'll try to make that," Lara said. Kristian and Deborah Srb were amusing, and good friends, and she enjoyed being with them.

"Kathy, how many of me do you see?"

"What?"

"Take a good look."

Kathy looked at her. "One of you, Miss Cameron."

"That's right. There's only one of me. How did you expect me to meet with the bankers from Metropolitan at two-thirty today, the City Planning Commission at four, then meet with the mayor at five, the architects at six-fifteen, the Housing Department at six-thirty, have a cocktail party at seven-thirty and my birthday dinner at eight? The next time you make up a schedule, try using your brain."

"I'm sorry. You wanted me to . . ."

"I wanted you to *think*. I don't need stupid people around me. Reschedule the appointments with the architects and the Housing Department."

"Right," Kathy said stiffly.

"How's the baby?"

The question caught the secretary by surprise. "David? He's . . . he's fine."

"He must be getting big by now."

"He's almost two."

"Have you thought about a school for him?"

"Not yet. It's too early to . . ."

"You're wrong. If you want to get him into a decent school in New York, you start before he's born."

Lara made a note on a desk pad. "I know the principal at Dalton. I'll arrange to have David registered there."

"I . . . thank you."

Lara did not bother to look up. "That's all."

"Yes, ma'am." Kathy walked out of the office not knowing whether to love her boss or hate her. When Kathy had first come to work at Cameron Enterprises, she had been warned about Lara Cameron. "The Iron Butterfly is a bitch on wheels," she had been told. "Her secretaries don't figure their employment there by the calendar—they use stopwatches. She'll eat you alive."

Kathy remembered her first interview with her. She had seen pictures of Lara Cameron in half a dozen magazines, but none of them had done her justice. In person, the woman was breathtakingly beautiful.

Lara Cameron had been reading Kathy's résumé. She looked up and said, "Sit down, Kathy." Her voice was husky and vibrant. There was an energy about her that was almost overpowering.

"This is quite a résumé."

"Thank you."

"How much of it is real?"

"I'm sorry?"

"Most of the ones that come across my desk are fiction. Are you good at what you do?"

"I'm very good at what I do, Miss Cameron."

"Two of my secretaries just quit. Everything's snowballing around here. Can you handle pressure?"

"I think so."

"This isn't a guessing contest. Can you handle pressure or can't you?"

At that moment Kathy was not sure she wanted the job. "Yes, I can."

"Good. You're on a one-week trial. You'll have to sign a form saying that at no time will you discuss me or your work here at Cameron Enterprises. That means no interviews, no books, nothing. Everything that happens here is confidential."

"I understand."

"Fine."

That was how it had begun five years earlier. During that time Kathy had learned to love, hate, admire, and despise her boss. In the beginning Kathy's husband had asked, "What is the legend like?"

It was a difficult question. "She's larger than life," Kathy had said.

"She's drop-dead beautiful. She works harder than anyone I've ever known. God only knows when she sleeps. She's a perfectionist, so she makes everyone around her miserable. In her own way, she's a genius. She can be petty and vengeful and incredibly generous."

Her husband had smiled. "In other words, she's a woman."

Kathy had looked at him and said, unsmiling, "I don't know what she is. Sometimes she scares me."

"Come on, honey, you're exaggerating."

"No. I honestly believe that if someone stood in Lara Cameron's way . . . she would kill."

When Lara finished with the faxes and overseas calls, she buzzed Charlie Hunter, an ambitious young man in charge of accounting. "Come in, Charlie."

"Yes, Miss Cameron."

A minute later he entered her office.

"Yes, Miss Cameron?"

"I read the interview you gave in *The New York Times* this morning," Lara said.

He brightened. "I haven't seen it yet. How was it?"

"You talked about Cameron Enterprises and about some of the problems we're having."

He frowned. "Well, you know, that reporter fellow probably misquoted some of my . . ."

"You're fired."

"What? Why? I . . ."

"When you were hired, you signed a paper agreeing not to give any interviews. I'll expect you out of here this morning."

"I . . . you can't do that. Who would take my place?"

"I've already arranged that," Lara told him.

The luncheon was almost over. The *Fortune* reporter, Hugh Thompson, was an intense, intellectual-looking man with sharp brown eyes behind black horn-rimmed glasses.

"It was a great lunch," he said. "All my favorite dishes. Thanks."

"I'm glad you enjoyed it."

"You really didn't have to go to all that trouble for me."

"No trouble at all." Lara smiled. "My father always told me that the way to a man's heart was through his stomach."

"And you wanted to get to my heart before we started the interview?"

Lara smiled. "Exactly."

"How much trouble is your company really in?"

Lara's smile faded. "I beg your pardon?"

"Come on. You can't keep a thing like that quiet. The word on the street is that some of your properties are on the verge of collapse because of the principal payments due on your junk bonds. You've done a lot of leveraging, and with the market down, Cameron Enterprises has to be pretty overextended."

Lara laughed. "Is that what the street says? Believe me, Mr. Thompson, you'd be wise not to listen to silly rumors. I'll tell you what I'll do. I'll send you a copy of my financials to set the record straight. Fair enough?"

"Fair enough. By the way, I didn't see your husband at the opening of the new hotel."

Lara sighed. "Philip wanted so much to be there, but unfortunately he had to be away on a concert tour."

"I went to one of his recitals once about three years ago. He's brilliant. You have been married a year now, haven't you?"

"The happiest year of my life. I'm a very lucky woman. I travel a lot, and so does Philip, but when I'm away from him, I can listen to his recordings wherever I am."

Thompson smiled. "And he can see your buildings wherever he is."

Lara laughed. "You flatter me."

"It's pretty true, isn't it? You've put up buildings all over this fair country of ours. You own apartment buildings, office buildings, a hotel chain . . . How do you do it?"

She smiled. "With mirrors."

"You're a puzzle."

"Am I? Why?"

"At this moment you're arguably the most successful builder in New York. Your name is plastered on half the real estate in this town. You're putting up the world's tallest skyscraper. Your competitors call you the Iron Butterfly. You've made it big in a business traditionally dominated by men."

"Does that bother you, Mr. Thompson?"

"No. What bothers me, Miss Cameron, is that I can't figure out who you are. When I ask two people about you, I get three opinions. Everyone grants that you're a brilliant businesswoman. I mean . . . you didn't fall off a hay wagon and become a success. I know a lot about construction crews—they're a rough, tough bunch of men. How does a woman like you keep them in line?"

She smiled. "There *are* no women like me. Seriously, I simply hire the best people for the job, and I pay them well."

Too simplistic, Thompson thought. *Much too simplistic. The real story is what she's not telling me.* He decided to change the direction of the interview.

"Every magazine on the stands has written about how successful you are. I'd like to do a more personal story. There's been very little printed about your background."

"I'm very proud of my background."

"Good. Let's talk about that. How did you get started in the real estate business?"

Lara smiled, and he could see that her smile was genuine. She suddenly looked like a little girl.

"Genes."

"Your genes?"

"My father's." She pointed to a portrait on a wall behind her. It showed a handsome-looking man with a leonine head of silver hair. "That's my father—James Hugh Cameron." Her voice was soft. "He's responsible for my success. I'm an only child. My mother died when I was very young, and my father brought me up. My family left Scotland a long time ago, Mr. Thompson, and emigrated to Nova Scotia—New Scotland, Glace Bay."

"Glace Bay?"

"It's a fishing village in the northeast part of Cape Breton, on the Atlantic shore. It was named by early French explorers. It means 'ice bay.' More coffee?"

"No, thanks."

"My grandfather owned a great deal of land in Scotland, and my father acquired more. He was a very wealthy man. We still have our castle there near Loch Morlich. When I was eight years old, I had my own horse, my dresses were bought in London, we lived in an enormous house with a lot of servants. It was a fairy tale life for a little girl."

Her voice was alive with echoes of long-ago memories.

"We would go ice skating in the winter, and watch hockey games, and go swimming at Big Glace Bay Lake in the summer. And there were dances at the Forum and the Venetian Gardens."

The reporter was busily making notes.

"My father put up buildings in Edmonton, and Calgary, and Ontario. Real estate was like a game to him, and he loved it. When I was very young, he taught me the game, and I learned to love it, too."

Her voice was filled with passion. "You must understand something, Mr. Thompson. What I do has nothing to do with the money or the bricks and steel that make a building. It's the people who matter. I'm able to give them a comfortable place to work or to live, a place where they can raise families and have decent lives. That's what was important to my father, and it became important to me."

Hugh Thompson looked up. "Do you remember your first real estate venture?"

Lara leaned forward. "Of course. On my eighteenth birthday my father asked me what I would like as a gift. A lot of newcomers were arriving in Glace Bay, and it was getting crowded. I felt the town needed more places for them to live. I told my father I wanted to build a small apartment house. He gave me the money as a present, but two years later I was able to pay him back. Then I borrowed money from a bank to put up a second building. By the time I was twenty-one, I owned three buildings, and they were all successful."

"Your father must have been very proud of you."

There was that warm smile again. "He was. He named me Lara. It's an old Scottish name that comes from the Latin. It means 'well known' or 'famous.' From the time I was a little girl, my father always told me I would be famous one day." Her smile faded. "He died of a heart attack, much too young." She paused. "I go to Scotland to visit his grave every year. I . . . I found it very difficult to stay on in the house without him. I decided to move to Chicago. I had an idea for small boutique hotels, and I persuaded a banker there to finance me. The hotels were a success." She shrugged. "And the rest, as the cliché goes, is history. I suppose that a psychiatrist would say that I haven't created this empire just for myself. In a way, it's a tribute to my father. James Cameron was the most wonderful man I've ever known."

"You must have loved him a lot."

"I did. And he loved me a lot." A smile touched her lips. "I've heard that on the day I was born, my father bought every man in Glace Bay a drink."

"So, really," Thompson said, "everything started in Glace Bay."

"That's right," Lara said softly, "everything started in Glace Bay. That's where it all began, almost forty years ago. . . ."

Chapter Three

Glace Bay, Nova Scotia
September 10, 1952

James Cameron was in a whorehouse, drunk, the night his daughter and son were born. He was in bed, sandwiched in between the Scandinavian twins, when Kirstie, the madam of the brothel, pounded on the door.

"James!" she called out. She pushed open the door and walked in.

"Och, ye auld hen!" James yelled out indignantly. "Can't a mon have any privacy even here?"

"Sorry to interrupt your pleasure, James. It's about your wife."

"Fuck my wife," Cameron roared.

"You did," Kirstie retorted, "and she's having your baby."

"So? Let her have it. That's what you women are guid for, nae?"

"The doctor just called. He's been trying desperately to find you. Your wife is bad off. You'd better hurry."

James Cameron sat up and slid to the edge of the bed, bleary-eyed, trying to clear his head. "Damned woman. She niver leaves me in peace." He looked up at the madam. "All right, I'll go." He glanced at the naked girls in the bed. "But I'll nae pay for these two."

"Never mind that now. You'd just better get back to the boardinghouse." She turned to the girls. "You two come along with me."

James Cameron was a once-handsome man whose face reflected fulfilled sins. He appeared to be in his early fifties. He was thirty years old and the manager of one of the boardinghouses owned by Sean MacAllister, the town banker. For the past five years James Cameron and his wife, Peggy, had divided the chores: Peggy did the cleaning and cooking for the two dozen boarders, and James did the drinking. Every Friday it was his responsibility to collect the rents from the four other boardinghouses in Glace Bay owned by MacAllister. It was another reason, if he needed one, to go out and get drunk.

James Cameron was a bitter man, who reveled in his bitterness. He was a failure, and he was convinced that everyone else was to blame. Over the years he had come to enjoy his failure. It made him feel like a martyr. When James was a year old, his family had emigrated to Glace Bay from Scotland with nothing but the few possessions they could carry, and they had struggled to survive. His father had put James to work in the coal mines when the boy was fourteen. James had suffered a slight back injury in a mining accident when he was sixteen, and had promptly quit the mine. One year later his parents were killed in a train disaster. So it was that James Cameron had decided that he was not responsible for his adversity—it was the Fates that were against him. But he had two great assets: He was extraordinarily handsome, and when he wished to, he could be charming. One weekend in Sydney, a town near Glace Bay, he met an impressionable young American girl named Peggy Maxwell, who was there on vacation with her family. She was not attractive, but the Maxwells were very wealthy, and James Cameron was very poor. He swept Peggy Maxwell off her feet, and against the advice of her father, she married him.

"I'm giving Peggy a dowry of five thousand dollars," her father told James. "The money will give you a chance to make something of yourself. You can invest it in real estate, and in five years it will double. I'll help you."

But James was not interested in waiting five years. Without consulting anyone, he invested the money in a wildcat oil venture with a friend, and sixty days later he was broke. His father-in-law, furious, refused to help him any further. "You're a fool, James, and I will not throw good money after bad."

The marriage that was going to be James Cameron's salvation turned out to be a disaster, for he now had a wife to support, and no job.

It was Sean MacAllister who had come to his rescue. The town banker was a man in his mid-fifties, a stumpy, pompous man, a pound short of being obese, given to wearing vests adorned with a heavy gold watch chain. He had come to Glace Bay twenty years earlier and had immediately seen the possibilities there. Miners and lumbermen were pouring into the town and were unable to find adequate housing. Mac-

Allister could have financed homes for them, but he had a better plan. He decided it would be cheaper to herd the men together in boardinghouses. Within two years he had built a hotel and five boardinghouses, and they were always full.

Finding managers was a difficult task because the work was exhausting. The manager's job was to keep all the rooms rented, supervise the cooking, handle the meals, and see that the premises were kept reasonably clean. As far as salaries were concerned, Sean MacAllister was not a man to throw away his money.

The manager of one of his boardinghouses had just quit, and MacAllister decided that James Cameron was a likely candidate. Cameron had borrowed small amounts of money from the bank from time to time, and payment on a loan was overdue. MacAllister sent for the young man.

"I have a job for you," MacAllister said.

"You have?"

"You're in luck. I have a splendid position that's just opened up."

"Working at the bank, is it?" James Cameron asked. The idea of working in a bank appealed to him. Where there was a lot of money, there was always a possibility of having some stick to one's fingers.

"Not at the bank," MacAllister told him. "You're a very personable young man, James, and I think you would be very good at dealing with people. I'd like you to run my boardinghouse on Cablehead Avenue."

"A *boarding*house, you say?" There was contempt in the young man's voice.

"You need a roof over your head," MacAllister pointed out. "You and your wife will have free room and board and a small salary."

"How sma?"

"I'll be generous with you, James. Twenty-five dollars a week."

"Twenty-fi . . . ?"

"Take it or leave it. I have others waiting."

In the end James Cameron had no choice. "I'll tach it."

"Good. By the way, every Friday I'll also expect you to collect the rents from my other boardinghouses and deliver the money to me on Saturday."

When James Cameron broke the news to Peggy, she was dismayed. "We don't know anything about running a boardinghouse, James."

"We'll learn. We'll share the work."

And she had believed him. "All right. We'll manage," she said.

And in their own fashion they had managed.

* * *

Over the years, several opportunities had come along for James Cameron to get better jobs, employment that would give him dignity and more money, but he was enjoying his failure too much to leave it.

"Why bother?" he would grumble. "When Fate's agin you, naething guid can happen."

And now, on this September night, he thought, *They won't even let me enjoy my whores in peace. God damn my wife.*

When he stepped out of Madam Kirstie's establishment, a chilly September wind was blowing.

I'd best fortify myself for the troubles aheid, James Cameron decided. He stopped in at the Ancient Mariner.

One hour later he wandered toward the boardinghouse in New Aberdeen, the poorest section of Glace Bay.

When he finally arrived, half a dozen boarders were anxiously waiting for him.

"The doctor is in wi' Peggy," one of the men said. "You'd better hurry, mon."

James staggered into the tiny, dreary back bedroom he and his wife shared. From another room he could hear the whimpering of a newborn baby. Peggy lay on the bed, motionless. Dr. Patrick Duncan was leaning over her. He turned as he heard James enter.

"Wass goin' on here?" James asked.

The doctor straightened up and looked at James with distaste. "You should have had your wife come to see me," he said.

"And throw guid money away? She's only haein' a baby. Wass the big . . . ?"

"Peggy's dead. I did everything I could. She had twins. I couldn't save the boy."

"Oh, Jesus," James Cameron whimpered. "It's the Fates agin."

"What?"

"The Fates. They've always been agin me. Now they've taine my bairn frae me. I dinna . . ."

A nurse walked in, carrying a tiny baby wrapped in a blanket. "This is your daughter, Mr. Cameron."

"A *daughter*? Wha' the hell will I dae wi' a daughter?" His speech was becoming more slurred.

"You disgust me, mon," Dr. Duncan said.

The nurse turned to James. "I'll stay until tomorrow and show you how to take care of her."

James Cameron looked at the tiny, wrinkled bundle in the blanket and thought, hopefully: *Maybe she'll die, too.*

For the first three weeks no one was sure whether the baby would live or not. A wet nurse came in to tend to her. And finally, the day came when the doctor was able to say, "Your daughter is going to live."

And he looked at James Cameron and said under his breath, "God have mercy on the poor child."

The wet nurse said, "Mr. Cameron, you must give the child a name."

"I dinna care wha' the hell ye call it. Ye gie her a name."

"Why don't we name her Lara? That's such a pretty . . ."

"Suit your bloody self."

And so she was christened Lara.

There was no one in Lara's life to care for her or nurture her. The boardinghouse was filled with men too busy with their own lives to pay attention to the baby. The only woman around was Bertha, the huge Swede who was hired to do the cooking and handle the chores.

James Cameron was determined to have nothing to do with his daughter. The damned Fates had betrayed him once again by letting her live. At night he would sit in the living room with his bottle of whiskey and complain. "The bairn murdered my wife and my son."

"You shouldn't say that, James."

"Weel, it's sae. My son would hae grown up to be a big strapping mon. He would hae been smart and rich and taine good care of his father in his auld age."

And the boarders let him ramble on.

James Cameron tried several times to get in touch with Maxwell, his father-in-law, hoping he would take the child off his hands, but the old man had disappeared. *It would be just my luck the auld fool's daid,* he thought.

Glace Bay was a town of transients who moved in and out of the boardinghouses. They came from France and China and the Ukraine. They were Italian and Irish and Greek, carpenters and tailors and plumbers and shoemakers. They swarmed into lower Main Street, Bell Street, North Street, and Water Street, near the waterfront area. They came to work the mines and cut timber and fish the seas. Glace Bay was a frontier town, primitive and rugged. The weather was an abomination.

The winters were harsh with heavy snowfalls that lasted until April, and because of the heavy ice in the harbor, even April and May were cold and windy, and from July to October it rained.

There were eighteen boardinghouses in town, some of them accommodating as many as seventy-two guests. At the boardinghouse managed by James Cameron, there were twenty-four boarders, most of them Scotsmen.

Lara was hungry for affection, without knowing what the hunger was. She had no toys or dolls to cherish nor any playmates. She had no one except her father. She made childish little gifts for him, desperate to please him, but he either ignored or ridiculed them.

When Lara was five years old, she overheard her father say to one of the boarders, "The wrong child died, ye ken. My son is the one who should hae lived."

That night Lara cried herself to sleep. She loved her father so much. And she hated him so much.

When Lara was six, she resembled a Keane painting, enormous eyes in a pale, thin face. That year a new boarder moved in. His name was Mungo McSween, and he was a huge bear of a man. He felt an instant affection for the little girl.

"What's your name, wee lassie?"

"Lara."

"Ah. 'Tis a braw name for a braw bairn. Dae ye gan to school then?"

"School? No."

"And why not?"

"I don't know."

"Weel, we maun find out."

And he went to find James Cameron. "I'm tauld your bairn daes nae gae to school."

"And why should she? She's only a girl. She dinna need no school."

"You're wrong, mon. She maun have an education. She maun be gien a chance in life."

"Forget it," James said. "It wad be a waste."

But McSween was insistent, and finally, to shut him up, James Cameron agreed. It would keep the brat out of his sight for a few hours.

* * *

Lara was terrified by the idea of going to school. She had lived in a world of adults all her short life, and had had almost no contact with other children.

The following Monday Big Bertha dropped her off at St. Anne's Grammar School, and Lara was taken to the principal's office.

"This is Lara Cameron."

The principal, Mrs. Cummings, was a middle-aged gray-haired widow with three children of her own. She studied the shabbily dressed little girl standing before her. "Lara. What a pretty name," she said, smiling. "How old are you, dear?"

"Six." She was fighting back tears.

The child is terrified, Mrs. Cummings thought. "Well, we're very glad to have you here, Lara. You'll have a good time, and you're going to learn a lot."

"I can't stay," Lara blurted out.

"Oh? Why not?"

"My papa misses me too much." She was fiercely determined not to cry.

"Well, we'll only keep you here for a few hours a day."

Lara allowed herself to be taken into a classroom filled with children, and she was shown to a seat near the back of the room.

Miss Terkel, the teacher, was busily writing letters on a blackboard.

"*A* is for apple," she said. "*B* is for boy. Does anyone know what *C* is for?"

A tiny hand was raised. "Candy."

"Very good! And *D*?"

"Dog."

"And *E*?"

"Eat."

"Excellent. Can anyone think of a word beginning with *F*?"

Lara spoke up. "Fuck."

Lara was the youngest one in her class, but it seemed to Miss Terkel that in many ways she was the oldest. There was a disquieting maturity about her.

"She's a small adult, waiting to grow taller," her teacher told Mrs. Cummings.

The first day at lunch, the other children took out their colorful little lunch pails and pulled out apples and cookies and sandwiches wrapped in wax paper.

No one had thought to pack a lunch for Lara.
"Where is your lunch, Lara?" Miss Terkel asked.
"I'm not hungry," Lara said stubbornly. "I had a big breakfast."
Most of the girls at school were nicely dressed in clean skirts and blouses. Lara had outgrown her few faded plaid dresses and threadbare blouses. She had gone to her father.
"I need some clothes for school," Lara said.
"Dae ye now? Weel, I'm nae made of money. Get yourself something frae the Salvation Army Citadel."
"That's charity, Papa."
And her father had slapped her hard across the face.

The children at school were familiar with games Lara had never even heard of. The girls had dolls and toys, and some of them were willing to share them with Lara, but she was painfully aware that nothing belonged to her. And there was something more. Over the next few years Lara got a glimpse of a different world, a world where children had mothers and fathers who gave them presents and birthday parties and loved them and held them and kissed them. And for the first time Lara began to realize how much was missing in her life. It only made her feel lonelier.

The boardinghouse was a different kind of school. It was an international microcosm. Lara learned to tell where the boarders came from by their names. Mac was from Scotland . . . Hodder and Pyke were from Newfoundland . . . Chiasson and Aucoin were from France . . . Dudash and Kosick from Poland. The boarders were lumbermen, fishermen, miners, and tradesmen. They would gather in the large dining room in the morning for breakfast and in the evening for supper, and their talk was fascinating to Lara. Each group seemed to have its own mysterious language.

There were thousands of lumbermen in Nova Scotia, scattered around the peninsula. The lumbermen at the boardinghouse smelled of sawdust and burned bark, and they spoke of arcane things like chippers and edging and trim.
"We should get out almost two hundred million board feet this year," one of them announced at supper.
"How can feet be bored?" Lara asked.
There was a roar of laughter. "Child, board foot is a piece of lumber a foot square by an inch thick. When you grow up and get married,

if you want to build a five-room, all-wood house, it will take twelve thousand board feet."

"I'm not going to get married," Lara swore.

The fishermen were another breed. They returned to the boardinghouse stinking of the sea, and they talked about the new experiment of growing oysters on the Bras d'Or Lake and bragged to one another of their catches of cod and herring and mackerel and haddock.

But the boarders who fascinated Lara the most were the miners. There were thirty-five hundred miners in Cape Breton, working the collieries at Lingan and Prince and Phalen. Lara loved the names of the mines. There was the Jubilee and the Last Chance and the Black Diamond and the Lucky Lady.

She was fascinated by their discussion of the day's work.

"What's this I hear about Mike?"

"It's true. The poor bastard was traveling inbye in a man-rake, and a box jumped the track and crushed his leg. The son of a bitch of a foreman said it was Mike's fault for not gettin' out of the way fast enough, and he's having his lamp stopped."

Lara was baffled. "What does that mean?"

One of the miners explained. "It means Mike was on his way to work—going inbye—in a man-rake—that's a car that takes you down to your working level. A box—that's a coal train—jumped the track and hit him."

"And stopped his lamp?" Lara asked.

The miner laughed. "When you've had your lamp stopped, it means you've been suspended."

When Lara was fifteen, she entered St. Michael's High School. She was gangly and awkward, with long legs, stringy black hair, and intelligent gray eyes still too large for her pale, thin face. No one quite knew how she was going to turn out. She was on the verge of womanhood, and her looks were in a stage of metamorphosis. She could have become ugly or beautiful.

To James Cameron, his daughter was ugly. "Ye hae best marry the first mon fool enough to ask ye," he told her. "Ye'll nae hae the looks to make a guid bargain."

Lara stood there, saying nothing.

"And tell the poor mon nae to expect a dowry frae me."

Mungo McSween had walked into the room. He stood there listening, furious.

"That's all, girl," James Cameron said. "Gae back to the kitchen." Lara fled.

"Why dae ye dae that to your daughter?" McSween demanded.

James Cameron looked up, his eyes bleary. "Nane of your business."

"You're drunk."

"Aye. And what else is there? If it isn't women, it's the whiskey, isn't it?"

McSween went into the kitchen, where Lara was washing dishes at the sink. Her eyes were hot with tears. McSween put his arms around her. "Niver ye mind, lassie," he said. "He dinna mean it."

"He hates me."

"Nae, he doesna."

"He's never given me one kind word. Never once. Never!"

There was nothing McSween could say.

In the summer the tourists would arrive at Glace Bay. They came in their expensive cars, wearing beautiful clothes and shopped along Castle Street and dined at the Cedar House and at Jasper's, and they visited Ingonish Beach and Cape Smoky and the Bird Islands. They were superior beings from another world, and Lara envied them and longed to escape with them when they left at the end of summer. But how?

Lara had heard stories about Grandfather Maxwell.

"The auld bastard tried to keep me frae marryin' his precious daughter," James Cameron would complain to any of the boarders who would listen. "He was filthy rich, but do ye think he wad gie me aught? Nae. But I took guid care of his Peggy anyway. . . ."

And Lara would fantasize that one day her grandfather would come to take her away to glamorous cities she had read about: London and Rome and Paris. *And I'll have beautiful clothes to wear. Hundreds of dresses and new shoes.*

But as the months and the years went by, and there was no word, Lara finally came to realize that she would never see her grandfather. She was doomed to spend the rest of her life in Glace Bay.

Chapter Four

There were myriad activities for a teenager growing up in Glace Bay: There were football games and hockey games, skating rinks and bowling, and in the summer, swimming and fishing. Carl's Drug Store was the popular after-school hangout. There were two movie theaters, and for dancing, the Venetian Gardens.

Lara had no chance to enjoy any of those things. She rose at five every morning to help Bertha prepare breakfast for the boarders and make up the beds before she left for school. In the afternoon she would hurry home to begin preparing supper. She helped Bertha serve, and after supper Lara cleared the table and washed and dried the dishes.

The boardinghouse served some favorite Scottish dishes: *howtowdie* and *hairst bree, cabbieclaw* and *skirlie*. Black Bun was a favorite, a spicy mixture encased in a short paste jacket made from half a pound of flour.

The conversation of the Scotsmen at supper made the Highlands of Scotland come alive for Lara. Her ancestors had come from the Highlands, and the stories about them gave Lara the only sense of belonging that she had. The boarders talked of the Great Glen containing loch Ness, Lochy, and Linnhe and of the rugged islands off the coast.

There was a battered piano in the sitting room, and sometimes at night, after supper, half a dozen boarders would gather around and sing the songs of home: "Annie Laurie," and "Comin' Through the Rye," and "The Hills of Home," and "The Bonnie Banks O'Loch Lomon."

Once a year there was a parade in town, and all the Scotsmen in Glace Bay would proudly put on their kilts or tartans and march through the streets to the raucous accompaniment of bagpipes.

"Why do the men wear skirts?" Lara asked Mungo McSween.

He frowned. "It's *nae* a skirt, lass. It's a kilt. Our ancestors invented it long ago. In the Highlands a plaid covered a mon's body agin the bitter cold but kept his legs free sae he could race across the heather and peat and escape his enemies. And at night, if he was in the open, the great length of the cloth was both bed and tent for him."

The names of the Scottish places were poetry to Lara. There was Breadalbane, Glenfinnan, and Kilbride, Kilninver, and Kilmichael. Lara learned that "kil" referred to a monk's cell of medieval times. If a name began with "inver" or "aber," it meant the village was at the mouth of a stream. If it began with "strath," it was in a valley. "Bad" meant the village was in a grove.

There were fierce arguments every night at the supper table. The Scotsmen argued about everything. Their ancestors had belonged to proud clans, and they were still fiercely protective of their history.

"The House of Bruce produced cowards. They lay down for the English like groveling dogs."

"You dinna ken wha' you're talking aboot, as usual, Ian. 'Twas the great Bruce himself who stood up to the English. 'Twas the House of Stuart that groveled."

"Och, you're a fool, and your clan comes from a long line of fools."

The argument would grow more heated.

"You ken wha' Scotland needed? Mair leaders like Robert the Second. Now, there was a great mon. He sired twenty-one bairns?"

"Aye, and half of them were bastards!"

And another argument would start.

Lara could not believe that they were fighting over events that had happened more than six hundred years earlier.

Mungo McSween said to Lara, "Dinna let it bother ye, lassie. A Scotsman wi' start a fight in an empty house."

It was a poem by Sir Walter Scott that set Lara's imagination on fire:

Oh, young Lochinvar is come out of the west:
Through all the wide Border his steed was the best;
And save his good broadsword he weapon had none;
He rode all unarmed and he rode all alone.
So faithful in love, and so dauntless in war,
There never was knight like the young Lochinvar.

And the glorious poem went on to tell how Lochinvar risked his life to rescue his beloved, who was being forced to marry another man.

So daring in love, and so dauntless in war,
Have ye e'er heard of gallant like young Lochinvar?

Someday, Lara thought, *a handsome Lochinvar will come and rescue me.*

One day Lara was working in the kitchen when she came across an advertisement in a magazine, and her breath caught in her throat. It showed a tall, handsome man, blond, elegantly dressed in tails and white tie. He had blue eyes and a warm smile, and he looked every inch a prince. *That's what my Lochinvar will look like,* Lara thought. *He's out there somewhere, looking for me. He'll come and rescue me from here. I'll be at the sink washing dishes, and he'll come up behind me, put his arms around me, and whisper, "Can I help you?" And I'll turn and look into his eyes. And I'll say, "Do you dry dishes?"*

Bertha's voice said, "Do I *what?*"

Lara whirled around. Bertha was standing behind her. Lara had not realized she had spoken aloud.

"Nothing." Lara blushed.

To Lara, the most fascinating dinner conversations revolved around the stories of the notorious Highland clearances. She had heard them told over and over but could never get enough of it.

"Tell me again," she would ask. And Mungo McSween was eager to oblige . . . .

"Weel, it began in the year 1792, and it went on for more than sixty years. At first they called it *Bliadhna nan Co-arach*—The Year of the Sheep. The landowners in the Highlands had decided that their land would be more profitable with sheep than with tenant farmers, so they brought flocks of sheep into the Highlands and found that they could survive the cold winters. That was when the clearances began."

"The cry became *Mo thruaighe ort a thir, tha'n caoraich mhor a' teachd!* 'Woe to thee, oh, land, the great sheep is coming.' First there were a hundred sheep, then a thousand, then ten thousand. It was a bloody invasion.

"The lairds saw riches beyond their dreams, but they maun first get rid of the tenants, who worked their wee patches of land. They had little enough to begin with, God knows. They lived in sma stone houses with nae chimneys and nae windows. But the lairds forced them out."

The young girl was wide-eyed. "How?"

"The government regiments were ordered to attack the villages and evict the tenants. The soldiers wad come to a little village and gie the tenants six hours to remove their cattle and furniture and get out. They maun leave their crops behind. Then the soldiers burned their huts to the ground. More than a quarter of a million men, women, and children were forced frae their holdings and driven to the shores of the sea."

"But how could they drive them from their own land?"

"Ah, they niver owned the land, you see. They had the use of an acre or two frae a laird, but it was niver theirs. They paid a fee in goods or labor in order to till the land and grow some tatties and raise a few cattle."

"What happened if the people wouldn't move?" Lara asked breathlessly.

"The old folk that didn't get out in time were burned in their huts. The government was ruthless. Och, it was a terrible time. The people had naething to eat. Cholera struck, and diseases spread like wildfire."

"How awful," Lara said.

"Aye, lassie. Our people lived on tatties and bread and porridge, when they could git it. But there's one thing the government could nae take away frae the Highlanders—their pride. They fought back as best they could. For days after the burning was o'er, the homeless people remained in the glen, trying to salvage what they could frae the ruins. They put canvas over their heids for protection agin the night rain. My great-great-grandfather and my great-great-grandmother were there and suffered through it all. It's part of our history, and it's been burned into our very souls."

Lara could visualize the thousands of desperate, forlorn people robbed of everything they possessed, stunned by what had happened to them. She could hear the crying of the mourners and the screams of the terrified children.

"What finally happened to the people?" Lara asked.

"They left for other lands on ships that were deathtraps. The crowded passengers died of fever or frae dysentery. Sometimes the ship would hit storms that delayed them for weeks, sae they ran out of food. Only the strong were still alive when the ships landed in Canada. But once they landed here, they were able to hae somethin' they niver had before."

"Their own land," Lara said.

"That's right, lass."

Someday, Lara thought fiercely, *I will have my own land, and no one —no one—will ever take it away from me.*

On an evening in early July, James Cameron was in bed with one of the whores at Kirstie's bawdy house when he suffered a heart attack. He was quite drunk, and when he suddenly toppled over, his playmate assumed he had simply fallen asleep.

"Oh, no, you don't! I have other customers waitin' for me. Wake up, James! Wake up!"

He was gasping for breath and clutching his chest.

"For Gude's sake," he moaned, "git me a doctor."

An ambulance took him to the little hospital on Quarry Street. Dr. Duncan sent for Lara. She walked into the hospital, her heart pounding. Duncan was waiting for her.

"What happened?" Lara asked urgently. "Is my father dead?"

"No, Lara, but I'm afraid he's had a heart attack."

She stood there, frozen. "Is he . . . is he going to live?"

"I don't know. We're doing everything we can for him."

"Can I see him?"

"It would be better if you came back in the morning, lass."

She walked home, numb with fear. *Please don't let him die, God. He's all I have.*

When Lara reached the boardinghouse, Bertha was waiting for her. "What happened?"

Lara told her.

"Oh, God!" Bertha said. "And today is Friday."

"What?"

"Friday. The day the rents have to be collected. If I know Sean MacAllister, he'll use this as an excuse to throw us all out into the streets."

At least a dozen times in the past when James Cameron had been too drunk to handle it himself, he had sent Lara around to collect the rents from the other boardinghouses that Sean MacAllister owned. Lara had given the money to her father, and the next day he had taken it to the banker.

"What are we going to do?" Bertha moaned.

And suddenly Lara knew what had to be done.

"Don't worry," she said. "I'll take care of it."

In the middle of supper that evening Lara said, "Gentlemen, would you listen to me, please?" The conversations stopped. They were all watching her. "My father has had a . . . a little dizzy spell. He's in the hospital. They want to keep him under observation for a bit. So, until he comes back, I'll be collecting the rents. After supper I'll wait for you in the parlor."

"Is he going to be all right?" one of the boarders asked.

"Oh, yes," Lara said with a forced smile. "It's nothing serious."

After supper the men came into the parlor and handed Lara their week's rent.

"I hope your father recovers soon, child . . ."

"If there's anything I can do, let me know . . ."

"You're a braw lassie to do this for your father . . ."

"What about the other boardinghouses?" Bertha asked Lara. "He has to collect from four more."

"I know," Lara said. "If you'll take care of the dishes, I'll go collect the rents."

Bertha looked at her dubiously. "I wish you luck."

It was easier than Lara had expected. Most of the boarders were sympathetic and happy to help out the young girl.

Early the following morning Lara took the rent envelopes and went to see Sean MacAllister. The banker was seated in his office when Lara walked in.

"My secretary said you wanted to see me."

"Yes, sir."

MacAllister studied the scrawny, unkempt girl standing before him. "You're James Cameron's daughter, aren't you?"

"Yes, sir."

"Sarah."

"Lara."

"Sorry to hear about your father," MacAllister said. There was no sympathy in his voice. "I'll have to make other arrangements, of course, now that your father's too ill to carry out his job. I . . ."

"Oh, no, sir!" Lara said quickly. "He asked me to handle it for him."

"You?"

"Yes, sir."

"I'm afraid that won't . . ."

Lara put the envelopes on his desk. "Here are this week's rents."

MacAllister looked at her, surprised. "All of them?"

She nodded.

"And you collected them?"

"Yes, sir. And I'll do it every week until Papa gets better."

"I see." He opened the envelopes and carefully counted the money. Lara watched him enter the amount in a large green ledger.

For some time now MacAllister had intended to replace James Cameron because of his drunkenness and erratic performance, and now he saw his opportunity to get rid of the family.

He was sure that the young girl in front of him would not be able to carry out her father's duties, but at the same time he realized what the town's reaction would be if he threw James Cameron and his daughter out of the boardinghouse into the street. He made his decision.

"I'll try you for one month," he said. "At the end of that time we'll see where we stand."

"Thank you, Mr. MacAllister. Thank you very much."

"Wait." He handed Lara twenty-five dollars. "This is yours."

Lara held the money in her hand, and it was like a taste of freedom. It was the first time she had ever been paid for what she had done.

From the bank, Lara went to the hospital. Dr. Duncan was just coming out of her father's room. Lara felt a sudden sense of panic. "He isn't . . . ?"

"No . . . no . . . he's going to be all right, Lara." He hesitated. "When I say 'all right,' I mean he is not going to die . . . not yet, at least . . . but he is going to have to stay in bed for a few weeks. He'll need someone to take care of him."

"I'll take care of him," Lara said.

He looked at her and said, softly, "Your father doesn't know it, my dear, but he's a very lucky man."

"May I go in and see him now?"

"Yes."

Lara walked into her father's room and stood there staring at him. James Cameron lay in bed, looking pale and helpless, and he suddenly seemed very old. Lara was engulfed by a wave of tenderness. She was finally going to be able to do something for her father, something that would make him appreciate her and love her. She approached the bed.

"Papa . . ."

He looked up and muttered, "What the bluidy hell are you doin' here? You've work to dae at the boardin'house."

Lara froze. "I . . . I know, Papa. I just wanted to tell you that I saw Mr. MacAllister. I told him I would collect the rents until you got better and . . ."

"*Ye* collect the rents? Dinna make me laugh." He was shaken with a sudden spasm. When he spoke again, his voice was weak. "It's the Fates," he moaned. "I'm gang to be thrown oot into the streets."

He was not even thinking about what would happen to her. Lara stood there looking at him for a long time. Then she turned and walked out.

James Cameron was brought home three days later, and put to bed.

"You're not to get out of bed for the next couple of weeks," Dr. Duncan told him. "I'll come back and check on you in a day or two."

"I canna stay in bed," James Cameron protested. "I'm a busy mon. I have a lot to dae."

The doctor looked at him and said, quietly, "You have a choice. You can either stay in bed and live, or get up and die."

MacAllister's boarders were, at first, delighted to see the innocent young girl come around to collect their rents. But when the novelty wore off, they had a myriad of excuses:

"I was sick this week, and I had medical bills . . ."

"My son sends me money every week, but the mail's been delayed . . ."

"I had to buy some equipment . . ."

"I'll have the money for you next week for sure . . ."

But the young girl was fighting for her life. She listened politely and said, "I'm so sorry, but Mr. MacAllister says that the money is due today, and if you don't have it, you'll have to vacate immediately."

And somehow, they all managed to come up with the money.

Lara was inflexible.

"It was easier dealing with your father," one of the boarders grumbled. "He was always willing to wait a few days."

But in the end they had to admire the young girl's spunk.

* * *

If Lara had thought that her father's illness would bring him closer to her, she was sadly mistaken. Lara tried to anticipate his every need, but the more solicitous she was, the more badly he behaved.

She brought him fresh flowers every day, and little treats.

"For Gude's sakes!" he cried. "Stop hoverin' aboot. Hae you nae work to dae?"

"I just thought you'd like . . ."

"Oot!" He turned his face to the wall.

I hate him, Lara thought. *I hate him.*

At the end of the month, when Lara walked into Sean MacAllister's office with the envelopes filled with rent money, and he had finished counting it, he said, "I don't mind admitting, young lady, that you've been quite a surprise to me. You've done better than your father."

The words were thrilling. "Thank you."

"As a matter of fact, this is the first month that everybody has paid on time in full."

"Then my father and I can stay on at the boardinghouse?" Lara asked eagerly.

MacAllister studied her a moment. "I suppose so. You must love your father very much."

"I'll see you next Saturday, Mr. MacAllister."

Chapter Five

At seventeen, the spindly, gaunt little girl had grown into a woman. Her face bore the imprint of her Scottish forebears: the gleaming skin, the arched, fine eyebrows, the thundercloud gray eyes, the stormy black hair. And in addition, there was a strain of melancholy that seemed to hover around her, the bleed-through of a people's tragic history. It was hard to look away from Lara Cameron's face.

Most of the boarders were without women, except for the companions they paid for at Madam Kirstie's and some of the other houses of prostitution, and the beautiful young girl was a natural target for them. One of the men would corner her in the kitchen or in his bedroom when she was cleaning it and say, "Why don't you be nice to me, Lara? I could do a lot for you."

Or, "You don't have a boyfriend, do you? Let me show you what a man is like."

Or, "How would you like to go to Kansas City? I'm leaving next week, and I'd be glad to take you with me."

After one or another of the boarders had tried to persuade Lara to go to bed with him, she would walk into the small room where her father lay helpless, and say, "You were wrong, Father. All the men want me." And she would walk out, leaving him staring after her.

James Cameron died on an early morning in spring, and Lara buried him at the Greenwood Cemetery in the Passiondale area. The only other person at the funeral was Bertha. There were no tears.

A new boarder moved in, an American named Bill Rogers. He was in his seventies, bald and fat, an affable man who liked to talk. After supper he would sit and chat with Lara. "You're too damned pretty to be stuck in a hick town like this," he advised her. "You should go to Chicago or New York. Big time."

"I will one day," Lara said.

"You've got your whole life ahead of you. Do you know what you want to do with it?"

"I want to own things."

"Ah, pretty clothes and . . ."

"No. Land. I want to own land. My father never owned anything. He had to live off other people's favors all his life."

Bill Rogers's face lit up. "Real estate was the business I was in."

"Really?"

"I had buildings all over the Midwest. I even had a chain of hotels once." His tone was wistful.

"What happened?"

He shrugged. "I got greedy. Lost it all. But it was sure fun while it lasted."

After that they talked about real estate almost every night.

"The first rule in real estate," Rogers told her, "is OPM. Never forget that."

"What's OPM?"

"Other people's money. What makes real estate a great business is that the government lets you take deductions on interest and depreciation while your assets keep growing. The three most important things in real estate are location, location, and location. A beautiful building up on a hill is a waste of time. An ugly building downtown will make you rich."

Rogers taught Lara about mortgages and refinancing and the use of bank loans. Lara listened and learned and remembered. She was like a sponge, eagerly soaking up every bit of information.

The most meaningful thing Rogers said to her was: "You know, Glace Bay has a big housing shortage. It's a great opportunity for someone. If I were twenty years younger . . ."

From that moment on Lara looked at Glace Bay with different eyes, visualizing office buildings and homes on vacant lots. It was exciting, and it was frustrating. Her dreams were there, but she had no money to carry them out.

The day Bill Rogers left town he said, "Remember—other people's money. Good luck, kid."

A week later Charles Cohn moved into the boardinghouse. He was a small man in his sixties, neat and trim and well dressed. He sat at the supper table with the other boarders but said very little. He seemed cocooned in his own private world.

He watched Lara as she worked around the boardinghouse, smiling, never complaining.

"How long do you plan to stay with us?" Lara asked Cohn.

"I'm not sure. It could be a week or a month or two . . ."

Charles Cohn was a puzzle to Lara. He did not fit in with the other boarders at all. She tried to imagine what he did. He was certainly not a miner or a fisherman, and he did not look like a merchant. He seemed superior to the other boarders, better educated. He told Lara that he had tried to get into the one hotel in town but that it was full. Lara noticed that at mealtimes he ate almost nothing.

"If you have a little fruit," he would say, apologetically, "or some vegetables . . ."

"Are you on some special kind of diet?" Lara asked.

"In a way. I eat only kosher food, and I'm afraid Glace Bay doesn't have any."

The next evening, when Charles Cohn sat down to supper, a plate of lamb chops was placed in front of him. He looked up at Lara in surprise. "I'm sorry. I can't eat this," he said. "I thought I explained . . ."

Lara smiled. "You did. This is kosher."

"What?"

"I found a kosher meat market in Sydney. The *shochet* there sold me this. Enjoy it. Your rent includes two meals a day. Tomorrow you're having a steak."

From that time on, whenever Lara had a free moment, Cohn made it a point to talk to her, to draw her out. He was impressed by her quick intelligence and her independent spirit.

One day Charles Cohn confided to Lara what he was doing in Glace Bay. "I'm an executive with Continental Supplies." It was a famous national chain. "I'm here to find a location for our new store."

"That's exciting," Lara said. *I knew he was in Glace Bay for some important reason.* "You're going to put up a building?"

"No. We'll find someone else to do that. We just lease our buildings."

At three o'clock in the morning Lara awakened out of a sound sleep and sat up in bed, her heart pounding wildly. Had it been a dream? No. Her mind was racing. She was too excited to go back to sleep.

When Charles Cohn came out of his room for breakfast, Lara was waiting for him.

"Mr. Cohn . . . I know a great place," she blurted out.

He stared at her, puzzled. "What?"

"For the location you're looking for."

"Oh? Where?"

Lara evaded the question. "Let me ask you something. If I owned a location that you liked, and if I put up a building on it, would you agree to lease it from me for five years?"

He shook his head. "That's a rather hypothetical question, isn't it?"

"Would you?" Lara persisted.

"Lara, what do you know about putting up a building?"

"I wouldn't be putting it up," she said. "I'd hire an architect and a good construction firm to do that."

Charles Cohn was watching her closely. "I see. And where is this wonderful piece of land?"

"I'll show it to you," Lara said. "Believe me, you're going to love it. It's perfect."

After breakfast Lara took Charles Cohn downtown. At the corner of Main and Commercial streets in the center of Glace Bay was a vacant square block. It was a site Cohn had examined two days earlier.

"This is the location I had in mind," Lara said.

Cohn stood there, pretending to study it. "You have an *ahf*—a nose. It's a very good location."

He had already made discreet inquiries and learned that the property was owned by a banker, Sean MacAllister. Cohn's assignment was to locate a site, arrange for someone to construct the building, and then lease it from them. It would not matter to the company who put up the building as long as its specifications were met.

Cohn was studying Lara. *She's too young,* he thought. *It's a foolish idea. And yet . . . "I found a kosher meat market in Sydney . . . Tomorrow you're having a steak."* She had such *rachmones*—compassion.

Lara was saying, excitedly, "If I could acquire this land and put up a building to meet your specifications, would you give me a five-year lease?"

He paused, and then said slowly, "No, Lara. It would have to be a ten-year lease."

That afternoon Lara went to see Sean MacAllister. He looked up in surprise as she walked into his office.

"You're a few days early, Lara. Today's only Wednesday."

"I know. I want to ask a favor, Mr. MacAllister."

Sean MacAllister sat there, watching her. *She has really turned into a beautiful-looking girl. Not a girl, a woman.* He could see the swell of her breasts against the cotton blouse she was wearing.

"Sit down, my dear. What can I do for you?"

Lara was too excited to sit. "I want to take out a loan."

It took him by surprise. "What?"

"I'd like to borrow some money."

He smiled indulgently. "I don't see why not. If you need a new dress or something, I'll be happy to advance . . ."

"I want to borrow two hundred thousand dollars."

MacAllister's smile died. "Is this some kind of joke?"

"No, sir." Lara leaned forward and said earnestly, "There's a piece of land I want to buy to put up a building. I have an important tenant who's willing to give me a ten-year lease. That will guarantee the cost of the land and the building."

MacAllister was studying her, frowning. "Have you discussed this with the owner of the land?"

"I'm discussing it with him now," Lara said.

It took a moment for it to sink in. "Wait a minute. Are you telling me that this is land that *I* own?"

"Yes. It's the lot on the corner of Main and Commercial streets."

"You came here to borrow money from *me* to buy *my* land?"

"That lot is worth no more than twenty thousand dollars. I checked. I'm offering you thirty. You'll make a profit of ten thousand dollars on the land plus interest on two hundred thousand dollars you're going to loan me to put up the building."

MacAllister shook his head. "You're asking me to loan you two hundred thousand dollars with no security. It's out of the question."

Lara leaned forward. "There *is* security. You'll hold the mortgage on the building and the land. You can't lose."

MacAllister sat there studying her, turning her proposal over in his mind. He smiled. "You know," he said, "you have a lot of nerve. But I could never explain a loan like that to my board of directors."

"You have no board of directors," Lara told him.

The smile turned to a grin. "True."

Lara leaned forward, and he could see her breasts touching the edge of his desk.

"If you say yes, Mr. MacAllister, you'll never regret it. I promise."

He could not take his eyes off her breasts. "You're not a bit like your father, are you?"

"No, sir." *Nothing like him,* Lara thought fiercely.

"Supposing for the sake of argument," MacAllister said carefully, "that I was interested. Who is this tenant of yours?"

"His name is Charles Cohn. He's an executive with Continental Supplies."

"The chain store?"

"Yes."

MacAllister was suddenly very interested.

Lara went on. "They want to have a big store built here to supply the miners and lumbermen with equipment."

To MacAllister, it had the smell of instant success.

"Where did you meet this man?" he asked casually.

"He's staying at the boardinghouse."

"I see. Let me think about it, Lara. We'll discuss it again tomorrow."

Lara was almost trembling with excitement. "Thank you, Mr. MacAllister. You won't be sorry."

He smiled. "No, I don't think I will be."

That afternoon Sean MacAllister went to the boardinghouse to meet Charles Cohn.

"I just dropped by to welcome you to Glace Bay," MacAllister said. "I'm Sean MacAllister. I own the bank here. I heard you were in town. But you shouldn't be staying at my boardinghouse; you should be staying at my hotel. It's much more comfortable."

"It was full," Mr. Cohn explained.

"That's because we didn't know who you were."

Mr. Cohn said pleasantly, "Who am I?"

Sean MacAllister smiled. "We don't have to play games, Mr. Cohn.

Word gets around. I understand that you're interested in leasing a building to be put up on a property I own."

"What property would that be?"

"The lot at Main and Commercial. It's a great location, isn't it? I don't think we'll have any problem making a deal."

"I already have a deal with someone."

Sean MacAllister laughed. "Lara? She's a pretty little thing, isn't she? Why don't you come down to the bank with me and we'll draw up a contract?"

"I don't think you understand, Mr. MacAllister. I said I already have a deal."

"I don't think *you* understand, Mr. Cohn. Lara doesn't own that land. I do."

"She's trying to buy it from you, isn't she?"

"Yes. I don't have to sell it to her."

"And I don't have to use that lot. I've seen three other lots that will do just as nicely. Thanks for dropping by."

Sean MacAllister looked at him for a long moment. "You mean . . . you're serious?"

"Very. I never go into a deal that's not kosher, and I never break my word."

"But Lara doesn't know anything about building. She . . ."

"She plans to find people who do. Naturally, we'll have final approval."

The banker was thoughtful. "Do I understand that Continental Supplies is willing to sign a ten-year lease?"

"That's correct."

"I see. Well, under the circumstances, I . . . let me think about it."

When Lara arrived at the boardinghouse, Charles Cohn told her about his conversation with the banker.

Lara was upset. "You mean Mr. MacAllister went behind my back and . . . ?"

"Don't worry," Cohn assured her, "he'll make the deal with you."

"Do you really think so?"

"He's a banker. He's in business to make a profit."

"What about you? Why are you doing this for me?" Lara asked.

He had asked himself the same question. *Because you're achingly young*, he thought. *Because you don't belong in this town. Because I wish I had a daughter like you.*

But he said none of those things.

"I have nothing to lose, Lara. I found some other locations that would serve just as well. If you can acquire this land, I'd like to do this for you. It doesn't matter to my company who I deal with. If you get your loan, and I approve your builder, we're in business."

A feeling of elation swept over Lara. "I . . . I don't know how to thank you. I'll go to see Mr. MacAllister and . . ."

"I wouldn't if I were you," Cohn advised her. "Let him come to you."

She looked worried. "But what if he doesn't . . . ?"

Cohn smiled. "He will."

He handed her a printed lease. "Here's the ten-year lease we discussed. It's contingent, you understand, on your meeting all our requirements for the building." He handed her a set of blueprints. "These are our specifications."

Lara spent the night studying the pages of drawings and instructions.

The following morning Sean MacAllister telephoned Lara.

"Can you come down to see me, Lara?"

Her heart was pounding. "I'll be there in fifteen minutes."

He was waiting for her.

"I've been thinking about our conversation," MacAllister said. "I would need a written agreement for a ten-year lease from Mr. Cohn."

"I already have it," Lara said. She opened her bag and took out the contract.

Sean MacAllister examined it carefully. "It seems to be in order."

"Then we have a deal?" Lara asked. She was holding her breath.

MacAllister shook his head. "No."

"But I thought . . ."

His fingers were drumming restlessly on his desk. "To tell you the truth, I'm really in no hurry to sell that lot, Lara. The longer I hold on to it, the more valuable it will become."

She looked at him blankly. "But you . . ."

"Your request is completely unorthodox. You've had no experience. I would need a very special reason to make this loan to you."

"I don't under . . . what kind of reason?"

"Let's say . . . a little bonus. Tell me, Lara, have you ever had a lover?"

The question caught her completely off-guard.

"I . . . no." She could feel the deal slipping away from her. "What does that have . . . ?"

MacAllister leaned forward. "I'm going to be frank with you, Lara. I find you very attractive. I'd like to go to bed with you. *Quid pro quo.* That means . . ."

"I know what it means." Her face had turned to stone.

"Look at it this way. This is your chance to make something of yourself, isn't it? To own something, to be somebody. To prove to yourself that you're not like your father."

Lara's mind was spinning.

"You'll probably never have another chance like this again, Lara. Perhaps you'd like some time to think it over, and . . ."

"No." Her voice sounded hollow in her own ears. "I can give you my answer now." She pressed her arms tightly against her sides to stop her body from trembling. Her whole future, her very life, hung on her next words.

"I'll go to bed with you."

Grinning, MacAllister rose and moved toward her, his fat arms outstretched.

"Not now," Lara said. "After I see the contract."

The following day Sean MacAllister handed Lara a contract for the bank loan.

"It's a very simple contract, my dear. It's a ten-year two-hundred-thousand-dollar loan at eight percent." He gave her a pen. "You can just sign here on the last page."

"If you don't mind, I'd like to read it first," Lara said. She looked at her watch. "But I don't have time now. May I take it with me? I'll bring it back tomorrow."

Sean MacAllister shrugged. "Very well." He lowered his voice. "About our little date. Next Saturday I have to go into Halifax. I thought we might go there together."

Lara looked at his leering smile and felt sick to her stomach. "All right." It was a whisper.

"Good. You sign the contract and bring it back and we're in business." He was thoughtful for a moment. "You're going to need a good builder. Are you familiar with the Nova Scotia Construction Company?"

Lara's face lit up. "Yes. I know their foreman, Buzz Steele."

He had put up some of the biggest buildings in Glace Bay."
"Good. It's a fine outfit. I would recommend them."
"I'll talk to Buzz tomorrow."

That evening Lara showed the contract to Charles Cohn. She did not dare tell him about the private deal she had made with MacAllister. She was too ashamed. Cohn read the contract carefully, and when he finished, he handed it back to Lara. "I would advise you not to sign this."

She was dismayed. "Why?"

"There's a clause in there that stipulates that the building must be completed by December thirty-first, or title reverts to the bank. In other words, the building will belong to MacAllister, and my company will become *his* tenant. You forfeit the deal and are still obligated to repay the loan with interest. Ask him to change that."

MacAllister's words rang in Lara's ears. *"I'm really in no hurry to sell that lot. The longer I hold on to it, the more valuable it will become."*

Lara shook her head. "He won't."

"Then you're taking a big gamble, Lara. You could wind up with nothing, and a debt of two hundred thousand dollars plus interest."

"But if I bring the building in on time . . ."

"That's a big 'if.' When you put up a building, you're at the mercy of a lot of other people. You'd be surprised at the number of things that can go wrong."

"There's a very good construction company in Sydney. They've put up a lot of buildings around here. I know the foreman. If he says he can have the building up in time, I want to go ahead."

It was the desperate eagerness in Lara's voice that made him put aside his doubts. "All right," he finally said, "talk to him."

Lara found Buzz Steele walking the girders of a five-story building he was erecting in Sydney. Steele was a grizzled, weather-beaten man in his forties. He greeted Lara warmly. "This is a nice surprise," he said. "How did they let a pretty girl like you get out of Glace Bay?"

"I sneaked out," Lara told him. "I have a job for you, Mr. Steele."

He smiled. "You do? What are we building—a dollhouse?"

"No." She pulled out the blueprints Charles Cohn had given her. "This is the building."

Buzz Steele studied it a moment. He looked up, surprised. "This is a pretty big job. What does it have to do with you?"

"I put the deal together," Lara said proudly. "I'm going to own the building."

Steele whistled softly. "Well, good for you, honey."

"There are two catches."

"Oh?"

"The building has to be finished by December thirty-first or it reverts to the bank, and the building can't cost more than one hundred seventy thousand dollars. Can it be done?"

Steele looked at the blueprints again. Lara watched him silently calculating.

Finally he spoke. "It can be done."

It was all Lara could do not to shout out loud.

"Then you've got a deal."

They shook hands. "You're the prettiest boss I've ever had," Buzz Steele said.

"Thank you. How soon can you get started?"

"Tell you what. I'll go into Glace Bay tomorrow to look over the lot. I'm going to give you a building you'll be proud of."

When Lara left, she felt that she had wings.

Lara returned to Glace Bay and told Charles Cohn the news.

"Are you sure this company is reliable, Lara?"

"I know it is," Lara assured him. "They've put up buildings here and in Sydney and Halifax and . . ."

Her enthusiasm was contagious.

Cohn smiled. "Well, then, it looks like we're in business."

"It does, doesn't it?" Lara beamed. And then she remembered the deal she had made with Sean MacAllister, and her smile faded. *"Next Saturday I have to go into Halifax. I thought we might go there together."* Saturday was only two days away.

Lara signed the contracts the following morning. As Sean MacAllister watched her leave the office, he was very pleased with himself. He had no intention of letting her have the new building. And he almost laughed aloud at her naïveté. He would loan her the money, but he would really be loaning it to himself. He thought about making love to that wonderful young body, and he began to get an erection.

Lara had been to Halifax only twice. Compared to Glace Bay, it was a bustling town, full of pedestrians and automobiles and shops crammed with merchandise. Sean MacAllister drove Lara to a motel on the outskirts of town. He pulled into the parking lot and patted her on the knee. "You wait here while I register for us, honey."

Lara sat in the car, waiting, panicky. *I'm selling myself*, she thought. *Like a whore. But it's all I've got to sell, and at least he thinks I'm worth two hundred thousand dollars. My father never saw two hundred thousand dollars in his life. He was always too* . . .

The car door opened, and MacAllister was standing there, grinning. "All set. Let's go."

Lara suddenly found it hard to breathe. Her heart was pounding so hard she thought it was going to fly out of her chest. *I'm having a heart attack*, she thought.

"Lara . . ." He was looking at her strangely. "Are you all right?"

No. I'm dying. They'll take me to the hospital, and I'll die there. A virgin. "I'm fine," she said.

Slowly she got out of the car and followed MacAllister into a drab cabin with a bed, two chairs, a battered dressing table, and a tiny bathroom.

She was caught up in a nightmare.

"So this is your first time, eh?" MacAllister said.

She thought of the boys at school who had fondled her and kissed her breasts and tried to put their hands between her legs. "Yes," she said.

"Well, you mustn't be nervous. Sex is the most natural thing in the world."

Lara watched as MacAllister began to strip off his clothes. His body was pudgy.

"Get undressed," MacAllister ordered.

Slowly Lara took off her blouse and skirt and shoes. She was wearing a brassiere and panties.

MacAllister looked at her figure and walked over to her. "You're beautiful, you know that, baby?"

She could feel his male hardness pressing against her body. MacAllister kissed her on the lips, and she felt disgust.

"Get the rest of your clothes off," he said urgently. He walked over to the bed and stripped off his shorts. His penis was hard and red.

That will never fit inside me, Lara thought. *It will kill me.*

"Hurry up."

Slowly Lara took off her brassiere and stepped out of her panties.

"My God," he said, "you're fantastic. Come over here."

Lara walked over to the bed and sat down. MacAllister squeezed her breasts hard, and she cried aloud with the pain.

"That felt good, didn't it? It's time you had yourself a man." MacAllister pushed her down on her back and spread her legs.

Lara was suddenly panicky. "I'm not wearing anything," she said. "I mean . . . I could get pregnant."

"Don't worry," MacAllister promised her, "I won't come inside you."

An instant later Lara felt him pushing inside her, hurting her.

"Wait!" she cried. "I . . ."

MacAllister was past the waiting. He rammed himself into her, and the pain was excruciating. He was pounding into her body now, harder and harder, and Lara put her hand to her mouth to keep from screaming. *It will be over in a minute,* she thought, *and I'll own a building. And I can put up a second building. And another . . .*

The pain was becoming unbearable.

"Move your ass," MacAllister cried. "Don't just lay there. Move it!"

She tried to move, but it was impossible. She was in too much pain.

Suddenly MacAllister gave a gasp, and Lara felt his body jerk. He let out a satisfied sigh and lay limp against her.

She was horrified. "You said you wouldn't . . ."

He lifted himself up on his elbows and said earnestly, "Darling, I couldn't help it, you're just so beautiful. But don't worry. If you get pregnant, I know a doctor who'll take care of you."

Lara turned her face away so he could not see her revulsion. She limped into the bathroom, sore and bleeding. She stood in the shower, letting the warm water wash over her body, and she thought, *It's over with. I've done it. I own the land. I'm going to be rich.*

Now all she had to do was get dressed and go back to Glace Bay and get her building started.

She walked out of the bathroom, and Sean MacAllister said, "That was so good we're going to do it again."

Chapter Six

Charles Cohn had inspected five buildings erected by the Nova Scotia Construction Company.

"They're a first-rate outfit," he had told Lara. "You shouldn't have any problem with them."

Now Lara, Charles Cohn, and Buzz Steele were inspecting the new site.

"It's perfect," Buzz Steele said. "The measurements come to forty-three thousand five hundred sixty square feet. That will give you the twenty-thousand-square-foot building you want."

Charles Cohn asked, "Can you have the building finished by December thirty-first?" He was determined to protect Lara.

"Sooner," Steele said. "I can promise it to you by Christmas Eve."

Lara was beaming. "How soon can you get started?"

"I'll have my crew here by the middle of next week."

Watching the new building going up was the most exciting thing Lara had ever experienced. She was there every day. "I want to learn," she told Charles Cohn. "This is just the beginning for me. Before I'm through, I'm going to put up a hundred buildings."

Cohn wondered whether Lara really knew what she was getting into.

The first men to set foot on the project site were members of the survey team. They established the legal geometric borders of the property and drove hubs into the ground at each corner, every hub painted with a fluorescent color for easy identification. The survey work was finished in two days, and early the following morning, heavy earth-moving equipment—a truck-mounted Caterpillar front-end loader—arrived at the site.

Lara was there, waiting. "What happens now?" she asked Buzz Steele.

"We clear and grub."

Lara looked at him. "What does that mean?"

"The Caterpillar is gonna dig up tree stumps and do some rough grading."

The next piece of equipment that came in was a backhoe to dig the trenches for foundations, utility conduits, and drainage piping.

By now the boarders at the house had all heard what was happening, and it became the main topic of conversation at breakfast and supper. They were all cheering for Lara.

"What happens next?" they would ask.

She was becoming an expert. "This morning they put the underground piping in place. Tomorrow they start to put in the wood and concrete formwork, so they can wire-tie the steel bars into the skeletal gridiron." She grinned. "Do you understand what I'm saying?"

Pouring the concrete was the next step, and when the concrete foundation was cured, large truckloads of lumber rolled in, and crews of carpenters began to assemble the wooden frames. The noise was horrendous, but to Lara it was music. The place was filled with the sounds of rhythmic hammers and whining power saws. After two weeks the wall panels, punctuated with window and door openings, were stood upright as if the building had suddenly been inflated.

To passersby, the building was a maze of wood and steel, but to Lara it was something else. It was her dream come to life. Every morning and every evening she went downtown and stared at what was being built. *I own this,* Lara thought. *This belongs to me.*

After the episode with MacAllister, Lara had been terrified that she might become pregnant. The thought of it made her sick to her stomach. When her period came, she was weak with relief. *Now all I have to worry about is my building.*

She continued to collect the rents for Sean MacAllister because she needed a place to live, but she had to steel herself to go into his office and face him.

"We had a good time in Halifax, didn't we, honey? Why don't we do it again?"

"I'm busy with my building," Lara said firmly.

The level of activity began to heighten as the sheet metal crews, roofers, and carpenters worked simultaneously, the number of men, materials, and trucks tripling.

Charles Cohn had left Glace Bay, but he telephoned Lara once a week.

"How is the building going?" he had asked the last time he called.

"Great!" Lara said enthusiastically.

"Is it on schedule?"

"It's ahead of schedule."

"That's wonderful. I can tell you now that I wasn't really sure you could do it."

"But you gave me a chance anyway. Thank you, Charles."

"One good turn deserves another. Remember, if it hadn't been for you, I might have starved to death."

From time to time Sean MacAllister would join Lara at the building site.

"It's coming along just fine, isn't it?"

"Yes," Lara said.

MacAllister seemed genuinely pleased. Lara thought: *Mr. Cohn was wrong about him. He's not trying to take advantage of me.*

By the end of November the building was progressing rapidly. The windows and doors were in place, and the exterior walls were set. The structure was ready to accept the network of nerves and arteries.

On Monday, the first week of December, work on the building began to slow down. Lara went to the site one morning, and there were only two men there, and they seemed to be doing very little.

"Where's the rest of the crew today?" Lara asked.

"They're on another job," one of the men explained. "They'll be here tomorrow."

The following day no one was there.

Lara took a bus into Halifax to see Buzz Steele. "What's happening?" Lara asked. "The work has stopped."

"Nothing to worry about," Steele assured her. "We ran into a little snag on another job, and I had to pull my men off temporarily."

"When will they be coming back to work?"

"Next week. We'll be on schedule."

"Buzz, you know how much this means to me."

"Sure, Lara."

"If the building's not completed on time, I lose it. I lose everything."

"Don't worry, kid. I won't let that happen."

When Lara left, she had a feeling of unease.

The following week the workmen still had not appeared. She went into Halifax again to see Steele.

"I'm sorry," the secretary said, "Mr. Steele is not in."

"I must talk to him. When will he be back?"

"He's out of town on a job. I don't know when he'll be back."

Lara felt the first stirrings of panic. "This is very important," Lara insisted. "He's putting up a building for me. It has to be finished in three weeks."

"I wouldn't worry, Miss Cameron. If Mr. Steele said it will be finished, it will be finished."

"But nothing's happening," Lara cried. "No one's working on it."

"Would you like to talk to Mr. Ericksen, his assistant?"

"Yes, please."

Ericksen was a giant of a man, broad-shouldered and amiable. He radiated reassurance.

"I know why you're here," he said, "but Buzz told me to assure you that you have nothing to worry about. We've been held back a little on your project because of some problems on a couple of big construction jobs we're handling, but your building is only three weeks away from completion."

"There's still so much to do . . ."

"Not to worry. We'll have a crew out there first thing on Monday morning."

"Thank you," Lara said, relieved. "I'm sorry to have bothered you, but I'm a little nervous. This means a great deal to me."

"No problem," Ericksen smiled. "You just go home and relax. You're in good hands."

Monday morning there was not a single workman at the site. Lara was frantic. She telephoned Charles Cohn.

"The men have stopped working," she told him, "and I can't find out why. They keep making promises and breaking them."

"What's the name of the company—Nova Scotia Construction?"

"That's right."

"I'll call you back," Cohn said.

Two hours later Charles Cohn telephoned. "Who recommended the Nova Scotia Construction Company to you?"

She thought back. "Sean MacAllister."

"I'm not surprised. He owns the company, Lara."

Lara felt suddenly faint. "And he's stopping the men from finishing it on time . . . ?"

"I'm afraid it looks that way."

"Oh, my God."

"He's a *nahash tzefa*—a poisonous snake."

He was too kind to say that he had warned her. All he managed was: "Maybe . . . maybe something will turn up."

He admired the young girl's spirit and ambition, and he despised Sean MacAllister. But he was helpless. There was nothing he could do.

Lara lay awake all night thinking about her folly. The building she had put up would belong now to Sean MacAllister, and she would be left with a staggering debt which she would spend the rest of her life working to repay. The thought of how MacAllister might exact payment made her shudder.

When Lara awakened, she went to see Sean MacAllister.

"Good morning, my dear. You're looking lovely today."

Lara came right to the point. "I need an extension. The building won't be ready by the thirty-first."

MacAllister sat back in his chair and frowned. "Really? That's bad news, Lara."

"I need another month."

MacAllister sighed. "I'm afraid that's not possible. Oh, dear, no. You signed a contract. A deal is a deal."

"But . . ."

"I'm sorry, Lara. On the thirty-first, the property reverts to the bank."

When the boarders at the house heard what was happening, they were furious.

"That son of a bitch!" one of them cried. "He can't do this to you."

"He's done it," Lara said, despairingly. "It's over."

"Are we going to let him get away with this?"

"Hell, no. What have you got left—three weeks?"

Lara shook her head. "Less. Two and a half weeks."

The man turned to the others. "Let's go down and take a look at that building."

"What good will . . . ?"

"We'll see."

Soon half a dozen boarders were standing at the building site, carefully inspecting it.

"The plumbing hasn't been put in," one of the men said.

"Nor the electricity."

They stood there, shivering in the freezing December wind, discussing what still remained to be done.

One of the men turned to Lara. "Your banker's a tricky fellow. He's had the building almost finished so that he wouldn't have much to do when your contract was up." He turned to the others. "I would say that this could be finished in two and a half weeks."

There was a chorus of agreement.

Lara was bewildered. "You don't understand. The workmen won't come."

"Look, lassie, in your boardinghouse you've got plumbers and carpenters and electricians, and we've got lots of friends in town who can handle the rest."

"I don't have any money to pay you," Lara said. "Mr. MacAllister won't give me . . ."

"It will be our Christmas gift to you."

What happened after that was incredible. Word quickly spread around Glace Bay of what was happening. Construction workers on other buildings came to take a look at Lara's property. Half of them were there because they liked Lara, and the other half because they had had dealings with Sean MacAllister and hated him.

"Let's fix the bastard," they said.

They dropped by to lend a hand after work, working past midnight and on Saturdays and Sundays, and the sound of construction began again, filling the air with a joyful noise. Beating the deadline became a challenge, and the building was soon swarming with carpenters and electricians and plumbers, all eager to pitch in. When Sean MacAllister heard what was happening, he rushed over to the site.

He stood there, stunned. "What's going on?" he demanded. "Those aren't my workmen."

"They're mine," Lara said defiantly. "There's nothing in the contract that says I can't use my own men."

"Well, I . . ." MacAllister sputtered. "That building had better be up to specifications."

"It will be," Lara assured him.

The day before New Year's Eve the building was completed. It stood proud against the sky, solid and strong, and it was the most beautiful thing Lara had ever seen. She stood there staring at it, dazed.

"It's all yours," one of the workmen said proudly. "Are we going to have a party or what?"

That night it seemed that the whole town of Glace Bay celebrated Lara Cameron's first building.

It was the beginning.

There was no stopping Lara after that. Her mind was brimming with ideas.

"Your new employees are going to need places to live in Glace Bay," she told Charles Cohn. "I'd like to build houses for them. Are you interested?"

He nodded. "I'm very interested."

Lara went to see a banker in Sydney and borrowed enough money on her building to finance the new project.

When the houses were finished, Lara said to Charles Cohn, "Do you know what else this town needs, Charles? Cabins to accommodate the summer tourists who come here to fish. I know a wonderful place near the bay where I could build . . ."

Charles Cohn became Lara's unofficial financial adviser, and during the next three years Lara built an office building, half a dozen seashore cottages, and a shopping mall. The banks in Sydney and Halifax were happy to loan her money.

Two years later, when Lara sold out her real estate holdings, she had a certified check for three million dollars. She was twenty-one years old.

The following day she said good-bye to Glace Bay and left for Chicago.

Chapter Seven

Chicago was a revelation. Halifax had been the largest city Lara had ever seen, but it was like a hamlet compared to the giant of the Midwest. Chicago was a loud and noisy city, bustling and energetic, and everyone seemed to be hurrying to some important destination.

Lara checked into the Stevens Hotel. She took one look at the smartly dressed women walking through the lobby and became self-conscious about the clothes she was wearing. *Glace Bay, yes,* Lara thought. *Chicago, no.* The following morning, Lara went into action. She visited Kane's and Ultimo for designer dresses, Joseph's for shoes, Saks Fifth Avenue and Marshall Field's for lingerie, Trabert and Hoeffer for jewelry, and Ware for a mink coat. And every time she bought something, she heard her father's voice saying, *"I'm nae made of money. Get yourself something frae the Salvation Army Citadel."* Before her shopping spree was over, the closets in her hotel suite were filled with beautiful clothes.

Lara's next move was to look in the yellow pages of the telephone book under "Real Estate Brokers." She selected the one that had the largest advertisement, Parker & Associates. Lara telephoned and asked to speak to Mr. Parker.

"May I tell him who's calling?"

"Lara Cameron."

A moment later a voice said, "Bruce Parker speaking. How can I help you?"

"I'm looking for a location where I can put up a beautiful new hotel," Lara said.

The voice at the other end of the phone grew warmer. "Well, we're experts at that, Mrs. Cameron."

"*Miss* Cameron."

"Right. Did you have any particular area in mind?"

"No. To tell you the truth, I'm not really familiar with Chicago."

"That's no problem. I'm sure we can line up some very interesting properties for you. Just to give me an idea of what we're looking for, how much equity do you have?"

Lara said proudly, "Three million dollars."

There was a long silence. "Three million dollars?"

"Yes."

"And you want to build a beautiful new hotel?"

"Yes."

Another silence.

"Were you interested in building or acquiring something in the inner city area, Miss Cameron?"

"Of course not," Lara said. "What I have in mind is exactly the opposite. I want to build an exclusive boutique hotel in a nice area that . . ."

"With an equity of three million dollars?" Parker chuckled. "I'm afraid we're not going to be able to help you."

"Thank you," Lara said. She replaced the receiver. She had obviously called the wrong broker.

She went back to the yellow pages again and made half a dozen more calls. By the end of the afternoon Lara was forced to face reality. None of the brokers was interested in trying to find a prime location where she could build a hotel with a down payment of three million dollars. They had offered Lara a variety of suggestions, and they had all come down to the same thing: a cheap hotel in an inner city area.

Never, Lara thought. *I'll go back to Glace Bay first.*

She had dreamed for months about the hotel she wanted to build, and in her mind it was already a reality—beautiful, vivid, three-dimensional. Her plan was to turn a hotel into a real home away from home. It would have mostly suites, and each suite would have a living room and a library with a fireplace in each room, and be furnished with comfortable couches, easy chairs, and a grand piano. There would be two large bedrooms and an outside terrace running the length of the apartment. There would be a Jacuzzi and a minibar. Lara knew exactly what she wanted. The question was how she was going to get it.

Lara walked into a printshop on Lake Street. "I would like to have a hundred business cards printed up, please."

"Certainly. And how will the cards read?"

" 'Miss Lara Cameron,' and at the bottom, 'Real Estate Developer.' "

"Yes, Miss Cameron. I can have them for you in two days."

"No. I would like them this afternoon, please."

The next step was to get acquainted with the city.

Lara walked along Michigan Avenue and State Street and La Salle, strolled along Lake Shore Drive and wandered through Lincoln Park with its zoo and golf course and lagoon. She visited the Merchandise Mart and went to Kroch-Brentano's and bought books about Chicago. She read about the famous who had made Chicago their home: Carl Sandburg, Frank Lloyd Wright, Louis Sullivan, Saul Bellow. She read about the pioneer families of Chicago—the John Bairds and Gaylord Donnelleys, the Marshall Fields and Potter Palmers, and Walgreens— and she passed by their homes on Lake Shore Drive and their huge estates in suburban Lake Forest. Lara visited the South Side, and she felt at home there because of all the ethnic groups: Swedes, Poles, Irish, Lithuanians. It reminded her of Glace Bay.

She took to the streets again, looking at buildings with For Sale signs, and she went to see the listed brokers. "What's the price of that building?"

"Eighty million dollars . . ."

"Sixty million dollars . . ."

"A hundred million dollars . . ."

Her three million dollars was becoming more and more insignificant. Lara sat in her hotel room considering her options. Either she could go to one of the slum sections of the city and put up a little hotel there, or she could return home. Neither choice appealed to her.

I've too much at stake to give up now, Lara thought.

The following morning Lara stopped in at a bank on La Salle Street. She walked up to a clerk behind the counter. "I would like to speak to your vice-president, please."

She handed the clerk her card.

Five minutes later she was in the office of Tom Peterson, a flaccid middle-aged man, with a nervous tic. He was studying her card.

"What can I do for you, Miss Cameron?"

"I'm planning to put up a hotel in Chicago. I'll need to borrow some money."

He gave her a genial smile. "That's what we're here for. What kind of hotel were you planning to build?"

"A beautiful boutique hotel in a nice area."

"Sounds interesting."

"I have to tell you," Lara said, "that I only have three million dollars to put down, and . . ."

He smiled. "No problem."

She felt a thrill of excitement. "Really?"

"Three million can go a long way if you know what to do with it." He looked at his watch. "I have another appointment now. I wonder if we could get together for dinner tonight and talk about this."

"Certainly," Lara said. "That would be fine."

"Where are you staying?"

"At the Palmer House."

"Why don't I pick you up at eight?"

Lara got to her feet. "Thank you so much. I can't tell you how good you make me feel. Frankly, I was beginning to get discouraged."

"No need," he said. "I'm going to take good care of you."

At eight o'clock Tom Peterson picked up Lara and took her to Henrici's for dinner. When they were seated, he said, "You know, I'm glad that you came to me. We can do a lot for each other."

"We can?"

"Yes. There's a lot of ass around this town, but none of it as beautiful as yours, honey. You can open a luxury whorehouse and cater to an exclusive . . ."

Lara froze. "I beg your pardon?"

"If you can get half a dozen girls together, we . . ."

Lara was gone.

The following day Lara visited three more banks. When she explained her plans to the manager of the first bank, he said, "I'm going to give you the best advice you'll ever get: Forget it. Real estate development is a man's game. There's no place for women in it."

"And why is that?" Lara asked tonelessly.

"Because you'd be dealing with a bunch of macho roughnecks. They'd eat you alive."

"They didn't eat me alive in Glace Bay," Lara said.

He leaned forward. "I'm going to let you in on a little secret. Chicago is not Glace Bay."

At the next bank the manager said to her, "We'll be glad to help you out, Miss Cameron. Of course, what you have in mind is out of the question. What I would suggest is to let us handle your money and invest it . . ."

Lara was out of his office before he finished his sentence.

At the third bank Lara was ushered into the office of Bob Vance, a pleasant-looking gray-haired man who looked exactly as the president of a bank should look. In the office with him was a pale, thin, sandy-haired man in his early thirties, wearing a rumpled suit and looking completely out of place.

"This is Howard Keller, Miss Cameron, one of our vice-presidents."

"How do you do?"

"What can I do for you this morning?" Bob Vance asked.

"I'm interested in building a hotel in Chicago," Lara said, "and I'm looking for finance."

Bob Vance smiled. "You've come to the right place. Do you have a location in mind?"

"I know the general area I want. Near the Loop, not too far from Michigan Avenue . . ."

"Excellent."

Lara told him about her boutique hotel idea.

"That sounds interesting," Vance said. "And how much equity do you have?"

"Three million dollars. I want to borrow the rest."

There was a thoughtful pause. "I'm afraid I can't help you. Your problem is that you have big ideas and a small purse. Now, if you would like us to invest your money for you . . ."

"No, thank you," Lara said. "Thanks for your time. Good afternoon, gentlemen." She turned and left the office, fuming. In Glace Bay three million dollars was a fortune. Here people seemed to think it was nothing.

As Lara reached the street, a voice said, "Miss Cameron!"

Lara turned. It was the man she had been introduced to—Howard Keller. "Yes?"

"I'd like to talk to you," he said. "Perhaps we could have a cup of coffee."

Lara stiffened. *Was everyone in Chicago a sex maniac?*

"There's a good coffee shop just around the corner."

Lara shrugged. "All right."

When they had ordered, Howard Keller said, "If you don't mind my butting in, I'd like to give you some advice."

Lara was watching him, wary. "Go ahead."

"In the first place, you're going about this all wrong."

"You don't think my idea will work?" she asked stiffly.

"On the contrary. I think a boutique hotel is a really great idea."

She was surprised. "Then why . . . ?"

"Chicago could use a hotel like that, but I don't think you should build it."

"What do you mean?"

"I would suggest that instead you find an old hotel in a good location and remodel it. There are a lot of run-down hotels that can be bought at a low figure. Your three million dollars would be enough equity for a down payment. Then you could borrow enough from a bank to refurbish it and turn it into your boutique hotel."

Lara sat there thinking. He was right. It was a better approach.

"Another thing, no bank is going to be interested in financing you unless you come in with a solid architect and builder. They'll want to see a complete package."

Lara thought about Buzz Steele. "I understand. Do you know a good architect and builder?"

Howard Keller smiled. "Quite a few."

"Thanks for your advice," Lara said. "If I find the right site, could I come back and talk to you about it?"

"Any time. Good luck."

Lara was waiting for him to say something like "Why don't we talk it over at my apartment?" Instead all Howard Keller said was: "Would you care for more coffee, Miss Cameron?"

Lara roamed the downtown streets again, but this time she was looking for something different. A few blocks from Michigan Avenue, on Delaware, Lara passed a prewar run-down transient hotel. A sign outside said, CONG ESSI NAL HOTEL. Lara started to pass it, then suddenly stopped. She took a closer look. The brick facade was so dirty that it was difficult to tell what its original color had been. It was eight stories high. Lara turned and entered the hotel lobby. The interior was even worse than the exterior. A clerk dressed in jeans and a torn sweater was pushing a derelict out the door. The front desk looked more like a ticket window than a reception area. At one end of the lobby was a staircase leading to what once were meeting rooms, now turned into rented offices. On the mezzanine Lara could see a travel agency, a theater ticket service, and an employment agency.

The clerk returned to the front desk. "You wanna room?"

"No. I wanted to know . . ." She was interrupted by a heavily made-up young woman in a tight-fitting skirt. "Give me a key, Mike." There was an elderly man at her side.

The clerk handed her a key.

Lara watched the two of them head for the elevator.

"What can I do for you?" the clerk asked.

"I'm interested in this hotel," Lara said. "Is it for sale?"

"I guess everything's for sale. Is your father in the real estate business?"

"No," Lara said, "I am."

He looked at her in surprise. "Oh. Well, the one you want to talk to is one of the Diamond brothers. They own a chain of these dumps."

"Where would I find them?" Lara asked.

The clerk gave her an address on State Street.

"Would you mind if I looked around?"

He shrugged. "Help yourself." He grinned. "Who knows, you might wind up being my boss."

Not if I can help it, Lara thought.

She walked around the lobby, examining it closely. There were old marble columns lining the entrance. On a hunch, Lara pulled up an edge of the dirty, worn carpet. Underneath was a dull marble floor. She walked up to the mezzanine. The mustard-colored wallpaper was peeling. She pulled away an edge of it, and underneath was the same marble. Lara was becoming more and more excited. The handrail of the staircase was painted black. Lara turned to make sure that the room clerk was not watching and took out her key from the Stevens Hotel and scratched away some of the paint. She found what she was hoping for, a solid brass railing. She approached the elevators that were painted with the same black paint, scratched a bit away, and found more brass.

Lara walked back to the clerk, trying to conceal her excitement. "I wonder if I might look at one of the rooms."

He shrugged. "No skin off my nose." He handed her a key. "Fourten."

"Thank you."

Lara got in the elevator. It was slow and antiquated. *I'll have it redone*, Lara thought. *And I'll put a mural inside.*

In her mind she was already beginning to decorate the hotel.

Room 410 looked like a disaster, but the possibilities were immediately evident. It was a surprisingly large room with antiquated facilities and tasteless furniture. Lara's heart began to beat faster. *It's perfect,* she thought.

She walked downstairs. The stairway was old and had a musty smell. The carpets were worn, but underneath she found the same marble.

Lara returned the key to the desk clerk.

"Did you see what you wanted?"

"Yes," Lara said. "Thank you."

He grinned at her. "You really going to buy this joint?"

"Yes," Lara said. "I'm really going to buy this joint."

"Cool," he said.

The elevator door opened, and the young hooker and her elderly john emerged. She handed the key and some money to the clerk. "Thanks, Mike."

"Have a nice day," Mike called. He turned to Lara. "Are you coming back?"

"Oh, yes," Lara assured him, "I'm coming back."

Lara's next stop was at the City Hall of Records. She asked to see the records on the property that she was interested in. For a fee of ten dollars, she was handed a file on the Congressional Hotel. It had been sold to the Diamond brothers five years earlier for six million dollars.

The office of the Diamond brothers was in an old building on a corner of State Street. An Oriental receptionist in a tight red skirt greeted Lara as she walked in.

"Can I help you?"

"I'd like to see Mr. Diamond."

"Which one?"

"Either of them."

"I'll give you John."
She picked up the phone and spoke into it. "There's a lady here to see you, John." She listened a moment, then looked up at Lara. "What's it about?"
"I want to buy one of his hotels."
She spoke into the mouthpiece again. "She says she wants to buy one of your hotels. Right." She replaced the receiver. "Go right in."
John Diamond was a huge man, middle-aged and hairy, and he had the pushed-in face of a man who had once played a lot of football. He was wearing a short-sleeved shirt and smoking a large cigar. He looked up as Lara entered his office.
"My secretary said you wanted to buy one of my buildings." He studied her a moment. "You don't look old enough to vote."
"Oh, I'm old enough to vote," Lara assured him. "I'm also old enough to buy one of your buildings."
"Yeah? Which one?"
"The Cong essi nal Hotel."
"The *what*?"
"That's what the sign says. I assume it means 'Congressional.' "
"Oh. Yeah."
"Is it for sale?"
He shook his head. "Gee, I don't know. That's one of our big money-makers. I'm not sure we could let it go."
"You *have* let it go," Lara said.
"Huh?"
"It's in terrible shape. The place is falling apart."
"Yeah? Then what the hell do *you* want with it?"
"I'd like to buy it and fix it up a little. Of course, it would have to be delivered to me vacant."
"That's no problem. Our tenants are on a week-to-week basis."
"How many rooms does the hotel have?"
"A hundred and twenty-five. The gross building area is a hundred thousand square feet."
Too many rooms, Lara thought. *But if I combine them to create suites, I would end up with sixty to seventy-five keys. It could work.*
It was time to discuss price.
"If I decided to buy the building, how much would you want for it?"
Diamond said, "*If* I decided to sell the building, I'd want ten million dollars, a six-million cash down payment . . ."
Lara shook her head, "I'll offer . . ."

"... period. No negotiating."

Lara sat there, mentally figuring the cost of renovation. It would be approximately eighty dollars per square foot, or eight million dollars, plus furniture, fixtures, and equipment.

Lara's mind was furiously calculating. She was sure she could get a bank to finance the loan. The problem was that she needed six million dollars in equity, and she only had three million. Diamond was asking too much for the hotel, but she wanted it. She wanted it more than anything she had ever wanted in her life.

"I'll make you a deal," Lara said.

He was listening. "Yeah?"

"I'll give you your asking price . . ."

He smiled. "So far so good."

"And I'll give you a down payment of three million in cash."

He shook his head. "Can't do it. I've got to have six million in cash up front."

"You'll have it."

"Yeah? Where's the other three coming from?"

"From you."

"What?"

"You're going to give me a second mortgage for three million."

"You want to borrow money from *me* to buy my building?"

It was the same thing Sean MacAllister had asked her in Glace Bay.

"Look at it this way," Lara said. "You're really borrowing the money from yourself. You'll own the building until I pay it off. There's no way you can lose."

He thought about it and grinned. "Lady, you just bought yourself a hotel."

Howard Keller's office in the bank was a cubicle with his name on the door. When Lara walked in, he looked more rumpled than ever.

"Back so soon?"

"You told me to come and see you when I found a hotel. I found one."

Keller leaned back in his chair. "Tell me about it."

"I found an old hotel called the Congressional. It's on Delaware. It's a few blocks from Michigan Avenue. It's run-down and seedy, and I want to buy it and turn it into the best hotel in Chicago."

"Tell me the deal."

Lara told him.

Keller sat there, thinking. "Let's run it past Bob Vance."

Bob Vance listened and made some notes. "It might be possible," he said, "but . . ." He looked at Lara. "Have you ever run a hotel before, Miss Cameron?"

Lara thought about all the years of running the boardinghouse in Glace Bay, making the beds, scrubbing the floors and doing the laundry and the dishes, trying to please the different personalities and keep peace.

"I ran a boardinghouse full of miners and lumbermen. A hotel will be a cinch."

Howard Keller said, "I'd like to take a look at the property, Bob."

Lara's enthusiasm was irresistible. Howard Keller watched Lara's face as they walked through the seedy hotel rooms, and he saw them through her eyes.

"This will be a beautiful suite with a sauna," Lara said excitedly. "The fireplace will be here, and the grand piano in that corner." She began to pace back and forth. "When affluent travelers come to Chicago, they stay at the best hotels, but they're all the same—cold rooms without any character. If we can offer them something like this, even though it may cost a little more, there's no doubt about which they'll choose. This will *really* be a home away from home."

"I'm impressed," Howard Keller said.

Lara turned to him eagerly. "Do you think the bank will loan me the money?"

"Let's find out."

Thirty minutes later Howard Keller was in a conference with Vance.

"What do you think about it?" Vance asked.

"I think the lady's on to something. I like her idea about a boutique hotel."

"So do I. The only problem is that she's so young and inexperienced. It's a gamble." They spent the next half hour discussing costs and projected earnings.

"I think we should go ahead with it," Keller finally said. "We can't lose." He grinned. "If worse comes to worst, you and I can move into the hotel."

* * *

Howard Keller telephoned Lara at the Stevens Hotel. "The bank has just approved your loan."

Lara let out a shriek. "Do you mean it? That's wonderful! Oh, thank you, thank you!"

"We have a few things to talk about," Howard Keller said. "Are you free for dinner this evening?"

"Yes."

"Fine. I'll pick you up at seven-thirty."

They had dinner at the Imperial House. Lara was so excited that she barely touched her food.

"I can't tell you how thrilled I am," she said. "It's going to be the most beautiful hotel in Chicago."

"Easy," Keller warned, "there's a long way to go." He hesitated. "May I be frank with you, Miss Cameron?"

"Lara."

"Lara. You're a dark horse. You have no track record."

"In Glace Bay . . ."

"This isn't Glace Bay. To mix metaphors, it's a different ball park."

"Then why is the bank doing this?" Lara asked.

"Don't get me wrong. We're not a charitable organization. The worst thing that can happen is that the bank will break even. But I have a feeling about you. I believe you're going to make it. I think there could be a big upside. You don't intend to stop with this one hotel, do you?"

"Of course not," Lara said.

"I didn't think so. What I want to say is that when we make a loan, we don't usually get personally involved in the project. But in this case I'd like to give you whatever help you might need."

And Howard Keller intended to get personally involved with her. He had been attracted to Lara from the moment he had seen her. He was captivated by her enthusiasm and determination. She was a beautiful woman-child. He wanted desperately to impress her. *Maybe,* Keller thought, *one day I'll tell her how close I came to being famous.* . . .

Chapter Eight

It was the final game of the World Series, and Wrigley Field was packed with 38,710 screaming fans. "It's the top of the ninth, with the score Cubs one, Yankees zero. The Yankees are up at bat, with two outs. The bases are loaded with Tony Kubek on first, Whitey Ford on second, and Yogi Berra on third."

As Mickey Mantle stepped up to the plate, the crowd roared. "The Mick" had hit .304 for the season and had forty-two home runs under his belt for the year.

Jack Brickhouse, the Wrigley Field announcer, said, excitedly, "Oh, oh . . . it looks like they're going to change pitchers. They're taking out Moe Drabowsky. . . . Cub Manager Bob Scheffing is talking to the umpire . . . let's see who's coming in . . . it's Howard Keller! Keller is walking up to the pitcher's mound, and the crowd is screaming! The whole burden of the World Series rests on this youngster's shoulders. Can he strike out the great Mickey Mantle? We'll know in a moment! Keller is on the mound now . . . he looks around the loaded bases . . . takes a deep breath, and winds up. Here's the pitch . . . Mantle hauls back the bat . . . takes a swing, and misses! Strike one!"

The crowd had become hushed. Mantle moved forward a little, his face grim, his bat cocked, ready to swing. Howard Keller checked the runners. The pressure was enormous, but he seemed to be cool and composed. He turned to the catcher, looked in for the sign, and wound up for another pitch.

"There's the windup and the pitch!" the announcer yelled. "It's Keller's famous curve ball . . . Mantle swings on and misses! Strike two! If young Keller can strike out the Mick, the Chicago Cubs will win the World Series! We're watching David and Goliath, ladies and gentlemen! Young Keller has only played in the big leagues for one year, but during that time he has made an enviable reputation for himself. Mickey Mantle is Goliath . . . can the rookie Keller beat him? Everything is riding on this next pitch.

"Keller checks the runners again . . . here's the windup . . . and here we go! It's the curve . . . Mantle bails out as it curves right over the heart of the plate . . . Strike three called!" The announcer was screaming now. *"Mantle is caught looking! The mighty Mick has struck out, ladies and gentlemen! Young Howard Keller struck out the great Mickey Mantle! The game is over—the World Series belongs to the Chicago Cubs! The fans are on their feet going crazy!"*

On the field, Howard Keller's teammates raced up to him and picked him up on their shoulders and started to cross the . . .

"Howard, what in the world are you doing?"

"My homework, Mom." Guiltily the fifteen-year-old Howard Keller turned off the television set. The ball game was almost over anyway.

Baseball was Howard's passion and his life. He knew that one day he would play in the major leagues. At the age of six he was competing against kids twice his age in stickball, and when he was twelve, he began pitching for an American Legion team. When Howard was fifteen, a scout for the Chicago Cubs was told about the young boy. "I've never seen anything like him," his informant said. "The kid has an outstanding curve, and a mean slider, and a change-up you wouldn't believe!"

The scout was skeptical. Grudgingly, he said, "All right. I'll take a look at the kid." He went to the next American Legion game that Howard Keller played in, and he became an instant convert. He sought out the young boy after the game. "What do you want to do with your life, son?"

"Play baseball," said Keller promptly.

"I'm glad to hear that. We're going to sign you to a contract with our minor-league team."

Howard couldn't wait to tell his parents the exciting news.

The Kellers were a close-knit Catholic family. They went to mass every Sunday, and they saw to it that their son attended church. Howard Keller, Sr., was a typewriter salesman, and he was on the road a great deal. When he was at home, he spent as much time as possible with his son. Howard was close to both his parents. His mother made it a point to attend all the ball games when her son was playing, and cheer him on. Howard got his first glove and uniform when he was six years old. Howard was a fanatic about baseball. He had an encyclopedic memory for the statistics of games that were played before he was even born. He knew all the stats of the winning pitchers—the strikes, the outs, the number of saves and shutouts. He won money betting with his schoolmates that he could name the starting pitchers in any team lineup.

"Nineteen forty-nine."

"That's easy," Howard said. "Newcombe, Roe, Hatten, and Branca for the Dodgers. Reynolds, Raschi, Byrne, and Lopat for the Yankees."

"All right," one of his teammates challenged. "Who played the most consecutive games in major-league history?" The challenger was holding the *Guinness Book of Records* in front of him.

Howard Keller didn't even pause. "Lou Gehrig—two thousand one hundred thirty."

"Who had the record for the most shutouts?"

"Walter Johnson—one hundred and thirteen."

"Who hit the most home runs in his career?"

"Babe Ruth—seven hundred and fourteen."

Word of the young player's ability began to circulate, and professional scouts came to take a look at the young phenomenon who was playing on the Chicago Cubs minor-league team. They were stunned. By the time Keller was seventeen, he had been approached by scouts from the St. Louis Cardinals and the Baltimore Orioles and the New York Yankees.

Howard's father was proud of him. "He takes after me," he would boast. "I used to play baseball when I was a youngster."

During the summer of his senior year in high school, Howard Keller worked as a junior clerk in a bank owned by one of the sponsors of his American Legion team.

Howard was going steady with a pretty schoolmate named Betty Quinlan. It was understood that when they finished college, they would get married. Howard would talk baseball by the hour with her, and because she cared for him, she listened patiently. Howard loved the anecdotes about his favorite ballplayers, and every time he heard a new one, he would rush to tell it to Betty.

"Casey Stengel said, 'The secret of managing is to keep the five guys who hate you away from the five who are undecided.'"

"Someone asked Yogi Berra what time it was, and he said, 'You mean right now?'"

"And when a player was hit in the shoulder by a pitched ball, his teammate said, 'There's nothing wrong with his shoulder except some pain—and pain doesn't hurt you.'"

Young Keller knew that he was soon going to join the pantheon of the great players. But the gods had other plans for him.

Howard came home from school one day with his best friend, Jesse, who played shortstop on the team. There were two letters waiting for Keller. One offered him a baseball scholarship at Princeton, and the other a baseball scholarship at Harvard.

"Gee, that's great!" Jesse said. "Congratulations!" And he meant it. Howard Keller was his idol.

"Which one do you think you're going to take?" Howard's father asked.

"Why do I have to go to college at all?" Howard wondered. "I could get on one of the big-league teams now."

His mother said firmly, "There's plenty of time for that, son. You're going to get a good education first; then, when you're through playing baseball, you'll be fit to do anything you like."

"All right," Howard said. "Harvard. Betty is going to Wellesley and I can be near her."

Betty Quinlan was delighted when Howard told her what he had decided.

"We'll get to see each other over the weekends!" she said.

His buddy, Jesse, said, "I'm sure going to miss you."

The day before Howard Keller was to leave for the university, his father ran off with the secretary of one of his customers.

The young boy was stunned. "How could he do that?"

His mother was in shock. "He . . . he must be going through a change of life," she stammered. "Your . . . your father loves me very much. He'll . . . he'll come back. You'll see . . ."

The following day Howard's mother received a letter from an attorney, formally stating that his client, Howard Keller, Sr., wanted a divorce and, since he had no money to pay for alimony, was willing to let his wife have their small house.

Howard held his mother in his arms. "Don't worry, Mom, I'm going to stay here and take care of you."

"No. I don't want you to give up college for me. From the day you were born, your father and I planned for you to go to college." Then quietly, after a moment: "Let's talk about it in the morning. I'm very tired."

Howard stayed up all night, thinking about his choices. He could go to Harvard on a baseball scholarship or take one of the offers in the major leagues. Either way he would be leaving his mother alone. It was a difficult decision.

When his mother didn't appear at breakfast the next morning, Howard went into her bedroom. She was sitting up in bed, unable to move, her face pulled up on one side. She had suffered a stroke.

With no money to pay for the hospital or doctors, Howard went back to work at the bank, full-time. He was finished at four o'clock, and each afternoon he hurried home to take care of his mother.

It was a mild stroke, and the doctor assured Howard that in time his mother would be fine. "She's had a terrible shock, but she's going to recover."

Howard still got calls from scouts from the major leagues, but he knew that he could not leave his mother. *I'll go when she's better*, he told himself.

The medical bills kept piling up.

In the beginning he talked to Betty Quinlan once a week, but after a few months the calls became less and less frequent.

Howard's mother did not seem to be improving. Howard talked to the doctor. "When is she going to be all right?"

"In a case like this, it's hard to tell, son. She could go on for months like this, or even years. Sorry I can't be more specific."

The year ended and another began, and Howard was still living with his mother and working at the bank. One day he received a letter from Betty Quinlan, telling him that she had fallen in love with someone else and that she hoped his mother was feeling better. The calls from scouts became less frequent and finally stopped altogether. Howard's life centered on taking care of his mother. He did the shopping and the cooking and carried on with his job. He no longer thought about baseball. It was difficult enough just getting through each day.

When his mother died four years later, Howard Keller was no longer interested in baseball. He was now a banker.

His chance of fame had vanished.

Chapter Nine

Howard Keller and Lara were having dinner.

"How do we get started?" Lara asked.

"First of all, we're going to get you the best team money can buy. We'll start out with a real estate lawyer to work out the contract with the Diamond brothers. Then we want to get you a top architect. I have someone in mind. After that, we want to hire a top construction company. I've done a little arithmetic of my own. The soft costs for the project will come to about three hundred thousand dollars a room. The cost of the hotel will be about seven million dollars. If we plan it right, it can work."

The architect's name was Ted Tuttle, and when he heard Lara's plans, he grinned and said, "Bless you. I've been waiting for someone to come along with an idea like this."

Ten working days later he had rendered his drawings. They were everything Lara had dreamed of.

"Originally the hotel had a hundred and twenty-five rooms," the architect said. "As you can see, I've cut it down to seventy-five keys, as you've asked."

In the drawing there were fifty suites and twenty-five deluxe rooms.

"It's perfect," Lara said.

Lara showed the plans to Howard Keller. He was equally enthusiastic.

"Let's go to work. I've set up a meeting with a contractor. His name is Steve Rice."

Steve Rice was one of the top contractors in Chicago. Lara liked him immediately. He was a rugged, no-nonsense, down-to-earth type.

Lara said, "Howard Keller tells me that you're the best."

"He's right," Rice said. "Our motto is 'We build for posterity.'"

"That's a good motto."

Rice grinned. "I just made it up."

The first step was to break down each element into a series of drawings. The drawings were sent to potential subcontractors: steel manufacturers, bricklayers, window companies, electrical contractors. All in all, more than sixty subcontractors were involved.

The day escrow closed, Howard Keller took the afternoon off to celebrate with Lara.

"Does the bank mind your taking this time off?" Lara asked.

"No," Keller lied. "It's part of my job." The truth was that he was enjoying this more than he had enjoyed anything in years. He loved being with Lara: he loved talking to her, looking at her. He wondered how she felt about marriage.

Lara said, "I read this morning that they've almost completed the Sears Tower. It's a hundred and ten stories—the tallest building in the world."

"That's right," Keller said.

Lara said gravely, "Someday I'm going to build a higher one, Howard."

He believed her.

They were having lunch with Steve Rice at the Whitehall. "Tell me what happens next," Lara asked.

"Well," Rice said, "first we're going to clean up the interior of the building. We'll keep the marble. We'll remove all the windows and gut the bathrooms. We'll take out the electrical risers for the installation of the new electrical wiring and update the plumbing. When the demolition company is through, we'll be ready to begin building your hotel."

"How many people will be working on it?"

Rice laughed. "A mob, Miss Cameron. There'll be a window team, a bathroom team, a corridor team. These teams work floor by floor, usually from the top floor down. The hotel is scheduled to have two restaurants, and you'll have room service."

"How long is all this going to take?"

"I would say—equipped and furnished—eighteen months."

"I'll give you a bonus if you finish it in a year," Lara told him.

"Great. The Congressional should . . ."

"I'm changing the name. It's going to be called the Cameron Palace." Lara felt a thrill just saying the words. It was almost a sexual feeling. Her name was going to be on a building for all the world to see.

At six o'clock on a rainy September morning, the reconstruction of the hotel began. Lara was at the site eagerly watching as the workmen trooped into the lobby and began to tear it apart.

To Lara's surprise, Howard Keller appeared.

"You're up early," Lara said.

"I couldn't sleep." Keller grinned. "I have a feeling this is the beginning of something big."

Twelve months later the Cameron Palace opened to rave reviews and land office business.

The architectural critic for the Chicago *Tribune* wrote, "Chicago finally has a hotel that lives up to the motto 'Your home away from home!' Lara Cameron is someone to keep an eye on. . . ."

By the end of the first month the hotel was full and had a long waiting list.

Howard Keller was enthusiastic. "At this rate," he said, "the hotel will be paid off in twelve years. That's wonderful. We . . ."

"Not good enough," Lara said. "I'm raising the rates." She saw the expression on Keller's face. "Don't worry. They'll pay it. Where else can they get two fireplaces, a sauna, and a grand piano?"

Two weeks after the Cameron Palace opened, Lara had a meeting with Bob Vance and Howard Keller.

"I found another great site for a hotel," Lara said. "It's going to be like the Cameron Palace, only bigger and better."

Howard Keller grinned. "I'll take a look at it."

The site was perfect, but there was a problem.

"You're too late," the broker told Lara. "A developer named Steve

Murchison was here this morning, and he made me an offer. He's going to buy it."

"How much did he offer?"

"Three million."

"I'll give you four. Draw up the papers."

The broker blinked only once. "Right."

Lara received a telephone call the following afternoon.

"Lara Cameron?"

"Yes."

"This is Steve Murchison. I'm going to let it go this time, bitch, because I don't think you know what the hell you're doing. But in the future stay out of my way—you could get hurt."

And the line went dead.

It was 1974, and momentous events were occurring around the world. President Nixon resigned to avoid impeachment, and Gerald Ford stepped into the White House. OPEC ended its oil embargo, and Isabel Perón became the president of Argentina. And in Chicago Lara started construction on her second hotel, the Chicago Cameron Plaza. It was completed eighteen months later, and it was an even bigger success than the Cameron Palace. There was no stopping Lara after that. As *Forbes* magazine was to write later, "Lara Cameron is a phenomenon. Her innovations are changing the concept of hotels. Miss Cameron has invaded the traditionally male turf of real estate developers and has proved that a woman can outshine them all."

Lara received a telephone call from Charles Cohn.

"Congratulations," he said. "I'm proud of you. I've never had a protégé before."

"I've never had a mentor before. Without you, none of this would have happened."

"You would have found a way," Cohn said.

In 1975 the movie *Jaws* swept the country, and people stopped going into the ocean. The world population passed four billion, reduced by one when Teamster President James Hoffa disappeared. When Lara heard the four billion population figure, she said to Keller, "Do you have any idea how much housing that would require?"

He was not sure whether she was joking.

* * *

Over the next three years, two apartment buildings and a condominium were completed. "I want to put up an office building next," Lara told Keller, "right in the heart of the Loop."

"There's an interesting piece of property coming on the market," Keller told her. "If you like it, we'll finance you."

That afternoon they went to look at it. It was on the waterfront, in a choice location.

"What's it going to cost?" Lara asked.

"I've done the numbers. It will come to a hundred and twenty million dollars."

Lara swallowed. "That scares me."

"Lara, in real estate the name of the game is to borrow."

Other people's money, Lara thought. That's what Bill Rogers had told her at the boardinghouse. All that seemed so long ago, and so much had happened since then. *And it's only the beginning,* Lara thought. *It's only the beginning.*

"Some developers put up buildings with almost no cash of their own."

"I'm listening."

"The idea is to rent or resell the building for enough money to pay off the debt on it, and still have money left over to buy some more property with that cash, and borrow more money for another property. It's an inverted pyramid—a real estate pyramid—that you can build on a very small initial cash investment."

"I understand," Lara said.

"Of course, you have to be careful. The pyramid is built on paper—the mortgages. If anything goes wrong, if the profit from one investment fails to cover the debt on the next one, the pyramid can topple and bury you."

"Right. How can I acquire the waterfront property?"

"We'll set up a joint venture for you. I'll talk to Vance about it. If it's too big for our bank to handle, we'll go to an insurance company or a savings and loan. You'll take out a fifty-million-dollar mortgage loan. You'll get their mortgage coupon rate—that would be five million and a ten percent rate, plus amortization on the mortgage—and they'll be your partners. They'll take the first ten percent of the earnings, but you'll get your property, fully financed. You can get your cash repaid and keep one hundred percent of the depreciation, because financial institutions have no use for losses."

Lara was listening, absorbing every word.

"Are you with me so far?"

"I'm with you."

"In five or six years, after the building is leased, you sell it. If the property sells for seventy-five million, after you pay off the mortgage, you'll net twelve and a half million dollars. Besides that, you'll have a tax-sheltered earning stream of eight million in depreciation that you can use to reduce taxes on other income. All of this for a cash investment of ten million."

"That's fantastic!" Lara said.

Keller grinned. "The government wants you to make money."

"How would *you* like to make some money, Howard? Some real money?"

"I beg your pardon?"

"I want you to come to work for me."

Keller was suddenly quiet. He knew he was facing one of the most important decisions of his life, and it had nothing to do with money. It was Lara. He had fallen in love with her. There had been one painful episode when he had tried to tell her. He had practiced his marriage proposal all night, and the following morning he had gone to her and stammered, "Lara, I love you," and before he could say more, she had kissed him on the cheek and said, "I love you, too, Howard. Take a look at this new production schedule." And he had not had the nerve to try again.

Now she was asking him to be her partner. He would be working near her every day, unable to touch her, unable to . . .

"Do you believe in me, Howard?"

"I'd be crazy not to, wouldn't I?"

"I'll pay you twice whatever you're making now, and give you five percent of the company."

"Can I . . . can I think about it?"

"There's really nothing to think about, is there?"

He made his decision. "I guess not . . . partner."

Lara gave him a hug. "That's wonderful! You and I are going to build beautiful things. There are so many ugly buildings around. There's no excuse for them. Every building should be a tribute to this city."

He put his hand on her arm. "Don't ever change, Lara."

She looked at him hard.

"I won't."

Chapter Ten

The late 1970s were years of growth and change and excitement. In 1976 there was a successful Israeli raid on Entebbe, and Mao Zedong died, and James Earl Carter, Jr., was elected President of the United States.

Lara erected another office building.

In 1977 Charlie Chaplin died, and Elvis Presley temporarily died.

Lara built the largest shopping mall in Chicago.

In 1978 Reverend Jim Jones and 911 followers committed mass suicide in Guyana. The United States recognized Communist China, and the Panama Canal treaties were ratified.

Lara built a series of high-rise condominiums in Rogers Park.

In 1979 Israel and Egypt signed a peace treaty at Camp David, there was a nuclear accident at Three-Mile Island, and Muslim fundamentalists seized the United States Embassy in Iran.

Lara built a skyscraper and a glamorous resort and country club in Deerfield, north of Chicago.

Lara seldom went out socially, and when she did, she usually went to a club where jazz was played. She liked Andy's, a club where the top jazz artists performed. She listened to Von Freeman, the great saxophonist, and Eric Schneider, and reed man Anthony Braxton, and Art Hodes at the piano.

Lara had no time to feel lonely. She spent every day with her family: the architects and the construction crew, the carpenters, the electricians and surveyors and plumbers. She was obsessed with the buildings she was putting up. Her stage was Chicago, and she was the star.

Her professional life was proceeding beyond her wildest dreams, but she had no personal life. Her experience with Sean MacAllister had soured her on sexual relationships, and she never met anyone she was interested in seeing for more than an evening or two. In the back of Lara's mind was an elusive image, someone she had once met and wanted to meet again. But she could never seem to capture it. For a fleeting moment she would recall it, and then it was gone.

There were plenty of suitors. They ranged from business executives to oilmen to poets, and even included some of her employees. Lara was pleasant to all of the men, but she never permitted any relationship to go further than a good-night handshake at the door.

But then Lara found herself attracted to Pete Ryan, the head foreman on one of Lara's building jobs, a handsome, strapping young man with an Irish brogue and a quick smile, and Lara started visiting the project Ryan was working on more and more often. They would talk about construction problems, but underneath they were both aware that they were speaking about other things.

"Are you going to have dinner with me?" Ryan asked. The word "dinner" was stretched out slowly.

Lara felt her heart give a little jump. "Yes."

Ryan picked Lara up at her apartment, but they never got to dinner. "My God, you're a lovely thing," he said. And his strong arms went around her.

She was ready for him. Their foreplay had been going on for months. Ryan picked her up and carried her into the bedroom. They undressed together, quickly, urgently. He had a lean, hard build, and Lara had a quick mental picture of Sean MacAllister's heavy, pudgy body. The next moment she was in bed and Ryan was on top of her, his hands and tongue all over her, and she cried aloud with the joy of what was happening to her.

When they were both spent, they lay in each other's arms. "My God," Ryan said softly, "you're a bloody miracle."

"So are you," Lara whispered.

She could not remember when she had been so happy. Ryan was everything she wanted. He was intelligent and warm, and they understood each other, they spoke the same language.

Ryan squeezed her hand. "I'm starved."

"So am I. I'll make us some sandwiches."

"Tomorrow night," Ryan promised, "I'll take you out for a proper dinner."

Lara held him close. "It's a date."

The following morning Lara went to visit Ryan at the building site. She could see him high up on one of the steel girders, giving orders to his men. As Lara walked toward the work elevator, one of the workmen grinned at her. "Mornin', Miss Cameron." There was an odd note in his voice.

Another workman passed her and grinned. "Mornin', Miss Cameron."

Two other workmen were leering at her. "Morning, boss."

Lara looked around. Other workmen were watching her, all smirking. Lara's face turned red. She stepped into the work elevator and rode up to the level where Ryan was. As she stepped out, Ryan saw her and smiled.

"Morning, sweetheart," Ryan said. "What time is dinner tonight?"

"You'll starve first," Lara said fiercely. "You're fired."

Every building Lara put up was a challenge. She erected small office buildings with floor spaces of five thousand square feet, and large office buildings and hotels. But no matter what type of building it was, the most important thing to her was the location.

Bill Rogers had been right. *Location, location, location.*

Lara's empire kept expanding. She was beginning to get recognition from the city fathers and from the press and the public. She was a glamorous figure, and when she went to charity events or to the opera or a museum, photographers were always eager to take her picture. She began to appear in the media more and more often. All her buildings were successes, and still she was not satisfied. It was as though she were waiting for something wonderful to happen to her, waiting for a door to open, waiting to be touched by some unknown magic.

Keller was puzzled. "What do you want, Lara?"

"More."

And it was all he could get out of her.

* * *

One day Lara said to Keller, "Howard, do you know how much we're paying every month for janitors and linen service and window washers?"

"It goes with the territory," Keller said.

"Then let's buy the territory."

"What are you talking about?"

"We're going to start a subsidiary. We'll supply those services to ourselves and to other builders."

The idea was a success from the beginning. The profits kept pouring in.

It seemed to Keller that Lara had built an emotional wall around herself. He was closer to her than anyone else, and yet Lara never spoke to him about her family or her background. It was as though she had emerged full blown out of the mists of nowhere. In the beginning Keller had been Lara's mentor, teaching her and guiding her, but now Lara made all the decisions alone. The pupil had outgrown the teacher.

Lara let nothing stand in her way. She was becoming an irresistible force, and there was no stopping her. She was a perfectionist. She knew what she wanted and insisted on getting it.

At first some of the workmen tried to take advantage of her. They had never worked for a woman before, and the idea amused them. They were in for a shock. When Lara caught one of the foremen pencil-whipping—signing off for work that had not been done—she called him in front of the crew and fired him. She was at the building site every morning. The crew would arrive at six o'clock and find Lara already there, waiting for them. There was rampant sexism. The men would wait until Lara was in earshot and exchange lewd jokes.

"Did you hear about the talking pussy at the farm? It fell in love with a cock and . . ."

"So the little girl said, 'Can you get pregnant swallowing a man's seed?' And her mama said, 'No. From that, darling, you get jewelry . . .'"

There were some overt gestures. Occasionally one of the workmen passing Lara would "accidentally" brush his arm across her breasts or press against her bottom.

"Oops, sorry."

"No problem," Lara said. "Pick up your check and get out of here."

Their amusement eventually began to change to respect.

One day, when Lara was driving along Kedzie Avenue with Howard Keller, she came to a block filled with small shops. She stopped the car.

"This block is being wasted," Lara said. "There should be a high rise here. These little shops can't bring much of an income."

"Yeah, but the problem is, you'd have to persuade every one of these tenants to sell out," Keller said. "Some of them may not want to."

"We can buy them out," Lara declared.

"Lara, if even one tenant refuses to sell, you could be stuck for a bundle. You'll have bought a lot of little shops you don't want and you won't be able to put up your building. And if the tenants get wind that a big high rise is going up here, they'll hold you up."

"We won't let them know what we're doing," Lara said. She was beginning to get excited. "We'll have different people approach the owners of the shops."

"I've been through this before," Keller warned. "If word leaks out, they're going to gouge you for every penny they can get."

"Then we'll have to be careful. Let's get an option on the property."

The block on Kedzie Avenue consisted of more than a dozen small stores and shops. There was a bakery, a hardware store, a barbershop, a clothing store, a butcher, a tailor, a drugstore, a stationery store, a coffee shop, and a variety of other businesses.

"Don't forget the risk," Keller warned Lara. "If there's one holdout, you've lost all the money you've put in to buy those businesses."

"Don't worry," Lara said. "I'll handle it."

A week later a stranger walked into the two-chair barbershop. The barber was reading a magazine. As the door opened, he looked up and nodded. "Can I help you, sir? Haircut?"

The stranger smiled. "No," he said. "I just arrived in town. I had a barbershop in New Jersey, but my wife wanted to move here to be near her mother. I'm looking for a shop I can buy."

"This is the only barbershop in the neighborhood," the barber said. "It's not for sale."

The stranger smiled. "When you come right down to it, everything's for sale, isn't it? At the right price, of course. What's this shop worth—about fifty, sixty thousand dollars?"

"Something like that," the barber admitted.

"I really am anxious to have my own shop again. I'll tell you what. I'll give you seventy-five thousand dollars for this place."

"No, I couldn't think of selling it."

"A hundred."

"Really, mister, I don't . . ."

"And you can take all the equipment with you."

The barber was staring at him. "You'll give me a hundred thousand and let me take the barber chairs and the rest of the equipment?"

"That's right. I have my own equipment."

"Can I think about it? I'll have to talk to my wife."

"Sure. I'll drop back tomorrow."

Two days later the barbershop was acquired.

"That's one down," Lara said.

The bakery was next. It was a small family bakery owned by a husband and wife. The ovens in the back room permeated the store with the smell of fresh bread. A woman was talking to one of the owners.

"My husband died and left me his insurance money. We had a bakery in Florida. I've been looking for a place just like this. I'd like to buy it."

"It's a comfortable living," the owner said. "My wife and I have never thought about selling."

"If you *were* interested in selling, how much would you want?"

The owner shrugged. "I don't know."

"Would you say the bakery's worth sixty thousand dollars?"

"Oh, at least seventy-five," the owner said.

"I'll tell you what," the woman said. "I'll give you a hundred thousand dollars for it."

The owner stared at her. "Are you serious?"

"I've never been more serious in my life."

The next morning Lara said, "That's two down."

The rest of the deals went just as smoothly. They had a dozen men and women going around impersonating tailors, bakers, pharmacists, and butchers. Over the period of the next six months Lara bought out the stores, then hired people to come in and run the different operations. The architects had already started to draw up plans for the high rise.

Lara was studying the latest reports. "It looks like we've done it," she told Keller.

"I'm afraid we have a problem."

"Why? The only one left is the coffee shop."

"That's our problem. He's there on a five-year lease, but he won't give up the lease."

"Offer him more money . . ."

"He says he won't give it up at any price."

Lara was staring at him. "Does he know about the high rise going up?"

"No."

"All right. I'll go talk to him. Don't worry, he'll get out. Find out who owns the building he's in."

The following morning Lara paid a visit to the site. Haley's Coffee Shop was at the far end of the southwest corner of the block. The shop was small, with half a dozen stools along the counter and four booths. A man Lara presumed to be the proprietor was behind the counter. He appeared to be in his late sixties.

Lara sat down at a booth.

"Morning," the man said pleasantly. "What can I bring you?"

"Orange juice and coffee, please."

"Coming up."

She watched him squeeze some fresh orange juice.

"My waitress didn't show up today. Good help's hard to get these days." He poured the coffee and came from behind the counter. He was in a wheelchair. He had no legs. Lara watched silently as he brought the coffee and orange juice to the table.

"Thank you," Lara said. She looked around. "Nice place you have here."

"Yep. I like it."

"How long have you been here?"

"Ten years."

"Did you ever think of retiring?"

He shook his head. "You're the second person who asked me that this week. No, I'll never retire."

"Maybe they didn't offer you enough money," Lara suggested.

"It has nothing to do with money, miss. Before I came here, I spent two years in a veterans hospital. No friends. Not much point to life. And then someone talked me into leasing this place." He smiled. "It changed my whole life. All the people in the neighborhood drop in here. They've become my friends, almost like my family. It's given me a reason for living." He shook his head. "No. Money has nothing to do with it. Can I bring you more coffee?"

* * *

Lara was in a meeting with Howard Keller and the architect. "We don't even have to buy out his lease," Keller was saying. "I just talked to the landlord. There's a forfeiture clause if the coffee shop doesn't gross a certain amount each month. For the last few months he's been under that gross, so we can close him out."

Lara turned to the architect. "I have a question for you." She looked down at the plans spread out on the table and pointed to the southwest corner of the drawing. "What if we built a setback here, eliminated this little area and let the coffee shop stay? Could the building still be put up?"

The architect studied the plan. "I suppose so. I could slope that side of the building and counterbalance it on the other side. Of course, it would look better if we didn't have to do that . . ."

"But it *could* work," Lara pressed.

"Yes."

Keller said, "Lara, I told you we can force him out of there."

Lara shook her head. "We've bought up the rest of the block, haven't we?"

Keller nodded. "You bet. You're the proud owner of a clothing store, a tailor shop, a stationery store, a drugstore, a bakery, a . . ."

"All right," Lara said. "The tenants of the new high rise are going to have a coffee shop to drop in on. And so do we. Haley stays."

On her father's birthday Lara said to Keller, "Howard, I want you to do me a favor."

"Sure."

"I want you to go to Scotland for me."

"Are we going to build something in Scotland?"

"We're going to buy a castle."

He stood there, listening.

"There's a place in the Highlands called Loch Morlich. It's on the road to Glenmore near Aviemore. There are castles all around there. Buy one."

"Kind of a summer home?"

"I don't plan to live in it. I want to bury my father in the grounds."

Keller said, slowly, "You want me to buy a castle in Scotland to bury your father in?"

"That's right. I haven't time to go over myself. You're the only one

I can trust to do it. My father is in the Greenwood Cemetery at Glace Bay."

It was the first real insight Keller ever had into Lara's feelings about her family.

"You must have loved your father very much."

"Will you do it for me?"

"Certainly."

"After he's buried, arrange for a caretaker to tend the grave."

Three weeks later Keller returned from Scotland and said, "It's all taken care of. You own a castle. Your father's resting in the grounds. It's a beautiful place near the hills and with a small lake close by. You'll love it. When are you going over?"

Lara looked up in surprise. "Me? I'm not," she said.

BOOK TWO

Chapter Eleven

In 1984 Lara Cameron decided that the time had come to conquer New York. When she told Keller her plan, he was appalled.

"I don't like the idea," he said flatly. "You don't know New York. Neither do I. It's a different city, Lara. We . . ."

"That's what they told me when I came from Glace Bay to Chicago," Lara pointed out. "Buildings are the same whether you put them up in Glace Bay, Chicago, New York, or Tokyo. We all play by the same rules."

"But you're doing so great here," Keller protested. "What is it you want?"

"I told you. *More.* I want my name up on the New York skyline. I'm going to build a Cameron Plaza there, and a Cameron Center. And one day, Howard, I'm going to build the tallest skyscraper in the world. *That's* what I want. Cameron Enterprises is moving to New York."

New York was in the middle of a building boom, and it was peopled by real estate giants—the Zeckendorfs, Harry Helmsley, Donald Trump, the Urises, and the Rudins.

"We're going to join the club," Lara told Keller.

They checked into the Regency and began to explore the city. Lara could not get over the size and dynamics of the bustling metropolis. It was a canyon of skyscrapers, with rivers of cars running through it.

"It makes Chicago look like Glace Bay!" Lara said. She could not wait to get started.

"The first thing we're going to do is assemble a team. We'll find the best real estate lawyer in New York. Then a great management team. Find out who Rudin uses. See if you can lure them away."

"Right."

Lara said, "Here's a list of buildings I like the looks of. Find out who the architects are. I want to meet with them."

Keller was beginning to feel Lara's excitement. "I'll open up a line of credit with the banks. With the assets we have in Chicago, that won't be any problem. I'll make contacts with some savings and loan companies and some real estate brokers."

"Fine."

"Lara, before we start to get involved in all this, don't you think you should decide what your next project is going to be?"

Lara looked up and asked innocently, "Didn't I tell you? We're going to buy Manhattan Central Hospital."

Several days earlier Lara had gone to a hairdresser on Madison Avenue. While she was having her hair done, she had overheard a conversation in the next booth.

"We're going to miss you, Mrs. Walker."

"Same here, Darlene. How long have I been coming here?"

"Almost fifteen years."

"Time certainly flies, doesn't it? I'm going to miss New York."

"When will you be leaving?"

"Right away. We just got the closing notice this morning. Imagine—a hospital like Manhattan Central closing down because they've run out of cash. I've been supervisor there for almost twenty years, and they send me a memo telling me I'm through! You'd think they'd have the decency to do it in person, wouldn't you? What's the world coming to?"

Lara was now listening intently.

"I haven't seen anything about the closing in the papers."

"No. They're keeping it quiet. They want to break the news to the employees first."

Her beautician was in the middle of blow-drying Lara's hair. Lara started to get up.

"I'm not through yet, Miss Cameron."

"Never mind," Lara said, "I'm in a hurry."

* * *

Manhattan Central Hospital was a dilapidated, ugly-looking building located on the East Side, and it took up an entire block. Lara stared at it for a long time, and what she was seeing in her mind was a majestic new skyscraper with chic retail stores on the ground floor and luxury condominiums on the upper floors.

Lara walked into the hospital and asked the name of the corporation that owned it. She was sent to the offices of a Roger Burnham on Wall Street.

"What can I do for you, Miss Cameron?"

"I hear that Manhattan Central Hospital is for sale."

He looked at her in surprise. "Where did you hear that?"

"Is it true?"

He hedged. "It might be."

"I might be interested in buying it," Lara said. "What's your price?"

"Look, lady . . . I don't know you from Adam. You can't walk in off the street and expect me to discuss a ninety-million-dollar deal with you. I . . ."

"Ninety million?" Lara had a feeling it was high, but she wanted that site. It would be an exciting beginning. "Is that what we're talking about?"

"We're not talking about anything."

Lara handed Roger Burnham a hundred-dollar bill.

"What's this for?"

"That's for a forty-eight-hour option. All I'm asking is forty-eight hours. You weren't ready to announce that it was for sale anyway. What can you lose? If I meet your asking price, you've got what you wanted."

"I don't know anything about you."

"Call the Mercantile Bank in Chicago. Ask for Bob Vance. He's the president."

He stared at her for a long moment, shook his head, and muttered something with the word "crazies" in it.

He looked up the telephone number himself. Lara sat there while his secretary got Bob Vance for him.

"Mr. Vance? This is Roger Burnham in New York. I have a Miss . . ." He looked up at her.

"Lara Cameron."

"Lara Cameron here. She's interested in buying a property of ours here, and she says that you know her."

He sat there listening.

"She is . . . ? I see. . . . Really . . . ? No, I wasn't aware of that. . . . Right. . . . Right." After a long time he said, "Thank you very much."

He replaced the receiver and stared at Lara. "You seem to have made quite an impression in Chicago."

"I intend to make quite an impression in New York."

Burnham looked at the hundred-dollar bill. "What am I supposed to do with this?"

"Buy yourself some Cuban cigars. Do I have the option if I meet your price?"

He sat there, studying her. "It's a little unorthodox . . . but yes. I'll give you forty-eight hours."

"We have to move fast on this," Lara had told Keller. "We have forty-eight hours to line up our financing."

"Do you have any figures on it?"

"Ball park. Ninety million for the property, and I estimate another two hundred million to demolish the hospital and put up the building."

Keller was staring at her. "That's two hundred and ninety million dollars."

"You were always quick with figures," Lara said.

He ignored it. "Lara, where's that kind of money coming from?"

"We'll borrow it," Lara said. "Between my collateral in Chicago and the new property, it shouldn't be any problem."

"It's a big risk. A hundred things could go wrong. You'll be gambling everything you have on . . ."

"That's what makes it exciting," Lara said, "the gamble. And winning."

Getting financing for a building in New York was even simpler than in Chicago. Mayor Koch had instituted a tax program called the 421-A, and under it a developer replacing a functionally obsolete building could claim tax exemptions, with the first two years tax-free.

When the banks and savings and loan companies checked on Lara Cameron's credit, they were more than eager to do business with her.

Before forty-eight hours had passed, Lara walked into Burnham's office and handed him a check for three million dollars.

"This is a down payment on the deal," Lara said. "I'm meeting your asking price. By the way, you can keep the hundred dollars."

* * *

During the next six months Keller worked with banks on financing, and Lara worked with architects on planning.

Everything was proceeding smoothly. The architects and builders and marketing people were on schedule. Work was to begin on the demolition of the hospital and the construction of the new building in April.

Lara was restless. At six o'clock every morning she was at the construction site watching the new building going up. She felt frustrated because at this stage the building belonged to the workmen. There was nothing for her to do. She was used to more action. She liked to have half a dozen projects going at once.

"Why don't we look around for another deal?" Lara asked Keller.

"Because you're up to your ears in this one. If you even breathe hard, this whole thing is going to collapse. Do you know you've leveraged every penny you have to put this building up? If anything goes wrong . . ."

"Nothing is going to go wrong." She was watching his expression. "What's bothering you?"

"The deal you made with the savings and loan company . . ."

"What about it? We got our financing, didn't we?"

"I don't like the completion date clause. If the building's not finished by March fifteenth, they'll take it over, and you stand to lose everything you have."

Lara thought of the building she had put up in Glace Bay and how her friends had pitched in and finished it for her. But this was different.

"Don't worry," she told Keller. "The building will be finished. Are you sure we can't look around for another project?"

Lara was talking to the marketing people.

"The downstairs retail stores are already signed up," the marketing manager told Lara. "And more than half the condominiums have been taken. We estimate we'll have sold three-fourths of them before the building is finished, and the rest of them shortly after."

"I want them *all* sold before the building is completed," Lara said. "Step up the advertising."

"Very well."

Keller came into the office. "I have to hand it to you, Lara. You were right. The building's on schedule."

"This is going to be a money machine."

On January 15, sixty days before the date of completion, the huge girders and walls were finished, and the workers were already installing the electrical wiring and plumbing lines.

Lara stood there watching the men working on the girders high above. One of the workmen stopped to pull out a pack of cigarettes, and as he did so, a wrench slipped from his hand and fell to the ground far below. Lara watched in disbelief as the wrench came hurtling down toward her. She leaped out of the way, her heart pounding. The workman was looking down. He waved a "sorry."

Grim-faced, Lara got into the construction elevator and took it to the level where the workman was. Ignoring the dizzying empty space below, she walked across the scaffolding to the man.

"Did you drop that wrench?"

"Yeah, sorry."

She slapped him hard across the face. "You're fired. Now get off my building."

"Hey," he said, "it was an accident. I . . ."

"Get out of here."

The man glared at her for a moment, then walked away and took the elevator down.

Lara took a deep breath to control herself. The other workers were watching her.

"Get back to work," she ordered.

Lara was having lunch with Sam Gosden, the New York attorney who handled her contracts for her.

"I hear everything's going very well," Gosden said.

Lara smiled. "Better than very well. We're only a few weeks away from completion."

"Can I make an admission?"

"Yes, but be careful not to incriminate yourself."

He laughed. "I was betting that you couldn't do it."

"Really? Why?"

"Real estate development on the level where you're operating is a man's game. The only women who should be in real estate are the little old blue-haired ladies who sell co-ops."

"So you were betting against me," Lara said.

Sam Gosden smiled. "Yeah."

Lara leaned forward. "Sam . . ."

"Yes?"

"No one on my team bets against me. You're fired."

He sat there openmouthed as Lara got up and walked out of the restaurant.

On the following Monday morning, as Lara drove toward the building site, she sensed that something was wrong. And suddenly she realized what it was. It was the silence. There were no sounds of hammers or drills. When Lara arrived at the construction site, she stared in disbelief. The workmen were collecting their equipment and leaving. The foreman was packing up his things. Lara hurried up to him.

"What's going on?" Lara demanded. "It's only seven o'clock."

"I'm pulling the men."

"What are you talking about?"

"There's been a complaint, Miss Cameron."

"What kind of complaint?"

"Did you slap one of the workmen?"

"What?" She had forgotten. "Yes. He deserved it. I fired him."

"Did the city give you a license to go around slapping the people who work for you?"

"Wait a minute," Lara said. "It wasn't like that. He dropped a wrench. It almost killed me. I suppose I lost my temper. I'm sorry, but I don't want him back here."

"He won't be coming back here," the foreman said. "None of us will."

Lara stared at him. "Is this some kind of joke?"

"My union doesn't think it's a joke," the foreman told her. "They gave us orders to walk. We're walking."

"You have a contract."

"You broke it," the foreman told her. "If you have any complaints, take it up with the union."

He started to walk away.

"Wait a minute. I said I'm sorry. I'll tell you what. I . . . I'm willing to apologize to the man, and he can have his job back."

"Miss Cameron, I don't think you get the picture. He doesn't want his job back. We've all got other jobs waiting for us. This is a busy city. And I'll tell you something else, lady. We're too goddamn busy to let our bosses slap us around."

Lara stood there watching him walk away. It was her worst nightmare.

Lara hurried back to the office to tell the news to Keller. Before she could speak, he said, "I heard. I've been on the phone talking to the union."

"What did they say?" Lara asked eagerly.

"They're going to hold a hearing next month."

Lara's face filled with dismay. "Next month! We've got less than two months to finish the building."

"I told them that."

"And what did they say?"

"That it's not their problem."

Lara sank onto the couch. "Oh, my God. What are we going to do?"

"I don't know."

"Maybe we could persuade the bank to . . ." She saw the look on his face. "I guess not." Lara suddenly brightened. "I know. We'll hire another construction crew and . . ."

"Lara, there isn't a union worker who will touch that building."

"I should have killed that bastard."

"Right. That would have helped a lot," Keller said dryly.

Lara got up and began pacing. "I could ask Sam Gosden to . . ." She suddenly remembered. "No, I fired him."

"Why?"

"Never mind."

Keller was thinking aloud. "Maybe if we got hold of a good labor lawyer . . . someone with clout."

"That's a good idea. Someone who can move fast. Do you know anybody?"

"No. But Sam Gosden mentioned someone in one of our meetings. A man named Martin. Paul Martin."

"Who is he?"

"I'm not sure, but we were talking about union problems, and his name came up."

"Do you know what firm he's with?"

"No."

Lara buzzed her secretary. "Kathy, there's a lawyer in Manhattan named Paul Martin. Get me his address."

Keller said, "Don't you want his phone number so you can make an appointment?"

"There's no time. I can't afford to sit around waiting for an appointment. I'm going to see him today. If he can help us, fine. If he can't, we'll have to come up with something else."

But Lara was thinking to herself, *There is nothing else.*

Chapter Twelve

Paul Martin's office was on the twenty-fifth floor in an office building on Wall Street. The frosted sign on the door read, PAUL MARTIN, ATTORNEY AT LAW.

Lara took a deep breath and stepped inside. The reception office was smaller than she had expected. It contained one scarred desk with a bottle-blond secretary behind it.

"Good morning. Can I help you?"

"I'm here to see Mr. Martin," Lara said.

"Is he expecting you?"

"Yes, he is." There was no time for explanations.

"And your name?"

"Cameron. Lara Cameron."

The secretary looked at her quizzically. "Just a moment. I'll see whether Mr. Martin can see you."

The secretary got up from behind the desk and disappeared into the inner office.

He's got to see me, Lara thought.

A moment later the secretary emerged. "Yes, Mr. Martin will see you."

Lara concealed a sigh of relief. "Thank you."

She walked into the inner office. It was small and simply furnished. A desk, two couches, a coffee table, and a few chairs. *Not exactly a citadel of power,* Lara thought. The man behind the desk appeared to be in his early sixties. He had a deeply lined face, a hawk nose, and a mane of white hair. There was a feral, animal-like vitality about him. He was wearing an old-fashioned pinstripe double-breasted gray suit and a white shirt with a narrow collar. When he spoke, his voice was raspy, low, somehow compelling.

"My secretary said that I was expecting you."

"I'm sorry," Lara said. "I had to see you. It's an emergency."

"Sit down, Miss . . ."

"Cameron. Lara Cameron." She took a chair.

"What can I do for you?"

Lara took a deep breath. "I have a little problem." *A skeleton twenty-four stories of uncompleted steel and concrete standing idle.* "It's about a building."

"What about it?"

"I'm a real estate developer, Mr. Martin. I'm in the middle of putting up an office building on the East Side, and I'm having a problem with the union."

He was listening, saying nothing.

Lara hurried on. "I lost my temper and slapped one of the workmen, and the union called a strike."

He was studying her, puzzled. "Miss Cameron . . . what does all this have to do with me?"

"I heard you might be able to help me."

"I'm afraid you heard wrong. I'm a corporate attorney. I'm not involved with buildings, and I don't deal with unions."

Lara's heart sank. "Oh, I thought . . . isn't there anything you can do?"

He placed the palms of his hands on the desk, as though he were about to rise. "I can give you a couple pieces of advice. Get hold of a labor lawyer. Have him take the union to court and . . ."

"There's no time. I'm up against a deadline. I . . . what's the second piece of advice?"

"Get out of the building business." His eyes were fixed on her breasts. "You don't have the right equipment for it."

"What?"

"It's no place for a woman."

"And what *is* the place for a woman?" Lara asked angrily. "Barefoot, pregnant, and in the kitchen?"

"Something like that. Yeah."

Lara rose to her feet. It was all she could do to control herself.

"You must come from a long line of dinosaurs. Maybe you haven't heard the news. Women are free now."

Paul Martin shook his head. "No. Just noisier."

"Good-bye, Mr. Martin. I'm sorry I took up your valuable time."

Lara turned and strode out of the office, slamming the door behind her. She stopped in the corridor and took a deep breath. *This was a mistake,* she thought. She had finally reached a dead end. She had risked everything it had taken her years to build up, and she had lost it in one swift instant. There was no one to turn to. Nowhere to go.

It was over.

Lara walked the cold, rainy streets. She was completely unaware of the icy wind and her surroundings. Her mind was filled with the terrible disaster that had befallen her. Howard Keller's warning was ringing in her ears: *You put up buildings and borrow on them. It's like a pyramid, only if you're not careful, that pyramid can fall down.* And it had. The banks in Chicago would foreclose on her properties there, and she would lose all the money she had invested in the new building. She would have to start all over, from the beginning. *Poor Howard,* she thought. *He believed in my dreams, and I've let him down.*

The rain had stopped, and the sky was beginning to clear. A pale sun was fighting its way through the clouds. She suddenly realized it was dawn. She had walked all night. Lara looked around and saw where she was for the first time. She was only two blocks from the doomed property. *I'll take a last look at it,* Lara thought, resignedly.

She was a full block away when she first heard it. It was the sound of pneumatic drills and hammers and the roar of cement mixers filling the air. Lara stood there, listening for an instant, then started running toward the building site. When she reached it, she stood there, staring, unbelievingly.

The full crew was there, hard at work.

The foreman came up to her, smiling. "Morning, Miss Cameron."

Lara finally found her voice. "What . . . what's happening? I . . . I thought you were pulling your men off the job."

He said sheepishly, "That was a little misunderstanding, Miss Cameron. Bruno could have killed you when he dropped that wrench."

Lara swallowed. "But he . . ."

"Don't worry. He's gone. Nothing like that will happen again. You don't have a thing to worry about. We're right back on schedule."

Lara felt as though she were in a dream. She stood there watching the men swarming over the skeleton of the building and she thought, *I got it all back again. Everything. Paul Martin.*

Lara telephoned him as soon as she returned to her office. His secretary said, "I'm sorry, Mr. Martin is not available."

"Would you ask him to call me, please?" Lara left her number.

At three o'clock in the afternoon she still had not heard from him. She called him again.

"I'm sorry. Mr. Martin is not available."

He did not return her call.

At five o'clock Lara went to Paul Martin's office.

She said to the blond secretary, "Would you please tell Mr. Martin that Lara Cameron is here to see him?"

The secretary looked uncertain. "Well, I'll . . . Just a moment." She disappeared into the inner office and returned a minute later. "Go right in, please."

Paul Martin looked up as Lara walked in.

"Yes, Miss Cameron?" His voice was cool, neither friendly nor unfriendly. "What can I do for you?"

"I came to thank you."

"Thank me for what?"

"For . . . for straightening things out with the union."

He frowned. "I don't know what you're talking about."

"All the workmen came back this morning, and everything's wonderful. The building is back on schedule."

"Well, congratulations."

"If you'll send me a bill for your fee . . ."

"Miss Cameron, I think you're a little confused. If your problem is solved, I'm glad. But I had nothing to do with it."

Lara looked at him for a long time. "All right. I'm . . . I'm sorry I bothered you."

"No problem." He watched her leave the office.

A moment later his secretary came in. "Miss Cameron left a package for you, Mr. Martin."

It was a small package, tied with bright ribbon. Curious, he opened it. Inside was a silver knight in full armor, ready to do battle. An apology. *What did she call me? A dinosaur.* He could still hear his grandfather's voice. *Those were dangerous times, Paul. The young men decided to take control of the Mafia, to get rid of the old-timers, the mustache Petes, the dinosaurs. It was bloody, but they did it.*

But all that was a long, long time ago, in the old country. Sicily.

Chapter Thirteen

Gibellina, Sicily—1879

The Martinis were *stranieri*—outsiders, in the little Sicilian village of Gibellina. The countryside was desolate, a barren land of death, bathed in blazing pitiless sunlight, a landscape painted by a sadistic artist. In a land where the large estates belonged to the *gabelloti*, the wealthy landowners, the Martinis had bought a small farm and tried to run it themselves.

The *soprintendente* had come calling on Giuseppe Martini one day. "This little farm of yours," he said, "the land is too rocky. You will not be able to make a decent living on it, growing olives and grapes."

"Don't worry about me," Martini said. "I've been farming all my life."

"We're all worried about you," the *soprintendente* insisted. "Don Vito has some good farmland that he is willing to lease to you."

"I know about Don Vito and his land," Giuseppe Martini snorted. "If I sign a *mezzadria* with him to farm his land, he will take three fourths of my crops and charge me a hundred percent interest for the seed. I will end up with nothing, like the other fools who deal with him. Tell him I said no, thank you."

"You are making a big mistake, signore. This is dangerous country. Serious accidents can happen here."

"Are you threatening me?"

"Certainly not, signore. I was merely pointing out . . ."

"Get off my land," Giuseppe Martini said.

The overseer looked at him for a long time, then shook his head sadly. "You are a stubborn man."

Giuseppe Martini's young son, Ivo, said, "Who was that, Papa?"

"He's the overseer for one of the large landowners."

"I don't like him," the young boy said.

"I don't like him either, Ivo."

The following night Giuseppe Martini's crops were set on fire and the few cattle he had disappeared.

That was when Giuseppe Martini made his second mistake. He went to the *guardia* in the village.

"I demand protection," he said.

The chief of police studied him noncommittally. "That's what we are here for," he said. "What is your problem, signore?"

"Last night Don Vito's men burned my crops and stole my cattle."

"That is a serious charge. Can you prove it?"

"His *soprintendente* came to me and threatened me."

"Did he tell you they were going to burn your crops and steal your cattle?"

"Of course not," Giuseppe Martini said.

"What *did* he say to you?"

"He said that I should give up my farm and lease land from Don Vito."

"And you refused?"

"Naturally."

"Signore, Don Vito is a very important man. Do you wish me to arrest him simply because he offered to share his rich farmland with you?"

"I want you to protect me," Giuseppe Martini demanded. "I'm not going to let them drive me off my land."

"Signore, I am most sympathetic. I will certainly see what I can do."

"I would appreciate that."

"Consider it done."

The following afternoon, as young Ivo was returning from town, he saw half a dozen men ride up to his father's farm. They dismounted and went into the house.

A few minutes later Ivo saw his father dragged out to the field.

One of the men took out a gun. "We are going to give you a chance to escape. Run for it."

"No! This is my land! I . . ."

Ivo watched, terrified, as the man shot at the ground near his father's feet.

"Run!"

Giuseppe Martini started to run.

The *campieri* got on their horses and began circling Martini, yelling all the while.

Ivo hid, watching in horror at the terrible scene that was unfolding before his eyes.

The mounted men watched the man run across the field, trying to escape. Each time he reached the edge of the dirt road, one of them raced to cut him off and knock him to the ground. The farmer was bleeding and exhausted. He was slowing down.

The *campieri* decided they had had enough sport. One of them put a rope around the man's neck and dragged him toward the well.

"Why?" he gasped. "What have I done?"

"You went to the *guardia*. You should not have done that."

The *campieri* pulled down the victim's trousers, and one of the men took out a knife, while the others held him down.

"Let this be a lesson to you."

The man screamed, "No, please! I'm sorry."

The *campiero* smiled. "Tell that to your wife."

He reached down, grabbed the man's member, and slashed through it with the knife.

His screams filled the air.

"You won't need this anymore," the captain assured him.

He took the member and stuffed it in the man's mouth. He gagged and spit it out.

The captain looked at the other *campieri*. "He doesn't like the taste of it."

"*Uccidi quel figlio di puttana!*"

One of the *campieri* dismounted from his horse and picked up some heavy stones from the field. He pulled up the victim's bloodied pants and filled his pockets with the stones.

"Up you go." They lifted the man and carried him to the top of the well. "Have a nice trip."

They dumped him into the well.

"That water's going to taste like piss," one of them said.

Another one laughed. "The villagers won't know the difference."

They stayed for a moment, listening to the diminishing sounds and finally the silence, then mounted their horses and rode toward the house.

Ivo Martini stayed in the distance, watching in horror, hidden by the brush. The ten-year-old boy hurried to the well.

He looked down and whispered, "Papa . . ."

But the well was deep, and he heard nothing.

When the *campieri* had finished with Giuseppe Martini, they went to find his wife, Maria. She was in the kitchen when they entered.

"Where's my husband?" she demanded.

A grin. "Getting a drink of water."

Two of the men were closing in on her. One of them said, "You're too pretty to be married to an ugly man like that."

"Get out of my house," Maria ordered.

"Is that a way to treat guests?" One of the men reached out and tore her dress. "You're going to be wearing widow's clothes, so you won't need that anymore."

"Animal!"

There was a boiling pot of water on the stove. Maria reached for it and threw it in the man's face.

He screamed in pain. *"Fica!"* He pulled out his gun and fired at her.

She was dead before she hit the floor.

The captain shouted, *"Idiot! First* you fuck them, *then* you shoot them. Come on, let's report back to Don Vito."

Half an hour later they were back at Don Vito's estate.

"We took good care of the husband and wife," the captain reported.

"What about the son?"

The captain looked at Don Vito in surprise. "You didn't say anything about a son."

"Cretino! I said to take care of the family."

"But he's only a boy, Don Vito."

"Boys grow up to be men. Men want their vengeance. Kill him."

"As you say."

Two of the men rode back to the Martini farm.

* * *

THE STARS SHINE DOWN

Ivo was in a state of shock. He had watched both his parents murdered. He was alone in the world with no place to go and no one to turn to. *Wait!* There *was* one person to turn to: his father's brother, Nunzio Martini, in Palermo. Ivo knew that he had to move quickly. Don Vito's men would be coming back to kill him. He wondered why they had not done so already. The young boy threw some food into a knapsack, slung it over his shoulder, and hurriedly left the farm.

Ivo made his way to the little dirt road that led away from the village, and started walking. Whenever he heard a cart coming, he moved off the road and hid in the trees.

An hour after he had started his journey, he saw a group of *campieri* riding along the road searching for him. Ivo stayed hidden, motionless until long after they were gone. Then he began walking again. At night, he slept in the orchards and he lived off the fruit from the trees and the vegetables in the fields. He walked for three days.

When he felt he was safe from Don Vito, he approached a small village. An hour later he was in the back of a wagon headed for Palermo.

Ivo reached the house of his uncle in the middle of the night. Nunzio Martini lived in a large, prosperous-looking house on the outskirts of the city. It had a spacious balcony, terraces, and a courtyard. Ivo pounded on the front door. There was a long silence, and then a deep voice called out, "Who the hell is it?"

"It's Ivo, Uncle Nunzio."

Moments later Nunzio Martini opened the door. Ivo's uncle was a large middle-aged man with a generous Roman nose and flowing white hair. He was wearing a nightshirt. He looked at the boy in surprise. "Ivo! What are you doing here in the middle of the night? Where are your mother and father?"

"They're dead," Ivo sobbed.

"Dead? Come in, come in."

Ivo stumbled into the house.

"That's terrible news. Was there some kind of an accident?"

Ivo shook his head. "Don Vito had them murdered."

"Murdered? But why?"

"My father refused to lease land from him."

"Ah."

"Why would he have them killed? They never did anything to him."

"It was nothing personal," Nunzio Martini said.

Ivo stared at him. *"Nothing personal?* I don't understand."

"Everyone knows of Don Vito. He has a reputation. He is an *uomo rispettato*—a man of respect and power. If he let your father defy him, then others would try to defy him, and he would lose his power. There is nothing that can be done."

The boy was watching him, aghast. "Nothing?"

"Not now, Ivo. Not now. Meanwhile, you look as though you could use a good night's sleep."

In the morning, at breakfast, they talked.

"How would you like to live in this fine house and work for me?" Nunzio Martini was a widower.

"I think I would like that," Ivo said.

"I can use a smart boy like you. And you look strong."

"I am strong," Ivo told him.

"Good."

"What business are you in, Uncle?" Ivo asked.

Nunzio Martini smiled. "I protect people."

The Mafia had sprung up throughout Sicily and other poverty-stricken parts of Italy to protect the people from a ruthless, autocratic government. The Mafia corrected injustices and avenged wrongs, and it finally became so powerful that the government itself feared it, and merchants and farmers paid tribute to it.

Nunzio Martini was the Mafia *capo* in Palermo. He saw to it that proper tribute was collected and that those who did not pay were punished. Punishment could range from a broken arm or leg to a slow and painful death.

Ivo went to work for his uncle.

For the next fifteen years Palermo was Ivo's school, and his uncle Nunzio was his teacher. Ivo started out as an errand boy, then moved up to collector, and finally became his uncle's trusted lieutenant.

When Ivo was twenty-five years old, he married Carmela, a buxom Sicilian girl, and a year later they had a son, Gian Carlo. Ivo moved his family into their own house. When his uncle died, Ivo took his position and became even more successful and prosperous. But he had some unfinished business to attend to.

One day he said to Carmela, "Start packing up. We're moving to America."

She looked at him in surprise. "Why are we going to America?"

Ivo was not accustomed to being questioned. "Just do as I say. I'm leaving now. I'll be back in two or three days."

"Ivo . . ."

"Pack."

Three black *macchine* pulled up in front of the *guardia* headquarters in Gibellina. The captain, now heavier by thirty pounds, was seated at his desk when the door opened and half a dozen men walked in. They were well dressed and prosperous-looking.

"Good morning, gentlemen. Can I help you?"

"We have come to help *you*," Ivo said. "Do you remember me? I'm the son of Giuseppe Martini."

The police captain's eyes widened. *"You,"* he said. "What are you doing here? It is dangerous for you."

"I came because of your teeth."

"My teeth?"

"Yes." Two of Ivo's men closed in on the captain and pinned his arms to his side. "You need dental work. Let me fix them."

Ivo shoved the gun into the chief's mouth and pulled the trigger.

Ivo turned to his companions. "Let's go."

Fifteen minutes later the three automobiles drove up to Don Vito's house. There were two guards outside. They watched the procession curiously. When the cars came to a stop, Ivo got out.

"Good morning. Don Vito's expecting us," he said.

One of the guards frowned. "He didn't say anything about . . ."

In the next instant the guards were gunned down. The guns were loaded with *lupare*, cartridges with large leaden balls, a hunter's trick to spread the pellets. The guards were cut to pieces.

Inside the house Don Vito heard the shooting. When he looked out the window and saw what was happening, he quickly crossed to a drawer and pulled out a gun. "Franco!" he called. "Antonio! Quickly!"

There were more sounds of shots from outside.

A voice said, "Don Vito . . ."

He spun around.

Ivo stood there, a gun in his hand. "Drop your gun."

"I . . ."

"Drop it."

Don Vito let his gun fall to the floor. "Take whatever you want and get out."

"I don't want anything," Ivo said. "As a matter of fact, I came here because I owe you something."

Don Vito said, "Whatever it is, I'm prepared to forget it."

"I'm not. Do you know who I am?"

"No."

"Ivo Martini."

The old man frowned, trying to remember. He shrugged. "It means nothing to me."

"More than fifteen years ago. Your men killed my mother and father."

"That's terrible," Don Vito exclaimed. "I will have them punished, I'll . . ."

Ivo reached out and smashed him across his nose with his gun. Blood started pouring out. "This isn't necessary," Don Vito gasped. "I . . ."

Ivo pulled out a knife. "Take down your trousers."

"Why? You can't . . ."

Ivo raised the gun. "Take down your trousers."

"No!" It was a scream. "Think about what you're doing. I have sons and brothers. If you harm me, they will track you down and kill you like a dog."

"If they can find me," Ivo said. "Your trousers."

"No."

Ivo shot one of his kneecaps. The old man screamed out in pain.

"Let me help you," Ivo said. He reached out and pulled the old man's trousers down, and then his underwear. "There's not much there, is there? Well, we'll have to do the best we can." He grabbed Don Vito's member and slashed it off with a knife.

Don Vito fainted.

Ivo took the penis and shoved it into the man's mouth. "Sorry I don't have a well to drop you into," Ivo said. As a parting gesture, he shot the old man in the head, then turned and walked out of the house to the car. His friends were waiting for him.

"Let's go."

"He has a large family, Ivo. They'll come after you."

"Let them."

Two days later Ivo, his wife, and son, Gian Carlo, were on a boat to New York.

* * *

At the end of the last century the New World was a land of opportunity. New York had a large population of Italians. Many of Ivo's friends had already emigrated to the big city and decided to use their expertise in what they knew best: the protection racket. The Mafia began spreading its tentacles. Ivo anglicized his family name from Martini to Martin and enjoyed an uninterrupted prosperity.

Gian Carlo was a big disappointment to his father. He had no interest in working. When he was twenty-seven, he got an Italian girl pregnant, married her in a quiet and hurried ceremony, and three months later they had a son, Paul.

Ivo had big plans for his grandson. Lawyers were very important in America, and Ivo decided that his grandson should be an attorney. The young boy was ambitious and intelligent, and when he was twenty-two, he was admitted to Harvard Law School. When Paul was graduated, Ivo arranged for him to join a prestigious law firm, and he soon became a partner. Five years later Paul opened his own law firm. By this time Ivo had invested heavily in legitimate businesses, but he still kept his contacts with the Mafia, and his grandson handled his business affairs for him. In 1967, the year Ivo died, Paul married an Italian girl, Nina, and a year later his wife gave birth to twins.

In the seventies Paul was kept busy. His main clients were the unions, and because of that, he was in a position of power. Heads of businesses and industries deferred to him.

One day Paul was having lunch with a client, Bill Rohan, a respected banker who knew nothing of Paul's family background.

"You should join Sunnyvale, my golf club," Bill Rohan said. "You play golf, don't you?"

"Occasionally," Paul said. "When I have time."

"Fine. I'm on the admissions board. Would you like me to put you up for membership?"

"That would be nice."

The following week the board met to discuss new members. Paul Martin's name was brought up.

"I can recommend him," Bill Rohan said. "He's a good man."

John Hammond, another member of the board, said, "He's Italian, isn't he? We don't need any dagos in this club, Bill."

The banker looked at him. "Are you going to blackball him?"

"You're damn right I am."

"Okay, then we'll pass on him. Next . . ."
The meeting continued.

Two weeks later Paul Martin was having lunch with the banker again. "I've been practicing my golf," Paul joked.

Bill Rohan was embarrassed. "There's been a slight hitch, Paul."

"A hitch?"

"I did propose you for membership. But I'm afraid one of the members of the board blackballed you."

"Oh? Why?"

"Don't take this personally. He's a bigot. He doesn't like Italians."

Paul smiled. "That doesn't bother me, Bill. A lot of people don't like Italians. This Mr. . . ."

"Hammond. John Hammond."

"The meat-packer?"

"Yes. He'll change his mind. I'll talk to him again."

Paul shook his head. "Don't bother. To tell you the truth, I'm really not that crazy about golf anyway."

Six months later, in the middle of July, four Hammond Meat Packing Company refrigerated trucks loaded with pork loins, strip steaks, and pork butts, headed from the packinghouse in Minnesota to supermarkets in Buffalo and New Jersey, pulled off the road. The drivers opened the back doors of the trucks and walked away.

When John Hammond heard the news, he was furious. He called in his manager.

"What the hell is going on?" he demanded. "A million and a half dollars' worth of meat spoiled in the sun. How could that happen?"

"The union called a strike," the supervisor said.

"Without telling us? What are they striking about? More money?"

The supervisor shrugged. "I don't know. They didn't say anything to me. They just walked."

"Tell the local union guy to come in and see me. I'll settle it," Hammond said.

That afternoon the union representative was ushered into Hammond's office.

"Why wasn't I told there was going to be a strike?" Hammond demanded.

The representative said, apologetically, "I didn't know it myself, Mr. Hammond. The men just got mad and walked out. It happened very suddenly."

"You know I've always been a reasonable man to deal with. What is it they want? A raise?"

"No sir. It's soap."

Hammond stared at him. "Did you say *soap?*"

"That's right. They don't like the soap you're using in their bathrooms. It's too strong."

Hammond could not believe what he was hearing. *"The soap was too strong?* And that's why I lost a million and a half dollars?"

"Don't blame me," the foreman said. "It's the men."

"Jesus," Hammond said. "I can't believe this. What kind of soap would they like—fairy soap?" He slammed his fist on the desk. "The next time the men have any problem, you come to me first. You hear me?"

"Yes, Mr. Hammond."

"You tell them to get back to work. There will be the best soap money can buy in those washrooms by six o'clock tonight. Is that clear?"

"I'll tell them, Mr. Hammond."

John Hammond sat there for a long time fuming. *No wonder this country is going to hell,* he thought. *Soap!*

Two weeks later, at noon on a hot day in August, five Hammond Meat Packing trucks on their way to deliver meat to Syracuse and Boston pulled off the road. The drivers opened the back doors of the refrigerated trucks and left.

John Hammond got the news at six o'clock that evening.

"What the hell are you talking about?" he screamed. "Didn't you put in the new soap?"

"I did," his manager said, "the same day you told me to."

"Then what the hell is it this time?"

The manager said helplessly, "I don't know. There haven't been any complaints. No one said a word to me."

"Get the goddamned union representative in here."

At seven o'clock that evening Hammond was talking to the union representative.

"Two million dollars' worth of meat was ruined this afternoon because of your men," Hammond screamed. "Have they gone crazy?"

"Do you want me to tell the president of the union you asked that, Mr. Hammond?"

"No, no," Hammond said quickly. "Look, I've never had any problem with you fellows before. If the men want more money, just come to me and we'll discuss it like reasonable people. How much are they asking for?"

"Nothing."

"What do you mean?"

"It isn't the money, Mr. Hammond."

"Oh? What is it?"

"Lights."

"Lights?" Hammond thought he had misunderstood him.

"Yes. The men are complaining that the lights in the washrooms are too dim."

John Hammond sat back in his chair, suddenly quiet. "What's going on here?" he asked softly.

"I told you, the men think that . . ."

"Never mind that crap. What's going on?"

The union representative said, "If I knew, I would tell you."

"Is someone trying to put me out of business? Is that it?"

The union representative was silent.

"All right," John Hammond said. "Give me a name. Who can I talk to?"

"There's a lawyer who might be able to help you. The union uses him a lot. His name is Paul Martin."

"Paul . . . ?" And John Hammond suddenly remembered. "Why, that blackmailing guinea bastard. Get out of here," he yelled. *"Out!"*

Hammond sat there seething. *No one blackmails me. No one.*

One week later six more of his refrigerated trucks were abandoned on side roads.

John Hammond arranged a luncheon with Bill Rohan. "I've been thinking about your friend Paul Martin," Hammond said. "I may have been a bit hasty in blackballing him."

"Why, it's very generous of you to say that, John."

"I'll tell you what. You propose him for membership next week and I'll give him my vote."

The following week, when Paul Martin's name came up, he was accepted unanimously by the membership committee.

John Hammond personally put in a call to Paul Martin. "Congratulations, Mr. Martin," he said. "You've just been accepted as a member of Sunnyvale. We're delighted to have you aboard."

"Thank you," Paul said. "I appreciate the call."

John Hammond's next call was to the district attorney's office. He made an appointment to meet him the following week.

On Sunday John Hammond and Bill Rohan were part of a foursome at the club.

"You haven't met Paul Martin yet, have you?" Bill Rohan asked.

John Hammond shook his head. "No. I don't think he's going to be playing a lot of golf. The grand jury is going to be keeping your friend too busy."

"What are you talking about?"

"I'm going to give information about him to the district attorney that will certainly interest a grand jury."

Bill Rohan was shocked. "Do you know what you're doing?"

"You bet I do. He's a cockroach, John. I'm going to step on him."

The following Monday, on his way to the district attorney's office, John Hammond was killed in a hit-and-run accident. There were no witnesses. The police never found the driver.

Every Sunday after that Paul Martin took his wife and the twins to the Sunnyvale Club for lunch. The buffet there was delicious.

Paul Martin took his marriage vows seriously. For instance, he would never have dreamed of dishonoring his wife by taking her and his mistress to the same restaurant. His marriage was one part of his life; his affairs were another. All of Paul Martin's friends had mistresses. It was part of their accepted life-style. What bothered Martin was to see old men taking out young girls. It was undignified, and Paul Martin placed great value on dignity. He resolved that when he reached the age of sixty, he would stop having mistresses. And on his sixtieth birthday, two years earlier, he had stopped. His wife, Nina, was a good companion to him. That was enough. *Dignity.*

It was this man to whom Lara Cameron had come to ask for help. Martin had been aware of Lara Cameron by name, but he was stunned by how young and beautiful she was. She was ambitious and angrily independent, and yet she was very feminine. He found himself strongly attracted to her. *No,* he thought, *she's a young girl. I'm an old man. Too old.*

When Lara had stormed out of his office on her first visit, Paul Martin sat there for a long time, thinking about her. And then he had picked up the telephone and made a call.

Chapter Fourteen

The new building was progressing on schedule. Lara visited the site every morning and every afternoon, and there was a new respect in the attitude of the men toward her. She sensed it in the way they looked at her, talked to her, and worked for her. She knew it was because of Paul Martin, and disturbingly, she found herself thinking more and more about the ugly-attractive man with the strangely compelling voice.

Lara telephoned him again.

"I wondered if we might have lunch, Mr. Martin?"

"Are you having another problem of some kind?"

"No. I just thought it would be nice if we got to know each other better."

"I'm sorry, Miss Cameron. I never have lunch."

"What about dinner one evening?"

"I'm a married man, Miss Cameron. I have dinner with my wife and children."

"I see. If . . ." The line went dead. *What's the matter with him?* Lara wondered. *I'm not trying to go to bed with the man. I just want to find some way to thank him.* She tried to put him out of her mind.

Paul Martin was disturbed by how pleased he was to hear Lara Cameron's voice. He told his secretary, "If Miss Cameron calls again, tell her I'm not in." He did not need temptation, and Lara Cameron was temptation.

THE STARS SHINE DOWN

* * *

Howard Keller was delighted with the way things were progressing.

"I must admit, you had me a little worried there for a while," he said. "It looked as though we were going right down the tube. You pulled off a miracle."

It wasn't my miracle, Lara thought. *It was Paul Martin's.* Perhaps he was angry with her because she had not paid him for his services.

On an impulse, Lara sent Paul a check for fifty thousand dollars. The following day, the check was returned with no note.

Lara telephoned him again. His secretary said, "I'm sorry, Mr. Martin is not available."

Another snub. It was as though he could not be bothered with her. *And if he can't be bothered with me,* Lara wondered, *why did he go out of his way to help me?*

She dreamed about him that night.

Howard Keller walked into Lara's office.

"I've got two tickets for the new Andrew Lloyd Webber musical, *Song & Dance.* I have to go to Chicago. Can you use the tickets?"

"No, I . . . wait." She was quiet for a moment. "Yes, I think I can use them. Thank you, Howard."

That afternoon Lara put one of the tickets in an envelope and addressed it to Paul Martin at his office.

When he received the ticket the next day, he looked at it, puzzled. Who would send him a single ticket to the theater? *The Cameron girl. I'll have to put a stop to this,* he thought.

"Am I free Friday evening?" he asked his secretary.

"You're having dinner with your brother-in-law, Mr. Martin."

"Cancel it."

Lara sat through the first act, and the seat next to her remained empty. *So he's not coming,* Lara thought. *Well, to hell with him. I've done everything I can.*

As the first act curtain came down, Lara debated whether she should stay for the second act or leave. A figure appeared at the seat next to hers.

"Let's get out of here," Paul Martin commanded.

* * *

They had dinner at a bistro on the East Side. He sat across the table from her, studying her, quiet and wary. The waiter came to take their drink order.

"I'll have a scotch and soda," Lara said.

"Nothing for me."

Lara looked at him in surprise.

"I don't drink."

After they had ordered dinner, Paul Martin said, "Miss Cameron, what do you want from me?"

"I don't like owing anyone anything," Lara said. "I owe you something, and you won't let me pay you. That bothers me."

"I told you before . . . you don't owe me anything."

"But I . . ."

"I hear your building is coming along well."

"Yes." She started to say "thanks to you," then thought better of it.

"You're good at what you do, aren't you?"

Lara nodded. "I want to be. It's the most exciting thing in the world to have an idea and watch it grow into concrete and steel, and become a building that people work in and live in. In a way, it becomes a monument, doesn't it?"

Her face was vibrant and alive.

"I suppose it does. And is one monument going to lead to another?"

"You bet it is," Lara said enthusiastically. "I intend to become the most important real estate developer in this city."

There was a sexuality about her that was mesmerizing.

Paul Martin smiled. "I wouldn't be surprised."

"Why did you decide to come to the theater tonight?" Lara asked.

He had come to tell her to leave him alone, but being with her now, being this close to her, he could not bring himself to say it. "I heard good things about the show."

Lara smiled. "Maybe we'll go again and see it together, Paul."

He shook his head. "Miss Cameron, I'm not only married, I'm very much married. I happen to love my wife."

"I admire that," Lara said. "The building will be finished on the fifteenth of March. We're having a party to celebrate. Will you come?"

He hesitated a long time trying to word his refusal as gently as possible. When he finally spoke, he said, "Yes, I'll come."

* * *

The celebration for the opening of the new building was a moderate success. Lara Cameron's name was not big enough to attract many members of the press or any of the city's important dignitaries. But one of the mayor's assistants was there, and a reporter from the *Post*.

"The building is almost fully leased out," Keller told Lara. "And we have a flood of inquiries."

"Good," Lara said absently. Her mind was on something else. She was thinking about Paul Martin and wondering whether he would appear. For some reason it was important to her. He was an intriguing mystery. He denied that he had helped her, and yet . . . She was pursuing a man old enough to be her father. Lara put the connection out of her mind.

Lara attended to her guests. Hors d'oeuvres and drinks were being served, and everyone seemed to be having a good time. In the midst of the festivities, Paul Martin arrived, and the tone of the party immediately changed. The workmen greeted him as though he were royalty. They were obviously in awe of him.

I'm a corporate attorney . . . I don't deal with unions.

Martin shook hands with the mayor's assistant and some of the union officials there, then went up to Lara.

"I'm glad you could come," Lara said.

Paul Martin looked around at the huge building and said, "Congratulations. You've done a good job."

"Thank you." She lowered her voice. "And I do mean thank you."

He was staring at her, bemused by how ravishing Lara looked and the way he felt, looking at her.

"The party's almost over," Lara said. "I was hoping you would take me to dinner."

"I told you, I have dinner with my wife and children." He was looking into her eyes. "I'll buy you a drink."

Lara smiled. "That will do nicely."

They stopped at a small bar on Third Avenue. They talked, but afterward neither of them would remember what they talked about. The words were camouflage for the sexual tension between them.

"Tell me about yourself," Paul Martin said. "Who are you? Where are you from? How did you get started in this business?"

Lara thought of Sean MacAllister and his repulsive body on top of hers. *"That was so good we're going to do it again."*

"I came from a little town in Nova Scotia," Lara said. "Glace Bay."

My father collected rents from some boardinghouses there. When he died, I took over. One of the boarders helped me buy a lot, and I put up a building on it. That was the beginning."

He was listening closely.

"After that I went to Chicago and developed some buildings there. I did well and came to New York." She smiled. "That's really the whole story." *Except for the agony of growing up with a father who hated her, the shame of poverty, of never owning anything, the giving of her body to Sean MacAllister . . .*

As though reading her mind, Paul Martin said, "I'll bet it wasn't really all that easy, was it?"

"I'm not complaining."

"What's your next project?"

Lara shrugged. "I'm not sure. I've looked at a lot of possibilities, but there's nothing I'm really wild about."

He could not take his eyes off her.

"What are you thinking?" Lara asked.

He took a deep breath. "The truth? I was thinking that if I weren't married, I would tell you that you're one of the most exciting women I've ever met. But I am married, so you and I are going to be just friends. Do I make myself clear?"

"Very clear."

He looked at his watch. "Time to go." He turned to the waiter. "Check, please." He rose to his feet.

"Can we have lunch next week?" Lara asked.

"No. Maybe I'll see you again when your next building is finished."

And he was gone.

That night Lara dreamed they were making love. Paul Martin was on top of her, stroking her body with his hands and whispering in her ear.

"You ken, I maun hae ye, and onie ye . . . Gude forgie me, my bonnie darlin', for I've niver tauld you how mickle I love ye, love ye, love ye. . . ."

And then he was inside her and her body was suddenly molten. She moaned, and her moans awakened her. She sat up in bed, trembling.

Two days later Paul Martin telephoned. "I think I have a location you might be interested in," he said crisply. "It's over on the West Side, on Sixty-ninth Street. It's not on the market yet. It belongs to a client of mine who wants to sell."

Lara and Howard Keller went to look at it that morning. It was a prime piece of property.

"How did you hear about this?" Keller asked.

"Paul Martin."

"Oh, I see." There was disapproval in his voice.

"What is that supposed to mean?"

"Lara . . . I checked on Martin. He's Mafia. Stay away from him."

She said indignantly, "He has nothing to do with the Mafia. He's a good friend. Anyway, what does that have to do with this site? Do you like it?"

"I think it's great."

"Then let's buy it."

Ten days later they closed the deal.

Lara sent Paul Martin a large bouquet of flowers. There was a note attached: "Paul—please don't send these back. They're very sensitive."

She received a call from him that afternoon.

"Thanks for the flowers. I'm not used to getting flowers from beautiful women." His voice sounded gruffer than usual.

"Do you know your problem?" Lara asked. "No one has ever spoiled you enough."

"Is that what you want to do, spoil me?"

"Rotten."

Paul laughed.

"I mean it."

"I know you do."

"Why don't we talk about it at lunch?" Lara asked.

Paul Martin had not been able to get Lara out of his mind. He knew that he could easily fall in love with her. There was a vulnerability about her, an innocence, and, at the same time, something wildly sensual. He knew that he would be smart never to see her again, but he was unable to control himself. He was drawn to her by something more powerful than his will.

They had lunch at the "21" Club.

"When you're trying to hide something," Paul Martin advised, "always do it out in the open. Then no one will believe you're doing anything wrong."

"Are we trying to hide something?" Lara asked softly.

He looked at her and made his decision. *She's beautiful and smart, but so are a thousand other women. It will be easy to get her out of my system. I'll go to bed with her once, and that will be the end of it.*

As it turned out, he was wrong.

When they arrived at Lara's apartment, Paul was unaccountably nervous.

"I feel like a fuckin' schoolboy," Paul said. "I'm out of practice."

"It's like riding a bicycle," Lara murmured. "It will come back to you. Let me undress you."

She took off his jacket and tie and started unbuttoning his shirt.

"You know that this could never become serious, Lara."

"I know that."

"I'm sixty-two years old. I could be your father."

She went still for an instant, remembering her dream. "I know." She finished undressing him. "You have a beautiful body."

"Thanks." His wife never told him that.

Lara slid her arms along his thighs. "You're very strong, aren't you?"

He found himself standing straighter. "I played basketball when I was in . . ."

Her lips were on his and they were in bed, and he experienced something that had never happened to him before in his life. He felt as though his body were on fire. They were making love, and it was without a beginning or an ending, a river that swept him along faster and faster, and the tide began to pull at him, sucking him down and down, deeper and deeper, into a velvet darkness that exploded into a thousand stars. And the miracle was that it happened again, and once again, until he lay there panting and exhausted.

"I can't believe this," he said.

His lovemaking with his wife had always been conventional, routine. But with Lara it was an incredibly sensual experience. Paul Martin had had many women before, but Lara was like no one he had ever known. She had given him a gift no woman had ever given him: She made him feel young.

When Paul was getting dressed, Lara asked, "Will I see you again?"

"Yes." *God help me.* "Yes."

* * *

The 1980s were a time of changes. Ronald Reagan was elected President of the United States and Wall Street had the busiest day in its history. The shah of Iran died in exile, and Anwar Sadat was assassinated. The public debt hit one trillion dollars, and the American hostages in Iran were freed. Sandra Day O'Connor became the first woman to serve on the Supreme Court.

Lara was in the right place at the right time. Real estate development was booming. Money was abundant, and banks were willing to finance projects that were both speculative and highly leveraged.

Savings and loan companies were a big source of equity. High-yield and high-risk bonds—nicknamed junk bonds—had been popularized by a young financial genius named Mike Milken, and they were manna to the real estate industry. The financing was there for the asking.

"I'm going to put up a hotel on the Sixty-ninth Street property, instead of an office building."

"Why?" Howard Keller asked. "It's a perfect location for an office building. With a hotel, you have to run it twenty-four hours a day. Tenants come and go like ants. With an office building, you only have to worry about a lease every five or ten years."

"I know, but in a hotel you have drop-dead power, Howard. You can give important people suites and entertain them in your own restaurant. I like that idea. It's going to be a hotel. I want you to set up meetings with the top architects in New York: Skidmore, Owings and Merrill, Peter Eisenman, and Philip Johnson."

The meetings took place over the next two weeks. Some of the architects were patronizing. They had never worked for a female developer before.

One of them said, "If you'd like us to copy . . ."

"No. We're going to build a hotel that *other* builders will copy. If you want a buzzword, try 'elegance.' I see an entryway flanked by twin fountains, a lobby with Italian marble. Off the lobby we'll have a comfortable conference room where . . ."

By the end of the meeting they were impressed.

Lara put together a team. She hired a lawyer named Terry Hill, an assistant named Jim Belon, a project manager named Tom Chriton, and an advertising agency headed by Tom Scott. She hired the architectural firm of Higgins, Almont & Clark, and the project was under way.

"We'll meet once a week," Lara told the group, "but I'll want daily reports from each of you. I want this hotel to go up on schedule and on budget. I selected all of you because you're the best at what you do. Don't let me down. Are there any questions?"

The next two hours were spent in answering them.

Later Lara said to Keller, "How do you think the meeting went?"

"Fine, boss."

It was the first time he had called her that. She liked it.

Charles Cohn telephoned.

"I'm in New York. Can we have lunch?"

"You bet we can!" Lara said.

They had lunch at Sardi's.

"You look wonderful," Cohn said. "Success agrees with you, Lara."

"It's only the beginning," Lara said. "Charles . . . how would you like to join Cameron Enterprises? I'll give you a piece of the company and . . ."

He shook his head. "Thanks, but no. You've just started the journey. I'm near the end of the road. I'll be retiring next summer."

"Let's stay in touch," Lara said. "I don't want to lose you."

The next time Paul Martin came to Lara's apartment, she said, "I have a surprise for you, darling."

She handed him half a dozen packages.

"Hey! It's not my birthday."

"Open them."

Inside were a dozen Bergdorf Goodman shirts and a dozen Pucci ties.

"I have shirts and ties." He laughed.

"Not like these," Lara told him. "They'll make you feel younger. I got the name of a good tailor for you, too."

The following week Lara had a new barber style Paul's hair.

Paul Martin looked at himself in the mirror and thought, *I do look younger.* Life had become exciting. *And all because of Lara,* he thought.

Paul's wife tried not to notice the change in her husband.

They were all there for the meeting: Keller, Tom Chriton, Jim Belon and Terry Hill.

"We're going to fast-track the hotel," Lara announced.

The men looked at one another. "That's dangerous," Keller said.

"Not if you do it right."

Tom Chriton spoke up. "Miss Cameron, the safe way to do this is to complete one phase at a time. You do your grading, and when that's done, you begin digging the trenches for foundations. When that's done, you put in the utility conduits and drainage piping. Then . . ."

Lara interrupted. "You put in the wooden concrete framework and the skeletal gridiron. I know all that."

"Then why . . . ?"

"Because that will take two years. I don't want to wait two years."

Jim Belon said, "If we fast-track it, that means starting all the different steps at once. If anything goes wrong, nothing will fit together. You could have a lopsided building with electric circuits in the wrong place and . . ."

"Then we have to see to it that nothing goes wrong, don't we?" Lara said. "If we do it this way, we'll get the building up in a year instead of two, and we'll save close to twenty million dollars."

"True, but it's taking a big chance."

"I like taking chances."

Chapter Fifteen

Lara told Paul Martin about her decision to fast-track the hotel and the discussion she had had with the committee.

"They may have been right," Paul said. "What you're doing could be dangerous."

"Trump does it. Uris does it."

Paul said gently, "Baby, you're not Trump or Uris."

"I'm going to be bigger than they are, Paul. I'm going to put up more buildings in New York than anyone ever has before. It's going to be my city."

He looked at her for a long moment. "I believe you."

Lara had an unlisted telephone installed in her office. Only Paul Martin had the number. He installed a telephone in his office for Lara's calls. They spoke to each other several times a day.

Whenever they could get away in the afternoon, they went to Lara's apartment. Paul Martin looked forward to those trysts more than he had ever believed possible. Lara had become an obsession with him.

When Keller became aware of what was happening, he was concerned.

"Lara," he said, "I think you're making a mistake. He's dangerous."

"You don't know him. He's wonderful."

"Are you in love with him?"

Lara thought about it. Paul Martin fulfilled a need in her life. But was she in love with him?

"No."

"Is he in love with you?"

"I think so."

"Be careful. Be very careful."

Lara smiled. Impulsively, she kissed Keller's cheek. "I love the way you take care of me, Howard."

Lara was at the construction site, studying a report.

"I notice we're paying for an awful lot of lumber," Lara said. She was talking to Pete Reese, the new project manager.

"I didn't want to mention it before, Miss Cameron, because I wasn't sure—but you're right. A lot of our lumber's missing. We've had to double order it."

She looked up at him. "You mean, someone is stealing it?"

"It looks that way."

"Do you have any idea who?"

"No."

"We have night watchmen here, don't we?"

"One watchman."

"And he hasn't seen anything?"

"No. But with all this activity going on, it could be happening during the day. It could be anybody."

Lara was thoughtful. "I see. Thanks for letting me know, Pete. I'll take care of it."

That afternoon Lara hired a private detective, Steve Kane.

"How does anyone walk away in broad daylight with a load of lumber?" Kane asked.

"You tell me."

"You say there's a night watchman at the site?"

"Yes."

"Maybe he's in on it."

"I'm not interested in maybes," Lara said. "Find out who's behind it and get back to me."

"Can you get me hired as a member of the construction crew?"

"I'll take care of it."

Steve Kane went to work at the site the next day.

When Lara told Keller what was happening, he said, "You didn't have to get involved in this. I could have handled it for you."

"I like handling things myself," Lara said.

That was the end of the conversation.

Five days later Kane appeared at Lara's office.

"Have you found out anything?"

"Everything," he said.

"Was it the watchman?"

"No. The lumber wasn't stolen from the building site."

"What do you mean?"

"I mean it never reached there. It was sent to another construction site in Jersey and double-billed. The invoices were doctored."

"Who's behind it?" Lara asked.

Kane told her.

The following afternoon there was a meeting of the committee. Terry Hill, Lara's lawyer, was there, Howard Keller, Jim Belon, the project manager, and Pete Reese. There was also a stranger at the conference table. Lara introduced him as Mr. Conroy.

"Let's have a report," Lara said.

Pete Reese said, "We're right on schedule. We estimate four more months. You were right about going fast track. It's all going smooth as silk. We've already started on the electrical and plumbing."

"Good," Lara said.

"What about the stolen lumber?" Keller asked.

"Nothing new on it yet," Pete Reese said. "We're keeping an eye open."

"I don't think we have to worry about that anymore," Lara announced. "We found out who's stealing it." She nodded toward the stranger. "Mr. Conroy is with the Special Fraud Squad. It's actually *Detective* Conroy."

"What's he doing here?" Pete Reese asked.

"He's come to take you away."

Reese looked up, startled. "What?"

Lara turned to the group. "Mr. Reese has been selling our lumber to another construction job. When he found out that I was checking the reports, he decided to tell me there was a problem."

"Wait a minute," Pete Reese said. "I . . . I . . . You have it wrong."

She turned to Conroy. "Would you please get him out of here?"

THE STARS SHINE DOWN

She turned to the others. "Now, let's discuss the opening of the hotel."

As the hotel grew nearer completion, the pressure became more intense. Lara was becoming impossible. She badgered everyone constantly. She made phone calls in the middle of the night.

"Howard, did you know the shipment of wallpaper hasn't arrived yet?"

"For God's sake, Lara, it's four o'clock in the morning."

"It's ninety days to the opening of the hotel. We can't open a hotel without wallpaper."

"I'll check it out in the morning."

"This *is* morning. Check it out now."

Lara's nervousness increased as the deadline grew closer. She met with Tom Scott, head of the advertising agency.

"Do you have small children, Mr. Scott?"

He looked at her in surprise. "No. Why?"

"Because I just went over the new advertising campaign and it seems to have been devised by a small retarded child. I can't believe that grown men sat down and thought up this junk."

Scott frowned. "If there's something about it that displeases you . . ."

"Everything about it displeases me," Lara said. "It lacks excitement. It's bland. It could be about any hotel anywhere. This isn't *any* hotel, Mr. Scott. This is the most beautiful, most modern hotel in New York. You make it sound like a cold, faceless building. It's a warm, exciting home. Let's spread the word. Do you think you can handle that?"

"I assure you we can handle it. We'll revise the campaign and in two weeks . . ."

"Monday," Lara said flatly. "I want to see the new campaign Monday."

The new ads went out in newspapers and magazines and billboards all over the country.

"I think the campaign turned out great," Tom Scott said. "You were right."

Lara looked at him and said quietly, "I don't want to be right. I want *you* to be right. That's what I pay you for."

She turned to Jerry Townsend, in charge of publicity.

"Have the invitations all been sent out?"

"Yes. We've gotten most of our replies already. Everybody's coming to the opening. It's going to be quite a party."

"It should be," Keller grumbled, "it's costing enough."

Lara grinned. "Stop being a banker. We'll get a million dollars' worth of publicity. We're going to have dozens of celebrities there and . . ."

He held up his hand. "All right, all right."

Two weeks before the opening, everything seemed to be happening at once. The wallpaper had arrived and carpets were being installed; halls were being painted and pictures were being hung. Lara inspected every suite, accompanied by a staff of five.

She walked into one suite and said, "The drapes are wrong. Switch them with the suite next door."

In another suite, she tried the piano. "It's out of tune. Take care of it."

In a third suite the electric fireplace didn't work. "Fix it."

It seemed to the harried staff that Lara was trying to do everything herself. She was in the kitchen and in the laundry room and in the utility closets. She was everywhere, demanding, complaining, fixing.

The man whom she had hired to manage the hotel said, "Don't get so excited, Miss Cameron. At the opening of any hotel, little things always go wrong."

"Not in my hotels," Lara said. "Not in my hotels."

The day of the opening, Lara was up at 4:00 A.M., too nervous to sleep. She wanted desperately to talk to Paul Martin, but there was no way she could call him at that hour. She dressed and went for a walk. *Everything is going to be fine,* she told herself. *The reservation computer is going to be fixed. They'll get the third oven working. The lock on Suite Seven will be repaired. We'll find a replacement for the maids who quit yesterday. The air-conditioning unit in the penthouse will work. . . .*

At six o'clock that evening the invited guests began to arrive. A uniformed guard at each entrance to the hotel examined their invitations before admitting them. There was a mix of celebrities, famous athletes, and corporation executives. Lara had gone over the list carefully, eliminating the names of the freeloaders and the hangers-on.

She stood in the spacious lobby greeting the newcomers as they arrived. "I'm Lara Cameron. So nice of you to come . . . Please feel free to look around."

Lara took Keller aside. "Why isn't the mayor coming?"
"He's pretty busy, you know, and . . ."
"You mean he thinks I'm not important enough."
"One day he'll change his mind."
One of the mayor's assistants arrived.
"Thank you for coming," Lara said. "This is an honor for the hotel."

Lara kept looking nervously for Todd Grayson, the architectural critic for *The New York Times,* who had been invited. *If he likes it,* Lara thought, *we have a winner.*

Paul Martin arrived with his wife. It was the first time Lara had seen Mrs. Martin. She was an attractive, elegant-looking woman. Lara felt an unexpected pang of guilt.

Paul walked up to Lara. "Miss Cameron, I'm Paul Martin. This is my wife, Nina. Thank you for inviting us."

Lara gripped his hand a second longer than necessary. "I'm delighted that you're here. Please make yourself at home."

Paul looked around the lobby. He had seen it half a dozen times before. "It's beautiful," he exclaimed. "I think you're going to be very successful."

Nina Martin was staring at Lara. "I'm sure she will be."
And Lara wondered if she knew.
The guests began to stream in.

An hour later Lara was standing in the lobby when Keller rushed up to her. "For God's sakes," he said, "everyone's looking for you. They're all in the ballroom, eating. Why aren't you in there?"

"Todd Grayson hasn't arrived. I'm waiting for him."
"The *Times'* architectural critic? I saw him an hour ago."
"What?"
"Yes. He went on a tour of the hotel with the others."
"Why didn't you tell me?"
"I thought you knew."
"What did he say?" Lara asked eagerly. "How did he look? Did he seem impressed?"
"He didn't say anything. He looked fine. And I don't know whether he was impressed or not."
"Didn't he say *anything*?"
"No."

Lara frowned. "He would have said something if he had liked it. It's a bad sign, Howard."

The party was a huge success. The guests ate and drank and toasted the hotel. When the evening was over, Lara was showered with compliments.

"It's such a lovely hotel, Miss Cameron . . ."

"I'll certainly stay here when I come back to New York . . ."

"What a great idea, having a piano in every living room . . ."

"I love the fireplaces . . ."

"I'll certainly recommend this to all my friends . . ."

Well, Lara thought, *even if The New York Times hates it, it's going to be a success.*

Lara saw Paul Martin and his wife as they were leaving.

"I think you really have a winner here, Miss Cameron. It's going to be the talk of New York."

"You're very kind, Mr. Martin," Lara said. "Thank you for coming."

Nina Martin said quietly, "Good night, Miss Cameron."

"Good night."

As they were walking out the lobby door, Lara heard her say, "She's very beautiful, isn't she, Paul?"

The following Thursday when the first edition of *The New York Times* came out, Lara was at the newsstand at Forty-second Street and Broadway at four o'clock in the morning, to pick up a copy. She hurriedly turned to the Home Section. Todd Grayson's article began:

Manhattan has long needed a hotel that does not remind travelers that they're staying in a hotel. The suites at the Cameron Plaza are large and gracious, and done in beautiful taste. Lara Cameron has finally given New York . . .

She yelled aloud with joy. She telephoned Keller and woke him up. "We're in!" she said. "The *Times* loves us."

He sat up in bed, groggy. "That's great. What did they say?"

Lara read the article to him. "All right," Keller said, "now you can get some sleep."

"Sleep? Are you joking? I have a new site picked out. As soon as the banks open, I want you to start negotiating a loan. . . ."

* * *

The New York Cameron Plaza was a triumph. It was completely booked, and there was a waiting list.

"It's only the beginning," Lara told Keller. "There are ten thousand builders in the metropolitan area—but only a handful of the big boys—the Tisches, the Rudins, the Rockefellers, the Sterns. Well, whether they like it or not, we're going to play in their sandbox. We're going to change the skyline. We're going to invent the future."

Lara began to get calls from banks offering her loans. She cultivated the important real estate brokers, taking them to dinner and the theater. She had power breakfasts at the Regency and was told about properties that were about to come on the market. She acquired two more downtown sites and began construction.

Paul Martin telephoned Lara at the office. "Have you seen *Business Week*? You're a hot ticket," he said. "The word's out that you're a shaker. You get things done."

"I try."

"Are you free for dinner?"

"I'll make myself free."

Lara was in a meeting with the partner of a top architectural firm. She was examining the blueprints and drawings they had brought.

"You're going to like this," the chief architect said. "It has grace and symmetry and the scope that you asked for. Let me explain some of the details . . ."

"That won't be necessary," Lara said. "I understand them." She looked up. "I want you to turn these plans over to an artist."

"What?"

"I want large color drawings of the building. I want drawings of the lobby, the corridors, and the offices. Bankers have no imagination. I'm going to *show* them what the building is going to look like."

"That's a great idea."

Lara's secretary appeared. "I'm sorry I'm late."

"This meeting was called for nine o'clock, Kathy. It's nine-fifteen."

"I'm sorry, Miss Cameron, my alarm didn't go off and . . ."

"We'll discuss it later."

She turned to the architects. "I want a few changes made . . ."

Two hours later Lara had finished discussing the changes she wanted. When the meeting was over, she said to Kathy, "Don't leave. Sit down."

Kathy sat.

"Do you like your job?"

"Yes, Miss Cameron."

"This is the third time you've been late this week. I won't put up with that again."

"I'm terribly sorry, I . . . I haven't been feeling well."

"What's your problem?"

"It's nothing, really."

"It's obviously enough to keep you from coming in on time. What is it?"

"I haven't been sleeping very well lately. To tell you the truth, I . . . I'm scared."

"Scared of what?" Lara asked impatiently.

"I . . . I have a lump."

"Oh." Lara was silent for a moment. "Well, what did the doctor say?"

Kathy swallowed. "I haven't seen a doctor."

"Not seen one!" Lara exploded. "For God's sakes, do you come from a family of ostriches? Of course you've got to see a doctor."

Lara picked up the phone. "Get me Dr. Peters."

She replaced the receiver. "It's probably nothing, but you can't let it go."

"I have a mother and brother who died of cancer," Kathy said miserably. "I don't want a doctor to tell me I have it."

The telephone rang. Lara picked it up. "Hello? He what? . . . I don't care if he is. You tell him I want to talk to him *now*."

She replaced the receiver.

A few moments later the phone rang again. Lara picked it up. "Hello, Alan . . . no, I'm fine. I'm sending my secretary over to see you. Her name is Kathy Turner. She'll be there in half an hour. I want her examined this morning, and I want you to stay on top of it . . . I know you are . . . I appreciate it . . . thanks."

She replaced the receiver. "Get over to Sloan-Kettering Hospital. Dr. Peters will be waiting for you."

"I don't know what to say, Miss Cameron."

"Say that you'll be on time tomorrow."

Howard Keller came into the office. "We have a problem, boss."

"Go."

"It's the property on Fourteenth Street. We've cleared the tenants out of the whole block except for one apartment house. The Dorchester

Apartments. Six of the tenants refuse to leave, and the city won't let us force them out."

"Offer them more money."

"It's not a question of money. Those people have lived there a long time. They don't want to leave. They're comfortable there."

"Then let's make them *un*comfortable."

"What do you mean?"

Lara got up. "Let's go take a look at the building."

On the drive down, they passed bag ladies and homeless people roaming the streets, asking for handouts.

"In a country as wealthy as this," Lara said, "that's a disgrace."

The Dorchester Apartments was a six-story brick building in the middle of a block filled with old structures waiting for the bulldozers.

Lara stood in front of it, examining it. "How many tenants are in there?"

"We got sixteen out of the apartment. Six are still hanging on."

"That means we have sixteen apartments available."

He looked at her, puzzled. "That's right. Why?"

"Let's fill those apartments."

"You mean, lease them? What's the point . . ."

"We're not going to lease them. We're going to donate them to the homeless. There are thousands of homeless people in New York. We're going to take care of some of them. Crowd in as many as you can. See that they're given some food."

Keller frowned. "What makes me think this isn't one of your better ideas?"

"Howard, we're going to become benefactors. We're going to do something the city can't do—shelter the homeless."

Lara was studying the building more closely, looking at the windows. "And I want those windows boarded up."

"What?"

"We're going to make the building look like an old derelict. Is the top floor apartment still occupied, the one with the roof garden?"

"Yes."

"Put up a big billboard on the roof to block the view."

"But . . ."

"Get to work on it."

When Lara returned to the office, there was a message for her. "Dr. Peters would like you to call him," Tricia said.

133

"Get him for me."

He came on the phone almost immediately.

"Lara, I examined your secretary."

"Yes?"

"She has a tumor. I'm afraid it's malignant. I recommend an immediate mastectomy."

"I want a second opinion," Lara said.

"Of course, if you wish, but I *am* head of the department and . . ."

"I still want a second opinion. Have someone else examine her. Get back to me as soon as possible. Where is Kathy now?"

"She's on her way back to your office."

"Thanks, Alan."

Lara replaced the receiver. She pressed down the intercom button. "When Kathy returns, send her in to me."

Lara studied the calendar on her desk. She had only thirty days left to clear out the Dorchester Apartments before construction was scheduled to start.

Six stubborn tenants. All right, Lara thought, *let's see how long they can hold out.*

Kathy walked into Lara's office. Her face was puffy and her eyes were red.

"I heard the news," Lara told her. "I'm so sorry, Kathy."

"I'm going to die," Kathy said.

Lara rose and put her arms around her, holding her close. "You're not going to do anything of the kind. They've made a lot of progress with cancer. You're going to have the operation, and you're going to be all right."

"Miss Cameron, I can't afford . . ."

"Everything will be taken care of. Dr. Peters is going to see that you have one more examination. If it verifies his diagnosis, you should have the operation right away. Now go home and get some rest."

Kathy's eyes filled with tears again. "I . . . thank you."

As Kathy walked out of the office, she thought, *No one really knows that lady.*

Chapter Sixteen

The following Monday Lara had a visitor.

"There's a Mr. O'Brian here to see you from the city planning commissioner's office, Miss Cameron."

"What about?"

"He didn't say."

Lara buzzed Keller on the intercom. "Will you come in here, Howard?" She said to the secretary, "Send Mr. O'Brian in."

Andy O'Brian was a burly red-faced Irishman with a slight brogue. "Miss Cameron?"

Lara remained seated behind her desk. "Yes. What can I do for you, Mr. O'Brian?"

"I'm afraid you're in violation of the law, Miss Cameron."

"Really? What is this all about?"

"You own the Dorchester Apartments on East Fourteenth Street?"

"Yes."

"We have a report that about a hundred homeless people have crowded into those apartments."

"Oh, that." Lara smiled. "Yes, I thought that since the city wasn't doing anything about the homeless, I would help out. I'm giving them shelter."

Howard Keller walked into the room.

"This is Mr. Keller. Mr. O'Brian."

The two men shook hands.

Lara turned to Keller. "I was just explaining how we're helping the city out by providing housing."

"You invited them in, Miss Cameron?"

"That's right."

"Do you have a license from the city?"

"A license for what?"

"If you're setting up a shelter, it has to be approved by the city. There are certain strict conditions that are enforced."

"I'm sorry. I wasn't aware of that. I'll arrange for the license immediately."

"I don't think so."

"What does that mean?"

"We've had complaints from the tenants in the building. They say you're trying to force them out."

"Nonsense."

"Miss Cameron, the city is giving you forty-eight hours to move those homeless people out of there. And when they leave, we have an order for you to take down the boards that you put up to cover the windows."

Lara was furious. "Is that all?"

"No, ma'am. The tenant who has the roof garden says you put up a sign blocking his view. You'll have to take that down, too."

"What if I won't?"

"I think you will. All this comes under harassment. You'll save yourself a lot of trouble and unpleasant publicity by not forcing us to take you to court." He nodded and said, "Have a nice day."

They watched him walk out of the office.

Keller turned to Lara. "We'll have to get all those people out of there."

"No." She sat there, thinking.

"What do you mean 'no'? The man said . . ."

"I know what he said. I want you to bring in *more* homeless. I want that building packed with street people. We're going to stall. Call Terry Hill. Tell him the problem. Have him get a stay or something. We've got to get those six tenants out by the end of the month or it's going to cost us three million dollars."

The intercom buzzed. "Dr. Peters is on the phone."

Lara picked up the telephone. "Hello, Alan."

"I just wanted to tell you that we finished the operation. It looks like we got it all. Kathy's going to be fine."

"That's wonderful news. When can I visit her?"

"You can come by this afternoon."

"I'll do that. Thanks, Alan. See that I get all the bills, will you?"

"Will do."

"And you can tell the hospital to expect a donation. Fifty thousand dollars."

Lara said to Tricia, "Fill her room with flowers." She looked at her schedule. "I'll go down to see her at four o'clock."

Terry Hill arrived at the office. "There's a warrant for your arrest coming in."

"What?"

"Weren't you warned to get those homeless people out of the building?"

"Yes, but . . ."

"You can't get away with this, Lara. There's an old adage: 'Don't fight City Hall, you can't win.' "

"Are they really going to arrest me?"

"You're damn right they are. You were given notice by the city to get those people out of there."

"All right," Lara said. "Let's get them out." She turned to Keller. "Remove them, but don't put them out on the street. That isn't right. . . . We have those empty rooming houses that we're waiting to convert in the West Twenties. Let's put them there. Take all the help you need. I want them gone in an hour."

She turned to Terry Hill. "I'll be out of here, so they can't serve me. By the time they do, the problem will be solved."

The intercom buzzed. "There are two gentlemen here from the district attorney's office."

Lara motioned to Howard Keller. He walked over to the intercom and said, "Miss Cameron isn't here."

There was a silence. "When do you expect her?"

Keller looked at Lara. Lara shook her head. Keller said into the intercom, "We don't know." He flicked the key up.

"I'll go out the back way," Lara said.

Lara hated hospitals. A hospital was her father lying in bed, pale and suddenly old. *What the bluidy hell are you doin' here? You've work to dae at the boardinghouse.*

Lara walked into Kathy's room. It was filled with flowers. Kathy was sitting up in bed.

"How do you feel?" Lara asked.

Kathy smiled. "The doctor said I'm going to be fine."

"You'd better be. Your work is piling up. I need you."

"I . . . I don't know how to thank you for all this."

"Don't."

Lara picked up the bedside phone and put a call through to her office. She spoke to Terry Hill.

"Are they still there?"

"They're still here. They intend to stay until you return."

"Check with Howard. As soon as he clears the street people out of the building, I'll come back."

Lara replaced the receiver.

"If you need anything, let me know," Lara said. "I'll be back to see you tomorrow."

Lara's next stop was at the architectural offices of Higgins, Almont & Clark. She was ushered in to see Mr. Clark. He rose as she walked into his office.

"What a nice surprise. What can I do for you, Miss Cameron?"

"Do you have the plans here for the project on Fourteenth Street?"

"Yes, indeed."

He went over to his drawing board. "Here we are."

There was a sketch of a beautiful high rise complex with apartment buildings and shops around it.

"I want you to redraw it," Lara said.

"What?"

Lara pointed to a space in the middle of the block. "There's a building still standing in this area. I want you to draw the same concept, but construct it *around* that building."

"You mean you want to put up the project with one of the old buildings still standing? It would never work. First of all, it would look terrible and . . ."

"Just do it, please. Send it over to my office this afternoon."

And Lara was gone.

From the car she telephoned Terry Hill. "Have you heard from Howard yet?"

"Yes. The squatters have all been cleared out."

"Good. Get the district attorney on the phone. Tell him that I had ordered those squatters out two days ago and that there was a lack of communication. The minute I heard about it, today, I had them moved out. I'm on my way back to the office now. See if he still wants to arrest me."

She said to the driver, "Drive through the park. Take your time."

Thirty minutes later, when Lara reached her office, the men with the warrant were gone.

Lara was in a meeting with Howard Keller and Terry Hill.

"The tenants still won't budge," Keller said. "I even went back and offered them more money. They're not leaving. We've only got five days left before we have to begin bulldozing."

Lara said, "I asked Mr. Clark to draw up a new blueprint for the project."

"I saw it," Keller said. "It doesn't make any sense. We can't leave that old building standing in the middle of a new giant construction. We're going to have to go to the bank and ask them if they'll move back the start date."

"No," Lara said. "I want to move it *up*."

"*What?*"

"Get hold of the contractor. Tell him we want to start bulldozing tomorrow."

"*Tomorrow?* Lara . . ."

"First thing in the morning. And take that blueprint and give it to the foreman of the construction crew."

"What good will that do?" Keller asked.

"We'll see."

The following morning the remaining tenants of the Dorchester Apartments were awakened by the roar of a bulldozer. They looked out of their windows. Halfway down the block, as they watched, a mechanical behemoth was moving toward them, leveling everything in its path. The tenants were stunned.

Mr. Hershey, who lived on the top floor, rushed outside and hurried over to the foreman. "What do you think you're doing?" he screamed. "You can't go ahead with this."

"Who says so?"

"The city does." Hershey pointed to the building he lived in. "You're not permitted to touch that building."

The foreman looked at the blueprint in front of him. "That's right," he said. "We have orders to leave that building standing."

Hershey frowned. "What? Let me see that." He looked at the plan and gasped. "They're going to put up the plaza and leave this building *standing*?"

"That's right, mister."

"But they can't do that! The noise and dirt!"

"That's not my problem. Now, if you'll get out of my way, I'd like to get back to work."

Thirty minutes later Lara's secretary said, "There's a Mr. Hershey on line two, Miss Cameron."

"Tell him I'm not available."

When Hershey called for the third time that afternoon, Lara finally picked up the phone and spoke with him.

"Yes, Mr. Hershey. What can I do for you?"

"I'd like to come in and see you, Miss Cameron."

"I'm afraid I'm rather busy. Whatever it is you have to say you can say on the phone."

"Well, you'll be glad to know that I've talked to the other tenants in our building and we've agreed that it might be best after all to take your offer and vacate our apartments."

"That offer is no longer good, Mr. Hershey. You can all stay where you are."

"If you build around us, we're never going to get any sleep!"

"Who told you we were going to build around you?" Lara demanded. "Where did you get that information?"

"The foreman on the job showed me a blueprint and . . ."

"Well, he's going to be fired." There was fury in Lara's voice. "That was confidential information."

"Wait a minute. Let's talk like two reasonable people, okay? Your project would be better off if we got out of here, and I think we'd be better off leaving. I don't want to live in the middle of a damned high rise."

Lara said, "It doesn't matter to me whether you go or stay, Mr. Hershey." Her voice softened. "I'll tell you what I'll do. If that building is vacated by next month I'm willing to go with our first offer."

She could hear him thinking it over.

Finally he said reluctantly, "Okay. I'll talk to the others, but I'm sure it will be all right. I really appreciate this, Miss Cameron."

Lara said, "It's been my pleasure, Mr. Hershey."

The following month, work on the new project began in earnest.

Lara's reputation was growing. Cameron Enterprises was putting up a high rise in Brooklyn, a shopping center in Westchester, a mall in Washington, D.C. There was a low-cost housing project being constructed in Dallas and a block of condominiums in Los Angeles. Capital flowed in from banks, savings and loan companies, and eager private investors. Lara had become a Name.

Kathy had returned to work.

"I'm back."

Lara studied her a moment. "How do you feel?"

Kathy smiled. "Great. Thanks to . . ."

"Do you have a lot of energy?"

She was surprised at the question. "Yes. I . . ."

"Good. You're going to need it. I'm making you my executive assistant. There will be a nice raise for you."

"I don't know what to say. I . . ."

"You've earned it."

Lara saw the memo in Kathy's hand. "What's that?"

"*Gourmet* magazine would like to publish your favorite recipe. Are you interested?"

"No. Tell them I'm too . . . wait a minute." She sat there a moment, lost in thought. Then she said softly, "Yes. I'll give them a recipe."

The recipe appeared in the magazine three months later.

It began:

Black Bun—A classic Scottish dish. A mixture encased in a short paste jacket made from half a pound of flour, a quarter pound of butter, a touch of cold water, and a half a teaspoon of baking power. Inside are two pounds of raisins, half a pound of chopped almonds, three-quarters of a pound of flour, half a pound of sugar, two teaspoons of allspice, a teaspoon of ground ginger, a teaspoon of cinnamon, a half teaspoon of baking powder, and a dash of brandy . . .

Lara looked at the article for a long time, and it brought back the taste of it, the smell of the boardinghouse kitchen, the noise of the boarders at supper. Her father helpless in his bed. She put the magazine away.

* * *

People recognized Lara on the street, and when she walked into a restaurant, there were always excited whispers. She was escorted around town by half a dozen eligible suitors and had flattering proposals, but she was not interested. In a strange, almost eerie way, she was still looking for someone. Someone familiar. Someone she had never met.

Lara would wake up at five o'clock every morning and have her driver, Max, take her to one of the buildings under construction. She would stand there, staring at what she was creating, and she thought, *You were wrong, Father. I can collect the rents.*

For Lara, the sounds of the day began with the rat-a-tat-tat of the jackhammers, the roar of the bulldozers, the clanging of heavy metal. She would ride the rickety construction elevator to the top and stand on the steel girders with the wind blowing in her face, and she thought, *I own this city.*

Paul Martin and Lara were in bed.

"I hear you chewed out a couple of your construction workers pretty good today."

"They deserved it," Lara said. "They were doing sloppy work."

Paul grinned. "At least you've learned not to slap them."

"Look what happened when I *did* slap one." She snuggled up to him. "I met you."

"I have to take a trip to L.A.," Paul said. "I'd like you to come with me. Can you get away for a few days?"

"I'd love to, Paul, but it's impossible. I schedule my days with a stopwatch."

He sat up and looked down at her. "Maybe you're doing too much, baby. Don't ever get too busy for me."

Lara smiled and began to stroke him. "Don't worry about that. It will never happen."

It had been there in front of her all the time, and she had not seen it. It was a huge waterfront property in the Wall Street area, near the World Trade Center. And it was for sale. Lara had passed it a dozen times, but she looked at it now and saw what should have been there all along: In her mind, she could see the world's tallest building. She knew what Howard was going to say: *"You're getting in over your head, Lara. You can't get involved with this."* But she knew that nothing was going to stop her.

When she got to the office, she called a meeting of her staff.

"The Wall Street property on the waterfront," Lara said. "We're going to buy it. We're going to put up the tallest skyscraper in the world."

"Lara . . ."

"Before you say anything, Howard, let me point out a few things. The location is perfect. It's in the heart of the business district. Tenants will be fighting to get office space there. And remember, it's going to be the tallest skyscraper in the world. That's a big sizzle. It's going to be our flagship. We'll call it Cameron Towers."

"Where's the money coming from?"

Lara handed him a piece of paper.

Keller was examining the figures. "You're being optimistic."

"I'm being realistic. We're not talking about just any building. We're talking about a jewel, Howard."

He was thinking hard. "You'll be stretching yourself thin."

Lara smiled. "We've done that before, haven't we?"

Keller said, thoughtfully, "The tallest skyscraper in the world . . ."

"That's right. And the banks call us every day, throwing money at us. They'll jump at this."

"They probably will," Keller said. He looked at Lara. "You really want this, don't you?"

"Yes."

Keller sighed. He looked around at the group. "All right. The first step is to take an option on the property."

Lara smiled. "I've already done that. And I have some other news for you. Steve Murchison was negotiating for that property."

"I remember him. We took that hotel site away from him in Chicago."

"I'm going to let it go this time, bitch, because I don't think you know what the hell you're doing. But in the future, stay out of my way—you could get hurt."

"Right." Murchison had become one of the most ruthless and successful real estate developers in New York.

Keller said, "Lara, he's bad news. He enjoys destroying people."

"You worry too much."

The financing for Cameron Towers went smoothly. Lara had been right. The bankers felt that there was a sizzle to the tallest skyscraper in the world. And the name of Cameron was an added cachet. They were eager to be associated with her.

Lara was more than a glamorous figure. She was a symbol to the women of the world, an icon. *If she can accomplish this, why not me?* A perfume was named after her. She was invited to all the important social events, and hostesses were eager to have her at their dinner parties. Her name on a building seemed to ensure success.

"We're going to start our own construction company," Lara decided one day. "We have the crews. We'll rent them out to other builders."

"That's not a bad idea," Keller said.

"Let's go for it. How soon are we going to break ground for Cameron Towers?"

"The deal's in place. I would say three months from now."

Lara sat back in her chair. "Can you imagine it, Howard? The tallest skyscraper in the world."

He wondered what Freud would have made of that.

The ground-breaking ceremony for Cameron Towers had the atmosphere of a three-ring circus. America's Princess, Lara Cameron, was the main attraction. The event had been heavily publicized in the newspapers and on television, and a crowd of more than two hundred people had gathered, waiting for Lara to arrive. When her white limousine pulled up to the building site, there was a roar from the crowd.

"There she is!"

As Lara stepped out of the car and moved toward the building site to greet the mayor, police and security guards held the crowd back. The people pushed forward, screaming and calling her name, and the photographers' flashbulbs began popping.

In a special roped-off section were the bankers, heads of advertising agencies, company directors, contractors, project managers, community representatives, and architects. One hundred feet away, large bulldozers and backhoes were standing by, ready to go to work. Fifty trucks were lined up to cart the rubble away.

Lara was standing next to the mayor and the Manhattan borough president. It had started to drizzle. Jerry Townsend, head of public relations for Cameron Enterprises, hurried toward Lara with an umbrella. She smiled and waved him away.

The mayor spoke into the cameras. "Today is a great day for Man-

THE STARS SHINE DOWN

hattan. This ground-breaking ceremony at Cameron Towers marks the beginning of one of the largest real estate projects in Manhattan's history. Six blocks of Manhattan real estate will be converted into a modern community that will include apartment buildings, two shopping centers, a convention center, and the tallest skyscraper in the world."

There was applause from the crowd.

"Wherever you look," the mayor continued, "you can see Lara Cameron's contribution written in concrete." He pointed. "Uptown is the Cameron Center. And near it, Cameron Plaza and half a dozen housing projects. And across the country is the great Cameron Hotel chain."

The mayor turned to Lara and smiled. "And she's not only brainy, she's beautiful."

There was laughter and more applause.

"Lara Cameron, ladies and gentlemen."

Lara looked into the television cameras and smiled. "Thank you, Mr. Mayor. I'm very pleased to have made some small contribution to this fabulous city of ours. My father always told me that the reason we were put on this earth was . . ." She hesitated. Out of the corner of her eye, she had seen a familiar figure in the crowd. Steve Murchison. She had seen his photograph in newspapers. . . . What was he doing here? Lara went on. . . . "was to leave it a better place than when we came into it. Well, I hope that in my own small way, I've been able to do that."

There was more applause. Lara was handed a ceremonial hard hat and a chrome-plated shovel.

"Time to go to work, Miss Cameron."

The flashbulbs began to pop again.

Lara pushed the shovel into the dirt and dug up the first bit of earth.

At the conclusion of the ceremony, refreshments were served, while the television cameras kept recording the event. When Lara looked around again, Murchison was nowhere in sight.

Thirty minutes later Lara Cameron was back in the limousine headed for the office. Jerry Townsend was seated next to her.

"I thought it went great," he said. "Just great."

"Not bad," Lara grinned. "Thanks, Jerry."

The executive suites of Cameron Enterprises occupied the entire fiftieth floor of Cameron Center.

Lara got off at the fiftieth floor, and by then the word had gotten around that she was arriving. The secretaries and staff were busily at work.

Lara turned to Jerry Townsend. "Come into my office."

The office was an enormous corner suite overlooking the city.

Lara glanced at some papers on her desk and looked up at Jerry. "How's your father? Is he any better?"

What did she know about his father?

"He's . . . he's not well."

"I know. He has Huntington's chorea, hasn't he, Jerry?"

"Yes."

It was a terrible disease. It was progressive and degenerative, characterized by spasmodic involuntary movements of the face and extremities, accompanied by the loss of mental faculties.

"How do you know about my father?"

"I'm on the board at the hospital where he's being treated. I heard some doctors discussing his case."

Jerry said tightly, "It's incurable."

"Everything is incurable until they find the cure," Lara said. "I did some checking. There's a doctor in Switzerland who's doing some advanced research on the disease. He's willing to take on your father's case. I'll handle the expenses."

Jerry stood there, stunned.

"Okay?"

He found it difficult to speak. "Okay." *I don't know her,* Jerry Townsend thought. *Nobody knows her.*

History was being made, but Lara was too busy to notice. Ronald Reagan had been re-elected, and a man named Mikhail Gorbachev had succeeded Chernenko as leader of the USSR.

Lara built a low-income housing development in Detroit.

In 1986 Ivan Boesky had been fined a hundred million dollars in an insider trading scandal and sentenced to three years in prison.

Lara started development on condominiums in Queens. Investors were eager to be a part of the magic of her name. A group of German investment bankers flew to New York to meet with Lara. She arranged for the meeting immediately after their plane landed. They had protested, but Lara said, "I'm so sorry, gentlemen. It's the only time I have. I'm leaving for Hong Kong."

The Germans were served coffee. Lara had tea. One of the Germans complained about the taste of the coffee. "It's a special brand made for me," Lara explained. "The flavor will grow on you. Have another cup."

By the end of the negotiations Lara had won all her points.

Life was a series of serendipities, except for one disturbing incident. Lara had had several run-ins with Steve Murchison over various properties, and she had always managed to outwit him.

"I think we should back off," Keller warned.

"Let him back off."

And one morning a beautiful package wrapped in rose paper arrived from Bendel's. Kathy laid it on Lara's desk.

"It's awfully heavy," Kathy said. "If it's a hat, you're in trouble."

Curious, Lara unwrapped it and opened the lid. The box was packed with dirt. A printed card inside read: *"The Frank E. Campbell Funeral Chapel."*

The building projects were all going well. When Lara read about a proposed inner-city playground that was stymied because of bureaucratic red tape, she stepped in, had her company build it, and donated it to the city. The publicity she received on it was enormous. One headline read: LARA CAMERON STANDS FOR "CAN DO."

She was seeing Paul once or twice a week, and she talked to him every day.

Lara bought a house in Southampton and lived in a fantasy world of expensive jewels and furs and limousines. Her closets were filled with beautiful designer clothes. *"I need some clothes for school." "Weel, I'm nae made of money. Get yourself something frae the Salvation Army Citadel."*

And Lara would order another outfit.

Her employees were her family. She worried about them and was generous with them. They were all she had. She remembered their birthdays and anniversaries. She helped get their children into good schools and set up scholarship funds for them. When they tried to thank her, Lara was embarrassed. It was difficult for her to express her emotions. Her father had ridiculed her when she had tried. Lara had built a protective wall around herself. *No one is ever going to hurt me again,* she vowed. *No one.*

BOOK THREE

Chapter Seventeen

"I'm leaving for London in the morning, Howard."

"What's up?" Keller asked.

"Lord MacIntosh has invited me to come over and take a look at a property he's interested in. He wants to go into partnership."

Brian MacIntosh was one of the wealthiest real estate developers in England.

"What time do we leave?" Keller asked.

"I've decided to go alone."

"Oh?"

"I want you to keep an eye on things here."

He nodded. "Right. I'll do that."

"I know you will. I can always count on you."

The trip to London was uneventful. The private 727 she had purchased took off in the morning and landed at the Magec Terminal at Luton Airport outside London. She had no idea her life was about to change.

When Lara arrived at the lobby of Claridges, Ronald Jones, the manager, was there to greet her. "It's a pleasure to have you back, Miss Cameron. I'll show you to your suite. By the way, we have some messages for you." There were more than two dozen.

The suite was lovely. There were flowers from Brian MacIntosh and from Paul Martin, and champagne and hors d'oeuvres from the management. The phone began to ring the minute Lara walked in. The calls were from all over the United States.

"The architect wants to make some changes in the plans. It will cost a fortune. . . ."

"There's a holdup on the cement delivery. . . ."

"The First National Savings and Loan wants in on our next deal. . . ."

"The mayor wants to know if you can be in L.A. for the opening. He'd like to plan a big ceremony. . . ."

"The toilets haven't arrived. . . ."

"Bad weather is holding us up. We're falling behind schedule. . . ."

Each problem required a decision, and when Lara finally finished with her calls, she was exhausted. She had dinner in her room alone and sat looking out the window, at the Rolls-Royces and Bentleys pulling up to the Brook Street entrance, and a feeling of elation swept over her. *The little girl from Glace Bay has come a long way, Daddy.*

The following morning Lara went with Brian MacIntosh to look at the proposed site. It was enormous—two miles of riverside frontage filled with old run-down buildings and storage sheds.

"The British government will give us a lot of tax relief on this," Brian MacIntosh explained, "because we're going to rehabilitate this whole section of the city."

"I'd like to think about it," Lara said. She had already made up her mind.

"By the way, I have tickets to a concert tonight," Brian MacIntosh told her. "My wife has a club meeting. Do you like classical music?"

Lara had no interest in classical music. "Yes."

"Philip Adler is playing Rachmaninoff." He looked at Lara as though expecting her to say something. She had never heard of Philip Adler.

"It sounds wonderful," Lara said.

"Good. We'll have supper afterward at Scotts. I'll pick you up at seven."

Why did I say I liked classical music? Lara wondered. It was going to be a boring evening. She would have preferred to take a hot bath and go to sleep. *Oh, well, one more evening won't hurt me. I'll fly back to New York in the morning.*

THE STARS SHINE DOWN

* * *

The Festival Hall was crowded with music aficionados. The men wore dinner jackets and the women were dressed in beautiful evening gowns. It was a gala evening, and there was a feeling of excited expectation in the large hall.

Brian MacIntosh purchased two programs from the usher, and they were seated. He handed Lara a program. She barely glanced at it. The London Philharmonic Orchestra . . . Philip Adler playing Rachmaninoff's Piano Concerto No. 3 in D Minor, Opus 30.

I've got to call Howard and remind him about the revised estimates on the Fifth Avenue site.

The conductor appeared onstage, and the audience applauded. Lara paid no attention. *The contractor in Boston is moving too slowly. He needs a carrot. I'll tell Howard to offer him a bonus.*

There was another loud round of applause from the audience. A man was taking his place at the piano at center stage. The conductor gave a downbeat, and the music began.

Philip Adler's fingers flashed across the keys.

A woman seated behind Lara said with a loud Texas accent, "Isn't he fantastic? I *told* you, Agnes!"

Lara tried to concentrate again. *The London deal is out. It's the wrong neighborhood,* Lara thought. *People aren't going to want to live there. Location. Location. Location.* She thought about a project that had been brought to her, near Columbus Circle. *Now that one could work.*

The woman behind Lara said, loudly, "His expression . . . he's fabulous! He's one of the most . . ."

Lara tried to tune her out.

The cost of an office building there would be approximately four hundred dollars per rentable square foot. If I can bring in the construction cost at one hundred fifty million, the land costs at one hundred twenty-five million, the soft costs . . .

"My God!" the woman behind Lara exclaimed.

Lara was startled out of her reverie.

"He's so brilliant!"

There was a drumroll from the orchestra, and Philip Adler played four bars alone, and the orchestra began to play faster and faster. The drums began to beat . . .

The woman could not contain herself. "Listen to that! The music is going from *più vivo* to *più mosso*. Have you ever heard anything so exciting?"

Lara gritted her teeth.

The minimum break-even should work out all right, she thought. *The cost of the rentable square feet would be three hundred fifty million, the interest at ten percent would be thirty-five million, plus ten million in operating expenses . . .*

The tempo of the music was increasing, reverberating through the hall. The music came to a sudden climax and stopped, and the audience was on its feet, cheering. There were calls of "bravo!" The pianist had risen and was taking bows.

Lara did not even bother to look up. *Taxes would be about six, free rent concessions would come to two. We're talking about fifty-eight million.*

"He's incredible, isn't he?" Brian MacIntosh said.

"Yes." Lara was annoyed at having her thoughts interrupted again.

"Let's go backstage. Philip is a friend of mine."

"I really don't . . ."

He took Lara's hand, and they were moving toward an exit.

"I'm glad I'll have a chance to introduce you to him," Brian MacIntosh said.

It's six o'clock in New York, Lara thought. *I'll be able to call Howard and tell him to start negotiations.*

"He's a once-in-a-lifetime experience, isn't he?"

Once is enough for me, Lara thought. "Yes."

They had reached the outside artists' entrance. There was a large crowd waiting. Brian MacIntosh knocked on the door. A doorman opened it.

"Yes, sir?"

"Lord MacIntosh to see Mr. Adler."

"Right, my lord. Come in, please." He opened the door wide enough to let Brian MacIntosh and Lara enter, then closed it against the crowd.

"What do all these people want?" Lara asked.

He looked at her in surprise. "They're here to see Philip."

She wondered why.

The doorman said, "Go right into the greenroom, my lord."

"Thank you."

Five minutes, Lara thought, *and I'll say I have to leave.*

The greenroom was noisy and already full. People were crowded around a figure Lara could not see. The crowd shifted, and for an instant he was clearly visible. Lara froze, and for a moment she felt her heart stop. The vague, evanescent image that had been at the back of her mind all those years had suddenly materialized out of nowhere. Lochinvar, the vision in her fantasies, had come to life! The man at the center of the crowd was tall and blond, with delicate, sensitive features. He was wearing white tie and tails, and a feeling of déjà vu swept over Lara: *She was standing at the kitchen sink in the boardinghouse, and the handsome young man in white tie and tails came up behind her and whispered, "Can I help you?"*

Brian MacIntosh was watching Lara, concerned. "Are you all right?"

"I . . . I'm fine." She was finding it difficult to breathe.

Philip Adler was moving toward them, smiling, and it was the same warm smile Lara had imagined. He held out his hand. "Brian, how good of you to come."

"I wouldn't have missed it," MacIntosh said. "You were simply marvelous."

"Thank you."

"Oh, Philip, I would like you to meet Lara Cameron."

Lara was looking into his eyes, and the words came out unbidden. "Do you dry?"

"I beg your pardon?"

Lara turned red. "Nothing. I . . ." She was suddenly tongue-tied.

People were crowding around Philip Adler, heaping praise on him.

"You've never played better . . ."

"I think Rachmaninoff was with you tonight . . ."

The praise went on and on. The women in the room were crowding around him, touching and pulling at him. Lara stood there watching, mesmerized. Her childhood dream had come true. Her fantasy had become flesh and blood.

"Are you ready to go?" Brian MacIntosh asked Lara.

No. She wanted nothing more than to stay. She wanted to talk to the vision again, to touch him, to make sure he was real. "I'm ready," Lara said reluctantly.

The following morning Lara was on her way back to New York. She wondered whether she would ever see Philip Adler again.

She was unable to get him out of her mind. She tried to tell herself that it was ridiculous, that she was trying to relive a childhood dream, but it was no use. She kept seeing his face, hearing his voice. *I must see him again,* Lara thought.

Early the next morning Paul Martin telephoned.

"Hi, baby. I missed you. How was London?"

"Fine," Lara said carefully. "Just fine."

When they had finished talking, Lara sat at her desk thinking about Philip Adler.

"They're waiting for you in the conference room, Miss Cameron."

"I'm coming."

"We lost the Queens deal," Keller said.

"Why? I thought it was all set."

"So did I, but the community board refuses to support the zoning change."

Lara looked around at the Executive Committee assembled in the room. There were architects, lawyers, publicity men, and construction engineers.

Lara said, "I don't understand. Those tenants have an average income of nine thousand dollars a year, and they're paying less than two hundred dollars a month in rent. We're going to rehabilitate the apartments for them, at no increase in rent, and we're going to provide new apartments for some of the other residents in the neighborhood. We're giving them Christmas in July and they turned you down? What's the problem?"

"It's not the board so much. It's their chairman. A lady named Edith Benson."

"Set up another meeting with her. I'll go there myself."

Lara took her chief construction supervisor, Bill Whitman, to the meeting.

Lara said, "Frankly, I was stunned when I heard that your board turned us down. We're going to put up over a hundred million dollars to improve this neighborhood, and yet you refuse to . . ."

Edith Benson cut her short. "Let's be honest, Miss Cameron. You're not putting up the money to improve the neighborhood. You're putting up the money so Cameron Enterprises can make more money."

"Of course, we expect to make money," Lara said. "But the only way we can do that is to help you people. We're going to make the living conditions in your area better, and . . ."

"Sorry. I don't agree. Right now, we're a quiet little neighborhood.

If we let you in, we're going to become a higher-density area—more traffic, more automobiles, more pollution. We don't want any of that."

"Neither do I," Lara said. "We don't intend to put up dingbats that . . ."

"Dingbats?"

"Yes, those ugly, stripped-down, three-story stucco boxes. We're interested in designs that won't increase the noise level or reduce the light or change the feel of the neighborhood. We're not interested in hot dog, show-off architecture. I've already hired Stanton Fielding, the top architect in the country, to design this project, and Andrew Burton from Washington to do the landscaping."

Edith Benson shrugged. "I'm sorry. It's no use. I don't think there's anything more to discuss." She started to rise.

I can't lose this, Lara thought desperately. *Can't they see it's for the good of their neighborhood? I'm trying to do something for them and they won't let me.* And suddenly she had a wild idea.

"Wait a minute," Lara said. "I understand that the other members of the board are willing to make the deal but you are the one blocking it."

"That's correct."

Lara took a deep breath. "There *is* something to discuss." She hesitated. "It's very personal." She was fidgeting now. "You say I'm not worried about pollution and what happens to the environment in this neighborhood if we move in? I'm going to tell you something that I hope you will keep in confidence. I have a ten-year-old daughter that I'm crazy about, and she's going to live in the new building with her father. He has custody of her."

Edith Benson was looking at her in surprise. "I . . . I didn't know you had a daughter."

"No one does," Lara said quietly. "I've never been married. That's why I'm asking you to keep this confidential. If it gets out, it could be very damaging to me. I'm sure you understand that."

"I do understand."

"I love my daughter very much, and I assure you that I would never do anything in the world that would hurt her. I intend to do everything I can to make this project wonderful for all the people who live here. And she'll be one of them."

There was a sympathetic silence. "I must say, this . . . this puts quite a different complexion on things, Miss Cameron. I'd like to have some time to think about it."

"Thank you. I appreciate that." *If I did have a daughter,* Lara thought, *it would be safe for her to live here.*

Three weeks later Lara got the approval from the City Planning Commission to go ahead with the project.

"Great," Lara said. "Now we'd better get hold of Stanton Fielding and Andrew Burton and see if they're interested in working on the project."

Howard Keller could not believe the news. "I heard what happened," he said. "You conned her! That's incredible. You don't *have* a daughter!"

"They need this project," Lara said. "This was the only way I could think of to change their minds."

Bill Whitman was listening. "There'll be hell to pay if they ever find out."

In January construction was completed on a new building on East Sixty-third Street. It was a forty-five-story apartment building, and Lara reserved the duplex penthouse for herself. The rooms were large, and the apartment had terraces that covered a full block. She brought in a top decorator to do the apartment. There was a housewarming for a hundred people.

"All it lacks is a man," one of the lady guests said cattily.

And Lara thought of Philip Adler and wondered where he was and what he was doing.

Lara and Howard Keller were in the middle of a discussion when Bill Whitman came into the office.

"Hi, boss. Got a minute?"

Lara looked up from her desk. "Just about, Bill. What's the problem?"

"My wife."

"If you're having marital difficulties . . ."

"It's not that. She thinks we ought to go away for a while on vacation. Maybe go to Paris for a few weeks."

Lara frowned. "Paris? We're in the middle of half a dozen jobs."

"I know, but I've been working long hours lately, and I don't get to see much of my wife. You know what she said to me this morning? She said, 'Bill, if you got a promotion and a nice raise, you wouldn't have to work so hard.' " He smiled.

Lara sat back in her chair, studying him. "You aren't due for a raise until next year."

Whitman shrugged. "Who knows what can happen in a year? We might run into problems with that Queens deal, for instance. You know, old Edith Benson might hear something that would make her change her mind. Right?"

Lara sat very still. "I see."

Bill Whitman got to his feet. "Think about it, and let me know."

Lara forced a smile. "Yes."

She watched him walk out of her office, her face grim.

"Jesus," Keller said. "What was that all about?"

"It's called blackmail."

The following day Lara had lunch with Paul Martin.

Lara said, "Paul, I have a problem. I'm not sure how to handle it." She told him about her conversation with Bill Whitman.

"Do you think he'll really go back to the old lady?" Paul Martin asked.

"I don't know. But if he does, I could get in a lot of trouble with the Housing Commission."

Paul shrugged. "I wouldn't worry about him. He's probably bluffing."

Lara sighed. "I hope so."

"How would you like to go to Reno?" Paul asked.

"I'd love to, but I can't get away."

"I'm not asking you to get away. I'm asking if you'd like to buy a hotel and casino there."

Lara studied him. "Are you serious?"

"I got word that one of the hotels is going to lose its license. The place is a gold mine. When the news gets out, everyone is going to be after it. The hotel's going on auction, but I think I can fix it for you to get it."

Lara hesitated. "I don't know. I'm pretty heavily committed. Howard Keller says the banks won't lend me any more until I can pay off some loans."

"You don't have to go to a bank."

"Then where . . . ?"

"Junk bonds. A lot of Wall Street firms offer them. There are savings and loan companies. You put up five percent equity, and a savings and loan company will put up sixty-five percent in high-yield notes. That leaves thirty percent uncovered. You can get that from a foreign bank that invests in casinos. You've got choices—Switzerland, Germany, Japan. There are half a dozen banks that will put up the thirty percent in commercial notes."

Lara was beginning to get excited. "It sounds great. Do you really think you can get the hotel for me?"

Paul grinned. "It will be your Christmas present."

"You're wonderful. Why are you so good to me?"

"I haven't the vaguest idea," he teased. But he knew the answer. He was obsessed with her. Lara made him feel young again, and she made everything exciting for him. *I never want to lose you,* he thought.

Keller was waiting for Lara when she walked into the office.

"Where have you been?" he asked. "There was a two o'clock meeting that . . ."

"Tell me about junk bonds, Howard. We've never dealt with them. How are bonds rated?"

"Well, at the top you have Triple A. That would be a company like AT and T. Down the ladder you have Double A, Single A, BAA, and at the bottom of the ladder, Double B—those are the junk bonds. An investment bond will pay nine percent. A junk bond will pay fourteen percent. Why do you ask?"

Lara told him.

"A *casino,* Lara? Jesus! Paul Martin is behind this, isn't he?"

"No, Howard. If I go ahead with this, *I'm* behind it. Did we get an answer on our offer on the Battery Park property?"

"Yes. She won't sell to us."

"The property is up for sale, isn't it?"

"In a way."

"Stop talking in circles."

"It's owned by a doctor's widow, Eleanor Royce. Every real estate developer in town has been bidding on that property."

"Have we been outbid?"

"It isn't that. The old lady isn't interested in money. She's loaded."

"What *is* she interested in?"

"She wants some kind of monument to her husband. Apparently she thinks she was married to Albert Schweitzer. She wants to keep his flame burning. She doesn't want her property turned into anything crass or commercial. I hear Steve Murchison has been trying to talk her into selling."

"Oh?"

Lara sat there quietly for a full minute. When she spoke, she said, "Who's your doctor, Howard?"

"What?"

"Who's your doctor?"

"Seymour Bennett. He's chief of staff at Midtown Hospital."

The following morning Lara's attorney, Terry Hill, was sitting in the office of Dr. Seymour Bennett.

"My secretary told me that you wanted to see me urgently and that it has nothing to do with a medical problem."

"In a sense," Terry Hill said, "it does concern a medical problem, Dr. Bennett. I represent an investment group that wants to put up a nonprofit clinic. We want to be able to take care of those unfortunate people who can't afford regular medical care."

"That's a splendid idea," Dr. Bennett said. "What can I do to help you?"

Terry Hill told him.

The following day Dr. Bennett was having tea in the home of Eleanor Royce.

"They've asked me to approach you on behalf of this group, Mrs. Royce. They want to build a beautiful clinic, and they want to name it after your late husband. They visualize it as sort of a shrine to him."

Mrs. Royce's face lit up. "They do?"

They discussed the group's plans for an hour, and at the end of that time Mrs. Royce said, "George would have loved this. You tell them that they have a deal."

Construction began six months later. When it was completed, it was gigantic. The entire square block was filled with huge apartment buildings, an enormous shopping mall, and a theater complex. In a remote corner of the property was a small one-story brick building. A simple sign over the door read: GEORGE ROYCE MEDICAL CLINIC.

Chapter Eighteen

On Christmas Day Lara stayed home. She had been invited to a dozen parties, but Paul Martin was going to drop by. "I have to be with Nina and the kids today," he had explained, "but I want to come by and see you."

She wondered what Philip Adler was doing on this Christmas Day.

It was a Currier & Ives postcard kind of day. New York was blanketed in a beautiful white snowfall, wrapped in silence. When Paul Martin arrived, he had a shopping bag full of gifts for Lara.

"I had to stop at the office to pick these up," he said. *So his wife wouldn't know.*

"You give me so much, Paul. You don't have to bring anything."

"I wanted to. Open them up now."

Lara was touched by his eagerness to see her reaction.

The gifts were thoughtful and expensive. A necklace from Cartier's, scarves from Hermès, books from Rizzoli, an antique carriage clock, and a small white envelope. Lara opened it. It read: "Cameron Reno Hotel & Casino" in large block letters. She looked up at him, in surprise. "I have the hotel?"

He nodded confidently. "You will have. The bidding starts next week. You're going to have fun with it," Paul Martin predicted.

"I don't know anything about running a casino."

"Don't worry. I'll put some professionals in to manage it for you. The hotel, you can handle yourself."

"I don't know how to thank you. You do so much for me."

He took her hands in his. "There isn't anything in the world that I wouldn't do for you. Remember that."

"I will," she said solemnly.

He was looking at his watch. "I have to get back home. I wish . . ." He hesitated.

"Yes?"

"Never mind. Merry Christmas, Lara."

"Merry Christmas, Paul."

She went to the window and looked out. The sky had become a delicate curtain of dancing snowflakes. Restless, Lara walked to the radio and turned it on. An announcer was saying, " . . . and now, for its holiday program, the Boston Symphony Orchestra presents Beethoven's Piano Concerto No. Five in E flat, with Philip Adler, soloist."

Lara listened with her eyes, seeing him at the piano, handsome and elegant. When the music ended, she thought, *I've got to see him again.*

Bill Whitman was one of the best construction supervisors in the business. He had risen through the ranks and was in great demand. He worked steadily and earned good money, but he was dissatisfied. For years he had watched builders reaping enormous fortunes while he got nothing but a salary. *In a way,* he thought, *they're making their money off of me. The owner gets the cake; I get the crumbs.* But the day Lara Cameron had gone before the community board, everything changed. She had lied to get the board's approval, and that lie could destroy her. *If I went to the board and told them the truth, she'd be out of business.*

But Bill Whitman had no intention of doing that. He had a better plan. He intended to use what had happened as leverage. The boss lady was going to give him anything he asked for. He could sense from their first meeting at which he had asked for a promotion and raise that she was going to give in. She had no choice. *I'll start small,* Bill Whitman thought happily, *and then I'll begin squeezing.*

Two days after Christmas, work began again on the Eastside Plaza project. Whitman looked around at the huge site and thought, *This one's going to be a real money-maker. Only this time, I'm going to cash in on it, too.*

The site was crowded with heavy equipment. Cranes were digging into the earth and lifting tons of it into waiting trucks. A crane wielding a giant saw-toothed scoop bucket seemed to be stuck. The huge arm hung suspended high in midair. Whitman strode toward the cab, under the huge metal bucket.

"Hey, Jesse," he called. "What's the matter up there?"

The man in the cab mumbled something that Whitman could not hear.

Whitman moved closer. "What?"

Everything happened in a split second. A chain slipped, and the huge metal bucket came crashing down on Whitman, smashing him to the ground. Men came running toward the body, but there was nothing to be done.

"The safety brake slipped," the operator explained later. "Gee, I feel really awful. I liked Bill a lot."

When she heard the news, Lara immediately telephoned Paul Martin. "Did you hear about Bill Whitman?"

"Yes. It was on television."

"Paul, you didn't . . . ?"

He laughed. "Don't go getting any crazy ideas. You've been seeing too many movies. Remember, the good guys always win in the end."

And Lara wondered, *Am I one of the good guys?*

There were more than a dozen bidders for the Reno hotel.

"When do I bid?" Lara asked Paul.

"You don't. Not until I tell you. Let the others jump in first."

The bidding was secret, and the bids were sealed, to be opened on the following Friday. By Wednesday Lara still had not made a bid. She telephoned Paul Martin.

"Sit tight," he said. "I'll tell you when."

They stayed in touch by phone several times a day.

At 5:00 P.M., one hour before the bidding was to close, Lara received a phone call.

"Now! The high bid is a hundred and twenty million. I want you to go five million over it."

Lara gasped. "But if I do that, I'll lose money on the deal."

"Trust me," Paul said. "After you get the hotel and start redoing it, you can cut corners on the changes. They'll all be endorsed by the supervising engineer. You'll make up the five million and then some."

The following day Lara was notified that hers was the winning bid.

Now Lara and Keller were on their way to Reno.

* * *

The hotel was called the Reno Palace. It was large and sumptuous, with fifteen hundred rooms and a huge, glittering casino that was empty. Lara and Howard Keller were being escorted through the casino by a man named Tony Wilkie.

"The people who owned this got a bum deal," Wilkie said.

"What kind of bum deal?" Keller asked.

"Well, it seems that a couple of the boys were pocketing a little money from the cash cage . . ."

"Skimming," Keller interjected.

"Yeah. Of course, the owners didn't know anything about it."

"Of course not."

"But someone blew the whistle, and the Gaming Commission pulled out the rug. It's too bad. It was a very profitable operation."

"I know." Keller had already studied the books.

When the tour of inspection was completed, and Lara and Howard were alone, she said, "Paul was right. This is a gold mine." She saw the expression on Howard's face. "What's the matter?"

He shrugged. "I don't know. I just don't like us getting involved in anything like this."

"What's 'anything like this'? It's a cash cow, Howard."

"Who's going to run the casino?"

"We'll find people," Lara said evasively.

"Where from? The Girl Scouts? It takes gamblers to run an operation like this. I don't know any, do you?"

Lara was silent.

"I'll bet Paul Martin does."

"Leave him out of this," Lara said.

"I'd like to, and I'd like to leave you out of it. I don't think this is such a great idea."

"You didn't think the Queens project was a great idea either, did you? Or the shopping center on Houston Street. But they're making money, aren't they?"

"Lara, I never said they weren't good deals. All I said was that I think we're moving too fast. You're swallowing up everything in sight, but you haven't digested anything yet."

Lara patted his cheek. "Relax."

The members of the Gaming Commission received Lara with elaborate courtesy.

"We don't often meet a beautiful young woman in here," the chairman said. "It brightens up our day."

Lara did look beautiful. She was wearing a Donna Karan beige wool suit, with a cream-colored silk blouse and, for good luck, one of the scarves Paul had given her for Christmas. She smiled. "Thank you."

"What can we do for you?" one of the gaming commissioners asked. They all knew perfectly well what they could do for her.

"I'm here because I would like to do something for Reno," Lara said earnestly. "I would like to give it the biggest, most beautiful hotel in Nevada. I'd like to add five stories to the Reno Palace, and put up a large convention center to attract more tourists here to gamble."

The members of the board glanced at one another. The chairman said, "I think something like that would have a very beneficial effect on the city. Of course, our job is to make sure that an operation like this would be run completely aboveboard."

"I'm not exactly an escaped convict," Lara smiled.

They chuckled at her little joke. "We know your record, Miss Cameron, and it is admirable. However, you've had no experience in running a casino."

"That's true," Lara admitted. "On the other hand, I'm sure it will be easy to find fine, qualified employees who will meet the approval of this commission. I would certainly welcome your guidance."

One of the members of the commission spoke up. "As far as the financing is concerned, can you guarantee . . . ?"

The chairman interrupted. "That's all right, Tom, Miss Cameron has submitted the financials on it. I'll see that you each get a copy."

Lara sat there, waiting.

The chairman said, "I can't promise anything at this moment, Miss Cameron, but I think I'm safe in saying that I don't see any obstacles to your being granted a license."

Lara beamed. "That's wonderful. I'd like to get moving as quickly as possible."

"I'm afraid things don't move quite that fast here. There will be a one-month waiting period before we can give you a definite answer."

Lara was dismayed. "A month?"

"Yes. We have a bit of checking to do."

"I understand," Lara said. "That will be fine."

There was a music store in the hotel's shopping complex. In the window was a large poster of Philip Adler, advertising his new compact disc.

Lara was not interested in the music. She bought the CD for Philip's photograph on the back of the case.

On their way back to New York, Lara said, "Howard, what do you know about Philip Adler?"

"Just what everybody else knows. He's probably the top concert pianist in the world today. He plays with the finest symphony orchestras. I read somewhere that he just set up a foundation for scholarships for minority musicians in inner cities."

"What's it called?"

"The Philip Adler Foundation, I think."

"I'd like to make a contribution," Lara said. "Send them a check for ten thousand dollars in my name."

Keller looked at her in surprise. "I thought you didn't care for classical music."

"I'm starting to get interested in it," Lara said.

The headline read:

DISTRICT ATTORNEY PROBE OF PAUL MARTIN—
ATTORNEY REPUTED TO HAVE MAFIA TIES

Lara read the story with dismay and telephoned Paul immediately. "What's going on?" Lara asked.

He chuckled. "The DA is on another fishing expedition. They've been trying to tie me in with the boys for years, and they haven't had any luck. Every time an election comes up, they try to use me as their whipping boy. Don't worry about it. What about dinner tonight?"

"Fine," Lara said.

"I know a little place on Mulberry Street where no one will bother us."

Over dinner Paul Martin said, "I hear that the meeting with the Gaming Commission went well."

"I think it did. They seemed friendly, but I've never done anything like this before."

"I don't think you'll have any problem. I'll get you some good boys for the casino. The man who owned the license got greedy." He changed the subject. "How are all the construction jobs going?"

"Fine. I have three projects in the works, Paul."

"You're not getting in over your head, are you, Lara?"

He sounded like Howard Keller. "No. Every job is on budget and on schedule."

"That's good, baby. I wouldn't want anything to ever go wrong for you."

"Nothing will." She put her hand on his. "You're my safety net."

"I'll always be there." He squeezed her hand.

Two weeks went by, and Lara had not heard from Philip Adler. She sent for Keller. "Did you make that ten-thousand dollar contribution to the Adler Foundation?"

"Yes, the day you mentioned it."

"Strange. I would have thought he would have called me."

Keller shrugged. "He's probably traveling somewhere."

"Probably." She tried to conceal her disappointment. "Let's talk about the building in Queens."

"That's going to take a big financial bite out of us," Keller said.

"I know how to protect us. I'd like to lock the deal in with one tenant."

"Do you have anyone in mind?"

"Yes. Mutual Security Insurance. The president is a man named Horace Guttman. I've heard they're looking for a new location. I'd like it to be our building."

"I'll check it out," Keller said.

Lara noticed that he made no notes. "You constantly amaze me. You remember everything, don't you?"

Keller grinned. "I have a photographic memory. It used to be for baseball statistics." *It all seems so long ago,* Howard thought. *The kid with the magic arm, the star of the Chicago Cubs minor league. Someone else and another time.* "Sometimes it's a curse. There are a few things in my life I'd like to forget."

"Howard, have the architect go ahead and draw up the plans for the Queens building. Find out how many floors Mutual Security will need, and how much floor space."

Two days later Keller walked into Lara's office. "I'm afraid I have some bad news."

"What's the problem?"

"I did a little snooping around. You were right about Mutual Security Insurance. They *are* looking for a new headquarters, but Guttman is thinking about a building in Union Square. It's your old friend Steve Murchison's building."

Murchison again! She was sure that the box of dirt had been sent by him. *I'm not going to let him bluff me.*

"Has Guttman committed to it?" Lara asked.

"Not yet."

"All right. I'll handle it."

That afternoon Lara made a dozen phone calls. She hit the jackpot on the last call. Barbara Roswell.

"Horace Guttman? Sure, I know him, Lara. What's your interest in him?"

"I'd like to meet him. I'm a big fan of his. I want you to do me a favor. Could you please invite him to dinner next Saturday night, Barbara?"

"You've got it."

The dinner party was simple but elegant. There were fourteen people at the Roswell residence. Alice Guttman wasn't feeling well that evening, so Horace Guttman had come to the party alone. Lara had been seated next to him. He was in his sixties, but he seemed much older. He had a stern, worn face and a stubborn chin. Lara looked enchanting, provocative. She was wearing a low-cut black Halston gown and simple but stunning jewelry. They had had their cocktails and were seated at the dining table.

"I've been wanting to meet you," Lara confessed. "I've heard so much about you."

"I've heard a lot about you, young lady. You've made quite a splash in this town."

"I hope I'm making a contribution," Lara said modestly. "It's such a wonderful town."

"Where are you from?"

"Gary, Indiana."

"Really?" He looked at her in surprise. "That's where I was born. So, you're a Hoosier, eh?"

Lara smiled. "That's right. I have such fond memories of Gary. My father worked for the *Post-Tribune*. I went to Roosevelt High. On weekends we'd go to Gleason Park for picnics and outdoor concerts, or we'd go bowling at the Twelve and Twenty. I hated having to leave."

"You've done well for yourself, Miss Cameron."

"Lara."

"Lara. What are you up to these days?"

"The project I'm most excited about," Lara told him, "is a new building I'm putting up in Queens. It's going to have thirty stories and two hundred thousand square feet of floor space."

"That's interesting," Guttman said, thoughtfully.

"Oh," Lara said innocently. "Why?"

"It happens that we're looking for a building just about that size for our new headquarters."

"Really? Have you chosen one yet?"

"Not exactly, but . . ."

"If you'd like, I can show you the plans for our new building. They've already been drawn up."

He studied her a moment. "Yes, I'd like to see them."

"I can bring them to your office Monday morning."

"I'll look forward to it."

The rest of the evening went well.

When Horace Guttman reached home that night, he walked into his wife's bedroom.

"How are you feeling?" he asked.

"Better, darling. How was the party?"

He sat down on the bed. "Well, they all missed you, but I had an interesting time. Have you ever heard of Lara Cameron?"

"Certainly. Everyone has heard of Lara Cameron."

"She's quite a woman. A little strange. Says she was born in Gary, Indiana, same as me. Knew all about Gary—Gleason Park and the Twelve and Twenty."

"What's strange about that?"

Guttman looked at his wife and grinned. "The little lady comes from Nova Scotia."

Early Monday morning Lara appeared at Horace Guttman's office, carrying the blueprints for the Queens project. She was ushered in immediately.

"Nice to see you, Lara. Sit down."

She laid the blueprints on his desk and sat across from him.

"Before you look at these," Lara said, "I have something to confess, Horace."

Guttman leaned back in his chair. "Yes?"

"That story I told on Saturday about Gary, Indiana . . ."

"What about it?"

"I've never even been to Gary, Indiana. I was trying to impress you."

He laughed. "Now you've succeeded in confusing me. I'm not sure I'm going to be able to keep up with you, young lady. Let's look at these blueprints."

Half an hour later he was through examining them.

"You know," he said reflectively, "I was pretty well set on another location."

"Were you?"

"Why should I change my mind and move into your building?"

"Because you're going to be happier there. I'll see that you have everything you need." She smiled. "Besides, it's going to cost your company ten percent less."

"Really? You don't know what my deal is for the other building."

"It doesn't matter. I'll take your word for it."

"You *could* have come from Gary, Indiana," Guttman said. "You've got a deal."

When Lara returned to her office, there was a message that Philip Adler had telephoned.

Chapter Nineteen

The ballroom at the Waldorf-Astoria was crowded with patrons of Carnegie Hall. Lara moved through the crowd, looking for Philip. She recalled the telephone conversation they had had a few days earlier.

"Miss Cameron, this is Philip Adler."

Her throat went suddenly dry.

"I'm sorry I wasn't able to thank you earlier for the donation you made to the foundation. I've just returned from Europe and learned about it."

"It was my pleasure," Lara said. She had to keep him talking. "As . . . as a matter of fact, I'm interested in knowing more about the foundation. Perhaps we could get together and discuss it."

There was a pause. "There's going to be a charity dinner at the Waldorf Saturday evening. We could meet there. Are you free?"

Lara quickly glanced at her schedule. She had a dinner meeting that evening with a banker from Texas.

She made a quick decision. "Yes. I'd be delighted to go."

"Wonderful. There will be a ticket at the door for you."

When Lara replaced the receiver, she was beaming.

Philip Adler was nowhere in sight. Lara moved through the huge ballroom, listening to the conversations around her.

" . . . so the leading tenor said, 'Dr. Klemperer, I have only two high C's left. Do you want to hear them now or tonight at the performance?' . . ."

" . . . oh, I admit that he has a good stick. His dynamics and tonal shadings are excellent . . . but the *tempi!* *Tempi!* Spare me! . . ."

" . . . you're insane! Stravinsky is too structured. His music could have been written by a robot. He holds back his feelings. Bartók, on the other hand, lets loose the floodgates, and we're bathed in emotions. . . ."

" . . . I simply can't stand her playing. Her Chopin is an exercise in tortured rubato, butchered textures, and purple passion . . ."

It was an arcane language that was beyond Lara's comprehension. And then she saw Philip, surrounded by an admiring coterie. Lara pushed her way through the crowd. An attractive young woman was saying, "When you played the B flat Minor Sonata, I felt that Rachmaninoff was smiling. Your tone and voicing, and the soft-grained readings . . . Wonderful!"

Philip smiled. "Thank you."

A middle-aged dowager was gushing, "I keep listening to your recording of the *Hammerklavier* over and over. My God! The vitality is irresistible! I think you must be the only pianist left in this world who really understands that Beethoven sonata . . ."

Philip saw Lara. "Ah. Excuse me," he said.

He made his way over to where she was standing and took her hand. His touch aroused her. "Hello. I'm glad you could come, Miss Cameron."

"Thank you." She looked around. "This is quite a crowd."

He nodded. "Yes. I assume that you're a lover of classical music?"

Lara thought of the music she had grown up with: "Annie Laurie," "Comin' through the Rye," "The Hills of Home" . . .

"Oh, yes," Lara said. "My father brought me up on classical music."

"I want to thank you again for your contribution. That was really very generous."

"Your foundation sounds so interesting. I would love to hear more about it. If . . ."

"Philip, darling! There are no words! Magnificent!" He was surrounded again.

Lara managed to make herself heard. "If you're free one evening next week . . ."

Philip shook his head. "I'm sorry, I leave for Rome tomorrow."

Lara felt a sudden sense of loss. "Oh."

"But I'll be back in three weeks. Perhaps then we could . . ."

"Wonderful!" Lara said.

" . . . spend an evening discussing music."

Lara smiled. "Yes. I'll look forward to that."

At that moment they were interrupted by two middle-aged men. One wore his hair in a ponytail; the other had on a single earring.

"Philip! You must settle an argument for us. When you're playing Liszt, which do you think is more important—a piano with heavy action that gives you a colorful sound or light action where you can do a colorful manipulation?"

Lara had no idea what they were talking about. They went off into a discussion about neutral sonority and long sounds and transparency. Lara watched the animation inPhilip's face as he talked, and she thought, *This is his world. I've got to find a way to get into it.*

The following morning Lara appeared at the Manhattan School of Music. She said to the woman at the reception desk, "I'd like to see one of the music professors, please."

"Anyone in particular?"

"No."

"Just a moment, please." She disappeared into another room.

A few minutes later a small gray-haired man appeared at Lara's side.

"Good morning. I'm Leonard Meyers. How may I help you?"

"I'm interested in classical music."

"Ah, you wish to enroll here. What instrument do you play?"

"I don't play any instrument. I just want to learn about classical music."

"I'm afraid you've come to the wrong place. This school is not for beginners."

"I'll pay you five thousand dollars for two weeks of your time."

Professor Meyers blinked. "I'm sorry, Miss . . . I didn't get your name."

"Cameron. Lara Cameron."

"You wish to pay me five thousand dollars for a two-week *discussion* of classical music?" He had trouble getting the words out.

"That's right. You can use the money for a scholarship fund if you wish."

Professor Meyers lowered his voice. "That will not be necessary. This can just be between you and me."
"That's fine."
"When . . . er . . . would you like to begin?"
"Now."
"I have a class at the moment, but give me five minutes . . ."

Lara and Professor Meyers were seated in a classroom alone.
"Let us start at the beginning. Do you know anything about classical music?"
"Very little."
"I see. Well, there are two ways to understand music," the professor began. "Intellectually and emotionally. Someone once said that music reveals to man his hidden soul. Every great composer was able to accomplish that."
Lara was listening intently.
"Are you familiar with *any* composers, Miss Cameron?"
She smiled. "Not too many."
The professor frowned. "I don't really understand your interest in . . ."
"I want to get enough of a background so that I can talk intelligently to a professional musician about the classics. I'm . . . particularly interested in piano music."
"I see." Meyers thought for a moment. "I'll tell you how we're going to begin. I'm going to give you some CDs to play."
Lara watched him walk over to a shelf and pull down some compact discs.
"We'll start with these. I want you to listen carefully to the allegro in Mozart's Piano Concerto No. Twenty-one in C, Köchel 467, and the adagio in Brahms Piano Concerto No. One, and the moderato in Rachmaninoff's Piano Concerto No. Two in C Minor, Opus Eighteen, and finally, the romanze in Chopin's Piano Concerto No. One. They're all marked."
"Right."
"If you would like to play these and come back in a few days . . ."
"I'll be back tomorrow."

The following day, when Lara came in, she was carrying half a dozen CDs of Philip Adler's concerts and recitals.

"Ah, splendid!" Professor Meyers said. "Maestro Adler is the best. You are particularly interested in his playing?"

"Yes."

"The maestro has recorded many beautiful sonatas."

"Sonatas?"

He sighed. "You don't know what a sonata is?"

"I'm afraid I don't."

"A sonata is a piece, usually in several movements, that has a certain basic musical form. And when that form is used in a piece for a solo instrument, like a piano or violin, the piece is called a sonata. A symphony is a sonata for orchestra."

"I understand." *That shouldn't be difficult to work into a conversation.*

"The piano was originally known as the pianoforte. That is Italian for 'soft-loud' . . ."

They spent the next few days discussing tapes that Philip had recorded—Beethoven, Liszt, Bartók, Mozart, Chopin.

Lara listened, and absorbed, and remembered.

"He likes Liszt. Tell me about him."

"Franz Liszt was a boy genius. Everyone admired him. He was brilliant. He was treated like a pet by the aristocracy, and he finally complained that he had become on par with a juggler or a performing dog. . . ."

"Tell me about Beethoven."

"A difficult man. He was such an unhappy person that in the middle of his great success he decided he didn't like the work that he had done, and he changed to longer and more emotional compositions, like the *Eroica* and the *Pathétique*. . . ."

"Chopin?"

"Chopin was criticized for writing music for the piano, so the critics of his day called him limited . . ."

Later: "Liszt could play Chopin better than Chopin could. . . ."

Another day: "There's a difference between French pianists and American pianists. The French like clarity and elegance. Traditionally, their technical schooling is grounded in *jeu perlé*—perfectly pearly evenness of articulation with a steady wrist. . . ."

Each day they played one of Philip's recordings and discussed it.

At the end of the two weeks Professor Meyers said, "I must confess that I'm impressed, Miss Cameron. You are a truly dedicated pupil. Perhaps you should take up an instrument."

Lara laughed. "Let's not get carried away." She handed him a check. "Here you are."

She could not wait for Philip to return to New York.

Chapter Twenty

The day started with good news. Terry Hill called.

"Lara?"

"Yes?"

"We just heard from the Gaming Commission. You've got your license."

"That's wonderful, Terry!"

"I'll go over the details when I see you, but it's a green light. Apparently you impressed the hell out of them."

"I'll get everything started right away," Lara said. "Thanks."

Lara told Keller what had happened.

"That's great. We can sure use the cash flow. That will take care of a lot of our problems . . ."

Lara looked at her calendar. "We can fly there on Tuesday and get things moving."

Kathy buzzed her. "There's a Mr. Adler on line two. Shall I tell him . . . ?"

Lara was suddenly nervous. "I'll take it." She picked up the telephone. "Philip?"

"Hello. I'm back."

"I'm glad." *I missed you.*

"I know it's short notice, but I wondered whether you might be free for dinner this evening."

She had a dinner engagement with Paul Martin. "Yes. I'm free."

"Wonderful. Where would you like to dine?"

"It doesn't matter."

"La Côte Basque?"

"Fine."

"Why don't we meet there? Eight o'clock?"

"Yes."

"See you tonight."

When Lara hung up, she was smiling.

"Was that *Philip* Adler?" Keller asked.

"Uh-huh. I'm going to marry him."

Keller was looking at her, stunned. "Are you serious?"

"Yes."

It was a jolt. *I'm going to lose her,* Keller thought. And then?: *Who am I kidding? I could never have her.*

"Lara . . . you hardly know him!"

I've known him all my life.

"I don't want you to make a mistake."

"I'm not. I . . ." Her private telephone rang. The one she had had installed for Paul Martin. Lara picked it up. "Hello, Paul."

"Hi, Lara. What time would you like to make dinner tonight? Eight?"

She felt a sudden sense of guilt. "Paul . . . I'm afraid I can't make it tonight. Something came up. I was just going to call you."

"Oh? Is everything all right?"

"Yes. Some people just flew in from Rome"—that part at least was true—"and I have to meet with them."

"My bad luck. Another night, then."

"Of course."

"I hear the license came through for the Reno hotel."

"Yes."

"We're going to have fun with that place."

"I'm looking forward to it. I'm sorry about tonight. I'll talk to you tomorrow."

The line went dead.

Lara replaced the receiver slowly.

Keller was watching her. She could see the disapproval on his face.

"Is something bothering you?"

"Yeah. It's all this modern equipment."

"What are you talking about?"

"I think you have too many phones in your office. He's bad news, Lara."

Lara stiffened. "Mr. Bad News has saved our hides a few times, Howard. Anything else?"

Keller shook his head. "No."

"Right. Let's get back to work."

Philip was waiting for her when she arrived at La Côte Basque. People turned to stare at Lara as she walked into the restaurant. Philip stood up to greet her, and Lara's heart skipped a beat.

"I hope I'm not late," she said.

"Not at all." He was looking at her admiringly. His eyes were warm. "You look lovely."

She had changed clothes half a dozen times. *Should I wear something simple or elegant or sexy?* Finally, she had decided on a simple Dior. "Thank you."

When they were seated, Philip said, "I feel like an idiot."

"Oh? Why?"

"I never connected the name. You're *that* Cameron."

She laughed. "Guilty."

"My God! You're a hotel chain, you're apartment buildings, office buildings. When I travel, I see your name all over the country."

"Good." Lara smiled. "It will remind you of me."

He was studying her. "I don't think I need any reminding. Do you get tired of people telling you that you're very beautiful?"

She started to say, "I'm glad you think I'm beautiful." What came out was: "Are you married?" She wanted to bite her tongue.

He smiled. "No. It would be impossible for me to get married."

"Why?" For an instant she held her breath. *Surely he's not . . .*

"Because I'm on tour most of the year. One night I'm in Budapest, the next night in London or Paris or Tokyo."

There was a sweeping sense of relief. "Ah. Philip, tell me about yourself."

"What do you want to know?"

"Everything."

Philip laughed. "That would take at least five minutes."

"No, I'm serious. I really want to know about you."

He took a deep breath. "Well, my parents were Viennese. My father was a musical conductor, and my mother was a piano teacher. They left Vienna to escape Hitler and settled in Boston. I was born there."

"Did you always know you wanted to be a pianist?"
"Yes."

He was six years old. He was practicing the piano, and his father came storming into the room. "No, no, no! Don't you know a major chord from a minor?" His hairy finger slashed at the sheet music. "That's a minor chord. Minor. Do you understand?"

"Father, please, can I go? My friends are waiting for me outside."

"No. You will sit here until you get it right."

He was eight years old. He had practiced for four hours that morning and had had a terrible fight with his parents. "I hate the piano," he cried. "I never want to touch it again."

His mother said, "Fine. Now, let me hear the andante once more."

He was ten years old. The apartment was filled with guests, most of them old friends of his parents from Vienna. All of them were musicians.

"Philip is going to play something for us now," his mother announced.

"We'd love to hear little Philip play," they said in patronizing voices.

"Play the Mozart, Philip."

Philip looked into their bored faces and sat down at the piano, angry. They went on chatting among themselves.

He began to play, his fingers flashing across the keyboard. The talking suddenly stopped. He played a Mozart sonata, and the music was alive. And at that moment he was Mozart, filling the room with the magic of the master.

As Philip's fingers struck the last chord, there was an awed silence. His parents' friends rushed over to the piano, talking excitedly, effusive with their praise. He listened to their applause and adulation, and that was the moment of his epiphany, when he knew who he was and what he wanted to do with his life.

"Yes, I always knew I wanted to be a pianist," Philip told Lara.

"Where did you study piano?"

"My mother taught me until I was fourteen, and then they sent me to study at the Curtis Institute in Philadelphia."

"Did you enjoy that?"

"Very much."

He was fourteen years old, alone in the city with no friends. The Curtis Institute of Music was located in four turn-of-the-century mansions near Philadelphia's Rittenhouse Square. It was the closest American equivalent to the Moscow Conservatory of Viardo, Egorov, and Toradze. Its graduates included Samuel Barber, Leonard Bernstein, Gian Carlo Menotti, Peter Serkin, and dozens of other brilliant musicians.

"Weren't you lonely there?"

"No."

He was miserable. He had never been away from home before. He had auditioned for the Curtis Institute, and when they accepted him, the realization struck him that he was about to begin a new life, that he would never go home again. The teachers recognized the young boy's talent immediately. His piano teachers were Isabelle Vengerova and Rudolf Serkin, and Philip studied piano, theory, harmony, orchestration, and flute. When he was not in class, he played chamber music with the other students. The piano, which he had been forced to practice from the time he was three years old, was now the focus of his life. To him, it had become a magical instrument out of which his fingers could draw romance and passion and thunder. It spoke a universal language.

"I gave my first concert when I was eighteen with the Detroit Symphony."

"Were you frightened?"

He was terrified. He found that it was one thing to play before a group of friends. It was another to face a huge auditorium filled with people who had paid money to hear him. He was nervously pacing backstage when the stage manager grabbed his arm and said, "Go. You're on." He had never forgotten the feeling he had when he walked out onto the stage and the audience began to applaud him. He sat down at the piano, and his nervousness vanished in an instant. After that his life became a marathon of concerts. He toured all over Europe and Asia, and after each tour his reputation grew. William Ellerbee, an important artists' manager, agreed to represent him. Within two years Philip Adler was in demand everywhere.

Philip looked at Lara and smiled. "Yes. I still get frightened before a concert."

"What's it like to go on tour?"

"It's never dull. Once I was on a tour with the Philadelphia Symphony. We were in Brussels, on our way to give a concert in London. The airport was closed because of fog, so they took us by bus to Schiphol Airport in Amsterdam. The man in charge explained that the plane they had chartered for us was small and that the musicians could take either their instruments or their luggage. Naturally they chose their instruments. We arrived in London just in time to begin the concert. We played it in jeans, sneakers, and unshaven."

Lara laughed. "And I'll bet the audience loved it."

"They did. Another time I was giving a concert in Indiana, and the piano was locked away in a closet and no one had a key. We had to break the door down."

Lara giggled.

"Last year I was scheduled to do a Beethoven concerto in Rome, and one of the music critics wrote: 'Adler gave a ponderous performance, with his phrasing in the finale completely missing the point. The tempo was too broad, rupturing the pulse of the piece.'"

"That's awful!" Lara said sympathetically.

"The awful part was that I never even gave that concert. I had missed the plane!"

Lara leaned forward, eagerly. "Tell me more."

"Well, one time in São Paulo the pedals fell off the piano in the middle of a Chopin concert."

"What did you do?"

"I finished the sonata without pedals. Another time the piano slid clear across the stage."

When Philip talked about his work, his voice was filled with enthusiasm.

"I'm very lucky. It's wonderful to be able to touch people and transport them into another world. The music gives each of them a dream. Sometimes I think music is the only sanity left in an insane world." He laughed self-consciously. "I didn't mean to sound pompous."

"No. You make millions of people so happy. I love to hear you play." She took a deep breath. "When I hear you play Debussy's *Voiles*, I'm on a lonely beach, and I see the mast of a ship sailing in the distance . . ."

He smiled. "Yes, so do I."

"And when I listen to your Scarlatti, I'm in Naples, and I can hear the horses and the carriages, and see the people walking through the streets. . . ." She could see the pleasure in his face as he listened to her.

She was dredging up every memory of her sessions with Professor Meyers.

"With Bartók, you take me to the villages of Central Europe, to the peasants of Hungary. You're painting pictures, and I lose myself in them."

"You're very flattering," Philip said.

"No. I mean every word of it."

Dinner arrived. It consisted of a chateaubriand with pommes frites, a Waldorf salad, fresh asparagus, and a fruit tart for dessert. There was a wine for each course. Over dinner Philip said, "Lara, we keep talking about me. Tell me about you. What is it like to put up enormous buildings all over the country?"

Lara was silent for a moment. "It's difficult to describe. *You* create with your hands. *I* create with my mind. I don't physically put up a building, but I make it possible. I dream a dream of bricks and concrete and steel, and make it come true. I create jobs for hundreds of people: architects and bricklayers and designers and carpenters and plumbers. Because of me, they're able to support their families. I give people beautiful surroundings to live in and make them comfortable. I build attractive stores where people can shop and buy things they need. I build monuments to the future." She smiled, sheepishly. "I didn't mean to make a speech."

"You're quite remarkable, do you know that?"

"I want you to think so."

It was an enchanted evening, and by the time it was over, Lara knew that for the first time in her life she was in love. She had been so afraid that she might be disappointed, that no man could live up to the image in her imagination. But here was Lochinvar in the flesh, and she was stirred.

When Lara got home, she so excited she was unable to go to sleep. She went over the evening in her mind, replaying the conversation again and again and again. Philip Adler was the most fascinating man she had ever met. The telephone rang. Lara smiled and picked it up. She started to say, "Philip . . . ," when Paul Martin said, "Just checking to make sure you got home safely."

"Yes," Lara said.

"How did your meeting go?"

"Fine."

"Good. Let's have dinner tomorrow night."

Lara hesitated. "All right." *I wonder if there's going to be a problem.*

Chapter Twenty-one

The following morning, a dozen red roses were delivered to Lara's apartment. *So, he enjoyed the evening, too,* Lara thought happily. She hurriedly tore open the card attached to the flowers. It read: "Baby, looking forward to our dinner tonight. Paul."

Lara felt a sharp sense of disappointment. She waited all morning for a call from Philip. She had a busy schedule, but she was unable to keep her mind on her work.

At two o'clock Kathy said, "The new secretaries are here for you to interview."

"Start sending them in."

There were half a dozen of them, all of them highly qualified. Gertrude Meeks was the choice of the day. She was in her thirties, bright and upbeat, and obviously in awe of Lara.

Lara looked over her résumé. It was impressive. "You've worked in the real estate development field before."

"Yes, ma'am. But I've never worked for anyone like you. To tell you the truth, I'd take this job for no salary!"

Lara smiled. "That won't be necessary. These are good references. All right, we'll give you a try."

"Thank you so much." She was almost blushing.

"You'll have to sign a form agreeing not to give any interviews or ever to discuss anything that happens at this firm. Is that agreeable?"

"Of course."

"Kathy will show you to your desk."

There was an eleven o'clock publicity meeting with Jerry Townsend. "How's your father?" Lara asked.

"He's in Switzerland. The doctor says he may have a chance." His voice grew husky. "If he has, it's because of you."

"Everyone deserves a chance, Jerry. I hope he gets well."

"Thanks." He cleared his throat. "I . . . I don't know how to tell you how grateful I . . ."

Lara stood up. "I'm late for a meeting."

And she walked out, leaving him standing there, looking after her.

The meeting was with the architects on a New Jersey development. "You've done a good job," Lara said, "but I'd like some changes. I want an elliptical arcade with lobbies on three sides and marble walls. Change the roof to the shape of a copper pyramid, with a beacon to light up at night. Any problem with that?"

"I don't see any, Miss Cameron."

When the meeting was over, the intercom buzzed.

"Miss Cameron, Raymond Duffy, one of the construction foremen, is on the line for you. He says it's urgent."

Lara picked up the telephone. "Hello, Raymond."

"We have a problem, Miss Cameron."

"Go on."

"They just delivered a load of cement blocks. They won't pass inspection. There are cracks in them. I'm going to send them back, but I wanted to tell you first."

Lara was thoughtful for a moment. "How bad is it?"

"Bad enough. The point is, they don't meet our specifications, and . . ."

"Can they be fixed?"

"I guess they could, but it would be expensive."

"Fix them," Lara said.

There was a silence at the other end of the line.

"Right. You're the boss."

Lara replaced the receiver. There were only two cement suppliers in the city, and it would be suicide to antagonize them.

* * *

By five o'clock Philip still had not called. Lara dialed the number at his foundation. "Philip Adler, please."

"Mr. Adler is out of town on tour. Can I help you?"

He hadn't mentioned that he was leaving town. "No, thank you."

That's that, Lara thought. *For now.*

The day ended with a visit from Steve Murchison. He was a huge man, built like a stack of bricks. He stormed into Lara's office.

"What can I do for you, Mr. Murchison?" Lara asked.

"You can keep your nose out of my fucking business," Murchison said.

Lara looked at him calmly. "What's your problem?"

"You. I don't like people horning in on my deals."

"If you're talking about Mr. Guttman . . ."

"You're damn right I am."

" . . . he preferred my building to yours."

"You suckered him into it, lady. You've been getting in my hair long enough. I warned you once. I'm not going to warn you again. There's not room enough for both of us in this town. I don't know where you keep your balls, but hide 'em, because if you ever do that to me again, I'm going to cut them off."

And he stormed out.

The dinner at her apartment that evening with Paul was strained.

"You seem preoccupied, baby," Paul said. "Any problems?"

Lara managed a smile. "No. Everything's fine." *Why didn't Philip tell me he was going away?*

"When does the Reno project start?"

"Howard and I are going to fly there again next week. We should be able to open in about nine months."

"You could have a baby in nine months."

Lara looked at him in surprise. "What?"

Paul Martin took her hand in his. "You know I'm crazy about you, Lara. You've changed my whole life. I wish things could have turned out differently. I would have loved for us to have had kids together."

There was nothing Lara could say to that.

"I have a little surprise for you." He reached into his pocket and pulled out a jewelry box. "Open it."

"Paul, you've already given me so much . . ."

"Open it."

Inside the box was an exquisite diamond necklace.

"It's lovely."

He stood up, and she felt his hands on her as he put the necklace around her neck. His hands slid down, caressing her breasts, and he said huskily, "Let's check it out."

Paul was leading her into the bedroom. Lara's mind was spinning. She had never been in love with him, and going to bed with him had been easy—the payment for all he had done for her—but now there was a difference. She was in love. *I'm a fool,* Lara thought. *I'll probably never see Philip again.*

She undressed slowly, reluctantly, and then they were in bed, and Paul Martin was on top of her, inside her, moaning, "Baby, I'm nuts about you." And she looked up and it was Philip's face she saw.

Everything was progressing smoothly. The renovations on the Reno hotel were proceeding rapidly, Cameron Towers was going to be finished on schedule, and Lara's reputation kept growing. She had called Philip Adler several times over the past few months, but he was always away on tour.

"Mr. Adler is in Beijing . . ."

"Mr. Adler is in Paris . . ."

"Mr. Adler is in Sydney . . ."

To hell with him, Lara thought.

During the next six months Lara managed to outbid Steve Murchison on three properties he was after.

Keller came to Lara, worried. "The word around town is that Murchison is making threats against you. Maybe we should cool it with him. He's a dangerous enemy, Lara."

"So am I," Lara said. "Maybe he should get into another business."

"It's not a joking matter, Lara. He . . ."

"Forget about him, Howard. I just got a tip about a property in Los Angeles. It's not on the market yet. If we move fast, I think we can get it. We'll fly out in the morning."

The property was on the site of the old Biltmore Hotel and consisted of five acres. A real estate agent was showing Lara and Howard around the grounds.

"Prime property," he was saying. "Yes, sir. You can't go wrong with this. You can build a beautiful little city in this area . . . apartment buildings, shopping centers, theaters, malls . . ."

"No."

He looked at Lara in surprise. "I beg your pardon?"

"I'm not interested."

"You're not? Why?"

"The neighborhood," Lara said. "I don't think people are going to move into this area. Los Angeles is moving west. People are like lemmings. You aren't going to get them to reverse direction."

"But . . ."

"I'll tell you what I *am* interested in. Condos. Find me a good location."

Lara turned to Howard. "I'm sorry I wasted our time. We'll fly back this afternoon."

When they returned to their hotel, Keller bought a newspaper at the newsstand. "Let's see what the market is doing today."

They looked through the paper. In the entertainment section was a large advertisement that read: "TONIGHT AT THE HOLLYWOOD BOWL- PHILIP ADLER." Lara's heart gave a little jump.

"Let's go back tomorrow," Lara said.

Keller studied her a moment. "Are you interested in the music or the musician?"

"Get us two tickets."

Lara had never been to the Hollywood Bowl before. The largest natural amphitheater in the world, it is surrounded by the hills of Hollywood, the grounds a park, open year-round for visitors to enjoy. The Bowl itself seats eighteen thousand people. It was filled to capacity, and Lara could sense the anticipation of the crowd. The musicians began to come onto the stage, and they were greeted with expectant applause. André Previn appeared, and the applause grew more enthusiastic. There was a hush, then loud applause from the audience as Philip Adler walked out on the stage, elegant in white tie and tails.

Lara squeezed Keller's arm. "Isn't he handsome?" she whispered.

Keller did not answer.

Philip sat down at the piano, and the program began. His magic took over instantly, enveloping the audience. There was a mysticism about the night. The stars were shining down, lighting the dark hills surrounding the Bowl. Thousands of people sat there silently, moved by the majesty of the music. When the last notes of the concerto died away, there was a roar from the audience, as the people leaped to their feet, applauding and cheering. Philip stood there, taking bow after bow.

"Let's go backstage," Lara said.

Keller turned to look at her. Her voice was trembling with excitement.

The backstage entrance was at the side of the orchestra shell. A guard stood at the door, keeping the crowd out. Keller said, "Miss Cameron is here to see Mr. Adler."

"Is he expecting you?" the guard asked.

"Yes," Lara said.

"Wait here, please.." A moment later the guard returned. "You can go in, Miss Cameron."

Lara and Keller walked into the greenroom. Philip was in the center of a crowd that was congratulating him.

"Darling, I've never heard Beethoven played so exquisitely. You were unbelievable . . ."

Philip was saying, "Thank you . . ."

" . . . thank you . . . with music like that, it's easy to be inspired . . ."

" . . . thank you . . . André is such a brilliant conductor . . ."

" . . . thank you . . . I always enjoy playing at the Bowl . . ."

He looked up and saw Lara, and again there was that smile. "Excuse me," he said. He made his way through the crowd, toward her. "I had no idea you were in town."

"We just flew in this morning. This is Howard Keller, my associate."

"Hello," Keller said curtly.

Philip turned to a short, heavyset man, standing behind him. "This is my manager, William Ellerbee." They exchanged hellos.

Philip was looking at Lara. "There's a party tonight at the Beverly Hilton. I was wondering . . ."

"We'd love to," Lara said.

When Lara and Keller arrived at the Beverly Hilton's International Ballroom, it was filled with musicians and music lovers, talking music.

" . . . have you ever noticed that the closer you get to the equator, the more demonstrative and hot-blooded the fans are . . ."

" . . . when Franz Liszt played, his piano became an orchestra. . . ."

" . . . I disagree with you. De Groote's talent is not for Liszt or Paganini études, but more for Beethoven. . . ."

" . . . you have to dominate the concerto's emotional landscape. . . ."

Musicians speaking in tongues, Lara thought.

Philip was surrounded, as usual, by adoring fans. Just watching him gave Lara a warm glow.

When Philip saw her arrive, he greeted her with a broad smile. "You made it. I'm so glad."

"I wouldn't have missed it."

Howard Keller watched the two of them talking, and he thought, *Maybe I should have learned to play the piano. Or maybe I should just wake up to reality.* It seemed so long ago when he had first met the bright, eager, ambitious young girl. Time had been good to her, and it had stood still for him.

Lara was saying, "I have to go back to New York tomorrow, but perhaps we could have breakfast."

"I wish I could. I'm leaving for Tokyo early in the morning."

She felt a sharp pang of disappointment. "Why?"

He laughed. "That's what I do, Lara. I give a hundred and fifty concerts a year. Sometimes two hundred."

"How long will you be gone this time?"

"Eight weeks."

"I'll miss you," Lara said quietly. *You have no idea how much.*

Chapter Twenty-two

During the next few weeks Lara and Keller flew to Atlanta to investigate two sites at Ainsley Park and one at Dunwoody.

"Get me some prices on Dunwoody," Lara said. "We might put some condos there."

From Atlanta they flew to New Orleans. They spent two days exploring the central business district and a day at Lake Pontchartrain. Lara found two sites she liked.

A day after they returned, Keller walked into Lara's office. "We had some bad luck on the Atlanta project," he said.

"What do you mean?"

"Someone beat us to it."

Lara looked at him, surprised. "How could they? Those properties weren't even on the market."

"I know. Word must have leaked out."

Lara shrugged. "I guess you can't win them all."

That afternoon Keller had more bad news. "We lost the Lake Pontchartrain deal."

The following week they flew to Seattle and explored Mercer Island and Kirkland. There was one site that interested Lara, and when they returned to New York, she said to Keller, "Let's go after it. I think it could be a money-maker."

"Right."

At a meeting the next day Lara asked, "Did you put in the bid on Kirkland?"

Keller shook his head. "Someone got there ahead of us."

Lara was thoughtful. "Oh. Howard, see if you can find out who's jumping the gun on us."

It took him less than twenty-four hours. "Steve Murchison."

"Did he get all those deals?"

"Yes."

"So someone in this office has a big mouth."

"It looks that way."

Her face was grim. The next morning she hired a detective agency to find the culprit. They had no success.

"As far as we can tell, all your employees are clean, Miss Cameron. None of the offices is bugged, and your phones haven't been tapped."

They had reached a dead end.

Maybe they were just coincidences, Lara thought. She did not believe it.

The sixty-eight story residential tower in Queens was half completed, and Lara had invited the bankers to come and inspect its progress. The higher the number of floors, the more expensive the unit. Lara's sixty-eight stories had only fifty-seven actual floors. It was a trick she had learned from Paul Martin.

"Everybody does it," Paul had laughed. "All you do is change the floor numbers."

"How do you do that?"

"It's very simple. Your first bank of elevators is from the lobby to the twenty-fourth floor. The second bank of elevators is from the thirty-fourth floor to the sixty-eighth. It's done all the time."

Because of the unions, the construction jobs had half a dozen phantoms on salary—people who did not exist. There was a Director of Safety Practices, the Coordinator of Construction, the Supervisor of Materials, and others with impressive-sounding titles. In the beginning Lara had questioned it.

"Don't worry about it," Paul had told her. "It's all part of the CDB —the cost of doing business."

Howard Keller had been living in a small apartment in Washington Square, and when Lara had visited him one evening, she had looked around the tiny apartment and said, "This is a rattrap. You've got to move out of here." At Lara's urging, he had moved into a condominium uptown.

One night Lara and Keller were working late, and when they finally finished, Lara said, "You look exhausted. Why don't you go home and get some sleep, Howard?"

"Good idea," Keller yawned. "See you in the morning."

"Come in late," Lara told him.

Keller got into his car and started driving home. He was thinking about a deal they had just closed and how well Lara had handled it. It was exciting working with her. Exciting and frustrating. Somehow, in the back of his mind, he kept hoping that a miracle would happen. *I was blind not to have seen it before, Howard darling. I'm not interested in Paul Martin or Philip Adler. It's you I've loved all along.*

Fat chance.

When Keller reached his apartment, he took out his key and put it in the lock. It did not fit. Puzzled, he tried again. Suddenly the door flew open from the inside, and a stranger was standing there. "What the hell do you think you're doing?" the man asked.

Keller looked at him, bewildered. "I live here."

"The hell you do."

"But I . . ." Realization suddenly hit him. "I . . . I'm sorry," he stammered, red-faced. "I *used* to live here. I . . ."

The door was slammed in his face. Keller stood there, disconcerted. *How could I have forgotten that I moved? I've been working too hard.*

Lara was in the middle of a conference when her private phone rang. "You've been pretty busy lately, baby. I've missed you."

"I've been traveling a lot, Paul." She couldn't bring herself to say that she had missed him.

"Let's have lunch today."

Lara thought about all he had done for her.

"I'd like that," she said. The last thing in the world she wanted to do was to hurt him.

They had lunch at Mr. Chow's.

"You're looking great," Paul said. "Whatever you've been doing agrees with you. How's the Reno hotel coming?"

"It's coming along beautifully," Lara said enthusiastically. She spent the next fifteen minutes describing how the work was progressing. "We should be ready to open in two months."

A man and woman across the room were just leaving. The man's back was to Lara, but he looked familiar. When he turned for an instant, she caught a glimpse of his face. Steve Murchison. The woman with him looked familiar also. She stooped to pick up her purse, and Lara's heart skipped a beat. *Gertrude Meeks, my secretary.* "Bingo," Lara said softly.

"Is anything wrong?" Paul asked.

"No. Everything's fine."

Lara went on describing the hotel.

When Lara returned from lunch, she sent for Keller.

"Do you remember the property in Phoenix we looked at a few months ago?"

"Yeah, we turned it down. You said it was a dog."

"I've changed my mind." She pressed down the intercom. "Gertrude, would you come in here, please?"

"Yes, Miss Cameron."

Gertrude Meeks came into the office.

"I want to dictate a memo," Lara said. "To the Baron Brothers in Phoenix."

Gertrude started writing.

"Gentlemen, I have reconsidered the Scottsdale property and have decided to go ahead with it immediately. I think in time it is going to be my most valuable asset." Keller was staring at her. "I'll be in touch with you regarding price in the next few days. Best regards. I'll sign it."

"Yes, Miss Cameron. Is that all?"

"That's all."

Keller watched Gertrude leave the room. He turned to Lara. "Lara, what are you doing? We had that property analyzed. It's worthless! If you . . ."

"Calm down. We're not making a deal for it."

"Then why . . . ?"

"Unless I miss my guess, Steve Murchison will. I saw Gertrude having lunch with him today."

Keller was staring at Lara. "I'll be damned."

"I want you to wait a couple of days and then call Baron and ask about the property."

Two days later Keller came into Lara's office, grinning. "You were right," he said. "Murchison took the bait—hook, line, and sinker. He's now the proud owner of fifty acres of worthless land."

Lara sent for Gertrude Meeks.
"Yes, Miss Cameron?"
"You're fired," Lara said.
Gertrude looked at her in surprise. "Fired? Why?"
"I don't like the company you keep. Go back to Steve Murchison and tell him I said so."
Gertrude's face lost its color. "But I . . ."
"That's all. I'll have you escorted out of here."

At midnight Lara buzzed Max, her chauffeur. "Bring the car around to the front," Lara said.
"Yes, Miss Cameron."
The car was there waiting for her.
"Where would you like to go, Miss Cameron?" Max asked.
"Drive around Manhattan. I want to see what I've done."
He was staring at her. "I beg your pardon?"
"I want to look at my buildings."
They drove around the city and stopped at the shopping mall, the housing center, and the skyscraper. There was Cameron Square, Cameron Plaza, Cameron Center, and the skeleton of Cameron Towers. Lara sat in the car, staring at each building, thinking about the people living there and working there. She had touched all their lives. *I've made this city better,* Lara thought. *I've done everything I wanted to do. Then why am I restless? What is missing?* But she knew.

The following morning Lara telephoned William Ellerbee, Philip's concert manager.
"Good morning, Mr. Ellerbee."
"Good morning, Miss Cameron. What can I do for you?"
"I was wondering where Philip Adler is playing this week."
"Philip has a pretty heavy schedule. Tomorrow night he'll be in Amsterdam, then he goes on to Milan, Venice, and . . . do you want to know the rest of his . . . ?"
"No, no. That's fine. I was just curious. Thank you."
"No problem."
Lara walked into Keller's office. "Howard, I have to go to Amsterdam."

He looked at her in surprise. "What do we have going on there?"

"It's just an idea," Lara said evasively. "I'll let you know if it checks out. Have them get the jet ready for me, will you?"

"You sent Bert to London on it, remember? I'll tell them to have it back here tomorrow, and . . ."

"I want to leave today." There was an urgency in her that took her completely by surprise. "I'll fly commercial." She returned to her office and said to Kathy, "Get mea seat on the first flight to Amsterdam on KLM."

"Yes, Miss Cameron."

"Are you going to be gone long?" Keller asked. "We have some meetings coming up that . . ."

"I'll be back in a day or two."

"Do you want me to come with you?"

"Thanks, Howard. Not this time."

"I talked to a senator friend of mine in Washington. He thinks there's a chance they're going to pass a bill that will remove most of the tax incentives for building. If it passes, it's going to kill capital gains taxes and stop accelerated depreciation."

"That would be stupid," Lara said. "It would cripple the real estate industry."

"I know. He's against the bill."

"A lot of people will be against it. It will never pass," Lara predicted. "In the first place . . ."

The private phone on the desk rang. Lara stared at it. It rang again.

"Aren't you going to answer it?" Keller asked.

Lara's mouth was dry. "No."

Paul Martin listened to the hollow ring a dozen times before he replaced the receiver. He sat there a long time thinking about Lara. It seemed to him that lately she had been less accessible, a little cooler. *Could there be someone else? No.* Paul Martin thought. *She belongs to me. She'll always belong to me.*

The flight on KLM was pleasant. The first-class seats in the wide-bodied 747 were spacious and comfortable, and the cabin attendants were attentive.

Lara was too nervous to eat or drink anything. *What am I doing?* she wondered. *I'm going to Amsterdam uninvited, and he'll probably be too busy to even see me. Running after him is going to ruin whatever chance I might have had. Too late.*

She checked in at the Grand Hotel on Oudezijds Voorburgwal 197, one of the most beautiful hotels in Amsterdam.

"We have a lovely suite for you, Miss Cameron," the clerk said.

"Thank you. I understand that Philip Adler is giving a recital this evening. Do you know where he would be playing?"

"Of course, Miss Cameron. At the Concertgebouw."

"Could you arrange a ticket for me?"

"It will be my pleasure."

As Lara entered her suite, the telephone was ringing. It was Howard Keller.

"Did you have a nice flight?"

"Yes, thanks."

"I thought you'd like to know that I've spoken to the two banks about the Seventh Avenue deal."

"And?"

His voice was vibrant. "They're jumping at it."

Lara was elated. "I told you! This is going to be a big one. I want you to start assembling a team of architects, builders—our construction group—the works."

"Right. I'll talk to you tomorrow." She replaced the receiver and thought about Howard Keller. He was so dear. *I'm so lucky. He's always there for me. I have to find someone wonderful for him.*

Philip Adler was always nervous before playing. He had rehearsed with the orchestra in the morning, and had a light lunch, and then, to take his mind off the concert, had gone to see an English movie. As he watched the picture, his mind was filled with the music he was going to play that evening. He was unaware that he was drumming his fingers on the arm of his seat until the person next to him said, "Would you mind stopping that awful sound?"

"I beg your pardon," Philip said politely.

He got up and left the theater and roamed the streets of Amsterdam. He visited the Rijksmuseum, and he strolled through the Botanical Gardens of the Free University, and window-shopped along the P. C. Hooftstraat. At four o'clock he went back to his hotel to take a nap. He was unaware that Lara Cameron was in the suite directly above him.

At 7:00 P.M. Philip arrived at the artists' entrance of the Con-

THE STARS SHINE DOWN

certgebouw, the lovely old theater in the heart of Amsterdam. The lobby was already crowded with early arrivals.

Backstage, Philip was in his dressing room, changing into tails. The director of the Concertgebouw bustled into the room.

"We're completely sold out, Mr. Adler! And we had to turn away so many people. If it were possible for you to stay another day or two, I would . . . I know you are fully booked . . . I will talk to Mr. Ellerbee about your return here next year and perhaps . . ."

Philip was not listening. His mind was focused on the recital that lay ahead. The director finally shrugged apologetically and bowed his way out. Philip played the music over and over in his mind. A page knocked at the dressing-room door.

"They're ready for you onstage, Mr. Adler."

"Thank you."

It was time. Philip rose to his feet. He held out his hands. They were trembling slightly. The nervousness before playing never went away. It was true of all the great pianists—Horowitz, Rubenstein, Serkin. Philip's stomach was churning, and his heart was pounding. *Why do I put myself through this agony?* he asked himself. But he knew the answer. He took one last look in the mirror, then stepped out of the dressing room, and walked through the long corridor, and started to descend the thirty-three steps that led onto the stage. There was a spotlight on him as he moved toward the piano. The applause grew thunderous. He sat down at the piano, and as if by magic, his nervousness disappeared. It was as though another person were taking his place, someone calm, and poised, and completely in charge. He began to play.

Lara, seated in the audience, felt a thrill as she watched Philip walk out on the stage. There was a presence about him that was mesmerizing. *I am going to marry him,* Lara thought. *I know it.* She sat back in her seat and let his playing wash over her.

The recital was a triumph, and afterward the greenroom was packed. Philip had long ago learned to divide the crowd invited to the greenroom into two groups: the fans and other musicians. The fans were always enthusiastic. If the performance was a success, the congratulations of the other musicians were cordial. If it was a failure, their congratulations were *very* cordial.

Philip had many avid fans in Amsterdam, and on this particular evening the greenroom was crowded with them. He stood in the center of the room, smiling, signing autographs, and being patiently polite to a hundred strangers. Invariably someone would say, "Do you remember me?" And Philip would pretend to. "Your face looks so familiar . . ."

He remembered the story of Sir Thomas Beecham, who had hit upon a device to conceal his bad memory. When someone asked, "Do you remember me?" the great conductor would reply, "Of course, I do! How are you, and how is your father, and what is he doing?" The device worked well until a concert in London when a young woman in the greenroom said, "Your performance was wonderful, Maestro. Do you remember me?" and Beecham gallantly replied, "Of course, I do, my dear. How is your father, and what is he doing?" The young woman said, "Father is fine, thank you. And he's still king of England."

Philip was busily signing autographs, listening to the familiar phrases—"You made Brahms come alive for me!" . . . "I can't tell you how moved I was!" . . . "I have all your albums" . . . "Would you sign an autograph for my mother too? She's your biggest fan . . ." —when something made him look up. Lara was standing in the doorway, watching. His eyes widened in surprise. "Excuse me."

He made his way over to her and took her hand. "What a wonderful surprise! What are you doing in Amsterdam?"

Careful, Lara. "I had some business to attend to here, and when I heard you were giving a recital, I had to come." *That was innocent enough.* "You were wonderful, Philip."

"Thank you . . . I . . . " He stopped to sign another autograph. "Look, if you're free for supper . . ."

"I'm free," Lara said quickly.

They had supper at the Bali restaurant on Leidsestraat. As they entered the restaurant, the patrons rose and applauded. *In the United States,* Lara thought, *the excitement would have been for me.* But she felt a warm glow, simply being at Philip's side.

"It's a great honor to have you with us, Mr. Adler," the maître d' said as he led them to their table.

"Thank you."

As they were being seated, Lara looked around at all the people staring admiringly at Philip. "They really love you, don't they?"

He shook his head. "It's the music they love. I'm just the messenger. I learned that a long time ago. When I was very young and perhaps a little arrogant, I gave a concert, and when I had finished my solo, there was tremendous applause, and I was bowing to the audience and smugly smiling at them, and the conductor turned to the audience and held up the score over his head to remind everyone that they were really applauding Mozart. It's a lesson I've never forgotten."

"Don't you ever get tired of playing the same music over and over, night after night?"

"No, because no two recitals are the same. The music may be the same, but the conductor is different, and the orchestra is different."

They ordered a rijsttafel dinner, and Philip said, "We try to make each recital perfect, but there's no such thing as a completely successful one because we're dealing with music that is always better than we are. We have to rethink the music each time in order to recreate the sound of the composer."

"You're never satisfied?"

"Never. Each composer has his own distinctive sound. Whether it's Debussy, Brahms, Haydn, Beethoven . . . our goal is to capture that particular sound."

Supper arrived. The rijsttafel was an Indonesian feast, consisting of twenty-one courses, including a variety of meats, fish, chicken, noodles, and two desserts.

"How can anyone eat all this?" Lara laughed.

"The Dutch have hearty appetites."

Philip found it difficult to take his eyes off Lara. He found himself ridiculously pleased that she was there. He had been involved with more than his share of beautiful women, but Lara was like no one he had ever known. She was strong and yet very feminine and totally unselfconscious about her beauty. He liked her throaty, sexy voice. *In fact, I like everything about her,* Philip admitted to himself.

"Where do you go from here?" Lara was asking.

"Tomorrow I'll be in Milan. Then Venice and Vienna, Paris and London, and finally New York."

"It sounds so romantic."

Philip laughed. "I'm not sure romantic is the word I would choose. We're talking about iffy airline schedules, strange hotels, and eating out in restaurants every night. I don't really mind because the act of playing is so wonderful. It's the 'say cheese' syndrome that I hate."

"What's that?"

"Being put on exhibit all the time, smiling at people you care nothing about, living your life in a world of strangers."

"I know what that's like," Lara said slowly.

* * *

As they were finishing supper, Philip said, "Look, I'm always keyed up after a concert. Would you care to take a ride on the canal?"

"I'd love to."

They boarded a canalbus that cruised the Amstel. There was no moon, but the city was alive with thousands of sparkling lights. The canal trip was an enchantment. A loudspeaker poured out information in four languages:

"We are now passing centuries-old merchants' houses with their richly decorated gables. Ahead are ancient church towers. There are twelve hundred bridges on the canals, all in the shade of magnificent avenues of elm trees . . ."

They passed the Smalste Huis—the narrowest house in Amsterdam—which was only as wide as the front door, and the Westerkerk with the crown of the Hapsburg emperor Maximilian, and they went under the wooden lift bridge over the Amstel and the Magere Brug—the skinny bridge—and passed scores of houseboats that served as home for hundreds of families.

"This is such a beautiful city," Lara said.

"You've never been here before?"

"No."

"And you're here on business."

Lara took a deep breath. "No."

He looked at her puzzled. "I thought you said . . ."

"I came to Amsterdam to see you."

He felt a sudden frisson of pleasure. "I . . . I'm very flattered."

"And I have another confession to make. I told you I was interested in classical music. That's not true."

A smile touched the corner of Philip's lips. "I know."

Lara looked at him in surprise. "You know?"

"Professor Meyers is an old friend of mine," he said gently. "He called to tell me that he was giving you a crash course on Philip Adler. He was concerned that you might have designs on me."

Lara said softly, "He was right. Are you involved with anyone?"

"You mean seriously?"

Lara was suddenly embarrassed. "If you're not interested, I'll leave and . . ."

He took her hand in his. "Let's get off at the next stop."

* * *

When they arrived back at the hotel, there were a dozen messages from Howard Keller. Lara put them in her purse, unread. At this moment nothing else in her life seemed important.

"Your room or mine?" Philip asked lightly.

"Yours."

There was a burning urgency in her.

It seemed to Lara that she had waited all her life for this moment. This was what she had been missing. She had found the stranger she was in love with. They reached Philip's room, and there was an urgency in both of them. Philip took her in his arms and kissed her softly and tenderly, exploring, and Lara murmured, "Oh, my God," and they began to undress each other.

The silence of the room was broken by a sudden clap of thunder outside. Slowly, gray clouds in the sky spread their skirts open, wider and wider, and soft rain began to fall. It started quietly and gently, caressing the warm air erotically, licking at the sides of buildings, sucking at the soft grass, kissing all the dark corners of the night. It was a hot rain, wanton and sensuous, sliding down slowly, slowly, until the tempo began to increase and it changed to a driving, pounding storm, fierce and demanding, an orgiastic beat in a steady, savage rhythm, plunging down harder and harder, moving faster and faster until it finally exploded in a burst of thunder. Suddenly, as quickly as it had started, it was over.

Lara and Philip lay in each other's arms, spent. Philip held Lara close, and he could feel the beating of her heart. He thought of a line he had once heard in a movie. *Did the earth move for you?* By God, it did. Philip thought. *If she were music, she would be Chopin's* Barcarolle *or Schumann's* Fantasy.

He could feel the soft contours of her body pressed against him, and he began to get aroused again.

"Philip . . . " Her voice was husky.

"Yes?"

"Would you like me to go with you to Milan?"

He found himself grinning. "Oh, my God, yes!"

"Good," Lara murmured. She leaned over him, and her soft hair started to trail down his lean, hard body.

It began to rain again.

When Lara finally returned to her room, she telephoned Keller. "Did I wake you up, Howard?"

"No." His voice was groggy. "I'm always up at four in the morning. What's going on there?"

Lara was bursting to tell him, but she said, "Nothing. I'm leaving for Milan."

"What? We aren't doing anything in Milan."

Oh, yes, we are, Lara thought happily.

"Did you see my messages?"

She had forgotten to look at them. Guiltily, she said, "Not yet."

"I've been hearing rumors about the casino."

"What's the problem?"

"There have been some complaints about the bidding."

"Don't worry about it. If there's any problem, Paul Martin will take care of it."

"You're the boss."

"I want you to send the plane to Milan. Have the pilots wait for me there. I'll get in touch with them at the airport."

"All right, but . . ."

"Go back to sleep."

At four o'clock in the morning, Paul Martin was wide-awake. He had left several messages on Lara's private answering machine at her apartment, but none of his calls had been returned. In the past, she had always let him know when she was going to be away. Something was happening. What was she up to? *"Be careful, my darling,"* he whispered. *"Be very careful."*

Chapter Twenty-three

In Milan, Lara and Philip Adler checked into the Antica Locanda Solferino, a charming hotel with only twelve rooms, and they spent the morning making passionate love. Afterward, they took the drive to Cernobbia and had lunch at Lake Como, at the beautiful Villa d'Este.

The concert that night was a triumph, and the greenroom at La Scala Opera House was packed with well-wishers.

Lara stood to one side, watching as Philip's fans surrounded him, touching him, adoring him, asking for autographs, handing him little gifts. Lara felt a sharp pang of jealousy. Some of the women were young and beautiful, and it seemed to Lara that all of them were obvious. An American woman in an elegant Fendi gown was saying, coyly, "If you're free tomorrow, Mr. Adler, I'm having an intimate little dinner at my villa. *Very* intimate."

Lara wanted to strangle the bitch.

Philip smiled. "Er . . . thank you, but I'm afraid I'm not free."

Another woman tried to slip Philip her hotel key. He shook his head.

Philip looked over at Lara and grinned. Women kept crowding around him.

"*Lei era magnifico, maestro!*"

"*Molto gentile da parte sua,*" Philip replied.

"*L'ho sentita suonare il anno scorso. Bravo!*"
"*Grazie.*" Philip smiled.
A woman was clutching his arm. "*Sarebbe possibile cenare insieme?*"
Philip shook his head. "*Ma non credo che sarai impossibile.*"
To Lara, it seemed to go on forever. Finally, Philip made his way over to Lara and whispered, "Let's get out of here."
"*Sì!*" Lara grinned.

They went to Biffy, the restaurant in the opera house, and the moment they walked in, the patrons, dressed in black tie for the concert, rose to their feet and began applauding. The maître d' led Philip and Lara toward a table in the center of the room. "It's such an honor to have you with us, Mr. Adler."
A complimentary bottle of champagne arrived, and they drank a toast.
"To us," Philip said warmly.
"To us."
Philip ordered two of the specialties of the house, osso buco and penne all'arrabbiata. All during supper they talked, and it was as though they had known each other forever.
They were constantly interrupted by people coming up to the table to compliment Philip and to ask for autographs.
"It's always like this, isn't it?" Lara asked.
Philip shrugged. "It goes with the territory. For every two hours you spend onstage, you spend countless more signing autographs or giving interviews."
As if to punctuate what he was saying, he stopped to sign another autograph.
"You've made this tour wonderful for me." Philip sighed. "The bad news is that I have to leave for Venice tomorrow. I'm going to miss you a lot."
"I've never been to Venice," Lara said.

Lara's jet was waiting for them at Linate Airport. When they arrived there, Philip looked at the huge jet in astonishment.
"This is *your* plane?"
"Yes. It's going to take us to Venice."
"You're going to spoil me, lady."
Lara said softly, "I intend to."
They landed in Venice thirty-five minutes later at Marco Polo Air-

port where a limousine waited to drive them the short distance to the dock. From the dock they would take a motorboat to the island of Giudecca, where the Cipriani Hotel was located.

"I arranged for two suites for us," Lara said. "I thought it would be more discreet that way."

In the motorboat on the way to the hotel, Lara asked, "How long will we be here?"

"Only one night, I'm afraid. I'm giving a recital at La Fenice, and then we head for Vienna."

The "we" gave Lara a little thrill. They had discussed it the night before. "I'd like you to stay with me as long as you can," Philip had said, "but are you sure I'm not keeping you from something more important?"

"There *is* nothing more important."

"Are you going to be all right by yourself this afternoon? I'm going to be busy rehearsing."

"I'll be fine," Lara assured him.

After they had checked into their suites, Philip took Lara in his arms. "I have to go to the theater now, but there's a lot to see here. Enjoy Venice. I'll see you later this afternoon." They kissed. It was meant to be a brief one, but it turned into a long, lingering kiss. "I'd better get out of here while I can," Philip murmured, "or I'll never be able to make it through the lobby."

"Happy rehearsal." Lara grinned.

And Philip was gone.

Lara telephoned Howard Keller.

"Where are you?" Keller demanded. "I've been trying to reach you."

"I'm in Venice."

There was a pause. "Are we buying a canal?"

"I'm checking it out." Lara laughed.

"You really should be back here," Keller said. "There's a lot going on. Young Frank Rose brought in some new plans. I like them, but I need your approval so we can get . . ."

"If you like them," Lara interrupted, "go ahead."

"You don't want to see them?" Keller's voice was filled with surprise.

"Not now, Howard."

"All right. And on the negotiations for the West Side property, I need your okay to . . ."

"You have it."
"Lara . . . are you feeling all right?"
"I've never felt better in my life."
"When are you coming home?"
"I don't know. I'll stay in touch. Good-bye, Howard."

Venice was the kind of magical city that Prospero might have created. Lara spent the rest of the morning and all afternoon exploring. She roamed through St. Mark's Square, and visited the Doge's Palace and the Bell Tower, and wandered along the crowded Riva degli Schiavoni, and everywhere she went she thought of Philip. She walked through the winding little side streets, crammed with jewelry shops and leather goods and restaurants, and stopped to buy expensive sweaters and scarves and lingerie for the secretaries at the office, and wallets and ties for Keller and some of the other men. She stopped in at a jeweler's to buy Philip a Piaget watch with a gold band.

"Would you please inscribe it 'To Philip with Love from Lara'?" Just saying his name made her miss him.

When Philip returned to the hotel, they had coffee in the verdant garden of the Cipriani.

Lara looked across at Philip and thought, *What a perfect place this would be for a honeymoon.*

"I have a present for you," Lara said. She handed him the box with the watch in it.

He opened it and stared. "My God! This must have cost a fortune. You shouldn't have, Lara."

"Don't you like it?"

"Of course I do. It's beautiful, but . . ."

"Ssh! Wear it and think of me."

"I don't need this to think of you, but thank you."

"What time do we have to leave for the theater?" Lara asked.

"Seven o'clock."

Lara glanced at Philip's new watch and said innocently, "That gives us two hours."

The theater was packed. The audience was volatile, applauding and cheering each number.

When the concert was over, Lara went back to the greenroom to join Philip. It was London and Amsterdam and Milan all over again, and the women seemed even more nubile and eager. There were at least half a dozen beautiful women in the room, and Lara wondered which one Philip would have spent the night with if she were not there.

They had supper at the storied Harry's Bar and were warmly greeted by the affable owner, Arrigo Cipriani.

"What a pleasure to see you, signore. And signorina. Please!"

He led them to a corner table. They ordered Bellinis, the specialty of the house. Philip said to Lara, "I recommend starting with the pasta e fagioli. It's the best in the world."

Later Philip had no memory of what he had eaten for dinner. He was mesmerized by Lara. He knew he was falling in love with her, and it terrified him. *I can't make a commitment*, he thought. *It's impossible. I'm a nomad.* He hated to think about the moment when she would leave him to go back to New York. He wanted to prolong their evening as long as possible.

When they had finished supper, Philip said, "There's a casino out on the Lido. Do you gamble?"

Lara laughed aloud.

"What's so funny?"

Lara thought about the hundreds of millions of dollars she gambled on her buildings. "Nothing," she said. "I'd love to go."

They took a motorboat to Lido Island. They walked past the Excelsior Hotel and went to the huge white building that housed the casino. It was filled with eager gamblers.

"Dreamers," Philip said.

Philip played roulette and within half an hour had won two thousand dollars. He turned to Lara. "I've never won before. You're my good-luck charm."

They played until 3:00 A.M., and by that time they were hungry again.

A motorboat took them back to St. Mark's Square, and they wandered through the side streets until they came to the Cantina do Mori.

"This is one of the best *bacaros* in Venice," Philip said.

Lara said, "I believe you. What's a *bacaro?*"

"It's a wine bar where they serve cicchetti—little nibbles of local delicacies."

Bottle-glass doors led to a dark, narrow space where copper pots hung from the ceiling and dishes gleamed on a long banquette.

It was dawn before they got back to their hotel. They got undressed, and Lara said, "Speaking of nibbles . . ."

* * *

Early the following morning Lara and Philip flew to Vienna.

"Going to Vienna is like going into another century," Philip explained. "There's a legend that airline pilots say, 'Ladies and gentlemen, we're on our final approach to Vienna Airport. Please make sure your seat backs and table trays are in the upright position, refrain from smoking until inside the terminal, and set your watches back one hundred years.'"

Lara laughed.

"My parents were born here. They used to talk about the old days, and it made me envious."

They were driving along the Ringstrasse, and Philip was filled with excitement, like a small boy eager to share his treasures with her.

"Vienna is the city of Mozart, Haydn, Beethoven, Brahms." He looked at Lara and grinned. "Oh, I forgot—you're an expert on classical music."

They checked into the Imperial Hotel.

"I have to go to the concert hall," Philip told Lara, "but I've decided that tomorrow we're going to take the whole day off. I'm going to show you Vienna."

"I'd like that, Philip."

He held Lara in his arms. "I wish we had more time now," he said ruefully.

"So do I."

He kissed her lightly on the forehead. "We'll make up for it tonight."

She held him close. "Promises, promises."

The concert that evening took place at the Musikverein. The recital consisted of compositions by Chopin, Schumann, and Prokofiev, and it was another triumph for Philip.

The greenroom was packed again, but this time the language was German.

"Sie waren wunderbar, Herr Adler!"

Philip smiled. *"Das ist sehr nett von Ihnen. Danke."*

"Ich bin ein grosser Anhänger von Ihnen."

Philip smiled again. *"Sie sind sehr freundlich."*

He was talking to them, but he could not take his eyes off Lara.

After the recital Lara and Philip had a late supper in the hotel. They were greeted by the maître d'.

"What an honor!" he exclaimed. "I was at the concert tonight. You were magnificent! Magnificent!"

"You're very kind," Philip said modestly.

The dinner was delicious, but they were both too excited by each other to eat. When the waiter asked, "Would you like some dessert?" Philip said quickly, "Yes." And he was looking at Lara.

His instincts told him that something was wrong. She had never been gone this long without telling him where she was. Was she deliberately avoiding him? If she was, there could only be one reason. *And I can't allow that,* Paul Martin thought.

A beam of pale moonlight streamed through the window, making soft shadows on the ceiling. Lara and Philip lay in bed, naked, watching their shadows move above their heads. The ripple of the curtains made the shadows dance, in a soft, swaying motion. The shadows came slowly together and separated and came together again, until the two became entwined, became one, and the movement of the dance became faster, and faster, a wild savage pounding, and suddenly it stopped, and there was only the gentle ripple of the curtains.

Early the following morning Philip said, "We have a whole day and an evening here. I have a lot to show you."

They had breakfast downstairs in the hotel dining room, then walked over to the Karntnerstrasse, where no cars were permitted. The shops there were filled with beautiful clothes and jewelry and antiques.

Philip hired a horse-drawn Fiaker, and they rode through the wide streets of the city along the Ring Road. They visited Schönbrunn Palace and looked at the colorful imperial coach collection. In the afternoon they got tickets for the Spanish Riding School and saw the Lipizzaner stallions. They rode the huge Ferris wheel at the Prater, and afterward Philip said, "Now we're going to sin!"

"Ooh!"

"No," Philip laughed. "I had something else in mind."

He took Lara to Demel's for its incomparable pastry and coffee.

Lara was fascinated by the mix of architecture in Vienna: beautiful baroque buildings centuries old that faced neomodern buildings.

Philip was interested in the composers. "Did you know that Franz Schubert started as a singer here, Lara? He was in the Imperial Chapel choir, and when his voice changed at seventeen, he was thrown out. That's when he decided to compose music."

They had a leisurely dinner at a small bistro, and stopped at a wine tavern in Grinzing. Afterward Philip said, "Would you like to go for a cruise on the Danube?"

"I'd love to."

It was a perfect night, with a bright full moon and a soft summer breeze. The stars were shining down. *They're shining down on us,* Lara thought, *because we're so happy.* Lara and Philip boarded one of the cruise ships, and from the ship's loudspeaker came the soft strains of "The Blue Danube." In the distance they saw a falling star.

"Quick! Make a wish," Philip said.

Lara closed her eyes and was silent for a moment.

"Did you make your wish?"

"Yes."

"What did you wish for?"

Lara looked up at him and said seriously, "I can't tell you, or it won't come true." *I'm going to make it come true,* Lara thought.

Philip leaned back and smiled at Lara. "This is perfect, isn't it?"

"It can always be this way, Philip."

"What do you mean?"

"We could get married."

And there it was, out in the open. He had been thinking of nothing else for the past few days. He was deeply in love with Lara, but he knew he could not make a commitment to her.

"Lara, that's impossible."

"Is it? Why?"

"I've explained it to you, darling. I'm almost always on tour like this. You couldn't travel with me all the time, could you?"

"No," Lara said, "but . . ."

"There you are. It would never work. Tomorrow in Paris, I'll show you . . ."

"I'm not going to Paris with you, Philip."

He thought he had misunderstood her. "What?"

Lara took a deep breath. "I'm not going to see you again."

It was like a blow to the stomach. "Why? I love you, Lara. I . . ."

"And I love you. But I'm not a groupie. I don't want to be just another one of your fans, chasing you around. You can have all those you want."

"Lara, I don't want anyone but you. But don't you see, darling, our marriage could never work. We have separate lives that are important to both of us. I would want us to be together all the time, and we couldn't be."

"That's it then, isn't it?" Lara said tightly. "I won't see you again, Philip."

"Wait. Please! Let's talk about this. Let's go to your room, and . . ."

"No, Philip. I love you very much, but I won't go on like this. It's over."

"I don't want it to be over," Philip insisted. "Change your mind."

"I can't. I'm sorry. It's all or nothing."

They were silent the rest of the way back to their hotel. When they reached the lobby, Philip said, "Why don't I come up to your room? We can talk about this and . . ."

"No, my darling. There's nothing more to talk about."

He watched Lara get into the elevator and disappear.

When Lara reached her suite, the telephone was ringing. She hurried to pick it up. "Philip . . ."

"It's Howard. I've been trying to reach you all day."

She managed to hide her disappointment. "Is anything wrong?"

"No. Just checking in. There's a lot going on around here. When do you think you'll be coming back?"

"Tomorrow," Lara said. "I'll be back in New York tomorrow." Slowly, Lara replaced the receiver.

She sat there, staring at the telephone, willing it to ring. Two hours later, it was still silent. *I made a mistake,* Lara thought miserably. *I gave him an ultimatum, and I lost him. If I had only waited . . . If only I had gone to Paris with him . . . if . . . if . . .* She tried to visualize her life without Philip. It was too painful to think about. *But we can't go on this way,* Lara thought. *I want us to belong to each other.* Tomorrow she would have to return to New York.

Lara lay down on the couch, fully dressed, the telephone by her side. She felt drained. She knew it would be impossible to get any sleep.

She slept.

In his room Philip was pacing back and forth like a caged animal. He was furious with Lara, furious with himself. He could not bear the thought of not seeing her again, not holding her in his arms. *Damn all women!* he thought. His parents had warned him. *"Your life is music. If you want to be the best, there's no room for anything else."* And until he met Lara, he had believed it. But now everything had changed. *Damn it!*

What we had was wonderful. Why did she have to destroy it? He loved her, but he knew he could never marry her.

Lara was awakened by the ringing of the telephone. She sat up the couch, groggy, and looked at the clock on the wall. It was five o'clock in the morning. Sleepily, Lara picked up the telephone.
"Howard?"
It was Philip's voice. "How would you like to get married in Paris?"

Chapter Twenty-four

The marriage of Lara Cameron to Philip Adler made headlines around the world. When Howard Keller heard the news, he went out and got drunk for the first time in his life. He had kept telling himself that Lara's infatuation with Philip Adler would pass. *Lara and I are a team. We belong together. No one can come between us.* He stayed drunk for two days, and when he sobered up, he telephoned Lara in Paris.

"If it's true," he said, "tell Philip I said he's the luckiest man who ever lived."

"It's true," Lara assured him brightly.

"You sound happy."

"I've never been happier in my life!"

"I . . . I'm pleased for you, Lara. When are you coming home?"

"Philip is giving a concert in London tomorrow, and then we'll be back in New York."

"Did you talk to Paul Martin before the wedding?"

She hesitated. "No."

"Don't you think you should do it now?"

"Yes, of course." She had been more concerned about that than she wanted to admit to herself. She was not sure how he was going to take the news of her marriage. "I'll talk to him when I get back."

"I'll sure be glad to see you. I miss you."

"I miss you, too, Howard." And it was true. He was very dear. He had always been a good and loyal friend. *I don't know what I would have done without him,* Lara thought.

When the 727 taxied up to the Butler Aviation Terminal at New York's La Guardia Airport, the press was there in full force. There were newspaper reporters and television cameras.

The airport manager led Lara and Philip into the reception office. "I can sneak you out of here," he said, "or . . ."

Lara turned to Philip. "Let's get this over with, darling. Otherwise, they'll never let us have any peace."

"You're probably right."

The press conference lasted for two hours. "Where did you two meet . . . ?"

"Have you always been interested in classical music, Mrs. Adler . . . ?"

"How long have you known each other . . . ?"

"Are you going to live in New York . . . ?"

"Will you give up your touring, Mr. Adler . . . ?"

Finally, it was over.

There were two limousines waiting for them. The second one was for luggage.

"I'm not used to traveling in this kind of style," Philip said.

Lara laughed. "You'll get used to it."

When they were in the limousine, Philip asked, "Where are we going? I have an apartment on Fifty-seventh Street . . ."

"I think you might be more comfortable at my place, darling. Look it over, and if you like it, we'll have your things moved in."

They arrived at the Cameron Plaza. Philip looked up at the huge building.

"You *own* this?"

"A few banks and I."

"I'm impressed."

Lara squeezed his arm. "Good. I want you to be."

The lobby had been freshly decorated with flowers. A half dozen employees were waiting to greet them.

"Welcome home, Mrs. Adler, Mr. Adler."

Philip looked around and said, "My God! All this is yours?"

"*Ours,* sweetheart."

The elevator took them up to the penthouse. It covered the whole forty-fifth floor. The door was opened by the butler.

"Welcome home, Mrs. Adler."

"Thank you, Simms."

Lara introduced Philip to the rest of the staff and showed him through the duplex penthouse. There was a large white drawing room, filled with antiques, a large enclosed terrace, a dining room, four master bedrooms and three staff bedrooms, six bathrooms, a kitchen, a library, and an office.

"Do you think you could be comfortable here, darling?" Lara asked.

Philip grinned. "It's a little small—but I'll manage."

In the middle of the drawing room was a beautiful new Bechstein piano. Philip walked over to it and ran his fingers over the keys.

"It's wonderful!" he said.

Lara moved to his side. "It's your wedding present."

"Really?" He was touched. He sat down at the piano and began to play.

"I just had it tuned for you." Lara listened as the cascade of notes filled the room. "Do you like it?"

"I love it! Thank you, Lara."

"You can play here to your heart's content."

Philip rose from the piano bench. "I'd better give Ellerbee a call," Philip said. "He's been trying to reach me."

"There's a telephone in the library, darling."

Lara went into her office and turned on the answering machine. There were half a dozen messages from Paul Martin. "Lara, where are you? I miss you, darling" . . . "Lara, I assume you're out of the country, or I would have heard from you" . . . "I'm worried about you, Lara. Call me . . . " Then the tone changed. "I just heard about your marriage. Is it true? Let's talk."

Philip had walked into the room. "Who's the mysterious caller?" he asked.

Lara turned. "An . . . an old friend of mine."

Philip walked up to her and put his arms around her. "Is he someone I should be jealous of?"

Lara said softly, "You don't have to be jealous of anyone in the world. You're the only man I've ever loved." *And it's true.*

Philip held her closely. "You're the only woman I've ever loved."

Later that afternoon, while Philip sat at the piano, Lara went back into her office and returned Paul Martin's telephone calls.

He came on the line almost immediately. "You're back." His voice was tight.

"Yes." She had been dreading this conversation.

"I don't mind telling you that the news was quite a shock, Lara."

"I'm sorry, Paul . . . I . . . it happened rather suddenly."

"It must have."

"Yes." She tried to read his mood.

"I thought we had something pretty good going for us. I thought it was something special."

"It was, Paul, but . . ."

"We'd better talk about it."

"Well, I . . ."

"Let's make it lunch tomorrow. Vitello's. One o'clock." It was an order.

Lara hesitated. It would be foolish to antagonize him any further. "All right, Paul. I'll be there."

The line went dead. Lara sat there worried. How angry was Paul, and was he going to do anything about it?

Chapter Twenty-five

The following morning when Lara arrived at Cameron Center, the entire staff was waiting to congratulate her.

"It's wonderful news!"

"It was such a big surprise to all of us! . . ."

"I'm sure you'll be very happy. . . ."

And on it went.

Howard Keller was waiting in Lara's office for her. He gave her a big hug. "For a lady who doesn't like classical music, you sure went and did it!"

Lara smiled. "I did, didn't I?"

"I'll have to get used to calling you Mrs. Adler."

Lara's smile faded. "I think it might be better for business reasons if I keep using Cameron, don't you?"

"Whatever you say. I'm sure glad you're back. Everything is piling up here."

Lara settled in a chair opposite Howard. "Okay, tell me what's been happening."

"Well, the West Side hotel is going to be a money-losing proposition. We have a buyer lined up from Texas who's interested in it, but I went over to the hotel yesterday. It's in terrible shape. It needs a complete refurbishing, and that's going to run into five or six million dollars."

"Has the buyer seen it yet?"

"No. I told him I'd show it to him tomorrow."

"Show it to him next week. Get some painters in there. Make it look squeaky clean. Arrange for a crowd to be in the lobby when he's there."

He grinned. "Right. Frank Rose is here with some new sketches. He's waiting in my office."

"I'll take a look at them."

"The Midland Insurance Company that was going into the new building?"

"Yes."

"They haven't signed the deal yet. They're a little shaky."

Lara made a note. "I'll talk to them about it. Next?"

"Gotham Bank's seventy-five million loan on the new project?"

"Yes?"

"They're pulling back. They think you're getting overextended."

"How much interest were they going to charge us?"

"Seventeen percent."

"Set up a meeting with them. We're going to offer to pay twenty percent."

He was looking at her, aghast. "Twenty percent? My God, Lara! No one pays twenty percent."

"I would rather be alive at twenty percent than dead at seventeen percent. Do it, Howard."

"All right."

The morning went by swiftly. At twelve-thirty Lara said, "I'm going to meet Paul Martin for lunch."

Howard looked worried. "Make sure you aren't lunch."

"What do you mean?"

"I mean he's Sicilian. They don't forgive and they don't forget."

"You're being melodramatic. Paul would never do anything to harm me."

"I hope you're right."

Paul Martin was waiting for Lara at the restaurant when she arrived. He looked thin and haggard, and there were circles under his eyes, as though he had not been sleeping well.

"Hello, Lara." He did not get up.

"Paul." She sat down across from him.

"I left some stupid messages on your answering machine. I'm sorry. I had no idea . . . " He shrugged.

"I should have let you know, Paul, but it all happened so fast."

"Yeah." He was studying her face. "You're looking great."

"Thank you."

"Where did you meet Adler?"

"In London."

"And you fell in love with him just like that?" There was a bitter undertone to his words.

"Paul, what you and I had was wonderful, but it wasn't enough for me. I needed something more than that. I needed someone to come home to every night."

He was listening, watching her.

"I would never do anything in the world to hurt you, but this just . . . just happened."

More silence.

"Please understand."

"Yeah." A wintry smile crossed his face. "I guess I have no choice, have I? What's done is done. It was just kind of a shock to read about it in the newspapers and see it on television. I thought we were closer than that."

"You're right," Lara said again. "I should have told you."

His hand reached out and caressed her chin. "I was crazy about you, Lara. I guess I still am. You were my *miracolo*. I could have given you anything in the world you wanted except what he could give you—a wedding ring. I love you enough to want you to be happy."

Lara felt a wave of relief sweep through her. "Thank you, Paul."

"When am I going to meet your husband?"

"We're giving a party next week for our friends. Will you come?"

"I'll be there. You tell him that he had better treat you right, or he'll have to answer to me."

Lara smiled. "I'll tell him."

When Lara returned to her office, Howard Keller was waiting for her. "How did the luncheon go?" he asked nervously.

"Fine. You were wrong about Paul. He behaved beautifully."

"Good. I'm glad I was wrong. Tomorrow morning I've set up some meetings for you with . . ."

"Cancel them," Lara said. "I'm staying home with my husband tomorrow. We're honeymooning for the next few days."

"I'm glad you're so happy," Howard said.

"Howard, I'm so happy it scares me. I'm afraid that I'll wake up and find this is all a dream. I never knew anyone could be this happy."

He smiled. "All right, I'll handle the meetings."

"Thank you." She kissed him on the cheek. "Philip and I are giving a party next week. We expect you there."

The party took place the following Saturday at the penthouse. There was a lavish buffet and more than a hundred guests. Lara had invited the men and women she worked with: bankers, builders, architects, construction chiefs, city officials, the city planners, and the heads of unions. Philip had invited his musician friends and music patrons and benefactors. The combination proved to be disastrous.

It wasn't that the two groups did not *try* to mix. The problem was that most of them had nothing in common. The builders were interested in construction and architecture, and the musicians were interested in music and composers.

Lara introduced a city planner to a group of musicians. The commissioner stood there, trying to follow the discussion.

"Do you know what Rossini felt about Wagner's music? One day he sat his ass on the piano keys and said, 'That's what Wagner sounds like to me.'"

"Wagner deserved it. When a fire broke out at the Ring Theater in Vienna during a performance of *Tales of Hoffmann,* four hundred people burned to death. When Wagner heard about it, he said, 'That's what they get for listening to an Offenbach operetta.'"

The commissioner hastily moved on.

Lara introduced some of Philip's friends to a group of real estate men.

"The problem," one of the men said, "is that you need thirty-five percent of the tenants signed up before you can go co-op."

"If you want my opinion, that's a pretty stupid rule."

"I agree. I'm switching to hotels. Do you know the hotels in Manhattan now are averaging two hundred dollars a room per night? Next year . . ."

The musicians moved on.

Conversations seemed to be going on in two different languages.

"The trouble with the Viennese is that they love dead composers. . . ."

"There's a new hotel going up on two parcels, between Forty-seventh and Forty-eighth streets. Chase Manhattan is financing it. . . ."

"He might not be the greatest conductor in the world, but his stick technique is *genau*. . . ."

" . . . I remember a lot of the mavens said that the 1929 stock market crash wasn't a bad thing. It would teach people to put their money in real estate. . . ."

" . . . and Horowitz wouldn't play for years because he thought his fingers were made of glass . . ."

" . . . I've seen the plans. There's going to be a classic base rising from three floors from Eighth Avenue, and inside an elliptical arcade with lobbies on three sides. . . ."

" . . . Einstein loved the piano. He used to play with Rubenstein, but Einstein kept playing off beat. Finally, Rubenstein couldn't stand it anymore, and he yelled, 'Albert, can't you count?' . . ."

" . . . Congress must have been drunk to pass the Tax Reform Act. It's going to cripple the building industry. . . ."

" . . . and at the end of the evening when Brahms left the party he said, 'If there's anyone here I've forgotten to insult, I apologize.'"

The Tower of Babel.

Paul Martin arrived alone, and Lara hurried over to the door to greet him. "I'm so glad you could come, Paul."

"I wouldn't have missed it." He looked around the room. "I want to meet Philip."

Lara took him over to where Philip was standing with a group. "Philip, this is an old friend of mine, Paul Martin."

Philip held out his hand. "I'm pleased to meet you."

The two men shook hands.

"You're a lucky man, Mr. Adler. Lara's a remarkable woman."

"That's what I keep telling him." Lara smiled.

"She doesn't have to tell me," Philip said. "I know how lucky I am."

Paul was studying him. "Do you?"

Lara could feel the sudden tension in the air. "Let me get you a cocktail," she said to Paul.

"No, thanks. Remember? I don't drink."

Lara bit her lip. "Of course. Let me introduce you to some people." She escorted him around the room, introducing him to some of the guests.

One of the musicians was saying, "Leon Fleisher is giving a recital tomorrow night. I wouldn't miss it for the world." He turned to Paul

Martin, who was standing next to Howard Keller. "Have you heard him play?"

"No."

"He's remarkable. He plays only with his left hand, of course."

Paul Martin was puzzled. "Why would he do that?"

"Fleisher developed carpal-tunnel syndrome in his right hand about ten years ago."

"But how can he give a recital with one hand?"

"Half a dozen composers wrote concertos for the left hand. There's one by Demuth, Franz Schmidt, Korngold, and a beautiful concerto by Ravel."

Some of the guests were asking Philip to play for them.

"All right. This is for my bride." He sat down at the piano and began to play a theme from a Rachmaninoff piano concerto. The room was hushed. Everyone seemed mesmerized by the lovely strains that filled the penthouse. When Philip rose, there was loud applause.

An hour later the party began to break up. When they had seen the last guest to the door, Philip said, "That was quite a party."

"You hate big parties, don't you?" Lara said.

Philip took her in his arms and grinned. "Did it show?"

"We'll only do this every ten years," Lara promised. "Philip, did you have a feeling that our guests were from two different planets?"

He put his lips to her cheek. "It doesn't matter. We have our own planet. Let's make it spin. . . ."

Chapter Twenty-six

Lara decided to work at home mornings.

"I want us to be together as much as possible," she told Philip.

Lara asked Kathy to arrange for some secretaries to be interviewed at the penthouse. Lara talked to half a dozen before Marian Bell appeared. She was in her middle twenties with soft blond hair, attractive features, and a warm personality.

"Sit down," Lara said.

"Thank you."

Lara was looking over her résumé. "You were graduated from Wellesley College?"

"Yes."

"And you have a B.A. Why do you want a job as a secretary?"

"I think I can learn a lot working for you. Whether I get this job or not, I'm a big fan of yours, Miss Cameron."

"Really? Why?"

"You're my role model. You've accomplished a lot, and you've done it on your own."

Lara was studying the young woman. "This job would mean long hours. I get up early. You'd be working at my apartment. You'd start at six in the morning."

"That wouldn't be a problem. I'm a hard worker."

Lara smiled. She liked Marian. "I'll give you a one-week trial," she said.

By the end of the week Lara knew that she had found a jewel. Marian was capable and intelligent and pleasant. Gradually, a routine was established. Unless there was an emergency, Lara spent the mornings working at the apartment. In the afternoon she would go to the office.

Each morning Lara and Philip had breakfast together and afterward Philip would go to the piano and sit in a sleeveless athletic shirt and jeans and practice for two or three hours while Lara went into her office and dictated to Marian. Sometimes Philip would play old Scottish tunes for Lara: "Annie Laurie," and "Comin' Through the Rye." She was touched. They would have lunch together.

"Tell me what your life was like in Glace Bay," Philip said.

"It would take at least five minutes." Lara smiled.

"No, I'm serious. I really want to know."

She talked about the boardinghouse, but she could not bring herself to talk about her father. She told Philip the story of Charles Cohn, and Philip said, "Good for him. I'd like to meet him one day."

"I'm sure you will."

Lara told him about her experience with Sean MacAllister, and Philip said, "That bastard! I'd like to kill him!" He held Lara close and said, "No one is ever going to hurt you again."

Philip was working on a concerto. She would hear him play three notes at a time, over and over and then move on, practicing slowly and picking up the tempo until the different phrases finally flowed into one.

In the beginning Lara would walk into the drawing room while Philip was playing and interrupt him.

"Darling, we're invited to Long Island for the weekend. Would you like to go?"

Or, "I have theater tickets for the new Neil Simon play."

Or, "Howard Keller would like to take us out to dinner Saturday night."

Philip had tried to be patient. Finally, he said, "Lara, please don't interrupt me while I'm at the piano. It breaks my concentration."

"I'm sorry," Lara said. "But I don't understand why you practice every day. You're not giving a concert now."

"I practice every day so I *can* give a concert. You see, my darling, when you put up a building and a mistake is made, it can be corrected. You can change the plans or you can redo the plumbing or the lighting or whatever. But at a recital there is no second chance. You're live in front of an audience and every note has to be perfect."

"I'm sorry," Lara apologized. "I understand."

Philip took her in his arms. "There's the old joke about a man in New York carrying a violin case. He was lost. He stopped a stranger and said, 'How do you get to Carnegie Hall?' 'Practice,' the stranger said, 'practice.'"

Lara laughed. "Go back to your piano. I'll leave you alone."

She sat in her office listening to the faint strains of Philip playing and she thought, *I'm so lucky. Thousands of women would envy me sitting here listening to Philip Adler play.*

She just wished he did not have to practice so often.

They both enjoyed playing backgammon, and in the evening, after dinner, they would sit in front of the fireplace and have mock-fierce contests. Lara treasured those moments of being alone with him.

The Reno casino was getting ready to open. Six months earlier Lara had had a meeting with Jerry Townsend. "I want them to read about this opening in Timbuktu," Lara said. "I'm flying in the chef from Maxim's for the opening. I want you to get me the hottest talent available. Start with Frank Sinatra and work your way down. I want the invitation list to include the top names in Hollywood, New York, and Washington. I want people fighting to get on that list."

Now, as Lara looked it over, she said, "You've done a good job. How many turndowns have we had?"

"A couple dozen," Townsend said. "That's not bad from a list of six hundred."

"Not bad at all," Lara agreed.

Keller telephoned Lara in the morning. "Good news," he said. "I got a call from the Swiss bankers. They're flying in to meet with you tomorrow to discuss the joint venture."

"Great," Lara said. "Nine o'clock, my office."

"I'll set it up."

At dinner that evening Philip said, "Lara, I'm doing a recording session tomorrow. You've never been to one, have you?"

"No."

"Would you like to come and watch?"

Lara hesitated, thinking about the meeting with the Swiss. "Of course," she said.

Lara telephoned Keller. "Start the meeting without me. I'll get there as soon as I can."

The recording studio was located on West Thirty-fourth Street, in a large warehouse filled with electronic equipment. There were 130 musicians seated in the room and a glass-enclosed control booth where the sound engineers worked. It seemed to Lara that the recording was going very slowly. They kept stopping and starting again. During one of the breaks she telephoned Keller.

"Where are you?" he demanded. "I'm stalling but they want to talk to you."

"I'll be there in an hour or two," she said. "Keep them talking."

Two hours later the recording session was still going on.

Lara telephoned Keller again.

"I'm sorry, Howard, I can't leave. Have them come back tomorrow."

"What's so important?" Keller demanded.

"My husband," Lara said. And she replaced the receiver.

When they returned to the apartment, Lara said, "We're going to Reno next week."

"What's in Reno?"

"It's the opening of the hotel and casino. We'll fly down on Wednesday."

Philip's voice was filled with distress. "Damn!"

"What's the matter?"

"I'm sorry, darling, I can't."

She was staring at him. "What do you mean?"

"I thought I had mentioned it. I'm leaving on a tour Monday."

"What are you talking about?"

"Ellerbee has booked me on a six-week tour. I'm going to Australia and . . ."

"Australia?"

"Yes. Then Japan and Hong Kong."

"You can't, Philip. I mean . . . why are you doing this? You don't have to. I want to be with you."

"Well, come with me, Lara. I'd love that."

"You know I can't. Not now. There's too much happening here." Lara said miserably, "I don't want you to leave me."

"I don't want to. But, darling, I warned you before we were married that this is what my life is about."

"I know," Lara said, "but that was before. Now it's different. Everything has changed."

"Nothing has changed," Philip said gently, "except that I'm absolutely crazy about you, and when I go away, I'll miss you like the devil."

There was nothing Lara could say to that.

Philip was gone, and Lara had never known such loneliness. In the middle of a meeting she would suddenly think about Philip and her heart would melt.

She wanted him to go on with his career, but she needed him with her. She thought of the wonderful times they had together, and of his arms around her, and his warmth and gentleness. She had never known she could love anyone so much. Philip telephoned her every day, but somehow it made the loneliness worse.

"Where are you, darling?"

"I'm still in Tokyo."

"How's the tour going?"

"Beautifully. I miss you."

"I miss you, too." Lara could not tell him how much she missed him.

"I leave for Hong Kong tomorrow and then . . ."

"I wish you'd come home." She regretted it the moment she said it.

"You know I can't."

There was a silence. "Of course not."

They talked for half an hour and when Lara put the receiver down, she was lonelier than ever. The time differences were maddening. Sometimes her Tuesday would be his Wednesday, and he would call in the middle of the night or in the early hours of the morning.

"How's Philip?" Keller asked.

"Fine. Why does he do it, Howard?"

"Why does he do what?"

"This tour of his. He doesn't have to do it. I mean, he certainly doesn't need the money."

"Whoa. I'm sure he's not doing it for the money. It's what he does, Lara."

The same words that Philip had used. She understood it intellectually, but not emotionally.

"Lara," Keller said, "you only married the man—you don't own him."

"I don't want to own him. I was just hoping that I was more important to him than . . ." She stopped herself in mid-sentence. "Never mind. I know I'm being silly."

Lara telephoned William Ellerbee.

"Are you free for lunch today?" Lara asked.

"I can make myself free," Ellerbee said. "Is anything wrong?"

"No, no. I just thought we should have a talk."

They met at Le Cirque.

"Have you talked to Philip lately?" Ellerbee asked.

"I talk to him every day."

"He's having a successful tour."

"Yes."

Ellerbee said, "Frankly, I never thought Philip would get married. He's like a priest—dedicated to what he does."

"I know"—Lara hesitated—"but don't you think he's traveling too much?"

"I don't understand."

"Philip has a home now. There's no reason for him to be running all over the world." She saw the expression on Ellerbee's face. "Oh, I don't mean he should just stay in New York. I'm sure you could arrange concerts for him in Boston, Chicago, Los Angeles. You know . . . where he wouldn't have to travel so far from home."

Ellerbee said carefully, "Have you discussed this with Philip?"

"No. I wanted to talk to you first. It *would* be possible, wouldn't it? I mean, Philip doesn't need the money, not anymore."

"Mrs. Adler, Philip makes thirty-five thousand dollars a performance. Last year he was on tour for forty weeks."

"I understand, but . . ."

"Do you have any idea how few pianists make it to the top, or how hard they have to struggle to get there? There are thousands of pianists out there, playing their fingers to the bone, and there are only about four or five superstars. Your husband is one of them. You don't know much about the concert world. The competition is murderous. You can go to a recital and see a soloist on the stage dressed in tails, looking prosperous and glamorous, but when he gets off that stage, he can barely afford to pay his rent or buy a decent meal. It took Philip a long time to become a world class pianist. Now you're asking me to take that away from him."

"No, I'm not. I'm merely suggesting . . ."

"What you're suggesting would destroy his career. You don't really want to do that, do you?"

"Of course not, " Lara said. She hesitated. "I understand that you get fifteen percent of what Philip earns."

"That's right."

"I wouldn't want you to lose anything if Philip gave fewer concerts," Lara said carefully. "I'd be glad to make up the difference and . . ."

"Mrs. Adler, I think this is something you should discuss with Philip. Shall we order?"

Chapter Twenty-seven

Liz Smith's column read: "IRON BUTTERFLY ABOUT TO GET HER WINGS CLIPPED . . . What beautiful real estate tycoon is about to hit her penthouse roof when she learns that a book about her, written by a former employee, is going to be published by Candlelight Press? The word is that it's going to be hot! Hot! Hot!"

Lara slammed the newspaper down. It had to be Gertrude Meeks, the secretary she had fired! Lara sent for Jerry Townsend. "Have you seen Liz Smith's column this morning?"

"Yes, I just read it. There isn't much we can do about it, boss. If you . . ."

"There's a lot we can do. All my employees sign an agreement that they will not write anything about me during or after their employment here. Gertrude Meeks has no right to do this. I'm going to sue the publisher for all he's worth."

Jerry Townsend shook his head. "I wouldn't do that."

"Why not?"

"Because it will create a lot of unfavorable publicity. If you let it ride, it becomes a small wind that will blow over. If you try to stop it, it will become a hurricane."

She listened, unimpressed. "Find out who owns the company," Lara ordered.

One hour later Lara was speaking on the phone to Henry Seinfeld, the owner and publisher of Candlelight Press.

"This is Lara Cameron. I understand you intend to publish a book about me."

"You read the Liz Smith item, huh? Yes, it's true, Miss Cameron."

"I want to warn you that if you publish the book, I'm going to sue you for invasion of privacy."

The voice at the other end of the phone said, "I think perhaps you should check with your attorney. You're a public figure, Miss Cameron. You have no right of privacy. And according to Gertrude Meeks's manuscript, you're quite a colorful character."

"Gertrude Meeks signed a paper forbidding her to write anything about me."

"Well, that's between you and Gertrude. You can sue her . . ."

But by then, of course, the book would be out.

"I don't want it published. If I can make it worth your while not to publish it . . ."

"Hold on. I think you're treading on dangerous ground. I would suggest that we terminate this conversation. Good-bye." The line went dead.

Damn him! Lara sat there thinking. She sent for Howard Keller.

"What do you know about Candlelight Press?"

He shrugged. "They're a small outfit. They do exploitation books. They did a hatchet job on Cher, Madonna . . ."

"Thanks. That's all."

Howard Keller had a headache. It seemed to him that he was getting a lot of headaches lately. Not enough sleep. He was under pressure, and he felt that things were moving too rapidly. He had to find a way to slow Lara down. *Maybe this was a hunger headache.* He buzzed his secretary.

"Bess, order some lunch in for me, would you?"

There was a silence.

"Bess?"

"Are you joking, Mr. Keller?"

"Joking? No, why?"

"You just had your lunch."

Keller felt a chill go through him.

"But if you're still hungry . . ."

"No, no." He remembered now. He had had a salad and a roast beef sandwich and . . . *My God,* he thought, *what's happening to me?*

"Just kidding, Bess," he said. *Who am I kidding?*

* * *

The opening of the Cameron Palace in Reno was a smash. The hotel was fully booked, and the casino was crowded with players. Lara had spared no expense to see that the invited celebrities were well taken care of. Everyone was there. *There's only one person missing.* Lara thought. Philip. He had sent an enormous bouquet of flowers with a note: "You're the music in my life. I adore you and miss you. Hub."

Paul Martin arrived. He came up to Lara. "Congratulations. You've outdone yourself."

"Thanks to you, Paul. I couldn't have done it without you."

He was looking around. "Where's Philip?"

"He couldn't be here. He's on tour."

"He's out playing piano somewhere? This is a big night for you, Lara. He should be at your side."

Lara smiled. "He really wanted to be."

The manager of the hotel came up to Lara. "This is quite a night, isn't it? The hotel is fully booked for the next three months."

"Let's keep it that way, Donald."

Lara had hired a Japanese and a Brazilian agent to bring in big players from abroad. She had spent a million dollars on each of the luxury suites, but it was going to pay off.

"You've got a gold mine here, Miss Cameron," the manager said. He looked around. "By the way, where's your husband? I've been looking forward to meeting him."

"He couldn't be here," Lara said. *He's out playing the piano somewhere.*

The entertainment was brilliant, but Lara was the star of the evening. Sammy Cahn had written special lyrics for "My Kind of Town." It went, "My kind of gal, Lara is . . ." She got up to make a speech, and there was enthusiastic applause. Everyone wanted to meet her, to touch her. The press was there in full force, and Lara gave interviews for television, radio, and the press. It all went well until the interviewers asked, "Where's your husband tonight?" And Lara found herself getting more and more upset. *He should have been at my side. The concert could have waited.* But she smiled sweetly and said, "Philip was so disappointed he couldn't be here."

When the entertainment was over, there was dancing. Paul Martin walked up to Lara's table. "Shall we?"

Lara rose and stepped into his arms.

"How does it feel owning all this?" Paul asked.

"It feels wonderful. Thanks for all your help."

"What are friends for? I notice that you have some heavyweight gamblers here. Be careful with them, Lara. Some of them are going to lose big, and you have to make them feel like they're winners. Get them a new car or girls or anything that will make them feel important."

"I'll remember," Lara said.

"It's good to hold you again," Paul said.

"Paul . . ."

"I know. Do you remember what I said about your husband taking good care of you?"

"Yes."

"He doesn't seem to be doing a very good job."

"Philip wanted to be here," Lara said defensively. And even as she said it, she thought, *Did he really?*

He telephoned her late that night, and the sound of his voice made her twice as lonely.

"Lara, I've been thinking about you all day, darling. How did the opening go?"

"Wonderfully. I wish you could have been here, Philip."

"So do I. I miss you like crazy."

Then why aren't you here with me? "I miss you, too. Hurry home."

Howard Keller walked into Lara's office carrying a thick manila envelope.

"You're not going to like this," Keller said.

"What's up?"

Keller laid the envelope on Lara's desk. "This is a copy of Gertrude Meeks's manuscript. Don't ask me how I got hold of it. We could both go to jail."

"Have you read it?"

He nodded. "Yes."

"And?"

"I think you'd better read it yourself. She wasn't even working here when some of these things happened. She must have done a lot of digging."

"Thanks, Howard."

Lara waited until he left the office; then she pressed down the key on the intercom. "No calls."

She opened the manuscript and began to read.

It was devastating. It was a portrait of a scheming, domineering woman who had clawed her way to the top. It depicted her temper tantrums and her imperious manner with her employees. It was mean-spirited, filled with nasty little anecdotes. What the manuscript left out was Lara's independence and courage, her talent and vision and generosity. She went on reading.

" . . . One of the Iron Butterfly's tricks was to schedule her business meetings early on the first morning of negotiations, so that the others were jet-lagged and Cameron was fresh.

" . . . At a meeting with the Japanese, they were served tea with Valium in it, while Lara Cameron drank coffee with Ritalin, a stimulant that speeds up the thought process.

" . . . At a meeting with some German bankers, they were served coffee with Valium, while she drank tea with Ritalin.

" . . . When Lara Cameron was negotiating for the Queens property and the community board turned her down, she got them to change their mind by making up a story that she had a young daughter who was going to live in one of the buildings . . ."

" . . . When tenants refused to leave the building at the Dorchester Apartments, Lara Cameron filled it with homeless people. . . ."

Nothing had been left out. When Lara finished reading it, she sat at her desk for a long time, motionless. She sent for Howard Keller.

"I want you to run a Dun and Bradstreet on Henry Seinfeld. He owns Candlelight Press."

"Right."

He was back fifteen minutes later. "Seinfeld has a D–C rating."

"Which means?"

"That's the lowest rating there is. A fourth-line credit rating is poor, and he's four notches below that. A good stiff wind would blow him over. He lives from book to book. One flop and he's out of business."

"Thanks, Howard." She telephoned Terry Hill, her attorney.

"Terry, how would you like to be a book publisher?"

"What did you have in mind?"

"I want you to buy Candlelight Press in your name. It's owned by Henry Seinfeld."

"That should be no problem. How much do you want to pay?"

"Try to buy him out for five hundred thousand. If you have to, go to a million. Make sure that the deal includes all the literary properties he owns. Keep my name out of it."

* * *

The offices of Candlelight Press were downtown in an old building on Thirty-fourth Street. Henry Seinfeld's quarters consisted of a small secretarial office and a slightly larger office for himself.

Seinfeld's secretary said, "There's a Mr. Hill to see you, Mr. Seinfeld."

"Send him in."

Terry Hill had called earlier that morning.

He walked into the shabby little office. Seinfeld was sitting behind the desk.

"What can I do for you, Mr. Hill?"

"I'm representing a German publishing company that might be interested in buying your company."

Seinfeld took his time lighting a cigar. "My company's not for sale," he said.

"Oh, that's too bad. We're trying to break into the American market, and we like your operation."

"I've built this company up from scratch," Seinfeld said. "It's like my baby. I'd hate to part with it."

"I understand how you feel," the lawyer said sympathetically. "We'd be willing to give you five hundred thousand dollars for it."

Seinfeld almost choked on his cigar. "Five hundred? Hell, I've got one book coming out that's going to be worth a million dollars alone. No, sir. Your offer's an insult."

"My offer's a gift. You have no assets, and you're over a hundred thousand dollars in debt. I checked. Tell you what I'll do. I'll go up to six hundred thousand. That's my final offer."

"I'd never forgive myself. Now, if you could see your way clear to going to seven . . ."

Terry Hill rose to his feet. "Good-bye, Mr. Seinfeld. I'll find another company."

He started toward the door.

"Wait a minute," Seinfeld said. "Let's not be hasty. The fact is, my wife's been after me to retire. Maybe this would be a good time."

Terry Hill walked over to the desk and pulled a contract out of his pocket. "I have a check here for six hundred thousand dollars. Just sign where the X is."

Lara sent for Keller.

"We just bought Candlelight Press."

"Great. What do you want to do with it?"

"First of all, kill Gertrude Meeks's book. See that it doesn't get published. There are plenty of ways to keep stalling. If she sues to get her rights back, we can tie her up in court for years."

"Do you want to fold the company?"

"Of course not. Put someone in to run it. We'll keep it as a tax loss."

When Keller returned to his office, he said to his secretary, "I want to give you a letter. Jack Hellman, Hellman Realty. Dear Jack, I discussed your offer with Miss Cameron, and we feel that it would be unwise to go into your venture at this time. However, we want you to know that we would be interested in any future . . ."

His secretary had stopped taking notes.

Keller looked up. "Do you have that?"

She was staring at him. "Mr. Keller?"

"Yes."

"You dictated this letter yesterday."

Keller swallowed. "What?"

"It's already gone out in the mail."

Howard Keller tried to smile. "I guess I'm on overload."

At four o'clock that afternoon Keller was being examined by Dr. Seymour Bennett.

"You seem to be in excellent shape," Dr. Bennett said. "Physically, there's nothing wrong with you at all."

"What about these lapses of memory?"

"How long since you've had a vacation, Howard?"

Keller tried to think. "I guess it's been quite a few years," he said. "We've been pretty busy."

Dr. Bennett smiled. "There you are. You're on overload." *That word again.* "This is more common than you think. Go somewhere where you can relax for a week or two. Get business off your mind. When you come back, you'll feel like a new man."

Keller stood up, relieved.

Keller went to see Lara in her office. "Could you spare me for a week?"

"About as easily as I can spare my right arm. What did you have in mind?"

"The doctor thinks I should take a little vacation, Lara. To tell you the truth, I've been having some problems with my memory."

She was watching him, concerned. "Anything serious?"

"No, not really. It's just annoying. I thought I might go to Hawaii for a few days."

"Take the jet."

"No, no, you'll be using it. I'll fly commercial."

"Charge everything to the company."

"Thanks. I'll check in every . . ."

"No, you won't. I want you to forget about the office. Just take care of yourself. I don't want anything to happen to you."

I hope he's all right, Lara thought. *He's got to be all right.*

Philip telephoned the next day. When Marian Bell said, "Mr. Adler is calling from Taipei," Lara hurriedly picked up the telephone.

"Philip . . . ?"

"Hello, darling. There's been a phone strike. I've been trying to reach you for hours. How do you feel?"

Lonely. "Wonderful. How is the tour going?"

"It's the usual. I miss you."

In the background Lara could hear music and voices.

"Where are you?"

"Oh, they're giving a little party for me. You know how it is."

Lara could hear the sound of a woman laughing. "Yes, I know how it is."

"I'll be home Wednesday."

"Philip?"

"Yes?"

"Nothing, darling. Hurry home."

"I will. Good-bye."

She replaced the receiver. What was he going to do after the party? Who was the woman? She was filled with a sense of jealousy so strong that it almost smothered her. She had never been jealous of anyone in her life.

Everything is so perfect, Lara thought. *I don't want to lose it. I can't lose it.*

She lay awake thinking about Philip and what he was doing.

Howard Keller was stretched out on Kona Beach at a small hotel on the big island of Hawaii. The weather had been ideal. He had gone swimming every day. He had gotten a tan, played some golf, and had daily massages. He was completely relaxed and had never felt better. *Dr. Bennett was right,* he thought. *Overload. I'm going to have to slow down a little when I get back.* The truth was that the episodes of memory loss had frightened him more than he wanted to admit.

Finally, it was time to return to New York. He took a midnight flight back and was in Manhattan at four o'clock in the afternoon. He went directly to the office. His secretary was there, smiling. "Welcome back, Mr. Keller. You look great."

"Thank you . . ." He stood there, and his face drained of color.

He could not remember her name.

Chapter Twenty-eight

Philip arrived home Wednesday afternoon, and Lara took the limousine to the airport to meet him. Philip stepped off the plane, and the image of Lochinvar instantly sprang to Lara's mind.

My God, but he's handsome! She ran into his arms.

"I've missed you," she said, hugging him.

"I've missed you, too, darling."

"How much?"

He held his thumb and forefinger half an inch apart. "This much."

"You beast," she said. "Where's your luggage?"

"It's coming."

One hour later they were back at the apartment. Marian Bell opened the door for them. "Welcome back, Mr. Adler."

"Thanks, Marian." He looked around. "I feel as though I've been away for a year."

"Two years," Lara said. She started to add, "Don't ever leave me again," and bit her lip.

"Can I do anything for you, Mrs. Adler?" Marian asked.

"No. We're fine. You can run along now. I'll dictate some letters in the morning. I won't be going into the office today."

"Very well. Good-bye." Marian left.

"Sweet girl," Philip said.

"Yes, isn't she?" Lara moved into Philip's arms. "Now show me how much you missed me."

Lara stayed away from the office for the next three days. She wanted to be with Philip, to talk to him, touch him, assure herself that he was real. They had breakfast in the morning, and while Lara dictated to Marian, Philip was at the piano practicing.

At lunch on the third day Lara told Philip about the casino opening. "I wish you could have been there, darling. It was fantastic."

"I'm so sorry I missed it."

He's out playing the piano somewhere. "Well, you'll have your chance next month. The mayor is giving me the keys to the city."

Philip said unhappily, "Darling, I'm afraid I'm going to have to miss that, too."

Lara froze. "What do you mean?"

"Ellerbee's booked me for another tour. I leave for Germany in three weeks."

"You can't!" Lara said.

"The contracts have already been signed. There's nothing I can do about it."

"You just got back. How can you go away again so soon?"

"It's an important tour, darling."

"And our marriage isn't important?"

"Lara . . ."

"You don't have to go," Lara said angrily. "I want a husband, not a part-time . . ."

Marian Bell came into the room carrying some letters. "Oh, I'm sorry. I didn't mean to interrupt. I have these letters ready for you to sign."

"Thank you," Lara said stiffly. "I'll call you when I need you."

"Yes, Miss Cameron."

They watched Marian retreat to her office.

"I know you have to give concerts," Lara said, "but you don't have to give them this often. It's not as though you were some kind of traveling salesman."

"No, it isn't, is it?" His tone was cool.

"Why don't you stay here for the ceremony and then go on your tour?"

"Lara, I know that it's important to you, but you must understand that my concert tours are important to me. I'm very proud of you and what you're doing, but I want you to be proud of me."

"I am," Lara said. "Forgive me, Philip, I just . . ." She was trying hard not to cry.

"I know, darling." He took her in his arms. "We'll work it out. When I come back, we'll take a long vacation together."

A vacation's impossible, Lara thought. *There are too many projects in the works.*

"Where are you going this time, Philip?"

"I'll be going to Germany, Norway, Denmark, England, and then back here."

Lara took a deep breath. "I see."

"I wish you could come with me, Lara. It's very lonely out there without you."

She thought of the laughing lady. "Is it?" She shook herself out of her mood and managed to smile. "I'll tell you what. Why don't you take the jet? It will make it more comfortable for you."

"Are you sure you're . . . ?"

"Absolutely. I'll manage without it until you're back."

"There's no one in the world like you," Philip said.

Lara rubbed a finger slowly along his cheek. "Remember that."

Philip's tour was a huge success. In Berlin the audiences went wild and the reviews were ecstatic.

Afterward the greenrooms were always crowded with eager fans, most of them female:

"I've traveled three hundred miles to hear you play . . ."

"I have a little castle not far from here, and I was wondering . . ."

"I've prepared a midnight supper just for the two of us . . ."

Some of them were rich and beautiful, and most of them were very willing. But Philip was in love. He called Lara after the concert in Denmark. "I miss you."

"I miss you, too, Philip. How did the concert go?"

"Well, no one walked out while I was playing."

Lara laughed. "That's a good sign. I'm right in the middle of a meeting now, darling. I'll call you at your hotel in an hour."

Philip said, "I won't be going right to the hotel, Lara. The manager of the concert hall is giving a dinner party for me and . . ."

"Oh? Really? Does he have a beautiful daughter?" She regretted it the moment the words were out.

"What?"

"Nothing. I have to go now. I'll talk to you later."

She hung up and turned to the men in the office. Keller was watching her. "Is everything all right?"

"Fine," Lara said lightly. She found it difficult to concentrate on the meeting. She visualized Philip at the party, beautiful women handing him their hotel keys. She was consumed with jealousy, and she hated herself for it.

The mayor's ceremony honoring Lara was a standing-room-only event. The press was out in force.

"Could we get a shot of you and your husband together?"

And Lara was forced to say, "He wanted so much to be here . . ."

Paul Martin was there.

"He's gone again, huh?"

"He really wanted to be here, Paul."

"Bullshit! This is a big honor for you. He should be at your side. What the hell kind of husband is he? Someone should have a talk with him!"

That night she lay in bed alone, unable to sleep. Philip was ten thousand miles away. The conversation with Paul Martin ran through Lara's mind. *"What the hell kind of husband is he? Someone should have a talk with him!"*

When Philip returned from Europe, he seemed happy to be home. He brought Lara an armload of gifts. There was an exquisite porcelain figurine from Denmark, lovely dolls from Germany, silk blouses, and a gold purse from England. In the purse was a diamond bracelet.

"It's lovely," Lara said. "Thank you, darling."

The next morning Lara said to Marian Bell, "I'm going to work at home all day."

Lara sat in her office dictating to Marian, and from the drawing room she could hear the sounds of Philip at the piano. *Our life is so perfect like this,* Lara thought. *Why does Philip want to spoil it?*

William Ellerbee telephoned Philip. "Congratulations," he said. "I hear the tour went wonderfully."

"It did. The Europeans are great audiences."

"I got a call from the management at Carnegie Hall. They have an unexpected opening a week from Friday, on the seventeenth. They would like to book you for a recital. Are you interested?"

"Very much."

"Good. I'll work out the arrangements. By the way," Ellerbee said, "are you thinking of cutting back on your concerts?"

Philip was taken aback. "Cutting back? No. Why?"

"I had a talk with Lara, and she indicated that you might want to just tour the United States. Perhaps it would be best if you talked to her and . . ."

Philip said, "I will. Thank you."

Philip replaced the receiver and walked into Lara's office. She was dictating to Marian.

"Would you excuse us?" Philip asked.

Marian smiled. "Certainly." She left the room.

Philip turned to Lara. "I just had a call from William Ellerbee. Did you talk to him about my cutting down on foreign tours?"

"I might have mentioned something like that, Philip. I thought it might be better for both of us if . . ."

"Please, don't do that again," Philip said. "You know how much I love you. But apart from our lives together, you have a career and I have a career. Let's make a rule. I won't interfere in yours, and you won't interfere in mine. Is that fair enough?"

"Of course, it is," Lara said. "I'm sorry, Philip. It's just that I miss you so much when you're away." She went into his arms. "Forgive me?"

"It's forgiven and forgotten."

Howard Keller came to the penthouse to bring Lara contracts to sign. "How's everything going?"

"Beautifully," Lara said.

"The wandering minstrel is home?"

"Yes."

"So music is your life now, huh?"

"The musician is my life. You have no idea how wonderful he is, Howard."

"When are you coming into the office? We need you."

"I'll come in a few days."

Keller nodded. "Okay."

They began to examine the papers he had brought.

* * *

The following morning Terry Hill telephoned. "Lara, I just received a call from the Gaming Commission in Reno," the attorney said. "There's going to be a hearing on your casino license."

"Why?" Lara asked.

"There have been some allegations that the bidding was rigged. They want you to go there and testify on the seventeenth."

"How serious is this?" Lara asked.

The lawyer hesitated. "Are you aware of any irregularities in the bidding?"

"No, of course not."

"Then you have nothing to worry about. I'll fly to Reno with you."

"What happens if I don't go?"

"They'll subpoena you. It would look better if you went on your own."

"All right."

Lara telephoned Paul Martin's private number at the office. He picked up the phone immediately.

"Lara?"

"Yes, Paul."

"You haven't used this number in a long time."

"I know. I'm calling about Reno . . ."

"I heard."

"Is there a real problem?"

He laughed. "No. The losers are upset that you beat them to it."

"Are you sure it's all right, Paul?" She hesitated. "We did discuss the other bids."

"Believe me, it's done all the time. Anyway, they have no way of proving that. Don't worry about a thing."

"All right. I won't."

She replaced the receiver and sat there, worried.

At lunch Philip said, "By the way, they offered me a concert at Carnegie Hall. I'm going to do it."

"Wonderful." Lara smiled. "I'll buy a new dress. When is it?"

"The seventeenth."

Lara's smile faded. "Oh."

"What's the matter?"

"I'm afraid I won't be able to be there, darling. I have to be in Reno. I'm so sorry."

Philip put his hands over hers. "Our timing seems to be off, doesn't it? Oh, well. Don't worry. There will be plenty more recitals."

Lara was in her office at Cameron Center. Howard Keller had called her at home that morning.

"I think you'd better get down here," he had said. "We have a few problems."

"I'll be there in an hour."

They were in the middle of a meeting. "A couple of deals have gone sour," Keller told her. "The insurance company that was moving into our building in Houston has gone bankrupt. They were our only tenant."

"We'll find someone else," Lara said.

"It's not going to be that simple. The Tax Reform Act is hurting us. Hell, it's hurting everybody. Congress has wiped out corporate tax shelters and eliminated most deductions. I think we're heading for a goddamned recession. The savings and loan companies we're dealing with are in trouble. Drexel Burnham Lambert may go out of business. Junk bonds are turning into land mines. We're having problems with half a dozen of our buildings. Two of them are only half finished. Without financing, those costs are going to be eating us up."

Lara sat there, thinking. "We can handle it. Sell whatever properties we have to to keep up our mortgage payments."

"The bright side of it," Keller said, "is that we have a cash flow from Reno that's bringing us in close to fifty million a year."

Lara said nothing.

On Friday the seventeenth Lara left for Reno. Philip rode with her to the airport. Terry Hill was waiting at the plane.

"When will you be back?" Philip said.

"Probably tomorrow. This shouldn't take long."

"I'll miss you," Philip said.

"I'll miss you, too, darling."

He stood there watching the plane taking off. *I am going to miss her,* Philip thought. *She's the most fantastic woman in the world.*

In the offices of the Nevada Gaming Commission, Lara was facing the same group of men she had met with during the application for a casino license. This time, however, they were not as friendly.

Lara was sworn in, and a court reporter took down her testimony.

The chairman said, "Miss Cameron, some rather disturbing allegations have been made concerning the licensing of your casino."

"What kind of allegations?" Terry Hill demanded.

"We'll come to those in due course." The chairman turned his attention back to Lara. "We understood that this was your first experience in acquiring a gambling casino."

"That's right. I told you that at the first hearing."

"How did you arrive at the bid you put in? I mean . . . how did you come to that precise figure?"

Terry Hill interrupted. "I'd like to know the reason for the question."

"In a moment, Mr. Hill. Will you permit your client to answer the question?"

Terry Hill looked at Lara and nodded.

Lara said, "I had my comptroller and accountants give me an estimate on how much we could afford to bid, and we figured in a small profit we could add to that, and that became my bid."

The chairman scanned the paper in front of him. "Your bid was five million dollars more than the next highest bid."

"Was it?"

"You weren't aware of that at the time you made your bid?"

"No. Of course not."

"Miss Cameron, are you acquainted with Paul Martin?"

Terry Hill interrupted. "I don't see the relevance of this line of questioning."

"We'll come to that in a moment. Meanwhile, I'd like Miss Cameron to answer the question."

"I have no objection," Lara said. "Yes. I know Paul Martin."

"Have you ever had any business dealings with him?"

Lara hesitated. "No. He's just a friend."

"Miss Cameron, are you aware that Paul Martin is reputed to be involved with the Mafia, that . . ."

"Objection. It's hearsay, and it has no place in this record."

"Very well, Mr. Hill. I'll withdraw that. Miss Cameron, when was the last time you saw or talked to Paul Martin?"

Lara hesitated. "I'm not sure, exactly. To be perfectly candid, since I got married, I've seen very little of Mr. Martin. We run into each other at parties occasionally, that's all."

"But it wasn't your habit to speak regularly with him on the telephone?"

"Not after my marriage, no."

"Did you ever have any discussions with Paul Martin regarding this casino?"

Lara looked over at Terry Hill. He nodded. "Yes, I believe that after I won the bid for it, he called to congratulate me. And then once again after I got the license to operate the casino."

"But you did not talk to him at any other time?"

"No."

"I'll remind you that you're under oath, Miss Cameron."

"Yes."

"You're aware of the penalty for perjury?"

"Yes."

He held up a sheet of paper. "I have here a list of fifteen telephone calls between you and Paul Martin, made during the time sealed bids were being submitted for the casino."

Chapter Twenty-nine

Most soloists are dwarfed by the huge twenty-eight-hundred-seat space at Carnegie Hall. There are not many musicians who can fill the prestigious hall, but on Friday night it was packed. Philip Adler walked out onto the vast stage to the thunderous applause of the audience. He sat down at the piano, paused a moment, then began to play. The program consisted of Beethoven sonatas. Over the years he had disciplined himself to concentrate only on the music. But on this night Philip's thoughts drifted away to Lara and their problems, and for a split second his fingers started to fumble, and he broke out in a cold sweat. It happened so swiftly that the audience did not notice.

There was loud applause at the end of the first part of the recital. At intermission Philip went to his dressing room.

The concert manager said, "Wonderful, Philip. You held them spellbound. Can I get anything for you?"

"No, thanks." Philip closed the door. He wished the recital were over. He was deeply disturbed by the situation with Lara. He loved her a great deal, and he knew she loved him, but they seemed to have come to an impasse. There had been a lot of tension between them before Lara had left for Reno. *I've got to do something about it,* Philip thought. *But what? How do we compromise?* He was still thinking about it when there was a knock at the door, and the stage manager's voice said, "Five minutes, Mr. Adler."

"Thank you."

The second half of the program consisted of the *Hammerklavier* sonata. It was a stirring, emotional piece, and when the last notes had thundered out through the vast hall, the audience rose to its feet with wild applause. Philip stood on the stage bowing, but his mind was elsewhere. *I've got to go home and talk to Lara.* And then he remembered that she was away. *We'll have to settle this now,* Philip thought. *We can't go on like this.*

The applause continued. The audience was shouting "bravo" and "encore." Ordinarily, Philip would have played another selection, but on this evening he was too upset. He returned to his dressing room and changed into his street clothes. From outside he could hear the distant rumble of thunder. The papers had said rain, but that had not kept the crowd away. The greenroom was filled with well-wishers waiting for him. It was always exciting to feel and hear the approval of his fans, but tonight he was in no mood for them. He stayed in his dressing room until he was sure the crowd had gone. When he came out, it was almost midnight. He walked through the empty backstage corridors and went out the stage door. The limousine was not there. *I'll find a taxi,* Philip decided.

He stepped outside into a pouring rain. There was a cold wind blowing, and Fifty-seventh Street was dark. As Philip moved toward Sixth Avenue, a large man in a raincoat approached from the shadows.

"Excuse me," he said, "how do you get to Carnegie Hall?"

Philip thought of the old joke he had told Lara and was tempted to say "practice," but he pointed to the building behind him. "It's right there."

As Philip turned, the man shoved him hard up against the building. In his hand was a deadly-looking switchblade knife. "Give me your wallet."

Philip's heart was pounding. He looked around for help. The rain-swept street was deserted. "All right," Philip said. "Don't get excited. You can have it."

The knife was pressing against his throat.

"Look, there's no need to . . ."

"Shut up! Just give it to me."

Philip reached into his pocket and pulled out his wallet. The man grabbed it with his free hand and put it in his pocket. He was looking at Philip's watch. He reached down and tore it from Philip's wrist. As he took the watch, he grabbed Philip's left hand, held it tightly, and slashed the razor-sharp knife across Philip's wrist, slicing it to the bone. Philip screamed aloud with pain. Blood began to gush out. The man fled.

Philip stood there in shock, watching his blood mingling with the rain, dripping into the street.

He fainted.

BOOK FOUR

Chapter Thirty

Lara received the news about Philip in Reno.

Marian Bell was on the phone, near hysteria.

"Is he badly hurt?" Lara demanded.

"We don't have any details yet. He's at Roosevelt Hospital in the emergency room."

"I'll come back immediately."

When Lara arrived at the hospital six hours later, Howard Keller was waiting there for her. He looked shaken.

"What happened?" Lara asked.

"Apparently, Philip was mugged after he left Carnegie Hall. They found him in the street, unconscious."

"How bad is it?"

"His wrist was slashed. He's heavily sedated, but he's conscious."

They went into the hospital room. Philip was lying on a bed with IV tubes feeding liquid into his body.

"Philip . . . Philip." It was Lara's voice calling to him from a long way off. He opened his eyes. Lara and Howard Keller were there. There seemed to be two of each. His mouth was dry, and he felt groggy.

"What happened?" Philip mumbled.

"You were hurt," Lara said. "But you're going to be all right."

Philip looked down and saw that his left wrist was heavily bandaged. Memory came flooding back. "I was . . . how bad is it?"

"I don't know, darling," Lara said. "I'm sure it will be fine. The doctor is coming in to see you."

Keller said reassuringly, "Doctors can do anything these days."

Philip was drifting back to sleep. "I told him to take what he wanted. He shouldn't have hurt my wrist," he mumbled. "He shouldn't have hurt my wrist . . ."

Two hours later Dr. Dennis Stanton walked into Philip's room, and the moment Philip saw the expression on his face he knew what he was going to say.

Philip took a deep breath. "Tell me."

Dr. Stanton sighed. "I'm afraid I don't have very good news for you, Mr. Adler."

"How bad is it?"

"The flexor tendons have been severed, so you'll have no motion in your hand, and there will be a permanent numbness. In addition to that, there's median and ulnar nerve damage." He illustrated on his hand. "The median nerve affects the thumb and first three fingers. The ulnar nerve goes to all the fingers."

Philip closed his eyes tightly against the wave of sudden despair that engulfed him. After a moment he spoke. "Are you saying that I'll . . . I'll never have the use of my left hand again?"

"That's right. The fact is that you're lucky to be alive. Whoever did this cut the artery. It's a wonder you didn't bleed to death. It took sixty stitches to sew your wrist together again."

Philip said in desperation, "My God, isn't there *anything* you can do?"

"Yes. We could put in an implant in your left hand so you would have some motion, but it would be very limited."

He might as well have killed me, Philip thought despairingly.

"As your hand starts to heal, there's going to be a great deal of pain. We'll give you medication to control it, but I can assure you that in time the pain will go away."

Not the real pain, Philip thought. *Not the real pain.* He was caught up in a nightmare. And there was no escape.

* * *

A detective came to see Philip at the hospital. He stood by the side of Philip's bed. He was one of the old breed, in his sixties and tired, with eyes that had already seen it all twice.

"I'm Lieutenant Mancini. I'm sorry about what happened, Mr. Adler," he said. "It's too bad they couldn't have broken your leg instead. I mean . . . if it had to happen . . ."

"I know what you mean," Philip said curtly.

Howard Keller came into the room. "I was looking for Lara." He saw the stranger. "Oh, sorry."

"She's around here somewhere," Philip said. "This is Lieutenant Mancini. Howard Keller."

Mancini was staring at him. "You look familiar. Have we met before?"

"I don't think so."

Mancini's face lit up. "Keller! My God, you used to play baseball in Chicago."

"That's right. How do you . . . ?"

"I was a scout for the Cubs one summer. I still remember your sliders and your change-ups. You could have had a big career."

"Yeah. Well, if you'll excuse me . . ." He looked at Philip. "I'll wait for Lara outside." He left.

Mancini turned to Philip. "Did you get a look at the man who attacked you?"

"He was a male Caucasian. A large man. About six foot two. Maybe fifty or so."

"Could you identify him if you saw him again?"

"Yes." It was a face he would never forget.

"Mr. Adler, I could ask you to look through a lot of mug shots, but frankly, I think it would be a waste of your time. I mean, this isn't exactly a high-tech crime. There are hundreds of muggers all over the city. Unless someone nabs them on the spot, they usually get away with it." He took out his notebook. "What was taken from you?"

"My wallet and my wristwatch."

"What kind of watch was it?"

"A Piaget."

"Was there anything distinctive about it? Did it have an inscription, for example?"

It was the watch Lara had given him. "Yes. On the back of the case, it read 'To Philip with Love from Lara.'"

He made a note. "Mr. Adler . . . I have to ask you this. Had you ever seen this man before?"

Philip looked up at him in surprise. "Seen him before? No. Why?"

"I just wondered." Mancini put the notebook away. "Well, we'll see what we can do. You're a lucky man, Mr. Adler.'"

"Really?" Philip's voice was filled with bitterness.

"Yeah. We have thousands of muggings a year in this city, and we can't afford to spend much time on them, but our captain happens to be a fan of yours. He collects all your records. He's going to do everything he can to catch the SOB who did this to you. We'll send out a description of your watch to pawnshops around the country."

"If you catch him, do you think he can give me my hand back?" Philip asked bitterly.

"What?"

"Nothing."

"You'll be hearing from us. Have a nice day."

Lara and Keller were waiting in the corridor for the detective.

"You said you wanted to see me?" Lara asked.

"Yes. I'd like to ask you a couple of questions," Lieutenant Mancini said. "Mrs. Adler, does your husband have any enemies that you know of?"

Lara frowned. "Enemies? No. Why?"

"No one who might be jealous of him? Another musician maybe? Someone who wants to hurt him?"

"What are you getting at? It was a simple street mugging, wasn't it?"

"To be perfectly frank, this doesn't fit the pattern of an ordinary mugging. He slashed your husband's wrist *after* he took his wallet and watch."

"I don't see what difference . . ."

"That was a pretty senseless thing to do, unless it was deliberate. Your husband didn't put up any resistance. Now, a kid on dope might do a thing like that, but . . ." He shrugged. "I'll be in touch."

They watched him walk away.

"Jesus!" Keller said. "He thinks it was a setup."

Lara had turned pale.

Keller looked at her and said slowly, "My God! One of Paul Martin's hoods! But why would he do this?"

Lara found it difficult to speak. "He . . . he might have thought he was doing it for me. Philip has . . . has been away a lot, and Paul kept saying that it . . . it wasn't right, that someone should have a talk with him. Oh, Howard!" She buried her head in his shoulder, fighting back the tears.

"That son of a bitch! I warned you to stay away from that man."

Lara took a deep breath. "Philip is going to be all right. He *has* to be."

Three days later Lara brought Philip home from the hospital. He looked pale and shaken. Marian Bell was at the door, waiting for them. She had gone to the hospital every day to see Philip and to bring him his messages. There had been an outpouring of sympathy from all around the world—cards and letters and telephone calls from distraught fans. The newspapers had played the story up, condemning the violence on the streets of New York.

Lara was in the library when the telephone rang.

"It's for you," Marian Bell said. "A Mr. Paul Martin."

"I . . . I can't talk to him," Lara told her. And she stood there, fighting to keep her body from trembling.

Chapter Thirty-one

Overnight their lives together changed.

Lara said to Keller, "I'm going to be working at home from now on. Philip needs me."

"Sure. I understand."

The calls and get-well cards kept pouring in, and Marian Bell proved to be a blessing. She was self-effacing and never got in the way. "Don't worry about them, Mrs. Adler. I'll handle them, if you like."

"Thank you, Marian."

William Ellerbee called several times, but Philip refused to take his calls. "I don't want to talk to anyone," he told Lara.

Dr. Stanton had been right about the pain. It was excruciating. Philip tried to avoid taking pain pills until he could no longer stand it.

Lara was always at his side. "We're going to get you the best doctors in the world, darling. There must be *someone* who can fix your hand. I heard about a doctor in Switzerland . . ."

Philip shook his head. "It's no use." He looked at his bandaged hand. "I'm a cripple."

"Don't talk like that," Lara said fiercely. "There are a thousand things you can still do. I blame myself. If I hadn't gone to Reno that day, if I had been with you at the concert, this never would have happened. If . . ."

Philip smiled wryly. "You wanted me to stay home more. Well, now I have nowhere else to go."

Lara said huskily, "Someone said, 'Be careful what you wish for, because you might get it.' I did want you to stay home, but not like this. I can't stand to see you in pain."

"Don't worry about me," Philip said. "I just have to work a few things out in my mind. It's all happened so suddenly. I . . . I don't think I've quite realized it, yet."

Howard Keller came to the penthouse with some contracts. "Hello, Philip. How do you feel?"

"Wonderful," Philip snapped. "I feel just wonderful."

"It was a stupid question. I'm sorry."

"Don't mind me," Philip apologized. "I haven't been myself lately." He pounded his right hand against the chair. "If the bastard had only cut my *right* hand. There are a dozen left-handed concertos I could have played."

And Keller remembered the conversation at the party. *"Half a dozen composers wrote concertos for the left hand. There's one by Demuth, Franz Schmidt, Korngold, and a beautiful concerto by Ravel."*

And Paul Martin had been there and heard it.

Dr. Stanton came to the penthouse to see Philip. Carefully, he removed the bandage, exposing a long angry scar.

"Can you flex your hand at all?"

Philip tried. It was impossible.

"How's the pain?" Dr. Stanton asked.

"It's bad, but I don't want to take any more of those damned pain pills."

"I'll leave another prescription anyway. You can take them if you have to. Believe me, the pain will stop in the next few weeks." He rose to leave. "I really am sorry. I happen to be a big fan of yours."

"Buy my records," Philip said curtly.

Marian Bell made a suggestion to Lara. "Do you think it might help Mr. Adler if a therapist came to work on his hand?"

Lara thought about it. "We can try. Let's see what happens."

When Lara suggested it to Philip, he shook his head. "No. What's the point? The doctor said . . ."

"Doctors can be wrong," Lara said firmly. "We're going to try everything."

The next day a young therapist appeared at the apartment. Lara brought him in to Philip. "This is Mr. Rossman. He works at Columbia Hospital. He's going to try to help you, Philip."

"Good luck," Philip said bitterly.

"Let's take a look at that hand, Mr. Adler."

Philip held out his hand. Rossman examined it carefully. "Looks as though there's been quite a bit of muscle damage, but we'll see what we can to. Can you move your fingers?"

Philip tried.

"There's not much motion, is there? Let's try to exercise it."

It was unbelievably painful.

They worked for half an hour, and at the end of that time Rossman said, "I'll come back tomorrow."

"No," Philip said. "Don't bother."

Lara had come into the room. "Philip, won't you try?"

"I tried," he snarled. "Don't you understand? My hand is dead. Nothing's going to bring it back to life."

"Philip . . ." Her eyes filled with tears.

"I'm sorry," Philip said. "I just . . . Give me time."

That night Lara was awakened by the sound of the piano. She got out of bed and quietly walked over to the entrance of the drawing room. Philip was in his robe, seated at the piano, his right hand softly playing. He looked up when he saw Lara.

"Sorry if I woke you up."

Lara moved toward him. "Darling . . ."

"It's a big joke, isn't it? You married a concert pianist and you wound up with a cripple."

She put her arms around him and held him close. "You're not a cripple. There are so many things you can do."

"Stop being a goddamn Pollyanna!"

"I'm sorry. I just meant . . ."

"I know. Forgive me, I"—he held up his mutilated hand—"I just can't get used to this."

"Come back to bed."

"No. You go ahead. I'll be all right."

He sat up all night, thinking about his future, and he wondered angrily, *What future?*

* * *

Lara and Philip had dinner together every evening, and after dinner they read or watched television and then went to sleep.

Philip said apologetically, "I know I'm not being much of a husband, Lara. I just . . . I just don't feel like sex. Believe me, it has nothing to do with you."

Lara sat up in bed, her voice trembling. "I didn't marry you for your body. I married you because I was wildly head over heels in love with you. I still am. If we never make love again, it will be fine with me. All I want is for you to hold me and love me."

"I do love you," Philip said.

Invitations to dinner parties and charity events came in constantly, but Philip refused them all. He did not want to leave the apartment. "You go," he would tell Lara. "It's important to your business."

"Nothing is more important to me than you. We'll have a nice quiet dinner at home."

Lara saw to it that their chef prepared all of Philip's favorite dishes. He had no appetite. Lara arranged to hold her meetings at the penthouse. When it was necessary for her to go out during the day, she would say to Marian, "I'll be gone for a few hours. Keep an eye on Mr. Adler."

"I will," Marian promised.

One morning Lara said, "Darling, I hate to leave you, but I have to go to Cleveland for a day. Will you be all right?"

"Of course," Philip said. "I'm not helpless. Please go. Don't worry about me."

Marian brought in some letters she had finished answering for Philip. "Would you like to sign these, Mr. Adler?"

Philip said, "Sure. It's a good thing I'm right-handed, isn't it?" There was a bitter edge to his voice. He looked at Marian and said, "I'm sorry. I didn't mean to take it out on you."

Marian said quietly, "I know that, Mr. Adler. Don't you think it would be a good idea for you to go outside and see some friends?"

"My friends are all working," Philip snapped. "They're musicians. They're busy playing concerts. How can you be so stupid?"

He stormed out of the room.

Marian stood there looking after him.

An hour later Philip walked back into the office. Marian was at the typewriter. "Marian?"

She looked up. "Yes, Mr. Adler?"

"Please forgive me. I'm not myself. I didn't mean to be rude."

"I understand," she said quietly.

He sat down opposite her. "The reason I'm not going out," Philip said, "is that I feel like a freak. I'm sure that everybody's going to be staring at my hand. I don't want anyone's pity."

She was watching him, saying nothing.

"You've been very kind, and I appreciate it, I really do. But there's nothing anyone can do. You know the expression 'The bigger they are, the harder they fall'? Well, I was big, Marian—really big. Everybody came to hear me play . . . kings and queens and . . ." He broke off. "People all over the world heard my music. I've given recitals in China and Russia and India and Germany." His voice choked up, and tears began rolling down his cheeks. "Have you noticed I cry a lot lately?" he said. He was fighting to control himself.

Marian said softly, "Please don't. Everything's going to be all right."

"No! Nothing's going to be all right. Nothing! I'm a goddamn cripple."

"Don't say that. Mrs. Adler is right, you know. There are a hundred things you can do. When you get over this pain, you'll begin to do them."

Philip took out a handkerchief and wiped his eyes. "Jesus Christ, I'm becoming a damn crybaby."

"If it helps you," Marian said, "do it."

He looked up at her and smiled. "How old are you?"

"Twenty-six."

"You're a pretty wise twenty-six, aren't you?"

"No. I just know what you're going through, and I'd give anything if it hadn't happened. But it has happened, and I know that you're going to figure out the best way to deal with it."

"You're wasting your time here," Philip said. "You should have been a shrink."

"Would you like me to make a drink for you?"

"No, thanks. Are you interested in a game of backgammon?" Philip asked.

"I'd love it, Mr. Adler."

"If you're going to be my backgammon partner, you'd better start calling me Philip."

"Philip."

From that time on, they played backgammon every day.

Lara received a telephone call from Terry Hill.

"Lara, I'm afraid I have some bad news for you."

Lara readied herself. "Yes?"

"The Nevada Gaming Commission has voted to suspend your gambling license until further investigation. You may be facing criminal charges."

It was a shock. She thought of Paul Martin's words *"Don't worry. They can't prove anything."* "Isn't there something we can do about it, Terry?"

"Not for the present. Just sit tight. I'm working on it."

When Lara told Keller the news, he said, "My God! We're counting on the cash flow from the casino to pay off the mortgages on three buildings. Are they going to reinstate your license?"

"I don't know."

Keller was thoughtful. "All right. We'll sell the Chicago hotel and use the equity to pay the mortgage on the Houston property. The real estate market has gone to hell. A lot of banks and savings and loans are in deep trouble. Drexel Burnham Lambert has folded. It's the end of Milken honey."

"It will turn around," Lara said.

"It had better turn around *fast*. I've been getting calls from the banks about our loans."

"Don't worry," Lara said confidently. "If you owe a bank a million dollars, they own you. If you owe a bank a hundred million dollars, you own them. They can't afford to let anything happen to me."

The following day, an article appeared in *Business Week*. It was headlined: CAMERON EMPIRE SHAKY—LARA CAMERON FACING POSSIBLE CRIMINAL INDICTMENT IN RENO. CAN THE IRON BUTTERFLY KEEP HER EMPIRE TOGETHER?

Lara slammed her fist against the magazine. "How dare they print that? I'm going to sue them."

Keller said, "Not a great idea."

Lara said earnestly, "Howard, Cameron Towers is almost fully rented, right?"

"Seventy percent, so far, and climbing. Southern Insurance has taken twenty floors, and International Investment Banking has taken ten floors."

"When the building is finished, it will throw off enough money to take care of all our problems. How far away are we from completion?"

"Six months."

Lara's voice was filled with excitement. "Look what we'll have then. The biggest skyscraper in the world! It's going to be beautiful."

She turned to the framed sketch of it behind her desk. It showed a towering glass-sheathed monolith, whose facets reflected the other buildings around it. On the lower floors were a promenade and atrium, with expensive shops. Above were apartments and Lara's offices.

"We'll have a big publicity promotion," Lara said.

"Good idea." He frowned.

"What's the matter?"

"Nothing. I was just thinking about Steve Murchison. He wanted that site pretty bad."

"Well, we beat him to it, didn't we?"

"Yes," Keller said slowly. "We beat him to it."

Lara sent for Jerry Townsend.

"Jerry, I want to do something special for the opening of Cameron Towers. Any ideas?"

"I have a great idea. The opening is September tenth?"

"Yes."

"Doesn't that ring a bell?"

"Well, it's my birthday . . ."

"Right." A smile lit up Jerry Townsend's face. "Why don't we give you a big birthday party to celebrate the completion of the skyscraper?"

Lara was thoughtful for a moment. "I like it. It's a wonderful idea. We'll invite everybody! We'll make a noise that will be heard around the world. Jerry, I want you to make up a guest list. Two hundred people. I want you to handle it personally."

Townsend grinned. "You've got it. I'll give you the guest list to approve."

Lara slammed her fist down on the magazine again. "We're going to show them!"

"Excuse me, Mrs. Adler," Marian said. "I have the secretary of the National Builders Association on line three. You haven't responded to their invitation for the dinner Friday night."

"Tell them I can't make it," Lara said. "Give them my apologies."

"Yes, ma'am." Marian left the room.

Philip said, "Lara, you can't turn yourself into a hermit because of me. It's important for you to go to those things."

"Nothing is more important than my being here with you. That funny little man who married us in Paris said, 'For better or for worse.'" She frowned. "At least I *think* that's what he said. I don't speak French."

Philip smiled. "I want you to know how much I appreciate you. I feel like I'm putting you through hell."

Lara moved closer to him. "Wrong word," she said. "Heaven."

Philip was getting dressed. Lara was helping him with the buttons on his shirt. Philip looked in the mirror. "I look like a damned hippie," he said. "I need a haircut."

"Do you want me to have Marian make an appointment with your barber?"

He shook his head. "No. I'm sorry, Lara. I'm just not ready to go out."

The following morning Philip's barber and a manicurist appeared at the apartment. Philip was taken aback. "What's all this?"

"If Mohammed won't go to the mountain, the mountain comes to Mohammed. They'll be here every week for you."

"You're a wonder," Philip said.

"You ain't seen nothin' yet." Lara grinned.

The following day, a tailor arrived with some sample swatches for suits and shirts.

"What's going on?" Philip asked.

Lara said, "You're the only man I know who has six pairs of tails, four dinner jackets, and two suits. I think it's time we got you a proper wardrobe."

"Why?" Philip protested. "I'm not going anywhere."

But he allowed himself to be fitted for the suits and shirts.

A few days later a custom shoemaker arrived.

"Now what?" Philip asked.

"It's time you had some new shoes."

"I told you, I'm not going out."

"I know, baby. But when you do, your shoes will be ready."

Philip held her close. "I don't deserve you."

"That's what I keep telling you."

* * *

They were in a meeting at the office. Howard Keller was saying, "We're losing the shopping mall in Los Angeles. The banks have decided to call in the loans."

"They can't do that."

"They're doing it," Keller said. "We're overleveraged."

"We can pay the loans off by borrowing on one of the other buildings."

Keller said, patiently, "Lara, you're already leveraged to the hilt. You have a sixty-million-dollar payment coming up on the skyscraper."

"I know that, but completion is only four months away now. We can roll the loan over. The building's on schedule, isn't it?"

"Yes." Keller was studying her thoughtfully. It was a question she never would have asked one year ago. Then she would have known exactly where everything stood. "I think it might be better if you spent more time here in the office," Keller told her. "Too many things are becoming unraveled. There are some decisions that only you can make."

Lara nodded. "All right," she said reluctantly. "I'll be in tomorrow morning.

"William Ellerbee is on the telephone for you," Marian announced.

"Tell him I can't talk to him." Philip watched her as she returned to the phone.

"I'm sorry, Mr. Ellerbee. Mr. Adler is not available just now. Can I take a message?" She listened a moment. "I'll tell him. Thank you." She replaced the receiver and looked up at Philip. "He's really anxious to have lunch with you."

"He probably wants to talk about the commissions he's not getting anymore."

"You're probably right," Marian said mildly. "I'm sure he must hate you because you were attacked."

Philip said quietly, "Sorry. Is that the way I sounded?"

"Yes."

"How do you put up with me?"

Marian smiled. "It's not that difficult."

The following day William Ellerbee called again. Philip was out of the room. Marian spoke to Ellerbee for a few minutes, then went to find Philip.

"That was Mr. Ellerbee," Marian said.

"Next time tell him to stop calling."

"Maybe you should tell him yourself," Marian said. "You're having lunch with him Thursday at one o'clock."

"*I'm what?*"

"He suggested Le Cirque, but I thought a smaller restaurant might be better." She looked at the pad in her hand. "He's going to meet you at Fu's at one. I'll arrange for Max to drive you there."

Philip was staring at her, furious. "You made a lunch date for me without asking me?"

She said calmly, "If I had asked you, you wouldn't have gone. You can fire me if you want to."

He glared at her for a long moment, and then he broke into a slow smile. "You know something? I haven't had Chinese food in a long time."

When Lara arrived from the office, Philip said, "I'm going out for lunch on Thursday with Ellerbee."

"That's wonderful, darling! When did you decide that?"

"Marian decided it for me. She thought it would be a good idea for me to get out."

"Oh, really?" *But you wouldn't go out when I suggested it.* "That was very thoughtful of her."

"Yes. She's quite a woman."

I've been stupid, Lara thought. *I shouldn't have thrown them together like this. And Philip is so vulnerable right now.*

That was the moment when Lara knew she had to get rid of Marian.

When Lara arrived home the following day, Philip and Marian were playing backgammon in the game room.

Our game, Lara thought.

"How can I beat you if you keep rolling doubles?" Philip was saying, laughing.

Lara stood in the doorway watching. She had not heard Philip laugh in a long time.

Marian looked up and saw her. "Good evening, Mrs. Adler."

Philip sprang to his feet. "Hello, darling." He kissed her. "She's beating the pants off me."

Not if I can help it, Lara thought.

"Will you need me tonight, Mrs. Adler?"

"No, Marian. You can run along. I'll see you in the morning."

"Thank you. Good night."

"Good night, Marian."

They watched her leave.

"She's good company," Philip said.

Lara stroked his cheek. "I'm glad, darling."

"How's everything at the office?"

"Fine." She had no intention of burdening Philip with her problems. She would have to fly to Reno and talk to the Gaming Commission again. If she were forced to, she would find a way to survive their cutting off the gambling at the hotel, but it would make it a lot easier if she could dissuade them.

"Philip, I'm afraid I'm going to have to start spending more time at the office. Howard can't make all the decisions himself."

"No problem. I'll be fine."

"I'm going to Reno in the next day or two," Lara said. "Why don't you come with me?"

Philip shook his head. "I'm not ready yet." He looked at his crippled left hand. "Not yet."

"All right, darling. I shouldn't be gone more than two or three days."

Early the following morning when Marian Bell arrived for work, Lara was waiting for her. Philip was still asleep.

"Marian . . . you know the diamond bracelet that Mr. Adler gave me for my birthday?"

"Yes, Mrs. Adler?"

"When did you see it last?"

She stopped to think. "It was on the dressing table in your bedroom."

"So you did see it?"

"Why, yes. Is something wrong?"

"I'm afraid there is. The bracelet is missing."

Marian was staring at her. "Missing? Who could have . . . ?"

"I've questioned the staff here. They don't know anything about it."

"Shall I call the police and . . . ?"

"That won't be necessary. I don't want to do anything that might embarrass you."

"I don't understand."

"Don't you? For your sake, I think it would be best if we dropped the whole matter."

Marian was staring at Lara in shock. "You know I didn't take that bracelet, Mrs. Adler."

"I don't know anything of the kind. You'll have to leave." And she hated herself for what she was doing. *But no one is going to take Philip away from me. No one.*

When Philip came down to breakfast, Lara said, "By the way, I'm getting a new secretary to work here at the apartment."

Philip looked at her in surprise. "What happened to Marian?"

"She quit. She was offered a . . . a job in San Francisco."

He looked at Lara in surprise. "Oh. That's too bad. I thought she liked it here."

"I'm sure she did, but we wouldn't want to stand in her way, would we?" *Forgive me,* Lara thought.

"No, of course not," Philip said. "I'd like to wish her luck. Is she . . . ?"

"She's gone."

Philip said, "I guess I'll have to find a new backgammon partner."

"When things settle down a bit, I'll be here for you."

Philip and William Ellerbee were seated in a corner table at Fu's restaurant.

Ellerbee said, "It's so good to see you, Philip. I've been calling you, but . . ."

"I know, I'm sorry. I haven't felt like talking to anyone, Bill."

"I hope they catch the bastard who did this to you."

"The police have been good enough to explain to me that muggings are not a high priority in their lives. They equate it just below lost cats. They'll never catch him."

Ellerbee said hesitantly, "I understand that you're not going to be able to play again."

"You understand right." Philip held up his crippled hand. "It's dead."

Ellerbee leaned forward and said earnestly, "But *you're* not, Philip. You still have your whole life ahead of you."

"Doing what?"

"Teaching."

There was a wry smile on Philip's lips. "It's ironic, isn't it? I had thought about doing that one day when I was through giving concerts."

Ellerbee said quietly, "Well, that day is here, isn't it? I took the liberty of talking to the head of the Eastman School of Music in Rochester. They would give anything to have you teach there."

Philip frowned. "That would mean my moving up there. Lara's headquarters are in New York." He shook his head. "I couldn't do that to her. You don't know how wonderful she's been to me, Bill."

"I'm sure she has."

"She's practically given up her business to take care of me. She's the most thoughtful, considerate woman I've ever known. I'm crazy about her."

"Philip, would you at least think about the offer from Eastman?"

"Tell them I appreciate it, but I'm afraid the answer is no."

"If you change your mind, will you let me know?"

Philip nodded. "You'll be the first."

When Philip returned to the penthouse, Lara had gone to the office. He wandered around the apartment, restless. He thought about his conversation with Ellerbee. *I would love to teach,* Philip thought, *but I can't ask Lara to move to Rochester, and I can't go there without her.*

He heard the front door open. "Lara?"

It was Marian. "Oh, I'm sorry, Philip. I didn't know anyone was here. I came to return my key."

"I thought you'd be in San Francisco by now."

She looked at him, puzzled. "San Francisco? Why?"

"Isn't that where your new job is?"

"I have no new job."

"But Lara said . . ."

Marian suddenly understood. "I see. She didn't tell you why she fired me?"

"Fired you? She told me that you quit . . . that you had a better offer."

"That's not true."

Philip said slowly, "I think you'd better sit down."

They sat across from each other. "What's going on here?" Philip asked.

Marian took a deep breath. "I think your wife believes that I . . . that I had designs on you."

"What are you talking about?"

"She accused me of stealing the diamond bracelet you gave her, as an excuse to fire me. I'm sure she has it put away somewhere."

"I can't believe this," Philip protested. "Lara would never do anything like that."

"She would do anything to hold on to you."

He was studying her, bewildered. "I . . . I don't know what to say. Let me talk to Lara and . . ."

"No. Please don't. It might be better if you didn't let her know I was here." She rose.

"What are you going to do now?"

"Don't worry. I'll find another job."

"Marian, if there's anything I can do . . ."

"There is nothing."

"Are you sure?"

"I'm sure. Take care of yourself, Philip." And she was gone.

Philip watched her leave, disturbed. He couldn't believe that Lara could be guilty of such a deception, and he wondered why she hadn't told him about it. Perhaps, he thought, Marian *did* steal the bracelet, and Lara had not wanted to upset him. Marian was lying.

Chapter Thirty-two

The pawnshop was on South State Street in the heart of the Loop. When Jesse Shaw walked through the door, the old man behind the counter looked up.

"Good morning. Can I help you?"

Shaw laid a wristwatch on the counter. "How much will you give me for this?"

The pawnbroker picked up the watch and studied it. "A Piaget. Nice watch."

"Yeah. I hate like hell to part with it, but I've run into a little bad luck. You understand what I mean?"

The pawnbroker shrugged. "It's my business to understand. You wouldn't believe the hard-luck stories I hear."

"I'll redeem it in a few days. I'm starting a new job Monday. Meanwhile, I need to get as much cash as I can for it."

The pawnbroker was looking at the watch more closely. On the back of the case, some writing had been scratched off. He looked at the customer. "If you'll excuse me a minute, I'll take a look at the movement. Sometimes these watches are made in Bangkok, and they forget to put anything inside."

He took the watch into the back room. He put a loupe to his eye and studied the scratch marks. He could faintly make out the letters "T Phi p wi h L v fro L ra." The old man opened a drawer and took out a police flyer. It had a description of the watch and the engraving on the back, "To Philip with Love from Lara." He started to pick up the telephone when the customer yelled, "Hey, I'm in a hurry. Do you want the watch or don't you?"

"I'm coming," the pawnbroker said. He walked back into the next room. "I can loan you five hundred dollars on it."

"Five hundred? This watch is worth . . ."

"Take it or leave it."

"All right," Shaw said grudgingly. "I'll take it."

"You'll have to fill out this form," the pawnbroker said.

"Sure." He wrote down *John Jones, 21 Hunt Street*." As far as he knew, there was no Hunt Street in Chicago, and he sure as hell was not John Jones. He pocketed the cash. "Much obliged. I'll be back in a few days for it."

"Right."

The pawnbroker picked up the telephone and made a call.

A detective arrived at the pawnshop twenty minutes later.

"Why didn't you call while he was here?" he demanded.

"I tried. He was in a hurry, and he was jumpy."

The detective studied the form the customer had filled out.

"That won't do you no good," the pawnbroker said. "It's probably a false name and address."

The detective grunted. "No kidding. Did he fill this out himself?"

"Yes."

"Then we'll nail him."

At police headquarters it took the computer less than three minutes to identify the thumbprint on the form. *Jesse Shaw.*

The butler came into the drawing room. "Excuse me, Mr. Adler, there's a gentleman on the telephone for you. A Lieutenant Mancini. Shall I . . . ?"

"I'll take it." Philip picked up the telephone. "Hello?"

"Philip Adler?"

"Yes . . . ?"

"This is Lieutenant Mancini. I came to see you in the hospital."

"I remember."

"I wanted to bring you up-to-date on what's happening. We had a bit of luck. I told you that our chief was going to send out flyers to pawnshops with a description of your watch?"

"Yes."

"They found it. The watch was pawned in Chicago. They're tracking down the person who pawned it. You did say that you could identify your assailant, didn't you?"

"That's right."

"Good. We'll be in touch."

Jerry Townsend came into Lara's office. He was excited. "I've worked out the party list we talked about. The more I think about the idea, the better I like it. We'll celebrate your fortieth birthday on the day the tallest skyscraper in the world opens." He handed Lara the list. "I've included the Vice President. He's a big admirer of yours."

Lara scanned it. It read like a who's who from Washington, Hollywood, New York, and London. There were government officials, motion picture celebrities, rock stars . . . it was impressive.

"I like it," Lara said. "Let's go with it."

Townsend put the list in his pocket. "Right. I'll have the invitations printed up and sent out. I've already called Carlos and told him to reserve the Grand Ballroom and arrange your favorite menu. We're setting up for two hundred people. We can always add or subtract a few if we have to. By the way, is there any more news on the Reno situation?"

Lara had talked to Terry Hill that morning. *"A grand jury is investigating, Lara. There's a possibility that they'll hand down a criminal indictment."*

"How can they? The fact that I had some conversations with Paul Martin doesn't prove anything. We could have been talking about the state of the world, or his ulcers, or a dozen other damned things."

"Lara, don't get angry with me. I'm on your side."

"Then do something. You're my lawyer. Get me the hell out of this."

"No. Everything's fine," Lara told Townsend.

"Good. I understand that you and Philip are going to the mayor's dinner Saturday night."

"Yes." She had wanted to turn down the invitation at first, but Philip had insisted.

"You need these people. You can't afford to offend them. I want you to go."

"Not without you, darling."

He had taken a deep breath. "All right. I'll go with you. I guess it's time I stopped being a hermit."

* * *

Saturday evening Lara helped Philip get dressed. She put his studs and cuff links in his shirt and tied his tie for him. He stood there, silently, cursing his helplessness.

"It's like Ken and Barbie, isn't it?"

"What?"

"Nothing."

"There you are, darling. You'll be the most handsome man there."

"Thanks."

"I'd better get dressed," Lara said. "The mayor doesn't like to be kept waiting."

"I'll be in the library," Philip told her.

Thirty minutes later Lara walked into the library. She looked ravishing. She was dressed in a beautiful white Oscar de la Renta gown. On her wrist was the diamond bracelet Philip had given her.

Philip had difficulty sleeping Saturday night. He looked across the bed at Lara and wondered how she could have falsely accused Marian of stealing the bracelet. He knew he had to confront her with it, but he wanted to speak with Marian first.

Early Sunday morning, while Lara was still asleep, Philip quietly got dressed and left the penthouse. He took a taxi to Marian's apartment. He rang the bell and waited.

A sleepy voice said, "Who is it?"

"It's Philip. I have to talk to you."

The door opened and Marian stood there.

"Philip? Is something wrong?"

"We have to talk."

"Come in."

He entered the apartment. "I'm sorry if I woke you up," Philip said, "but this is important."

"What's happened?"

He took a deep breath. "You were right about the bracelet. Lara wore it last night. I owe you an apology. I thought . . . perhaps that you . . . I just wanted to say I'm sorry."

Marian said quietly, "Of course, you would have believed her. She's your wife."

"I'm going to confront Lara with it this morning, but I wanted to talk to you first."

Marian turned to him. "I'm glad you did. I don't want you to discuss it with her."

"Why not?" Philip demanded. "And why would she do such a thing?"

"You don't know, do you?"

"Frankly, no. It makes no sense."

"I think I understand her better than you do. Lara is madly in love with you. She would do anything to hold on to you. You're probably the only person she has ever really loved in her life. She needs you. And I think you need her. You love her very much, don't you, Philip?"

"Yes."

"Then let's forget all this. If you bring it up to her, it won't do any good, and it will only make things worse between the two of you. I can easily find another job."

"But it's unfair to you, Marian."

She smiled wryly. "Life isn't always fair, is it?" *If it were, I would be Mrs. Philip Adler.* "Don't worry. I'll be fine."

"At least let me do something for you. Let me give you some money to make up for . . ."

"Thank you, but no."

There was so much she wanted to say, but she knew that it was hopeless. He was a man in love. What she said was: "Go back to her, Philip."

The construction site was on Chicago's Wabash Avenue, south of the Loop. It was a twenty-five story office building, and it was half finished. An unmarked police car pulled up to the corner, and two detectives got out. They walked over to the site and stopped one of the workers passing by. "Where's the foreman?"

He pointed to a huge, burly man cursing out a workman. "Over there."

The detectives went over to him. "Are you in charge here?"

He turned and said impatiently, "I'm not only in charge, I'm very busy. What do you want?"

"Do you have a man in your crew named Jesse Shaw?"

"Shaw? Sure. He's up there." The foreman pointed to a man working on a steel girder a dozen stories up.

"Would you ask him to come down, please?"

"Hell, no. He has work to . . ."

One of the detectives pulled out a badge. "Get him down here."

"What's the problem? Is Jesse in some kind of trouble?"

"No, we just want to talk to him."

"Okay." The foreman turned to one of the men working nearby. "Go up top and tell Jesse to come down here."

"Right."

A few minutes later Jesse Shaw was approaching the two detectives.

"These men want to talk to you," the foreman said, and walked away.

Jesse grinned at the two men. "Thanks. I can use a break. What can I do for you?"

One of the detectives pulled out a wristwatch. "Is this your watch?"

Shaw's grin faded. "No."

"Are you sure?"

"Yeah." He pointed to his wrist. "I wear a Seiko."

"But you pawned this watch."

Shawn hesitated. "Oh, yeah. I did. The bastard only gave me five hundred for it. It's worth at least . . ."

"You said it wasn't your watch."

"That's right. It's not."

"Where did you get it?"

"I found it."

"Really? Where?"

"On the sidewalk near my apartment building." He was warming up to his story. "It was in the grass, and I got out of my car, and there it was. The sun hit the band and made it sparkle. That's how I happened to see it."

"Lucky it wasn't a cloudy day."

"Yeah."

"Mr. Shaw, do you like to travel?"

"No."

"That's too bad. You're going to take a little trip to New York. We'll help you pack."

When they got to Shaw's apartment, the two detectives began looking around.

"Hold it!" Shaw said. "You guys got a search warrant?"

"We don't need one. We're just helping you pack your things."

One of the men was looking in a clothes closet. There was a shoe box high up on a shelf. He took it down and opened it. "Jesus!" he said. "Look what Santa Claus left."

* * *

Lara was in her office when Kathy's voice came over the intercom. "Mr. Tilly is on line four, Miss Cameron."

Tilly was the project manager on Cameron Towers.

Lara picked up the phone. "Hello?"

"We had a little problem this morning, Miss Cameron."

"Yes?"

"We had a fire. It's out now."

"What happened?"

"There's was an explosion in the air-conditioning unit. A transformer blew. There was a short circuit. It looks like someone wired it up wrong."

"How bad is it?"

"Well, it looks like we'll lose a day or two. We should be able to clean everything up and rewire it by then."

"Stay on it. Keep me informed."

Lara came home late each evening, worried and exhausted.

"I'm concerned about you," Philip told her. "Is there anything I can do?"

"Nothing, darling. Thank you." She managed a smile. "Just a few problems at the office."

He took her in his arms. "Did I ever tell you that I'm mad about you?"

She looked up at him and smiled. "Tell me again."

"I'm mad about you."

She held him close and thought, *This is what I want. This is what I need.* "Darling, when my little problems are over, let's go away somewhere. Just the two of us."

"It's a deal."

Someday, Lara thought, *I must tell him what I did to Marian. I know it was wrong. But I would die if I lost him.*

The following day Tilly called again. "Did you cancel the order for the marble for the lobby floors?"

Lara said slowly, "Why would I do that?"

"I don't know. Somebody did. The marble was supposed to have been delivered today. When I called, they said it was canceled two months ago by your order."

Lara sat there fuming. "I see. How badly are we delayed?"

"I'm not sure yet."

"Tell them to put a rush on it."

Keller came into Lara's office.

"I'm afraid the banks are getting nervous, Lara. I don't know how much longer I can hold them off."

"Just until Cameron Towers is finished. We're almost there, Howard. We're only three months away from completion."

"I told them that," he sighed. "All right. I'll talk to them again."

Kathy's voice came over the intercom. "Mr. Tilly's on line one."

Lara looked at Keller. "Don't go." She picked up the phone. "Yes?" Lara said.

"We're having another problem here, Miss Cameron."

"I'm listening," Lara said.

"The elevators are malfunctioning. The programs are out of sync, and the signals are all screwed up. You press the button for down, and it goes up. Press the eighteenth floor, and it will take you to the basement. I've never seen anything like this before."

"Do you think it was done deliberately?"

"It's hard to say. Could have been carelessness."

"How long will it take to straighten it out?"

"I have some people on the way over now."

"Get back to me." She replaced the receiver.

"Is everything all right?" Keller asked.

Lara evaded the question. "Howard, have you heard anything about Steve Murchison lately?"

He looked at her, surprised. "No. Why?"

"I just wondered."

The consortium of bankers financing Cameron Enterprises had good reason to be concerned. It was not only Cameron Enterprises that was in trouble; a majority of their corporate clients had serious problems. The decline in junk bonds had become a full-fledged disaster, and it was a crippling blow to the corporations that had depended on them.

There were six bankers in the room with Howard Keller, and the atmosphere was grim.

"We're holding overdue notes for almost a hundred million dollars," their spokesman said. "I'm afraid we can't accommodate Cameron Enterprises any longer."

"You're forgetting a couple of things," Keller reminded them. "Number one, we expect the casino gambling license in Reno to be renewed any day now. That cash flow will more than take care of any deficit. Number two, Cameron Towers is right on schedule. It's going to be finished in ninety days. We already have a seventy percent tenancy, and you can be assured that the day it's finished everybody is going to be clamoring to get in. Gentlemen, your money couldn't be more secure. You're dealing with the Lara Cameron magic."

The men looked at one another.

The spokesman said. "Why don't we discuss this among ourselves and we'll get back to you?"

"Fine. I'll tell Miss Cameron."

Keller reported back to Lara.

"I think they'll go along with us," he told her. "But in the meantime, we're going to have to sell off a few more assets to stay afloat."

"Do it."

Lara was getting to the office early in the morning and leaving late at night, fighting desperately to save her empire. She and Philip saw very little of each other. Lara did not want him to know how much trouble she was facing. *He has enough problems,* Lara thought. *I can't burden him with any more.*

At six o'clock Monday morning Tilly was on the phone. "I think you'd better get over here, Miss Cameron."

Lara felt a sharp sense of apprehension. "What's wrong?"

"I'd rather you saw it for yourself."

"I'm on my way."

Lara telephoned Keller. "Howard, there's another problem at Cameron Towers. I'll pick you up."

Half an hour later they were on their way to the construction site.

"Did Tilly say what the trouble was?" Keller asked.

"No, but I don't believe in accidents anymore. I've been thinking about what you said. Steve Murchison wanted that property badly. I took it away from him."

When they arrived at the site, they saw large sheets of crated tinted glass lying on the ground, and more glass being delivered by trucks. Tilly hurried over to Lara and Keller.

"I'm glad you're here."

"What's the problem?"

"This isn't the glass we ordered. It's the wrong tint and the wrong cut. There's no way it will fit the sides of our building."

Lara and Keller looked at each other. "Can we recut it here?" Keller asked.

Tilly shook his head. "Not a chance. You'd wind up with a mountain of silicate."

Lara said, "Who did we order this from?"

"The New Jersey Panel and Glass Company."

"I'll call them," Lara said. "What's our deadline on this?"

Tilly stood there calculating. "If it got here in two weeks, we could be back on schedule. It would be a push, but we'd be okay."

Lara turned to Keller, "Let's go."

Otto Karp was the manager of the New Jersey Panel and Glass Company. He came on the phone almost immediately. "Yes, Miss Cameron? I understand you have a problem."

"No," Lara snapped. "*You* have a problem. You shipped us the wrong glass. If I don't get the right order in the next two weeks, I'm going to sue your company out of business. You're holding up a three-hundred-million-dollar project."

"I don't understand. Will you hold on, please?"

He was gone almost five minutes. When he came back on the line, he said, "I'm terribly sorry, Miss Cameron, the order was written up wrong. What happened is . . ."

"I don't care what happened," Lara interrupted. "All I want you to do is to get our order filled and shipped out.

"I'll be happy to do that."

Lara felt a sharp sense of relief. "How soon can we have it?"

"In two to three months."

"Two to three months! That's impossible! We need it *now*."

"I'd be happy to accommodate you," Karp said, "but unfortunately we're way behind in our orders."

"You don't understand," Lara said. "This is an emergency and . . ."

"I certainly appreciate that. And we'll do the best we can. You'll have the order in two to three months. I'm sorry we can't do better . . ."

Lara slammed down the receiver. "I don't believe this," Lara said. She looked over at Tilly. "Is there another company we can deal with?"

Tilly rubbed his hand across his forehead. "Not at this late date. If we went to anyone else, they'd be starting from scratch, and their other customers would be ahead of us."

Keller said, "Lara, could I talk to you for a minute?" He took her aside. "I hate to suggest this, but . . ."

"Go ahead."

". . . your friend Paul Martin might have some connections over there. Or he might know someone who knows someone."

Lara nodded. "Good idea, Howard. I'll find out."

Two hours later Lara was seated in Paul Martin's office.

"You don't know how happy I am that you called," the lawyer said. "It's been too long. God, you look beautiful, Lara."

"Thank you, Paul."

"What can I do for you?"

Lara said hesitantly, "I seem to come to you whenever I'm in trouble."

"I've always been there for you, haven't I?"

"Yes. You're a good friend." She sighed. "Right now I need a good friend."

"What's the problem? Another strike?"

"No. It's about Cameron Towers."

He frowned. "I heard that was on schedule."

"It is. Or it was. I think Steve Murchison is out to sabotage the project. He has a vendetta against me. Things have suddenly started to go wrong at the building. Up to now we've been able to handle them. Now . . . We have a big problem. It could put us past our completion date. Our two biggest tenants would pull out. I can't afford to let that happen."

She took a deep breath, trying to control her anger.

"Six months ago we ordered tinted glass from the New Jersey Panel and Glass Company. We received our delivery this morning. It wasn't our glass."

"Did you call them?"

"Yes, but they're talking about two or three months. I need that glass in four weeks. Until it's in, there's nothing for the men to do. They've stopped working. If that building isn't completed on schedule, I'll lose everything I have."

Paul Martin looked at her and said quietly, "No, you won't. Let me see what I can do."

Lara felt an overwhelming sense of relief. "Paul, I . . ." It was difficult to put into words. "Thank you."

He took her hand in his and smiled. "The dinosaur isn't dead yet," he said. "I should have some word for you by tomorrow."

The following morning Lara's private phone rang for the first time in months. She picked it up eagerly. "Paul?"

"Hello, Lara. I had a little talk with some of my friends. It's not going to be easy, but it can be done. They promised a delivery a week from Monday."

On the day the glass shipment was scheduled to arrive, Lara telephoned Paul Martin again.

"The glass hasn't come yet, Paul," Lara said.

"Oh?" There was a silence. "I'll look into it." His voice softened. "You know, the only good thing about this, baby, is that I get to talk to you again."

"Yes. I . . . Paul . . . if I don't get that glass on time . . ."

"You'll have it. Don't give up."

By the end of the week there was still no word.

Keller came into Lara's office. "I just talked to Tilly. Our deadline is Friday. If the glass arrives by then, we'll be okay. Otherwise we're dead."

By Thursday nothing had changed.

Lara went to visit Cameron Towers. There were no workmen there. The skyscraper rose majestically into the sky, overshadowing everything around it. It was going to be a beautiful building. Her monument. *I'm not going to let it fail,* Lara thought fiercely.

Lara telephoned Paul Martin again.

"I'm sorry," his secretary said. "Mr. Martin is out of the office. Is there any message?"

"Please ask him to call me," Lara said. She turned to Keller, "I have a hunch I'd like you to check out. See if the owner of that glass factory happens to be Steve Murchison."

Thirty minutes later Keller returned to Lara's office. His face was pale.

"Well? Did you find out who owns the glass company?"

"Yes," he said slowly. "It's registered in Delaware. It's owned by Etna Enterprises."

"Etna Enterprises?"

"Right. They bought it a year ago. Etna Enterprises is Paul Martin."

Chapter Thirty-three

The bad publicity about Cameron Enterprises continued. The reporters who had been so eager to praise Lara before now turned on her.

Jerry Townsend went in to see Howard Keller.

"I'm worried," Townsend said.

"What's the problem?"

"Have you been reading the press?"

"Yeah. They're having a field day."

"I'm worried about the birthday party, Howard. I've sent out the invitations. Since all this bad publicity, I've been getting nothing but turndowns. The bastards are afraid they might be contaminated. It's a fiasco."

"What do you suggest?"

"That we cancel the party. I'll make up some excuse."

"I think you're right. I don't want anything to embarrass her."

"Good. I'll go ahead and cancel it. Will you tell Lara?"

"Yes."

Terry Hill called.

"I just received notice that you're being subpoenaed to testify before the grandjury in Reno day after tomorrow. I'll go with you."

Transcript of Interrogation of Jesse Shaw by Detective Lieutenant Sal Mancini.

M: Good morning, Mr. Shaw. I'm Lieutenant Mancini.

	You're aware that a stenographer is taking down our conversation?
S:	Sure.
M:	And you've waived the right to an attorney?
S:	I don't need no attorney. All I did was find a watch, for Christ's sake, and they drug me all the way up here like I'm some kind of animal.
M:	Mr. Shaw, do you know who Philip Adler is?
S:	No. Should I?
M:	No one paid you to attack him?
S:	I told you—I never heard of him.
M:	The police in Chicago found fifty thousand dollars in cash in your apartment. Where did that money come from?
S:	[No response]
M:	Mr. Shaw . . . ?
S:	I won it gambling.
M:	Where?
S:	At the track . . . football bets . . . you know.
M:	You're a lucky man, aren't you?
S:	Yeah. I guess so.
M:	At present, you have a job in Chicago. Is that right?
S:	Yes.
M:	Did you ever work in New York?
S:	Well, one time, yeah.
M:	I have a police report here that says you were operating a crane at a development in Queens that killed a construction foreman named Bill Whitman. Is that correct?
S:	Yeah. It was an accident.
M:	How long had you been on that job?
S:	I don't remember.
M:	Let me refresh your memory. You were on that job seventy-two hours. You flew in from Chicago the day before the accident with the crane, and flew back to Chicago two days later. Is that correct?
S:	I guess so.
M:	According to American Airlines' records, you flew from Chicago to New York again two days before Philip Adler was attacked, and you returned to Chicago the following day. What was the purpose of such a short trip?
S:	I wanted to see some plays.

M: Do you remember the names of the plays you saw?
S: No. That was awhile ago.
M: At the time of the accident with the crane, who was your employer?
S: Cameron Enterprises.
M: And who is your employer on the construction job you're working on in Chicago?
S: Cameron Enterprises.

Howard Keller was in a meeting with Lara. For the past hour they had been talking about damage control to offset the bad publicity the company was receiving. As the meeting was about to break up, Lara said, "Anything else?"

Howard frowned. Someone had told him to tell Lara something, but he could not remember what it was. *Oh, well, it's probably not important.*

Simms, the butler, said, "There's a telephone call for you, Mr. Adler. A Lieutenant Mancini."

Philip picked up the telephone. "Lieutenant. What can I do for you?"

"I have some news for you, Mr. Adler."

"What is it? Did you find the man?"

"I'd prefer to come up and discuss it with you in person. Would that be all right?"

"Of course."

"I'll be there in half an hour."

Philip replaced the receiver, wondering what it was that the detective did not want to talk about on the telephone.

When Mancini arrived, Simms showed him into the library.

"Afternoon, Mr. Adler."

"Good afternoon. What's going on?"

"We caught the man who attacked you."

"You did? I'm surprised," Philip said. "I thought you said it was impossible to catch muggers."

"He's not an ordinary mugger."

Philip frowned. "I don't understand."

"He's a construction worker. He works out of Chicago and New York. He has a police record—assault, breaking and entering. He pawned your watch, and we got his prints." Mancini held up a wristwatch. "This is your watch, isn't it?"

Philip stared at it, not wanting to touch it. The sight of it brought back the horrible moment when the man had grabbed his wrist and slashed it. Reluctantly, he reached out and took the watch. He looked at the back of the case where some of the letters had been scratched off. "Yes. It's mine."

Lieutenant Mancini took the watch back. "We'll keep this for the moment, as evidence. I'd like you to come downtown tomorrow morning to identify the man in a police lineup."

The thought of seeing his attacker again, face-to-face, filled Philip with a sudden fury. "I'll be there."

"The address is One Police Plaza, Room Two-twelve. Ten o'clock?"

"Fine." He frowned. "What did you mean when you said he wasn't an ordinary mugger?"

Lieutenant Mancini hesitated. "He was paid to attack you."

Philip was staring at him, bewildered. *"What?"*

"What happened to you wasn't an accident. He got paid fifty thousand dollars to cut you up."

"I don't believe it," Philip said slowly. "Who would pay anyone fifty thousand dollars to cripple me?"

"He was hired by your wife."

Chapter Thirty-four

He *was hired by your wife!*

Philip was stunned. *Lara?* Could Lara have done such a terrible thing? What reason would she have?

"I don't understand why you practice every day. You're not giving a concert now . . ."

"You don't have to go. I want a husband. Not a part-time . . . It's not as though you were some kind of traveling salesman . . ."

"She accused me of stealing the diamond bracelet you gave her. . . . She would do anything to hold on to you . . ."

And Ellerbee: *"Are you thinking of cutting back on your concerts? . . . I had a talk with Lara."*

Lara.

At 1 Police Plaza a meeting was in progress with the district attorney, the police commissioner, and Lieutenant Mancini.

The district attorney was saying, "We're not dealing here with Jane Doe. The lady has a lot of clout. How much solid evidence do you have, Lieutenant?"

Mancini said, "I checked with personnel at Cameron Enterprises. Jesse Shaw was hired at the request of Lara Cameron. I asked them if she had ever personally hired anyone on the construction crew before. The answer was 'no.'"

"What else?"

"There was a rumor that a construction boss named Bill Whitman was bragging to his buddies that he had something on Lara Cameron that was going to make him a rich man. Shortly after that he was killed by a crane operated by Jesse Shaw. Shaw had been pulled off his job in Chicago to go to New York. After the accident he went right back to Chicago. There's no question but that it was a hit. Incidentally, his airline ticket was paid for by Cameron Enterprises."

"What about the attack on Adler?"

"Same MO. Shaw flew in from Chicago two days before the attack and left the next day. If he hadn't gotten greedy and decided to pick up a little extra money by pawning the watch, instead of throwing it away, we never would have caught him."

The police commissioner asked, "What about motive? Why would she do that to her husband?"

"I talked to some of the servants. Lara Cameron was crazy about her husband. The only thing they ever quarreled about was his going away on concert tours. She wanted him to stay home."

"And now he's staying home."

"Exactly."

The district attorney asked, "What's her story? Does she deny it?"

"We haven't confronted her yet. We wanted to talk to you first to see if we have a case."

"You say that Philip Adler can identify Shaw?"

"Yes."

"Good."

"Why don't you send one of your men over to question Lara Cameron? See what she has to say."

Lara was in a meeting with Howard Keller when the intercom buzzed. "There's a Lieutenant Mancini here to see you."

Lara frowned. "What about?"

"He didn't say."

"Send him in."

Lieutenant Mancini was treading on delicate ground. Without hard evidence, it was going to be difficult to get anything out of Lara Cameron. *But I've got to give it a try,* he thought. He had not expected to see Howard Keller there.

"Good afternoon, Lieutenant."

"Afternoon."

"You've met Howard Keller."

"I certainly have. Best pitching arm in Chicago."

"What can I do for you?" Lara asked.

This was the tricky part. *First establish that she knew Jesse Shaw and then lead her on from there.*

"We've arrested the man who attacked your husband." He was watching her face.

"You have? What . . . ?"

Howard Keller interrupted. "How did you catch him?"

"He pawned a watch that Miss Cameron gave her husband." Mancini looked at Lara again. "The man's name is Jesse Shaw."

There was not the faintest change of expression. *She's good*, Mancini thought. *The lady is really good.*

"Do you know him?"

Lara frowned. "No. Should I?"

That's her first slip, Mancini thought. *I've got her.*

"He worked on the construction crew of one of your buildings in Chicago. He also worked for you on a project in Queens. He was operating a crane that killed a man." He pretended to consult his notebook. "A Bill Whitman. The medical examiner put it down as an accident."

Lara swallowed. "Yes . . ."

Before she could go on, Keller spoke up. "Look, Lieutenant, we have hundreds of people working for this company. You can't expect us to know them all."

"You don't know Jesse Shaw?"

"No. And I'm sure Miss Cameron . . ."

"I'd rather hear it from her, if you don't mind."

Lara said, "I've never heard of the man."

"He was paid fifty thousand dollars to attack your husband."

"I . . . I can't believe it!" Her face was suddenly drained of color.

Now I'm getting to her, Mancini thought. "You don't know anything about it?"

Lara was staring at him, her eyes suddenly blazing. "Are you suggesting . . . ? How dare you! If someone put him up to that, I want to know who it was!"

"So does your husband, Miss Cameron."

"You discussed this with Philip?"

"Yes. I . . ."

A moment later Lara was flying out of the office.

* * *

When Lara reached the penthouse, Philip was in the bedroom packing, clumsily because of his crippled hand.

"Philip . . . what are you doing?"

He turned to face her, and it was as though he were seeing her for the first time. "I'm leaving."

"Why? You can't believe that . . . that terrible story?"

"No more lies, Lara."

"But I'm *not* lying. You've got to listen to me. I had nothing to do with what happened to you. I wouldn't hurt you for anything in the world. I love you, Philip."

He turned to face her. "The police say that the man worked for you. That he was paid fifty thousand dollars to . . . to do what he did."

She shook her head. "I don't know anything about it. I only know that I had nothing to do with it. Do you believe me?"

He stared at her, silent.

Lara stood there for a long moment, then turned and blindly walked out of the room.

Philip spent a sleepless night at a downtown hotel. Visions of Lara kept coming to his mind. *"I'm interested in knowing more about the foundation. Perhaps we could get together and discuss it . . ."*

"Are you married? . . . Tell me about yourself . . ."

"When I listen to your Scarlatti, I'm in Naples . . ."

"I dream a dream of bricks and concrete and steel, and make it come true . . ."

"I came to Amsterdam to see you . . ."

"Would you like me to go with you to Milan . . . ?"

"You're going to spoil me, lady. . . ." *"I intend to . . ."*

And Lara's warmth, compassion, and caring. *Could I have been that wrong about her?*

When Philip arrived at police headquarters, Lieutenant Mancini was waiting for him. He led Philip into a small auditorium with a raised platform at the far end.

"All we need is for you to identify him in the lineup."

So they can tie him in with Lara, Philip thought.

There were six men in the lineup, all roughly the same build and age. Jesse Shaw was in the middle. When Philip saw him, his head began to pound suddenly. He could hear his voice saying, *"Give me your wallet."* He could feel the terrible pain of the knife slashing across his wrist. *Could Lara have done that to me? "You're the only man I've ever loved."*

Lieutenant Mancini was speaking. "Take a good look, Mr. Adler."

"I'm going to be working at home from now on. Philip needs me . . ."

"Mr. Adler . . ."

"We're going to get you the best doctors in the world . . ." She had been there for him every moment, nurturing him, caring for him. *"If Mohammed won't go to the mountain . . ."*

"Would you point him out to me?"

"I married you because I was wildly head over heels in love with you. I still am. If we never make love again, it will be fine with me. All I want is for you to hold me and love me . . ." And she had meant it.

And then the last scene in the apartment. *"I had nothing to do with what happened to you. I wouldn't hurt you for anything in the world . . ."*

"Mr. Adler . . ."

The police must have made a mistake, Philip thought. *By God, I believe her. She couldn't have done it!*

Mancini was speaking again. "Which one is he?"

And Philip turned to him and said, "I don't know."

"What?"

"I don't see him."

"You told us you got a good look at him."

"That's right."

"Then tell me which one he is."

"I can't," Philip said. "He's not up there."

Lieutenant Mancini's face was grim. "You're sure about that?"

Philip stood up. "I'm positive."

"Then I guess that's all, Mr. Adler. Thanks a lot for your cooperation."

I've got to find Lara, Philip thought. *I've got to find Lara.*

She was seated at her desk, staring out the window. Philip had not believed her. That was what hurt so terribly. And Paul Martin. *Of course, he was behind it. But why did he do it? "Do you remember what I said about your husband taking care of you? He doesn't seem to be doing a very good job. Someone should have a talk with him!"* Was it because he loved her? Or was it an act of vengeance because he hated her?

Howard Keller walked in. His face looked white and drawn. "I just got off the phone. We lost Cameron Towers, Lara. Both Southern Insurance and Mutual Overseas Investment are pulling out because we can't meet our completion date. There's no way we can handle our mortgage payments. We almost made it, didn't we? The biggest skyscraper in the world. I'm . . . I'm sorry. I know how much it meant to you."

Lara turned to face him, and Keller was shocked by her appearance. Her face was pale, and there were black circles under her eyes. She seemed dazed, as though the energy had been drained from her.

"Lara . . . did you hear what I said? We've lost Cameron Towers."

When she spoke, her voice was unnaturally calm. "I heard you. Don't worry, Howard. We'll borrow on some of the other buildings and pay everything off."

She was frightening him. "Lara, there's nothing more to borrow on. You're going to have to file for bankruptcy and . . ."

"Howard . . . ?"

"Yes?"

"Can a woman love a man too much?"

"What?"

Her voice was dead. "Philip has left me."

It suddenly explained a lot. "I . . . I'm sorry, Lara."

She had a strange smile on her face. "It's funny, isn't it? I'm losing everything at once. First Philip, now my buildings. Do you know what it is, Howard? It's the Fates. They're against me. You can't fight the Fates, can you?"

He had never seen her in such pain. It tore at him. "Lara . . ."

"They're not through with me yet. I have to fly to Reno this afternoon. There's a grand jury hearing. If . . ."

The intercom buzzed. "There's a Lieutenant Mancini here."

"Send him in."

Howard Keller looked at Lara quizzically. "Mancini? What does he want?"

Lara took a deep breath. "He's here to arrest me, Howard."

"*Arrest* you? What are you talking about?"

Her voice was very quiet. "They think I arranged the attack on Philip."

"That's ridiculous! They can't . . ."

The door opened, and Lieutenant Mancini walked in. He stood there, looking at the two of them for a moment, then moved forward.

"I have a warrant here for your arrest."

Howard Keller's face was pale. He moved in front of Lara protectively and said hoarsely, "You can't do that. She hasn't done anything."

"You're right, Mr. Keller. I'm not arresting her. The warrant is for you."

Chapter Thirty-five

Transcript of Interrogation of Howard Keller by Detective Lieutenant Sal Mancini.
M: You have been read your rights, Mr. Keller?
K: Yes.
M: And you have waived the right to have an attorney present?
K: I don't need an attorney. I was going to come in anyway. I couldn't let anything happen to Lara.
M: You paid Jesse Shaw $50,000 to attack Philip Adler?
K: Yes.
M: Why?
K: He was making her miserable. She begged him to stay home with her, but he kept leaving her.
M: So you arranged to have him crippled.
K: It wasn't like that. I never meant for Jesse to go so far. He got carried away.
M: Tell me about Bill Whitman.
K: He was a bastard. He was trying to blackmail Lara. I couldn't let him do that. He could have ruined her.
M: So you had him killed?
K: For Lara's sake, yes.
M: Was she aware of what you were doing?
K: Of course not. She never would have allowed it. No. I was

there to protect her, you see. Anything I did, I did for her. I would die for her.
M: Or kill for her.
K: Can I ask you a question? How did you know I was involved in this?
End of Interrogation.

At 1 Police Plaza, Captain Bronson said to Mancini, "How *did* you know he was behind it?"

"He left a loose thread, and I unraveled it. I almost missed it. In Jesse Shaw's rap sheet, it mentioned that he took a fall when he was seventeen for stealing some baseball equipment from a Chicago Cubs minor league team. I checked it out, and sure enough, they were teammates. That's where Keller slipped up. When I asked him, he told me he had never heard of Jesse Shaw. I called a friend of mine who used to be a sports editor for the Chicago *Sun Times*. He remembered them both. They were buddies. I figured it was Keller who got Shaw the job with Cameron Enterprises. Lara Cameron hired Jesse Shaw because Howard Keller asked her to. She probably never even saw Shaw."

"Nice work, Sal."

Mancini shook his head. "You know something? In the end it really didn't matter. If I hadn't caught him, and if we had gone after Lara Cameron, Howard Keller would have come in and confessed."

Her world was collapsing. It was unbelievable to Lara that Howard Keller, of all people, could have been responsible for the terrible things that had happened. *He did it for me,* Lara thought. *I have to try to help him.*

Kathy buzzed her. "The car is here, Miss Cameron. Are you ready?"

"Yes." She was on her way to Reno to testify before the grand jury.

Five minutes after Lara left, Philip telephoned the office.

"I'm sorry, Mr. Adler. You just missed her. She's on her way to Reno."

He felt a sharp pang of disappointment. He was desperately eager to see her, to ask her forgiveness. "When you speak to her, tell her I'll be waiting for her."

"I'll tell her."

He made a second phone call, spoke for ten minutes, and then telephoned William Ellerbee.

"Bill . . . I'm going to stay in New York. I'm going to teach at Juilliard."

"What can they do to me?" Lara asked.

Terry Hill said, "That depends. They'll listen to your testimony. They can either decide that you're innocent, in which case you'll get your casino back, or they can recommend that there's enough evidence against you to indict you. If that's their verdict, you'll be tried on criminal charges and face prison."

Lara mumbled something.

"I'm sorry?"

"I said Papa was right. It's the Fates."

The grand jury hearing lasted for four hours. Lara was questioned about the acquisition of the Cameron Palace Hotel & Casino. When they came out of the hearing room, Terry Hill squeezed Lara's hand. "You did very well, Lara. I think you really impressed them. They have no hard evidence against you, so there's a good chance that . . ." He broke off, stunned. Lara turned. Paul Martin had come into the anteroom. He was dressed in an old-fashioned double-breasted suit with a vest, and his white hair was combed in the same style as when Lara had first met him.

Terry Hill said, "Oh, God! He's here to testify." He turned to Lara. "How much does he hate you?"

"What do you mean?"

"Lara, if they've offered him leniency to testify against you, you're finished. You'll go to prison."

Lara was looking across the room at Paul Martin. "But . . . then he would destroy himself, too."

"That's why I asked you how much he hates you. Would he do that to himself to destroy you?"

Lara said numbly, "I don't know."

Paul Martin was walking toward them. "Hello, Lara. I hear things have been going badly for you." His eyes revealed nothing. "I'm so sorry."

Lara remembered Howard Keller's words. *"He's Sicilian. They never forgive, and they never forget."* He had been carrying this burning thirst for vengeance inside him, and she had had no idea.

Paul Martin started to move away.

"Paul . . ."

He stopped. "Yes?"

"I need to talk to you."

He hesitated a moment. "All right."

He nodded toward an empty office down the corridor. "We can talk in there."

Terry Hill watched as the two of them went into the office. The door closed behind them. He would have given anything to have heard their conversation.

She did not know how to begin.

"What is it you want, Lara?"

It was much more difficult than she had anticipated. When she spoke, her voice was hoarse. "I want you to let me go."

His eyebrows were raised. "How can I? I don't have you." He was mocking her.

She was finding it hard to breathe.

"Don't you think you've punished me enough?"

Paul Martin stood there, stone, his expression unreadable.

"The time we had together was wonderful, Paul. Outside of Philip, you've meant more to me than anyone in my life. I owe you more than I could ever repay. I never meant to hurt you. You must believe that."

It was difficult to go on.

"You have the power to destroy me. Is that really what you want? Will sending me to prison make you happy?" She was fighting to hold back her tears. "I'm begging you, Paul. Give me back my life. Please, stop treating me like an enemy . . ."

Paul Martin stood there, his black eyes giving away nothing.

"I'm asking for your forgiveness. I . . . I'm too tired to fight anymore, Paul. You've won . . ." Her voice broke.

There was a knock on the door, and the bailiff peered into the room. "The grand jury is ready for you, Mr. Martin."

He stood there, looking at Lara for a long time; then he turned and left without a word.

It's all over, Lara thought. *It's finished.*

Terry Hill came hurrying into the office. "I wish to God I knew how he was going to testify in there. There's nothing to do now but wait."

* * *

They waited. It seemed an eternity. When Paul Martin finally emerged from the hearing room, he looked tired and drawn. *He's become old,* Lara thought. *He blames me for that.* He was watching her. He hesitated a moment, then walked over to her.

"I can never forgive you. You made a fool of me. But you were the best thing that ever happened to me. I guess I owe you something for that. I didn't tell them anything in there, Lara."

Her eyes filled with tears. "Oh, Paul. I don't know how to . . ."

"Call it my birthday present to you. Happy birthday, baby."

She watched him walk away, and his words suddenly hit her. *It was her birthday!* So many events had been piling on top of one another that she had completely forgotten about it. And the party. Two hundred guests were going to be waiting for her at the Manhattan Cameron Plaza!

Lara turned to Terry Hill. "I've got to get back to New York tonight. There's a big party for me. Will they let me go?"

"Just a minute," Terry Hill said. He disappeared inside the hearing room, and when he came out five minutes later, he said, "You can go to New York. The grand jury will give its verdict in the morning, but it's just a formality now. You can return here tonight. By the way, your friend told you the truth. He didn't talk in there."

Thirty minutes later Lara was headed for New York.

"Are you going to be all right?" Terry Hill asked.

She looked at him and said, "Of course I am." There would be hundreds of important people at the party to honor her that night. She would hold her head high. She was Lara Cameron . . .

She stood in the center of the deserted Grand Ballroom and looked around. *I created this. I created monuments that towered into the sky, that changed the lives of thousands of people all over America. And now it's all going to belong to the faceless bankers.* She could hear her father's voice so clearly. *"The Fates. They've always been agin me."* She thought of Glace Bay and the little boardinghouse where she had grown up. She remembered how terrified she had been on her first day at school: *"Can anyone think of a word beginning with f?"* She remembered the boarders. Bill Rogers . . . *"The first rule in real estate is OPM. Never forget that."* And Charles Cohn: *"I eat only kosher food, and I'm afraid Glace Bay doesn't have any."* . . .

"If I could acquire this land . . . would you give me a five-year lease?" . . .

"No, Lara. It would have to be a ten-year lease." . . .

And Sean MacAllister . . . "I would need a very special reason to make this loan to you! . . . have you ever had a lover?" . . .

And Howard Keller: " . . . you're going about this all wrong." . . .

"I want you to come to work for me." . . .

And then the successes. The wonderful, brilliant successes. And Philip. Her Lochinvar. The man she adored. That was the greatest loss of all.

A voice called, "Lara . . ."

She turned.

It was Jerry Townsend. "Carlos told me you were here." He walked up to her. "I'm sorry about the birthday party."

She looked at him. "What . . . what happened?"

He was staring at her. "Didn't Howard tell you?"

"Tell me what?"

"There were so many cancellations because of the bad publicity that we decided it would be best to call it off. I asked Howard to tell you."

"To tell you the truth, I've been having some problems with my memory."

Lara said softly, "It doesn't matter." She took one last look at the beautiful room. "I had my fifteen minutes, didn't I?"

"What?"

"Nothing." She started to walk toward the door.

"Lara, let's go up to the office. There are some things that have to be wound up."

"All right." *I'll probably never be in this building again,* Lara thought.

In the elevator on the way up to the executive offices, Jerry said, "I heard about Keller. It's hard to believe he was responsible for what happened."

Lara shook her head. "*I* was responsible, Jerry. I'll never forgive myself."

"It's not your fault."

She felt a sudden wave of loneliness. "Jerry, if you haven't had your dinner yet . . ."

"I'm sorry, Lara. I'm busy tonight."

"Oh. That's all right."

The elevator door opened, and the two of them stepped out.

"The papers that you have to sign are on the conference room table," Jerry said.

"Fine."

The door to the conference room was closed. He let Lara open the door and as she did, forty voices started to sing out, "Happy birthday to you, Happy birthday to you . . ."

Lara stood there, stunned. The room was filled with people she had worked with over the years—the architects and contractors and construction managers. Charles Cohn was there, and Professor Meyers. Horace Guttman and Kathy and Jerry Townsend's father. But the only one that Lara saw was Philip. He was moving toward her, his arms outstretched, and she suddenly found it difficult to breathe.

"Lara . . ." It was a caress.

And she was in his arms, fighting to hold back the tears, and she thought, *I'm home. This is where I belong,* and it was a healing, a blessed feeling of peace. Lara felt a warm glow as she held him. *This is all that matters,* Lara thought.

People were crowding around her, and everyone seemed to be talking at once.

"Happy birthday, Lara . . ."

"You look wonderful . . ."

"Were you surprised . . . ?"

Lara turned to Jerry Townsend. "Jerry, how did you . . . ?"

He shook his head. "Philip arranged it."

"Oh, darling!"

Waiters were coming in now with hors d'oeuvres and drinks.

Charles Cohn said, "No matter what happens, I'm proud of you, Lara. You said you wanted to make a difference, and you did."

Jerry Townsend's father was saying, "I owe my life to this woman."

"So do I." Kathy smiled.

"Let's drink a toast," Jerry Townsend said, "to the best boss I ever had, or ever will have!"

Charles Cohn raised his glass. "To a wonderful little girl who became a wonderful woman!"

The toasts went on, and finally, it was Philip's turn. There was too much to say, and he put it in five words: "To the woman I love."

Lara's eyes were brimming with tears. She found it difficult to speak. "I . . . I owe so much to all of you," Lara said. "There's no way

I can ever repay you. I just want to say"—she choked up, unable to go on—"thank you."

Lara turned to Philip. "Thank you for this, darling. It's the nicest birthday I've ever had." She suddenly remembered. "I have to fly back to Reno tonight!"

Philip looked at her and grinned. "I've never been to Reno . . ."

Half an hour later they were in the limousine on their way to the airport. Lara was holding Philip's hand, and thinking, *I haven't lost everything after all. I'll spend the rest of my life making it up to him. Nothing else matters. The only important thing is being with him and taking care of him. I don't need anything else.*

"Lara . . . ?"

She was looking out the window. "Stop, Max!"

The limousine braked to a quick stop.

Philip looked at her, puzzled. They had stopped in front of a huge empty lot, covered with weeds. Lara was staring at it.

"Lara . . ."

"Look, Philip! Look!"

He turned his head. "What?"

"Don't you see it?"

"See what?"

"Oh, it's beautiful! A shopping mall over there, in the far corner! In the middle we'll put up luxury apartment houses. There's room enough for four buildings. You see it now, don't you?"

He was staring at Lara, mesmerized.

She turned to him, her voice charged with excitement. "Now, here's my plan . . ."